In Search of Shiloh

A Journey Home Through Arkansas

Book I of the Shiloh Saga

Written by

Patricia Clark Blake

ISBN: 1547069228
ISBN 13: 9781547069224
Library of Congress Control Number: 2017909011
CreateSpace Independent Publishing Platform
North Charleston, South Carolina

Dedication

The scepter shall not depart from Judah, nor a lawgiver from between his feet, until Shiloh come; and unto Him shall the gathering of the people be.

Genesis 41:10

In gratitude, I dedicate <u>The Shiloh Saga</u> to God, Jesus Christ, and the Holy Spirit—the source of all creation, inspiration, and grace. I am indebted to and inspired by the pioneers of Arkansas for their industry and tenacity in building the beautiful wilderness God created here into the place we call Arkansas. We Arkansans are blessed to live in the Natural State and the Land of Opportunity, which continues to be a place where people honor God, help their neighbors, and seek to build homes where families flourish.

The Shiloh Saga is also dedicated to Gretchen Kopert Campbell, my dear friend, whose encouragement and support pushed me to complete the many stories in the series.

<u>In Search of Shiloh</u>, the first of the Shiloh books, is also dedicated to Beverly Thompson and Brenda Thakkar, both special friends, who edited the manuscript.

Finally, I would have no need to write any dedication had I not been raised by wonderful parents who provided me with the opportunity to get an excellent education and instilled in me a love of reading. Foremost though, in love and pride, I dedicate this work of my heart to my daughter Tara, my granddaughter Kennedy, my son-in-law Kinley, and my grandson Noah. They are my daily inspiration and blessing.

Patricia Clark Blake

1

And we know that all things work together for good to them that love the Lord, to them who are called according to His purpose.

KJV c 1850, Romans 8:28.

"**L**aurel, I wanna talk to you. Darlin', leave the dishes and come set with me a spell." Mark Campbell pointed to the chair near his bed.

With a confused look on her face, Laurel looked across the room to the nook on the other side of the hearth where her father lay. Mark Campbell was not given to endearments, nor had he ever ask her to leave morning chores to sit with him. "Papa, are you hurtin' this mornin'?"

"No more 'n usual. Come over here and set yerself down, like I asked."

Even at such an early hour, Laurel saw the weariness in her father's eyes. He was mortally ill, and she knew his main concern was what would become of her when he was no longer around. Laurel sat in her Granny Wilson's chair, brushed her fingertips across his cheeks, and breathed a sigh of relief that she felt no fever.

"Daughter, my time's short. This blamed cough's gettin' worse ever day and my strength's all but gone. Don't mind so much for me...." Her father glanced up at a pen and ink drawing of her beautiful mother which hung over the mantle. "Spendin' eternity with your mama in paradise ain't exactly a scary thought." A severe bout of coughing interrupted his remarks. Laurel handed him a handkerchief and turned her head. She knew the cloth would be stained with blood. He'd often told her that he hated this weakness. He closed his eyes and took a couple of sharp breaths.

"Rest now, Papa. We'll talk more after your nap. Just sleep a while."

"No." Laurel's father sharp reply suggested a renewed strength Laurel hadn't seen in days. "We gotta talk. Gotta tell you the plans I made for ya." Again, a hacking cough stopped him. Laurel walked across the room to the hearth to get hot water to make a tonic with honey, wild berries, and a bit of some amber colored elixir that Elizabeth Wilson had left. She knew her Papa didn't like the taste, but the hot brew seemed to help the cough.

"Here Papa, drink this. Whatever you want to tell me will wait." She bent down to pull the quilt over his shoulders, and brushed his forehead with her lips. "Sip this and then sleep, Papa, just for a spell."

"Can't wait, Laurel. Your Uncle Matthew found ya a place to teach at the subscription school at Shiloh Station. You got your schoolin', and you readin' all the time makes you more than suited. Good way for ya to earn your livin' once I'm gone."

"Papa, I can't go to Shiloh Station. We've worked so hard to build our homestead. I can take care of us here, Papa."

Her father attempted to push himself up. Laurel moved help him and placed a pillow at his back. He took her hand and spoke in a low, stern voice. "Laurel Grace Campbell, you ain't a hearin' me. I ain't a tellin' you what you might do. I am tellin' you what's gonna happen. Girl, you mean more to me than I ever told ya." Her father strangled and after several moments coughed up phlegm. He wiped his mouth with the bloody handkerchief he held. "Been real selfish lettin' you make us a home here after your mama died. You've been a comfort, 'specially since

I been laid up with this wastin' disease." He gasped for breath. "But it's been all about me." His attempt to explain to Laurel brought on another bout of coughing. "I gotta look to your well-bein' now." Mark Campbell lay back again and breathed deeply. Exhausted at the effort, he closed his eyes and slept.

She dropped another log onto the fire. Although Washington County had experienced an unusually mild winter, on this early March morning the weather was cold. She returned to the dishes, troubled by what her father said. How could Papa want her to move across the state and leave their home? Hawthorn Chapel had been home more than fifteen years. Even if she wanted to go to Shiloh Station to teach, travelling that distance alone would be impossible. She shrugged her shoulders to dismiss the ridiculous idea, dried her hands, and crossed the room to pick up her mother's seventy-five- year-old King James Bible. Laurel didn't have any special scripture in mind so she just opened the book and started to read. The first verse she found was Exodus 20:12. *Honour thy father and thy mother: that thy days may be long upon the land which the Lord thy God giveth thee.* She flipped to another page, hoping to find words to ease the foreboding. She turned to Proverbs 6:20. *My child, keep thy father's commandment and forsake not the law of thy mother.* Laurel was no fool. The word obey rang out to her as if spoken aloud. She made one final attempt to find solace. The New Testament nearly always lifted her spirits. She turned toward the back of the Bible and put her finger on Luke 22:41. *And He was withdrawn from them about a stone's cast, and kneeled down, and prayed, Saying Father, if thou be willing, remove this cup from me: nevertheless, not my will, but thine, be done.*

Laurel sank to her knees before the hearth and allowed her tears to fall. "Father, please let my Papa get well. You're the Great Healer. I'm so afraid. If it's Papa's time, I don't want to leave my home. With your help I can live here by myself. I'd be so unhappy trying to make a life with strangers. Please help me." She couldn't mistake the meaning of the lesson she'd just learned in the Scripture. She was to agree to her papa's plan. "Not my will, but Yours. If You will give me the strength, I will try, but I don't think I can." As she arose, the foreboding didn't cripple her anymore, but she felt no peace. She would go to Shiloh Station if her Papa asked her to go. At the same time, she prayed he wouldn't.

About an hour later, Laurel rushed to her father's side. He awoke to a severe bout of coughing. "Papa, let me get the honey tonic for you. You don't suffer so when you sleep."

"No, Laurel. Come here. I gotta tell you before it gets worse. I wrote a letter to your Uncle Matthew when I knew my congestion was more than a simple catarrh. People don't get rid of consumption. Matt arranged safe passage to Greene County." Again, as he talked, the cough grew worse and his voice fainter. "You just have to get to Shiloh by the end of April when the school term starts. Matthew helped me arrange a good future for you, so you just have to get there on time, and..." Laurel stared at her father, who said nothing. Her grandmother's mantle clock was the only sound, and it seemed to last eternally. Finally, her father gasped out, "And they won't hire an unmarried woman."

An involuntary grimace flickered on Laurel's face. She turned her face. What was he thinking? Had the pain addled his mind? Laurel was a spinster and likely to remain so. In rural Arkansas, an unwed woman beyond the age of twenty-five was destined to remain in her father's house...permanently. That was especially true if the woman was plain, spectacle-wearing, independent-minded, and self-sufficient. Laurel was all those things. She had never had a suitor. Now her Papa was telling her that she had a stable future ahead. All she had to do was find a mate and convince this man whom she didn't know to marry her within a month.

"Can't you say something, Laurel?"

"What can I say, Papa?" She had never shared the fears and hurts arising from her spinsterhood with her father. The foreboding pushed her to the edge of her control. "Papa, you spoke of a good life waiting for me and then added conditions that make the entire thing impossible. Haven't you ever looked at me?" Tears rolled down her cheeks. Laurel turned to go to the hearth, but before she could leave his nook, he called her back.

"Come back, girl. There's more you need to know." Laurel's papa drew his hands through his disheveled hair. With a voice so gravelly, the words were nearly indiscernible, he said, "I sold the homestead and all our stock."

"Did you say you sold our homestead?" He nodded.

"Why?" The sadness on his face told Laurel it was not by choice.

"The law, daughter...." After a few minutes, he continued. "I kept only your horse, the two mules, and the smaller wagon. You can take any of the family things you want. I want ya to safeguard the family records, Bibles, and all our family keepsakes. Amos Tomlin and his wife Lucinda will move into the homestead as soon as ya leave for Shiloh."

Laurel threw her arms in the air. "Papa, what good will it do for me to go to Shiloh? I have no husband. No one has ever asked for my hand. No one wants me. Papa, look at me. I'm plain!"

Deep sobs racked her body as she poured out her heart for the first time in her adult life. Covering her face with her hands, all the hurt, the shards of her broken dreams which she had carried and hidden, were laid bare for her father to witness. "Please excuse me. I need some time alone." She climbed the stairs to her loft and slumped in her mother's rocking chair. She wept.

After a long while, she wiped her face, smoothed her hair back and returned to her work. She went to the porch to bring in wood. As the sun set behind the cabin, sunbeams streamed through the limbs of the apple trees in the orchard. Were there new buds on the apple trees? Those trees would be glorious soon. The fruit from the orchard always provided for her family, giving fresh apples in the summer and plenty of fruit to preserve in apple butter, jelly, cider, and ample slices for canning and drying. A blessing every season...Laurel smiled at the beautiful sight before her. She could survive alone if Papa didn't get well. She knew how to care for animals, grow food in the garden, and harvest the fruits, grapes, and berries in the orchard. She knew where the nuts grew in the forest. But reality forced its way into her daydreams. Her father had sold the Campbell homestead to the Tomlins. She had no home. In her desperation she cried out, "Lord, what can I do?"

An almost audible reply came to her mind. "Child, remember My words. Honor your father and mother. Keep their commandment and follow their law. Live in My will. I am with you." She stared at the mountains around her. Shortly Laurel shook herself to awareness and returned to the kitchen to prepare supper. Within half an hour, she had warmed the brown beans and ham, baked a fresh corn pone, and cooked the stewed potatoes with a spoon of butter she had just churned the day before. Thanks to her bountiful orchard, she had dried apples from which she made an apple pie, hoping to encourage her father to eat. After Laurel prepared a tray for him, she went to eat dinner with him, anxious to know how he would respond to their last conversation. When she pulled back the curtain to his nook, she found him upright and leaning against the carved headboard of his bed.

"Thanks, daughter. I'm real hungry."

"That is a good sign, Papa. If you eat well, you can get your strength back." They ate in silence. The room was warm and comfortable as the last of the western sun found its way into the cabin. It was a beautiful spring evening in the Ozark. After supper, Laurel took her father his warm brew, but he refused the mixture. Laurel sat with her back to him. He waited for her to open the conversation. She called up her courage and in a quiet, steady voice she spoke. "Papa, please forgive my sass this afternoon. When I heard all that self-pity pour out of my mouth, I was ashamed. I just didn't think. I'm sorry."

"Laurel, don't apologize. Didn't know you felt that way. You never let on that you wanted to get married. Thought you were satisfied here with me. You're not plain, darlin'. You just never had a chance to learn womanly ways without your mama."

"Papa, please let's just speak truth to each other. I've known a long time I'm not pretty. That's all right because I have other blessings. I know I'm smart, and I've had my schoolin'. I've learned to work hard, and I can take care of myself. Don't worry about me."

"Laurel, you didn't let me finish tellin' you what Uncle Matthew and me planned. Mark Campbell squared his shoulders and in a steady, deliberate voice he spoke. "Your intended will arrive here sometime this weekend, probably Saturday."

She turned and stared at her father. She covered her face. How much more could she stand? Her father had arranged a marriage of convenience for her! She hardly heard another word he spoke.

"That's the news that came in Uncle Matthew's letter today. When he wrote me at the end of the summer to ask you to teach in Shiloh, I told him that I'd not consider such a dangerous trip through the mountains and foothills unless I was sure of a dependable guide. His letter told me he solved that problem. Matthew's friend wants a wife. He'd even thought he'd send for a mail order bride. When he found out a good woman of an age to marry and of his own faith lived just across the state, he asked for your hand."

"How can you match me with a man you never met?" Laurel couldn't believe her father would offer her up as a piece of chattel, passed from one man to another. Laurel's temper was near the surface. She felt her posture change. Her chin jutted out, her shoulders squared, and she lifted her head. Her voice was harsh and determined as she responded... "Papa, I <u>will not</u>...." But then her voice broke. No sooner were those rash words spoken than she saw the concern on her father's face. Mark Campbell looked so defeated. She remembered her prayer and the almost audible reply. She lowered her defiant eyes. She couldn't cause more distress for her sick father. "Papa, forgive my back talk...I will not disobey you. If you believe this is God's will for me, I will obey you. You've always been a loving father and wanted the best for me."

"Bless you, daughter. I should've told you more often, but I do love you, Laurel Grace. I hope you know I do."

2

Be not forgetful to entertain strangers: for thereby some have entertained angels unawares.

KJV c1850, Hebrews 13:2.

Laurel's Thursday morning began before the sun rose over the Boston Mountains. The dark gathering clouds and the heavy humidity foretold an approaching storm. She prayed but peace had evaded her since her father told her that she had been "given" to a stranger, without her knowledge or consent. The fact she had only two days to find a solution only increased her anxiety. She knew she'd turned her concerns over to the Lord, but surely He didn't intend for her to comply with her father's plan.

As the morning light filtered through the small window of her loft, Laurel took stock of where she stood. She peeked at the small peering glass over her bureau but turned her back immediately. Her reflection confirmed what she had told her father during her tirade last night. She saw the "spinster of Hawthorn". Other than two widows, she was the only unmarried female over seventeen in their congregation, and just last Sunday they had announced that Margie Wagoner, a sixteen-year-old, would be wed at Easter. Of course, Laurel understood exactly why she was unmarried. Her small almond- shaped eyes were gray...occasionally flecked with green and gold, but none of this was very noticeable because she constantly wore her German silver-framed glasses. Her non-descript brown curly tresses reached to her waist, not that anyone knew.

She pulled her hairbrush in long strokes. *All right, Spinster of Hawthorn, stop wasting time. You've got work to do.* Deftly, she divided the long tresses into three lengths, wove them into long braids which she wound into a severe coronet around her head. No comb or ribbon softened her profile. In fact, she didn't even own any. She put on a brown serge skirt and ecru blouse. The skirt was five inches shorter than the current fashion and too large for her small frame. The sleeves of her blouse didn't quite reach her wrist either. These things had once belonged to her much shorter mother. She pulled on her brown high-topped shoes over her stockings. The Spinster of Hawthorn was still alive and well in Mark Campbell's home.

Laurel climbed from the loft and crossed the room to her father's nook. He still slept. That was proof his consumption grew worse. He'd never been known to be a slugabed. Laurel knelt by his bed and softly touched his forehead. His fever had risen again. He needed the help of Elizabeth Wilson, the only healer in their area. She rushed to saddle Sassy Lady and rode as quickly as the rutted roads would allow. She hoped Elizabeth could come and provide the help she couldn't give. Thankfully, Elizabeth's knowledge about the medicinal properties of the plants found in the Boston Mountains had blessed many families at Hawthorn.

By God's providence, the two women were by Mark's side within the hour. He had awakened but in his weakened, feverish state, he couldn't sit by himself. The expression on Elizabeth's face showed doubt that her limited abilities would be enough. She took her satchel with home remedies to the kitchen, took the kettle from the hearth, and poured the hot water into a mixture of chamomile, willow root, honey, and grape juice. This old remedy usually reduced fevers and coughing. Blessedly, the person who drank this tonic slept more comfortably. She spooned a quarter cup of the tonic into Mark's mouth between bouts of his hacking, bloody cough. Shortly, Mark rested. "Laurel, you know your Papa has consumption. There's little I can do except keep him easy."

"I know, Elizabeth, and Papa's known for a good while that he is very sick."

"I'll leave you some tonic. Just give him a quarter a cup whenever he hurts or if the fever comes back. I'll return this afternoon if I can. All you can do now is to give it to the Lord, Laurel. Keep your faith, darlin'."

When Elizabeth left for home, Laurel went to the barn to do the chores, which she had neglected earlier. Because she mucked out the stalls and filled the troughs with fresh water the day before, all she had to do was milk and gather eggs. As she returned to the cabin, the storm, which had threatened all morning, broke. Confined to the cabin by both the needs of her father and the horrible weather outside, she thought about the changes coming in her life. She was grateful to have the time with her papa, what little remained. Laurel was her 'papa's girl.' Since she was born, there had been a special bond between them...her papa and her. Her brothers even called him pa because he was her papa. She simply couldn't imagine life without him. She would do her best to make his time calm, happy, and as stress-free as possible. *What would Papa want from me now?* Laurel shook her head in frustration. He wanted only the assurance she would follow his wishes for the new life he'd planned. He would worry until he knew her future was secure.

She would do what she could to let him pass peacefully. If it meant marriage to a stranger, so be it. Hadn't she felt the Lord tell her to obey? The Lord would not yoke her with a mate who wasn't her peer. Since this stranger had to seek a wife, he probably wasn't exactly anyone's dream himself, so he'd not expect a prize.

While her papa slept, she went up to her loft to see if anything she owned would make an appropriate trousseau. That was almost funny. Nothing she had fit well and the styles were seldom seen anymore. She found she had two outfits she liked. Her dove gray Sunday dress with its lace jabot was the best she had. She also had the brown serge skirt and ecru blouse she was wearing. The skirt was too large, but with a belt it didn't look too bad. Finally, she pulled her mother's wedding dress from the old cedar lined chest. The empire-styled gown, which had been fashionable in 1820 when her parents had wed, certainly would be serviceable even though it hardly fit the vision she had dreamed of. Of course, she didn't dream of an ideal wedding anymore...not for a very long time. Laurel tenderly laid the gown back in the chest. What difference did a dress make when her father lay downstairs--dying.

"Laurel, will you bring me a drink of water?" Mark Campbell awoke mid-morning. He was less feverish and somewhat stronger.

"Yes, Papa." Laurel took him a glass of cool water. "Do you feel better now, Papa? Are you able to eat some? Elizabeth left some good vegetable soup to perk up your appetite. Can I bring you some? I have fresh coffee ready if you..."

"Stop fussing, Laurel. Come sit. Matthew swore that you'll be well-treated and an honored part of the Shiloh congregation. They need you there. Matt said MacLayne is a good man, faithful to the Lord. He'll take care of you and support you. He'll treat you with respect. Will you go with him to Shiloh?"

Laurel closed her eyes to stop the tears lying just below the surface. Even a plain girl hoped she would merit more than respect and honor. She mentally scolded herself. *Laurel Grace, make your papa happy. Many women have less than respect and security, so why should you question the plans made for your own good. Hasn't the Lord promised to be with you?* "Yes, Papa. I will meet this man when he comes. We only need to deal with this one day at a time. Papa, I'll try to do what you ask me, but please try to get well, Papa. I need my father, even if it's my lot to be a teacher with a husband. Papa, I love you so much."

"Thank you, Sis. I can rest now I know you'll have a home...and a spouse." Clearly, Mark Campbell was exhausted by this brief conversation with his daughter. "Laurel, I believe one day you'll find happiness." Her father breathed heavily. "One more thing, Laurel, stay strong in your faith. Everything else will work itself out for good. Now get me another cup of that tonic." He slowly drank the warm liquid, and after a few minutes, he slept again.

Laurel went to the back porch on the sheltered side of the cabin. The storm continued, and as fierce as it was, there was a strange beauty in the lightning and wind. She'd always found God in the natural elements around her. She stood alone on the porch for some time, watching the storm and feeling the wind and rain caress her skin. Here she experienced more peace than any other place since her father had gotten ill. The lightning displayed silhouettes of trees and mountain peaks, and Laurel heard and felt the rumbling thunder as it rolled across the valley.

Water began to drip from her face. Chores needed to be done. No need to fret over things beyond her control. She kneaded bread as she usually did on Thursday, so they would have fresh bread for the weekend. On a chair, she found one of her papa's work shirts. When she picked it up, she found a small rip. She went to her notions basket before she realized that her papa wouldn't need the shirt. She held it to her nose and smelled the scent that was her papa's. As if it were the most precious shirt ever made, she gently folded it and put it in her papa's bureau, a tall walnut highboy, the most beautiful piece of furniture in their cabin. Mark Campbell carved it as a wedding present for her mother. Thirty-five years of care and polish had created a rich sheen to the beautiful walnut her papa had chosen. She could never part with her Papa's love gift to her mother.

Mark Campbell slept through the supper hour. Laurel warmed up what had remained from yesterday's lunch. Elizabeth would not be able to return through the fierceness of the storm. As the wind howled and lashed out at the tree limbs outside, Laurel decided to stay close to her father through the night. She added more wood to the fire and pulled a quilt from the back of his chair and cuddled up into its warmth and fell into a dreamless sleep.

Just before dawn on Friday, Mark Campbell awoke, coughed up blood, and gasped for breath. Laurel jumped to her feet to get the tonic, which seemed to help him sleep, even if it could not cure the terrible disease. Thankfully, Elizabeth had left enough fixings for several doses.

Like all good pioneer women, she knew they were all at the mercy of the elements. Perhaps it was a blessing after all. If Elizabeth couldn't get to the Campbell homestead, then a stranger to the area wouldn't be able to get here either. The storm may have provided a reprieve for Laurel.

With a hint of smile on her face, Laurel dressed in her father's old dungarees and a large flannel shirt. After all, the homestead couldn't take care of itself. As she walked onto the front porch, Laurel noticed the spring storm had left the valley fresh and vibrant. The trees held buds which would soon become full, lush leaves. Early flowers, sprouts of meadow grass, the birds singing in the trees...it was all so wonderful ...the beauty that is Arkansas in the springtime. She could hardly wait for summer. Then she remembered her father's words from the night before. "Laurel, I sold the homestead."

Laurel began the chores. Milking, collecting eggs, feeding the stock, and mucking out the stalls all waited for her. Then she had only one chore left--carrying in the wood. Sassy Lady deserved a good brushing, but that would wait. About noon, she was carrying the final load of wood to the porch, and just as she reached for the latch cord, a rider approach from the northwest. *Thank God, Elizabeth has come so soon.* She turned to greet her friend, but Elizabeth wasn't in the front yard. Here at her doorstep was a man she'd never seen before, a tall, well-dressed man atop a well-bred horse. Laurel gaped at this stranger momentarily. With lowered eyes and in a barely audible voice, she managed to ask, "You need directions, mister?"

"Not if Mr. Mark Campbell lives here."

"My father's inside, but he's very sick. If your business can wait, it'd be better." She shifted from one foot to the other.

"That's why I'm here. My pastor is Mr. Campbell's brother. He assured me he'd write to expect me." Reality struck Laurel. Her eyes made an involuntary trip from the tips of his sturdy boots to the brim of his hat before she realized she was gawking. She turned her head. This tall, well-dressed, well-spoken stranger was the man her father called her intended. Mortified, she stood before him, dressed like a slave—probably worse since one of the chores that morning included mucking out the stalls. This man was not supposed to have arrived until Saturday, but here he was on her front porch on Friday morning!

Laurel rubbed her dirty hands against her pants, turned her face toward the door, and whispered in a terse, cold whisper voice, "If you wait, I'll see if he's awake. I know he wasn't expecting any visitors today."

"Sorry I interrupted your work, but I've travelled nearly two weeks. Reverend Campbell said he'd write I was coming."

"Please wait here. I'll ask Papa if he can see you."

"I'm grateful, ma'am."

"It's alright," she replied without one glance at the stranger. Laurel picked up the last armload of firewood and started to the door. Before she reached the bottom step, the stranger took the wood from her.

"I'll add this to your stack while you see to Mr. Campbell."

"Who can I say is here?" Again, Laurel's voice reflected distance, constraint, and fear.

"My name is Patrick MacLayne, but my friends call me Mac." He tipped his hat and sat in the rocking chair on the porch.

When she opened the door, Laurel was surprised her father was awake and seated upright in his bed. The fire had burned out, but the cabin was still warm and comfortable. The sun was bright and light flooded into the only paned glass window in the cabin.

"Papa, should you be up? The tonic must've worked fast. Has your fever gone?"

"Stop the fussing, girl. Let that fella in here. I told you I expected him."

"I didn't expect anyone today. Look at me!" She held out her dirty hands and pulled at the torn pocket of the flannel shirt. "Perhaps it is all for the best. Surely he'll see I'm not the suitable wife he expected."

"Laurel, get up to the loft and get cleaned up. You got our noon meal to fix, and I expect you'll be a gracious hostess for our guest. Now put a pillow behind my back and let that man in." She did all her father asked and hastily climbed the ladder to the loft, grateful she didn't have to face this man--at least for a while, but more than annoyed at the orders her father had issued. Instead of bathing and dressing, Laurel chose to read.

She'd done the chores. She deserved some leisure, didn't she? Yet she'd read a few words and then a sound below would catch her attention, and she'd lose her place. She slung the book across the room to her bed. The old mantle clock struck 1:00 and then 1:30.

Reluctantly, Laurel bathed and changed her clothes. After a look into her peering glass, she tucked several strands of her hair back into her coronet. She picked up her German silver rimmed glasses from the chest of drawers, put them on, and left the safety of her loft. In the kitchen, she pushed the black kettle back onto the fire to warm the meat. She placed the apple cobbler into the hearth oven, and soon the scent of cinnamon and butter would fill the entire cabin. Finally, she ran the short distance to the springhouse for butter and buttermilk. This meal was more than adequate for any unexpected visitor, even her so-called intended.

How could a man be so inconsiderate as to appear a whole day early? How could he expect her to prepare company victuals a day early? She laid out the table with her mother's best dishes and put two candles on the table, as if a circuit rider were their guest for supper. She certainly didn't want her papa to be shamed by her lack of hospitality. When she was satisfied she'd done a presentable job, she sat stiff-backed on the edge of her father's chair and waited. She heard murmuring from the other room, but she understood nothing of the conversation, which was just loud enough to be annoying.

Shortly after 2:00, Patrick MacLayne entered in the main room with his arm supporting Mark Campbell, whose once handsome face sagged with obvious signs of exhaustion. He had been up more than two and a half hours. He coughed harshly and nearly non-stop, a common aftermath of his fatigue. Laurel stood as they approached the hearth.

"Mr. Patrick MacLayne, this is my daughter, Laurel. Laurel Grace, this is Patrick MacLayne. He asked me for the opportunity to seek your hand in marriage. I said I would agree to the match if you're agreeable to his suit."

"Miss Campbell, I'm honored to meet you. Your uncle Matthew has spoken so highly of you both."

Laurel nodded briefly and replied, "Welcome to our home, Mr. MacLayne. Won't you join us? Dinner is ready, Papa." The midday meal was rarely so late in the day. Regardless, the two men at the table carried on an easy, frank dialog for what seemed an hours. Laurel judged the time by the ticking of her grandmother's clock. Mark Campbell continued to break the conversation with strong bouts of coughing. Patrick MacLayne waited patiently and then continued the when he could. He possessed tremendous patience and compassion for the man whom he met only two hours ago. For Laurel the entire time was an ordeal. She found little to add to the conversation. Spilling the ewer of milk, dropping a spoon, and passing cornbread when her father had asked for butter were just signs of the awkwardness she felt.

"Afraid I used up all my strength for this day, Mr. MacLayne. Please pardon my lack of hospitality, but I gotta rest now. Laurel, see to our guest. Good night, Daughter. Mr. MacLayne, we'll talk again tomorrow." Laurel prepared the hot tonic to help her papa to sleep, carried the cup to his bed, and held it while he sipped between fits of coughs. Shortly, he slept.

The moment she dreaded came. The spinster of Hawthorn was forced to play hostess for the man who had come to claim her from her dying father. What could she say to him? She knotted her arms around her waist as she struggled to gain enough composure to face him. She jerked her head toward the sound of her Grandmother Wilson's clock on the massive oak mantle as it struck 4:00. *Lord, help me! How can my father expect me to entertain this man for the rest of the day? I can't do this.* Laurel stopped an arm's length from the end of the hewn plank table where he sat. She watched him from the corner of her eye but refused to make eye contact.

This friend of her Uncle Matthew sat with his long, lean legs crossed at the knees, just above his well-worn, but not shabby leather boots. The linen of his crisp white shirt lay across his relaxed broad shoulders in a way that suggested the shirt was made to fit his torso alone. His very presence at her papa's table oozed confidence. He poured himself another cup of coffee. The amber liquid was still hot enough to send the pleasant aroma throughout the cabin. "Please finish your coffee, Mr.

MacLayne. I'll just clean the table. Can I bring more apple cobbler?" Even before he had a chance to reply, Laurel had already piled the dishes at her father's place and started to hers.

"Laurel, please call me Mac. It's the name my friends use."

"I'll try to remember, Mr...I mean Mac." She reached to remove his dishes but realized she'd have to touch his arm so she turned toward the dry sink. However, before she put the dishes in the wash pan, Mac stood beside her, ready to pour hot water from the kettle. In a very short time, the dishes were finished. Neither of them spoke a word.

"Will you show me around your homestead, Laurel?"

"If that's what you'd like." Laurel opened the back door and walked down the path. "This is our orchard." What a silly statement! "The fruit for the cobbler we had was part of last summer's harvest." Another senseless remark. Clenching her fists, Laurel didn't speak again because she knew the next remark would probably be even more ridiculous. Small talk was a skill she'd never mastered. She despised feeling inadequate, and the more she thought about it the more she resented being put in this position in the first place.

"Look, Mr. MacLayne. You don't know anything about me nor do I know you, but I am a frank person. I am not easy with socializing. I don't have the least idea how I should treat you or what I should say."

Patrick continued to look at her. Laurel shifted from one foot to the other, unable to look at him directly. Looking at the scuffed toes of her work shoes, she spoke. "As you can obviously see, I'm no southern beauty. I have no sense of humor, and I never learned to flirt. I don't know what my Uncle Matthew said to bring you all the way across the state on this ridiculous quest, but I surely won't hold you to any agreement you made with my family. You're in no way bound to me, Mr. MacLayne. Obviously, I'm not a suitable match for you." Laurel stepped back two steps, turned around, and breathed a deep sigh of relief. She settled the whole matter.

"Laurel, I asked you to call me Mac." She turned back, her gray eyes wide with surprise.

Laurel raised her arms and set her jaw. "Didn't you understand what I just said? You're free to return home. I have no hold on you. There's no need for me to call you anything."

Mac walked toward her, but she lifted her skirt to walk away. Mac reached out and took her elbow, but Laurel jerked away as if his touch were painful. She looked up, momentarily, and then quickly lowered her gaze. Laurel wrapped her arms around her shoulders.

Mac grinned and then rubbed his palm against his neatly trimmed beard. "Can we continue our walk?"

Hesitantly, Laurel led him on a silent tour of the area around the homestead, speaking only to point out a landmark or two. They walked until just before the sun began to set behind the mountain peak. "Mr. MacLayne, I am sorry I couldn't offer you a more entertaining afternoon. We best go back before it gets dark."

"Laurel, I want you to call me Mac, and I enjoyed our walk very much." They climbed the stairs of the porch. "Let's sit here a while. The night will be beautiful here on your mountain." Mac held the chair as she sat, and he took the second rocker. Around them, the night chorus of the mountains began as the sun set. Cicadas, tree frogs, whippoorwills, and scores of other living creatures performed for them. The darkening sky encroached on the peaks of the Boston Mountains—gold, red, and orange streaked across the evening sky. Because the moon was in a new phase, there was little light to detract from the beauty of the stars. "I don't think I have ever seen so many stars as here. Shiloh nights are beautiful, but your stars surely put on a grand show."

"Yes, the Ozarks are beautiful in the spring."

Mac sat quietly for a while, and then his yawn broke the silence. "Laurel, thank you for a nice day. You served me a fine meal, and from the way your pa talked you didn't expected me until tomorrow. You graciously showed me your home. As much as I'd enjoy more conversation, I'm tired. I rode the last twelve miles here this morning. Your father offered me his hospitality so if you have no objection, I plan to stay a few days. I'll make myself at home in the barn. Good night."

As Mac left the porch, Lauren rose and pushed the palms of her hands against the porch rail. She watched him stride across the yard. *Who did he think he was? Hadn't she told him he had no obligation to her?* She dropped back into her mother's rocker. She pounded her fists on the arms of the chair and wanted to scream. Only knowing he'd hear stopped the screech from echoing across the mountains. She clasped her hands, closed her eyes, and moaned instead. How much more she needed to scream.

Then she realized that she'd not offered the visitor blankets or a pillow to use on the hay. She went to the cedar chest to retrieve the bedding. Shuddering at the thought of taking it, she walked quickly to the barn and edged open the door. Mac stood bare to the waist, preparing for bed. Embarrassed, she uttered not a word, threw the bedding, and fled. She heard him call after her, "Thank you, Laurel."

3

But he said, Yea, rather, blessed are they that hear the word of God and keep it.

KJV c185, Luke 11:28.

Out in the Campbell barn, Patrick MacLayne tossed and turned, pushed up more hay, and pushed some away. What sense could he make of the day he'd spent? Why had he ridden twelve days across dirt roads, barely discernible paths, and along river banks to get to Hawthorn Chapel only to find himself engaged to a woman who not only didn't want to be married to him but wasn't too shy to say so.

He rose from his none-too-comfortable bed and went to stroke Midnight's muzzle. At least the beloved horse was one thing he understood right then. "Boy, what have I done?" When he'd talked to Matthew, the plan was to meet Laurel Campbell and arrange a courtship. Her father had told her they would marry. She'd made it clear she wasn't interested in her father's plans. She was distant and painfully shy most of the day. At least, she had been thoughtful enough to bring him bedding. Of course, when she saw him, she fled as if the devil himself stalked her.

Laurel in no way resembled women he'd been attracted to in the past. He wouldn't call her beautiful in any stretch of the imagination, but her appearance was intriguing. Her uncle Matthew, his best friend, told him they'd make a good match. That certainly remained to be seen. Mac would wait to see where the Lord led. He climbed back to the loft and lay on the makeshift bed. He tossed and turned for a while longer but eventually got up to find a light. Mac took his Bible from his saddlebag and read from Genesis 30. When he read the story of Jacob and Leah, he thought God's word told him he had made the right decision. It wasn't difficult to see parallels between his present state and the story of Jacob. Jacob built a family with a woman he didn't love. He finally blew out the lantern and tried to sleep, only to find himself dreaming about the events that had lead him across the state.

Mac's interminable dream left him exhausted the next day, but when he did rise, he had no qualms that he was doing what God had asked him to do. He wasn't sure that Laurel would see things the same way. In the short time he'd known her, he'd learned she had a mind of her own, but her uncle said she was a woman of faith. What he didn't know was whether she would be obedient to God's plan when a stranger delivered the message. *Lord, please speak for me.* Nevertheless, he would do what he had pledged to do—with God's help.

❦

Shortly after daybreak, Laurel ran through the gentle spring rain to saddle her horse. She needed Elizabeth to help her papa. As she opened the barn door, Mr. MacLayne was feeding the stock. "Good morning. You sure seem to be in a hurry this morning. Is there something I can do?"

"Papa is worse. I have to get Elizabeth Wilson."

"I'll go to Engel's Mill for help."

"No need. No doctor there."

"Here, let me help." He took the horse blanket and saddle from the stall rail. "Which horse is yours?"

"Sassy Lady, the one nearest the door. I can do that."

"I'm sure you can, but I'll saddle the horse. I will go for the healer if you will tell me the way."

"I can go faster myself."

"Then I will stay with your father."

Laurel nodded, mounted Sassy, and galloped down the muddy road.

— —

Mac sprinted to the cabin to sit at the bedside of Mark Campbell, and he thought how much he would have enjoyed knowing this man. Even in their brief conversations, he found him to be wise, humorous, and faithful. What a good father-in-law he would have been. Mac felt the older man's cheek and found it hot. He jerked the blankets from the bed, opened his nightshirt, and sponged him with cool water in an attempt to reduce his temperature. He ladled the warm honey tonic Laurel made into Mark Campbell's mouth. With no other help to give, Mac prayed this good man would find ease.

Within half an hour, Mr. Campbell awoke. His fever had ebbed somewhat. Even his cough had lessened after he drank a second cup of the warm toddy. In a raspy, barely audible voice, he spoke to Mac. "Mr. MacLayne, I want to see my girl wed before the Lord takes me home. I know this ain't the way it's supposed to happen, but time is too short for me to give Laurel time to be a proper bride."

"Mr. Campbell, I know you gave me leave to court your daughter, but I'm not sure she will agree to this suit."

"Laurel will do what I ask. She's a godly daughter. I'm not worried 'bout her right now, but you've been pushed into a situation I know you didn't expect. Matthew told me you'd ask to pay court to Laurel, but I told her you asked for her hand." Mark's attempt to press his case with Mac was halted by a jolting cough.

"Try to rest, sir. We will talk more later."

"No time." Mark brought his feeble hand to his mouth to cover his cough again. "Will you speak vows with Laurel in front of our preacher when he can drive out here?"

Mac knew from the earlier conversation that Mark Campbell intended to see Laurel wed. He just hadn't expected the wedding to be that soon. A frown clearly showed the doubt...not on his part, for he believed God had planned this union long before he left Shiloh Station, but Laurel had expressed no interest in the match.

"There is more, MacLayne. You must promise you'll make a safe home for my girl. Pledge you'll treat her like the lady she is." A hacking cough again broke the conversation. "Laurel's a prize among women. She'll say she ain't pretty and not suitable, but if you're the man my brother thinks you are, you'll see her worth. You've got to help her see it too." Mark pushed up on his elbows, trying to lift himself to eye level with Mac. "Can you make me these promises? If not, I can't bless the marriage."

Mac took a deep breath and closed his eyes for a minute. *Lord, if this is your will, show me.* Again the thought *My Grace is sufficient for you* came to him. "Mr. Campbell, with God's help, I'll do all you've asked. If Laurel agrees, we will marry as soon as your pastor can say the words over us."

"Thank you, son. You lifted my burden." Mark Campbell closed his eyes and slept again.

 ⁓ ⁓

Within the hour, Laurel and Elizabeth Wilson arrived. "How is my papa?" Laurel looked at Patrick MacLayne for the first time since he had arrived...really looked at him. She saw compassion and empathy in his face. She didn't understand the connection that had developed so quickly between her father and this stranger.

"He's very tired, but the fever is not as high. Mrs. Wilson, your fever remedy is a wonder."

"The tonic works for a while. Just wish I knew something to fix the consumption. Best I can do is make Brother Mark easy. Laurel, you go and fix the midday meal. Your papa'll need something he can keep down so heat that chicken stock I made."

The last thing on her mind was food, but she did as Elizabeth asked. She started to the springhouse, but before she could open the door, Mac had done it. "I'd like to go along if you'll allow me."

"I am only going to the springhouse to get fresh butter and milk for dinner. No need to bother yourself."

"Not a bother, Miss Campbell." They walked along the path toward the creek. Laurel's father had built the springhouse on the creek bank under a grove of hickory trees. The dense shade helped to keep the water cool. The creek flowed through the small room and over a miniature rock waterfall so the food could sit on the ledges in the shallow water. Even in the hottest weather, the Campbell family had fresh food. Once inside, Laurel bent down to put her hand into the cool water, feeling it dance across her fingers. She drew her hand across the damp stones of the native rock walls and smiled.

"Are you all right, Miss Campbell? You seem quiet."

"I am fine. Just making a memory."

"Your father is blessed to have you caring for him. Do you have any other family around to help?"

"No. My older brother lives in Texas with his family. My mother and baby sister were laid in the Hawthorn cemetery nearly twelve years ago. Then in '55 we buried my brother Samuel next to them. I suppose we'll lay papa there soon."

"It's not easy to care for your father alone."

"I have friends and the members of our congregation have been good to us. Just last Saturday, seven or eight of the men came, plowed our garden, and tilled the hay fields so we could get our crops in this year." When they returned to the cabin, Laurel prepared dinner and warmed the chicken soup for her father. When she finished, Elizabeth came to get the broth.

"Laurel, if you'll go ahead and eat now, I'll feed your pa. You will need your strength to nurse him." Laurel started to object, but Elizabeth stopped the discussion. "Sit down a spell...I'll eat in a while."

Mac stood and held her chair where she drooped weary and frightened. Her father had little time left and she felt alone. Mac took her hand. She tried to pull away again, but Mac tightened his hold. "Will you allow me to say grace? I know it's your father's right to bless the food, but he's asleep." Laurel looked at him through her lashes. She found his deep, stormy blue eyes fixed on her, awaiting an answer.

She nodded. "Yes, please offer the blessing for the food."

"Dear Father, we offer You praise and thanksgiving for all the blessings You bring. We ask comfort for Mr. Campbell. Don't let him suffer unduly. Bless the food before us. Amen."

Laurel whispered amen. "Thank you for praying for my papa. That's a kind gesture."

"Will you give me some of those pole beans and mashed potatoes? And that bread smells good."

"Yes, of course." Again, Laurel fell quiet. With all her education and the books she'd read, she never learned the social graces needed to entertain a gentleman, not like the one seated at her table.

Mac ate well. He didn't seem to mind the silence. Twenty minutes passed, and still he showed no sign he wanted to leave the table.

"Can I get you more coffee and some bread pudding?"

"Not just now. I'm afraid I ate too much already."

"Well, I'll put away the dishes, then."

"Please, just sit with me a while. Your papa will need you soon, but I would like to learn more about you."

"Not much to know. What you see is what there is. Pretty ordinary."

"Your uncle said you finished common school before you were thirteen. That's certainly not ordinary. I don't know many women who can read and write, let alone have finished the eighth grade."

"Yes, I can read and write."

"What else makes you 'not ordinary', Laurel?" She flushed at the question. Couldn't this man see there was nothing the least extraordinary about her?

"Nothing."

"I'm sure--"

"I need to clean the table. Papa will need me when he wakes." She started to rise and Mac got up to pull her chair out. Laurel's temper rose. *Why did he treat her as he did?* She bit her tongue to stop the harsh words she'd not be able to take back if she spoke them. "Mr. MacLayne--"

"It's Mac, Laurel."

"Mac, you're very kind, but you're a guest here, not me. Now I have chores to do." She set about clearing the table. When that was finished, she laid in wood for the night, stirred batter for cornbread, gathered the laundry, trimmed the wicks in the lanterns...anything to keep busy and away from Patrick MacLayne. Finally, Elizabeth came from Mark Campbell's bedside.

"He asked for you, Laurel."

"Thank you. I set aside a meal in the hearth oven. Please eat and rest awhile."

"I'll eat. Go visit your papa. He is awake, but with the pain, I don't know how long he can go without the tonic."

Laurel went immediately. "Papa, it is so good to see you eat. Do you want more?" He shook his head. "The weather has been nice today, even with the rain. No storms and not too cool. Typical March..."

"Laurel, don't make idle chatter...we need to finish our talk. I'll not see another week out. My strength is gone, and my coughing is bloodier every day."

"Papa, don't say that. Good food and rest'll help."

"No, Laurel, it won't. I talked real frank with MacLayne while you were gone. He promised all I asked of him. I like that young man.... I like that he ain't no boy, he's a believer, and he's able to support you. He is obliged to marry you as soon as Reverend Caldwell can come. Laurel, I want you to marry Mr. MacLayne on Tuesday. Will you speak the words with him?"

Laurel stood and took the two steps to the wall. She laid her head against the hewn log of the cabin wall. Finally, she spoke. "Papa, I love you, and I want to honor your request, but he's a stranger. We know nothing of his character, his family, or his means to support a family." She turned to face her father and walked to kneel by his bed. "Surely, you don't believe marrying a stranger is right." She looked directly into her father's eyes, hoping desperately to find a reprieve. "Papa, I can take care of myself. I've taken care of us both since you've been sick."

"Laurel, I know enough. MacLayne's a good man who fears the Lord. You know that's the most important quality for any man. I'm at peace with this decision. I believe this marriage is God's will. Regardless of what I think, you got to choose for yourself. I see only two paths. Marry this fine man and have a family, or go back to Shiloh with him and let your Uncle Matthew take you into his household. Of course, the elders of the church won't let you teach since you're a spinster."

Concern and fatigue lined her father's face. He was in a great pain. "Papa, I'll get the tonic so you can sleep. I don't want the fever to rise up on you again."

"I want you to think on what I said. Pray about it. I'm tired now. Get that medicine." Laurel had been dismissed. He wanted no more discussion. She was amazed the stranger had agreed to go through with the arrangement. He had to be aware that she didn't want to be married and that she was not suited to be his wife. Mac was intelligent, learned, tall, attractive, and financially stable. He could have a choice of many brides, all of them more suitable, more beautiful, and more willing than the spinster of Hawthorn. She didn't want to be any man's obligation. What would his people say when he brought HER home?

Elizabeth came to bring more tonic and sit with her neighbor. The last thing Laurel wanted was to play the hostess to Mac but what else could she do? She felt trapped between the demands of obedience to father and her own independent, proud nature. She would not deny her father if he demanded she marry. He had spent much time and effort to arrange this marriage of convenience because he loved her. Regardless, Laurel didn't know if she could speak marriage vows with a stranger, a man who couldn't possibly care for her. She would simply have to make him understand he was free from his promise. Maybe she couldn't deny her father, but this man could stop this lunacy. She'd find the right words to make him understand. She returned to the kitchen where Mac already started the fire as the cabin had become chilled when the sun set.

"Mac--"

"Laurel--"

"Go on and speak first, Laurel."

"Are you're ready for dessert and coffee, yet."

"That'd be nice." While she went to get the sweets, Mac stoked the fire, moved the rocking chair, and placed Mark Campbell's armchair near the hearth. The chairs were near each other but not so close as to make Laurel uneasy. Laurel handed the cup and small pewter dish to Mac.

"Don't you want any?"

"No, I don't like coffee. I'm sorry. I didn't ask if you wanted sweetener or cream."

"No, you got it just right. I prefer things plain."

Laurel winched at the word. Mac hadn't meant anything with his comment, yet she'd still reacted. She didn't speak for some time. Neither did he. When the tension grew uncomfortable, Laurel asked, "Mac, do you know how old I am?"

"If you are asking if your uncle told me you are a spinster--yes, he told me during a not very flattering description of you. He said you're the same age as his oldest daughter, past twenty-seven."

"Yes, Susan's my beautiful, blonde, married cousin. She has been married for more than seven years and has three children. We haven't seen each other in years, but the family keeps in touch through letters."

"That's good news. When we get home, we will have family to welcome us."

Laurel shook her head in disbelief. "What else did my Uncle Matthew say about me?"

"Well, he said you're too smart for your own good. Personally, I think that's impossible. I enjoy intelligent people. Make for good conversation. He said you're shy around people you don't know, especially men. I haven't noticed that either. We only met yesterday, and you've given a piece of your mind twice already. He told me that you think you're plain...or maybe your father told me that. Anyway, beauty comes from inside, not outside."

"Mr. MacLayne, why do you want to marry me? You know nothing about me. As you've seen and been told by members of my own family, I am plain. Is the northeast side of the state without any marriageable women that you had to come three hundred miles to find one?"

"Since you refuse to call me Mac as I have asked several times, I won't be so forward as to use your Christian name. Before I answer your question, I need to correct something you said. Neither of your relatives said you were plain. They said you think you're plain. Big difference in those two statements. Miss Campbell, I will marry you because I gave my word to your father. I know all I need to know about you. If you agree, we'll marry within a few days, and then we'll have lots of time to get acquainted as we travel to Shiloh."

"I don't understand."

"We don't have to understand everything. We simply need to step out in faith. Miss Campbell, I'd like to escort you to church tomorrow."

"I can't leave my papa alone."

"I already asked Elizabeth to stay with him. Will you let me to take you to church tomorrow?"

Laurel had no good excuse to refuse. She hadn't gone for the last several weeks due to her father's health, and she missed church. She loved to sing the hymns with the congregation, and Brother Caldwell was an excellent preacher. "I'd like to go to church tomorrow. Thank you for asking me."

"Your father asked me to arrange for the preacher to come on Tuesday afternoon to read the vows over us."

"I can't say those vows! Can you make those vows before God? I can't promise to love and obey you. I doubt you can do it either, if what my Uncle said about you is true. I hardly know you, but surely you feel the same way. Can you speak those eternal promises before God?"

"You ask difficult questions. Let me give it some thought. I'll say goodnight to you." Mac picked up his hat and left through the back door.

～ ～

He walked toward the orchard, quite distracted. Mac hadn't thought about the marriage ceremony. Yesterday, he came here to ask a man for permission to court his daughter, and now she'd asked if he could swear to love her for the rest of his life. After the tragedy of his only love affair, he vowed never to give his heart away again, not for the rest of his life, not to that romantic, heart crushing kind of love that led to unhappiness and loss. He couldn't speak the vows from the marriage ceremony to Laurel Campbell. Yet, people entered into arranged marriages for centuries, so there had to be some way to make a legal marriage without speaking vows that he couldn't keep.

Even with the troublesome thoughts going through his mind, Mac enjoyed the quiet time in the orchard. He understood why Laurel loved this part of the Campbell homestead, a little piece of heaven on earth. The mountains were grand, so different from his property in Greene County. That may be another obstacle they would have to overcome if they were ever to be a family. Of course, he had more immediate problems to deal with. He made promises to Mark Campbell and to Laurel, but he wasn't sure he should have. He had no intention of falling in love ever again. He thought the marriage would be--what had he thought? He hadn't. When he spoke to Matthew about his desire to have a family and build a home on his land, never once had he given any thought to the woman he would bring back to Shiloh as his life mate. Now faced with the dilemma, he had to tell a preacher he didn't know that he would marry a woman he didn't love but would accept her as a part of his life anyway. *Matthew Campbell, where are you when I need a friend?* Mac spoke aloud, "Lord, what have I done. Did I misunderstand what you want me to do?" As the sun set behind the west peak, Mac's once again remembered the scripture that brought him to Washington County.... *My grace is sufficient for you...'til Shiloh come.*

4

And they called Rebekah, and said unto her, 'Wilt thou go with this man?'
And she said, 'I will go.'....And they blessed Rebekah.

KJV c1850, Genesis 24:57, 60.

Before the sun rose over the mountains, Mac entered the cabin. He laid a fire and put the kettle on to heat. The trip to Hawthorn church would be an easy one, since the road was well-travelled, but the distance of nearly four miles would require them to leave no later than 7:30. Mac then returned to the barn to make himself presentable to attend church and to meet the Campbells' friends.

Promptly, Laurel appeared at the front door, ready to spend the day alone with the man she was to marry. She wore her Sunday dress, a gray woolen, bell-shaped dress, very severe and ill-fitting. The only adornment was a white tiered jabot. As with her other dresses, the hem was five or six inches too short, and her plain brown shoes were clearly visible. Her hair was woven into the severe, unflattering coronet. She wore the oval-shaped glasses and carried her mother's leather-bound Bible. She was every bit the picture of the spinster she believed herself to be.

"Good morning, Mr...Mac. Since you didn't come into breakfast, I brought you a biscuit with ham and some coffee. Would you like to eat on the way to church?"

Mac smiled and replied, "Yes, I appreciate your thoughtfulness. And thank you for calling me Mac." He took the basket from her and placed the canteen of coffee on the seat beside him. He took his place and picked up the reins to guide Sassy Lady to the church. They rode in silence for a while, but the silence was not as ominous this morning. There was a tension obviously, but for the first time, being seated next to Laurel was not as stilted. After a time, Mac spoke, "Laurel, I'm glad you came to services with me. I always feel better after I've been to worship."

"I needed to attend church. I haven't been able to go with Papa so sick and all. Anyway, I need to talk to Reverend Caldwell. I promised I would. Would you like your breakfast now?"

"I would. You're a fine cook, Laurel. I've enjoyed all the meals you've fixed since I got here."

"Nothing fancy. Just plain food, mostly what we can grow and harvest from our land."

A bit farther down the road, Mac attempted to revive the conversation. "Beautiful spring day here in the mountains."

"Yes, it's nice today. Been a mild winter here." Another lull in the conversation. After a few minutes, Laurel tried, "I hope you've been comfortable in the barn. I am sorry we don't have a spare room, but with Elizabeth helping with Papa, she needs the loft."

"The barn's fine." Another long pause in conversation followed. Finally, Laurel clenched her fists and spoke in an angry tirade. "Mr. Mac...Mac. I told you I'm no southern belle schooled in all the nice things to say and ways to flirt with a suitor. Besides, there is so much to discuss if we are to come to an understanding. Time's a luxury we don't have. What exactly do you want from me? Please speak frankly. I want to know so I can answer my father when we return."

"I want you to become my wife. I already told you that."

"I have heard you say those words, but what do you expect from a marriage to me?"

Mac took several moments to reply. Eventually, he stopped the horse and turned on the wagon seat to look Laurel squarely in the face. He made no attempt to take her hand or play the suitor. "First, I expect a partner I can build a life with." A long pause followed. "I need a help mate to work beside me while I build my homestead at Shiloh." Another few seconds went by in silence. "I'd like to have a friend who would share good times as well as support me in the bad ones." Mac stopped and looked at Laurel. She sat without a response. "I expect a woman to help me build a peaceful, secure home." More silence. "As we have time to become friends and partners and helpmates, I want a lover to share my bed and a spouse to bear my children. Did I answer your question well enough?"

Laurel looked intensely at Mac. Nothing in Mac's demeanor suggested guile, deceit, mockery or any sense of sarcasm. He had answered honestly and candidly.

"I appreciate your frank answer. Tell me what obligations my father made on you."

"I have no obligation to your father."

"He told me you were obliged to marry me on Tuesday, if I will agree."

"Poor choice of words on your father's part, but he is sick. I am sure he didn't think how that would sound to you. He asked no more than any other father would ask for his daughter. I made the promises willingly."

"What exactly did you have to promise?"

"I didn't have to promise anything. Laurel, I told you I am under no obligation. I did promise we would be married as soon as we could arrange the ceremony. He wants to see you wed. I told him I'd give you a safe home. He asked me to treat you with respect. The last promise was to help you see your own worth."

"What? He didn't ask for a maid? Surely, he required you to build me a mansion."

"Sarcasm doesn't become you, Laurel. Your father asked for no more than any father would expect of a prospective son-in-law."

"One slight difference in this situation, don't you think? We have no foundation to build on. We are strangers raised in very different worlds. Life in the Boston Mountains is not the same as you live in the flat lands. More importantly, we don't know each other. We don't love each other. What can we possibly build on?"

"We will build a life on our common faith." Laurel turned again to look at this stranger, the man her father had given her to. She had no reply, for how could she respond to such a sincere, honest proposal. "Laurel, Hawthorn Chapel is on the hill. Once we arrive, we'll have to answer questions from your friends and pastor. You have to decide. And it is your decision. I asked for your hand. Your father has consented. I will not take back my proposal, regardless of all the reasons you think I should. If you won't step out in faith with me, just tell me so. The choice is completely yours."

The congregation began to fill the churchyard. Her time was short. Laurel still didn't understand why Patrick MacLayne wanted to marry her. She couldn't disappoint her father, and it didn't seem Mac would change his mind. "I don't know why you asked for my hand, but I will take up your challenge to step out in faith. I hope you won't regret your choice."

"Thank you for agreeing to become my wife. Your consent is a gift. Let's go in to worship. After church, we'll have that talk with Brother Caldwell."

Hawthorn Chapel was a small one room log building. The church, erected four years earlier, was a bright airy place with four windows on each side of the building. Like most churches in this part of the country, backless wooden benches sat on either side of a center aisle. Men sat on one side of the aisle, while the women sat on the other. Laurel and Mac walked in and sat down opposite each other near the front of the sanctuary. Behind the podium was a slate board used in past years by the teacher of the subscription school. Now, Brother Caldwell used it to record the attendance of the previous Sunday as a reminder to his flock of their duty to evangelize the 'sinners' among them. A few old hymnals were scattered about the room, but since few of the worshippers could read, the books were used rarely. The hymns they sang were familiar, well-loved lyrics sung by rote.

"Let's all join in praise to our Father. Please join me in singing *There is a Fountain*. Along with the congregation, Laurel and Mac sang the familiar old hymn. She felt the eyes of her friend Rachel and most of the other people of the congregation on her. The spinster of Hawthorn did not attend Sunday worship in the company of a man, especially a stranger. Laurel felt Mac's presence across the aisle, but her attention was not the only attention he received. The next hymn they sang was *Blessed Assurance*. Laurel noticed how well Mac sang and that he truly seemed to enjoy singing the hymns. At the close of the song, Brother Caldwell walked to the pulpit and read the scripture. He had chosen Exodus 20:12. "Children, Honor your father and your mother." Laurel could hardly believe her ears. She hadn't been to worship in weeks, and the first scripture out of her pastor's mouth was the same words she read and thought about several times since her father had told her his plan for her future, the very words she believed God had spoken to her. "Yes, Lord. I hear you."

Mac looked across the aisle at her. Laurel saw he'd heard her, so she focused her attention back on Brother Caldwell, trying to listen to the words of the sermon. As the service ended, Laurel walked with Mac toward the door, greeting friends as she left. She nodded to her pastor and she spoke, "Brother Caldwell, I would like you to meet..." What would she say about Mac? What would she call him? He was not a family friend, not a relative. Mac stepped behind her and intervened.

"I'm Patrick MacLayne, member of the Shiloh church in Greene County. I've been fortunate enough to find hospitality with the brother of my pastor, Reverend Matthew Campbell. At your convenience this afternoon, I'd like to talk with you for several minutes. Miss Campbell and I will eat our lunch near that large hickory tree."

"Happy to talk with ya'll shortly." Reverend Caldwell continued to speak with his people as they left Hawthorn church.

Laurel took the basket from the wagon and led Mac to the grove of trees. She'd made a small lunch because dinner on the grounds was a common event of the Hawthorn congregation when the weather was nice. She'd have to introduce Mac and make explanations to her friends. Rachel was the first person to make her way to Laurel.

"We've missed you the past several weeks, Laurel. You been all right?"

"I've been all right. How about your kids and Josh?"

"We've all been good. Planned to come and see ya'll, but the seven miles between your place and ours seems like a trip to the moon with the little ones dragging on my dress tails every minute of the day." During the entire conversation, Rachel looked at Mac, her curiosity more than obvious. "Who's your friend, Laurel?"

"Patrick MacLayne, meet my friend Rachel Wilson. Rachel and I've been close since my family came to Arkansas back in '43. We went to school together for a while until she married my cousin Joshua Wilson."

"My pleasure, Mrs. Wilson."

"You're quite a surprise around here, Mr. MacLayne. Usually when a stranger passes through, he don't come to services."

"Big loss to the stranger. Good music and the parson preached a fine lesson today. I'm more than glad that I came and grateful that Laurel let me come along." Mac picked up a quilt to spread on the ground, and Laurel put the basket down there. "Won't you join us, Mrs. Wilson?"

"Goodness no. I got to get back to my brood. I just wanted to speak to Laurel since I ain't had the chance to catch up with her in a spell. How is your papa, Laurel?"

"His consumption's so much worse. He's not able to make the trip to church anymore."

"I'm sorry, Laurel. We all miss your pa. He's been so good to everyone here at Hawthorn. You know we'll come if we can help. I got to get back. My bunch'll be screaming for dinner. Nice to meet you, Mr. MacLayne." She returned to her family.

"Shall we sit?"

"Yes, I brought bread, cheese, a couple of slices of ham, and some apple butter. Not much of a lunch, but we'll have a good supper. With

Papa so sick, I don't think we should stay for the afternoon singing or the service tonight."

"I know you are worried. After we talk with the Reverend, we will start back." They ate their simple lunch in a few minutes.

"Excuse me. I'd like to visit my family's graves."

"Will you let me go with you?" Laurel nodded. Together they walked the short distance to the place the Campbells were buried. Small hewn stones marked the two graves. Names and dates had been etched into them.

"Mac, this is my mama. Her name was Leah Wilson Campbell. She died so young. She was thirty-one when we laid her here with my baby sister, who we'd have called Mary. She couldn't deliver the baby. Papa was so lost for a long, long time when Mama died. He really loved her. Even after fourteen years of marriage, he always held her hand and kissed her like a bride. Took him a while to get on with living. Then two years ago my brother Samuel died. He was thrown from a skittish horse he was trying to tame. He was twenty-seven years old." Tears fell unchecked from Laurel's eyes. "Soon Papa will lie there. Somehow, I got to get a marker for him, too."

Mac brushed a tear from Laurel's cheek. She flinched from his touch and stepped back. With her eyes downcast, Laurel whispered, "I'm sorry."

"Laurel, your father will have a suitable stone. I promise."

Laurel glanced up with a wisp of a smile on her tear-stained face. She turned to look around the peaceful churchyard. The area around Hawthorn Chapel was serene. A few early daffodils bloomed at the hedgerow, and the dogwood trees were covered with buds. Laurel picked several daffodils and laid them on the two graves. *The tree would be beautiful the next time she came to church. No, she'd probably not see the beauty of the fully blossomed dogwoods.* Again, tears rolled down her cheeks—and as soon as she was aware, she wiped them away with the back of her hand.

"It's all right to feel the loss of things you love. Let your tears come if you want. I understand."

"Please don't be nice to me right now. I need to keep my resolve. I can't cry in front of these folks."

"We should go back. Perhaps Reverend Caldwell can talk with us soon." Mac and Laurel returned and sat down to wait. In the meantime, several other friends came over to visit. Introductions were made and small talk followed. Mac was at ease with the friends of the Campbell family. He smiled and chatted and listened to these people. Laurel envied his ability to make people feel welcome and accepted. How well he evaded the explanation for his presence here among them.

By 1:00, most of the mothers with young children had laid them down on pallets for a nap. Older children went off to spend time with friends, chatting or playing simple games. The adults gathered in groups to talk about their crops, livestock, local politics, and other pertinent issues at Hawthorn. Reverend Caldwell made his way over to the grove where Laurel and Mac sat. Laurel fidgeted. She couldn't change her mind after they had this conversation. Her life would permanently change.

"Laurel, my dear, how's Brother Mark?"

"I'm afraid he's no better. He can't come to services anymore, and he misses it very much. The consumption takes his strength more every day."

"I am sorry to hear the bad news. I'll ride out to visit him some day this week."

"Reverend Caldwell, that's why Laurel and I need to talk with you. We plan to wed this Tuesday. Laurel's father can't come to the church, but he wants to give us his blessing and to give Laurel away. If possible, we need you to come to the homestead on Tuesday afternoon and speak the words over us."

Reverend Caldwell looked at Mac in confusion. He turned to look at Laurel, but she'd averted her face. Not new to him, though, as Laurel rarely looked at people when she spoke. "Laurel, do you want this marriage?" She nodded. "I haven't heard anything about you courting or a betrothal. I don't know this man. Have you known each other long?"

"Brother Caldwell. My papa wants me to marry Mr. MacLayne. Mac is a man of faith...he's a good man. Please come on Tuesday. Papa is anxious to have things settled."

"Laurel, you didn't answer my question. Do you want to marry?"

"Reverend Caldwell, Miss Campbell and I made this decision and spoke our intentions to each other. Mr. Campbell is pleased with the plans. We have prayed earnestly about this decision, and I believe it's the path we should follow. We need you to speak the words because neither of us could start a marriage without the blessing of our church."

Brother Caldwell stared several seconds into the face of the stranger. "I'll come to the Campbell place on Tuesday. I'll talk to Mark, and if he supports this union, I'll perform the rites for you."

"Brother Caldwell, there's one more thing." There was strength in Laurel's voice, and she looked directly into his face, not her usual demeanor. She sat taller, and with resolve, she spoke. "We want to write our own words. Neither of us is comfortable with the traditional vows. Will you let us to do that?"

"Laurel ... and what did you tell me your name is?"

"Please just call me Mac."

"Laurel and Mac, what part of the standard marriage ceremony don't you like? Vows are serious and permanent...not frivolous things that can just be discarded."

"Brother Caldwell, I...the words...I think..." Laurel couldn't find the words to explain her request.

Again, the pastor looked at the young woman he had known so long. "Laurel Grace, I am puzzled by the hurried nature of this wedding. I know you are respectable and have not given yourself to this man outside the bonds of marriage. I know you are not with child. Why is your marriage to be done so quickly and in a slipshod manner?"

"Reverend Caldwell, Laurel and I will write the words we want to speak before you arrive. You may read them and study them before we speak them. If you approve, we will use them. I assure you, the vows will be reverent, binding, and offer the glory to our Lord." Brother Caldwell wanted to discuss this strange request further, but Rachel and a few other women of the church walked up to speak to Laurel. The private talk between the pastor and the young couple ended.

"Can we expect you?"

"I'll arrive by the noon hour."

After attempted small talk and evading questions she felt ill-prepared to answer, Laurel searched to find Mac. He had he'd gone to hitch the horse. Mac saw her and quickly moved toward her side.

"Laurel, we must return to your father. I promised Mrs. Wilson that we'd get home early enough for her to return to her family before dark. I apologize that I have to take you from your friends." A sigh of relief came from Laurel, and she made several hasty goodbyes and walked by Mac's side to the wagon. After they took their seat, Mac began to maneuver the wagon between others in the churchyard.

"Mac, I am so grateful. You saved me from too many questions. My friends didn't mean to embarrass me, but I felt very awkward."

"Maybe you need to rethink your decision, Laurel." Mac looked directly at her. "I am not ashamed to declare our intention to marry. Did I embarrass you with your friends?"

"How could you ever embarrass me? You have been--" Before Laurel could finish her explanation to Mac, laughter erupted from a shadowy area near the wagons. Both Laurel and Mac overheard pieces of conversation from a group of younger men. "Spinster of Hawthorn... stranger ... keeps company...maybe she's not such a prude...maybe I should visit her ..."

"Excuse me, Laurel. Hold these reins for me." He jumped down and walked deliberately toward the huddle of men. He stared directly at the man who had made the crude remark about Laurel. Mac's stature and demeanor made his purpose clear. "Did one of you make a tasteless remark about Miss Campbell?" The silence among the men was a guilty response to the question. Mac continued, "I believe Brother Caldwell teaches that we are to treat all our sisters with respect and to protect all of our womenfolk. If he hasn't taught that lesson yet, perhaps a word to him will remedy the problem. Any of you who is a man will ask Miss Campbell's pardon."

A series of tipped hats, uttered regrets, and hasty apologies followed. Laurel nodded, wishing they would just leave. Mac returned to his place beside her. He turned back to the men who still stood huddled. "Thank you for the apology to Miss Campbell, but if I hear any of you insult my future wife again, I won't be so forgiving." He urged Sassy Lady into a trot toward Campbell's homestead.

As they drove from the churchyard, they heard the start of the afternoon singing. In his strong, solid voice Mac sang the praise songs he loved. When he sang, every word was clear and touched with meaning. Laurel sensed these were not just words to him, but truths he believed to the core of his being. "On Christ, the solid rock I stand...all other ground is sinking sand." She sat and listened and she relaxed as he sang to her.

"Mac, thank you. I appreciate how you defended me. If my brother Daniel had been here to confront those boys, he'd have started a fight, and I'd been the subject of even more gossip."

"No one will belittle you in my presence, Laurel. That's one promise I made your father. You will be treated with the respect you deserve." She looked at the man beside her. She felt safe. "Laurel, I would like to settle the matter we spoke of earlier before we return to your father's house. I asked if you were embarrassed by my presence. You can still reconsider your answer to my proposal if you don't think I'll make an adequate husband."

"I don't know how to answer your question. What should I say so you will understand me?"

"Simply speak the truth to me. Always tell me the truth. If you do that, we can handle all the other things we will need to overcome. Tell what's in your heart and speak the truth."

Tears ran down Laurel's face. "I am afraid." She was quiet again. Mac waited for her to continue. Soon the homestead was in view, and Mac remained silent. He drove toward the barn and started to climb down from the wagon seat. Laurel laid her hand on his sleeve, the first time she had ever purposefully touched him. "Can we talk in the orchard after supper when Papa's in bed? That's my favorite place in the evening."

"Yes."

After a good Sunday dinner of roast chicken, greens, stewed potatoes, and cornbread, Mark Campbell said good night. He came to the table for supper, but the major exertion sapped his strength. Laurel prepared the tonic of honey, cherry bark, chamomile, and hot water in hopes her father could to rest all night. As Mac helped him to his room, Laurel began to clean up from supper. When Mac returned, he picked up Laurel's shawl and told her, "This will wait 'til we get back."

As they stepped to the porch, they witnessed the glory of an Ozark sunset. At the horizon, red, orange, gray, yellow, and gold set the western sky aflame. The rest of the deep blue sky, tinged with gray near the mountain ridges, was cloudless. The wind was gentle but cool. The mountains were breathtakingly beautiful at twilight. Mac breathed deeply and lifted his eyes, "Thank you, Father, for this beautiful day."

Laurel recalled his words from the afternoon. He had told her, 'Speak the truth to me, Laurel. Always speak the truth to me'. She saw how deeply his faith and integrity were engrained, producing an attraction she couldn't deny. To have a man of such strong faith ask her to marry was a dream beyond any she had allowed herself in a long time.

"Mac, I told you I was afraid. I am. I don't know you. You don't know me. Last Wednesday, I had no idea you existed. I planned to remain the spinster of Hawthorn. If my father were not dying, I would remain unmarried and his housekeeper. I believed my dreams of a family and home would never come to pass. I accepted my lot in life a long time ago.

"I'm nearly twenty-eight years old. All my friends married years ago. I am a spinster, and I have never had a suitor. Then on Friday, you arrived—more than a day early, by the way. You were my intended before we ever met, thanks to a terrible case of consumption and my uncle's attempt at matchmaking. Don't you feel overwhelmed? Now we've made wedding plans, all happening within three days." Laurel paused, put her head in her hands, and screamed.

"Feel better now?"

"I'm talking too much."

"There is still much to be said. Laurel, I appreciate your honest answer to my earlier question. Talk all you need to. I want to hear anything you want to tell me. I'm humbled you are sharing with me so soon. I want you to know you can always speak your heart to me."

"I don't see that I have much choice. There has been no time to court so I can get to know you, so I will just have to talk to a stranger. I will have to trust that God leads me where he wants me to be. Papa is a good man and he loves me, so I know he thinks he has planned for my good. After he told me to expect you, three verses of Scripture came to me, over and over. *Honor your mother and father...Heed the commands of your parents, and ... not my will, but thine.* Brother Caldwell used the first verse in his sermon today. I'd have to be a dunce to misunderstand what I should do."

"You are no dunce, Laurel. All you say shows how wise you are. I'm pleased you're so bright and educated. We'll enjoy many spirited discussions over supper. Besides, what a blessing you will be in Shiloh Station. We have several young families with children and more to come...we truly need a good teacher."

"You don't have to marry a spinster to hire a teacher, but thank you for the compliment. People have always called me smart, but usually their words weren't meant as a compliment. Most men are intimidated by smart women."

"No real man is intimidated by an intelligent woman. You've known too many males who just didn't grow up."

"Well, it doesn't matter now. I have learned to accept myself as I am"

"How are you?"

"What is that supposed to mean?"

"Tell me about those dreams you gave up."

"Changing the subject, aren't you?"

"I aim to keep this conversation going, if it goes around in circles. Tell me about those dreams you say you gave up."

"You know—the same thing every girl wants."

"No. I don't know. I am a male, in case you haven't noticed."

Laurel had noticed. Mac wasn't the most handsome man she had ever seen, but he was attractive. He was masculine, confident, and educated. Most importantly, he was a man who lived his faith. He was more than she had ever dreamed she'd have as her mate...so much more than she deserved.

"You asked me this afternoon if I needed to reconsider my decision... you asked if you had embarrassed me today. Of course, you didn't embarrass me. You were friendly and kind to all my friends. You defended me with those boys in such a respectful, confident way. You didn't get angry or violent...you just solved the problem."

"So why were you embarrassed?"

"I didn't know what to say about the arrangement we made. You heard those boys. They can't understand why a man like you would want a wife like me. They laughed at the idea that you had escorted me to church."

"I don't care what they think. I only care what you think and what I think."

"I think you—never mind—I have no idea what I think. We're surely a strange pair. You may live to regret your noble act of this arranged marriage. I know my Papa misunderstood the reason for your visit. If you tell my Papa you made a mistake, I won't hold a grudge."

"Laurel, I won't take back my proposal. I already told you that. Everything I've learned about you in the past few days only confirms my decision. I understand you wanted the dream you described...a virtuous gentleman to come and take you to live happily for the rest of your days. I know you wanted to fall in love, have all the romantic things that happen to brides, and go off and live a beautiful life. I wish you could have all that, but we have a solid foundation. We will be equally yoked. We share a common faith in a benevolent Father who wants only good for us. Isn't that in Romans somewhere?"

"Romans 28."

"If you will walk out in faith with me, the things I told you I expected of you will happen. We have a better chance of building a happy life than many people I know. Between you, me, and the Lord, we can answer all those questions that are still not answered."

"What if..."

"No what if's, Laurel. The choice is a simple one. You can choose to become my wife, or I will start home at sunrise."

"Mac, I know so little about being a wife. My mother died when I was young and before she had the chance to teach me much of what papa calls 'womanly ways'."

"Laurel, we will learn together what we need to know. I will make no demands on you until I've met the promises I made to your father. There will be no physical union between us until I have earned the right to be your husband. I make you that promise...I hope that will remove some of your fears. We have a three-hundred-mile trip to Shiloh. In that time, surely, we can get to know each other. Right now, let's just learn to be good friends. That is a good place for any marriage to start. Will you be my friend, Laurel?"

She remained quiet for a few minutes. She looked at the strange man who spoke with such wisdom. "Tomorrow I'd like to tell you about my home—I believe you will find much to love there when we get to Shiloh. Crowley's Ridge isn't like your mountains, but it has its own kind of beauty. It's late and will be dark very soon. We should return to the cabin. Tomorrow will be a busy day if you've decided I will do as a husband." Laurel grinned at the joke he had made. Mac would do...her father had planned that for her.

Laurel heard the hesitation in his voice as he repeated the question. "Laurel, will you be my friend?" She lowered her eyes. "Laurel, look at me."

She raised her head. "With God's help, I will try."

5

Houses and riches are the inheritance of fathers; and a prudent wife is
from the Lord.

KJV c1850, Proverbs 19:14.

Monday morning began with a heavy rainfall across the valley. Laurel arose early to prepare breakfast. She made biscuits and gravy, hoping to entice her father to eat. The aroma of the coffee spread throughout the cabin.

"Coffee smells good. Will you bring me a cup with a dribble of cream?"

"Yes, I will, Papa. I will run out to get some fresh cream." While she was outside, Mac entered the cabin and walked over to where Mark Campbell sat in his bed.

"Good morning, Mr. Campbell. Did you rest well last night?"

"I'd have slept better if I knew Laurel's decision." Mark Campbell lay back against his pillow. Already his strength was gone.

"Did you have a talk with Laurel this morning?"

"We talked about breakfast. She went out to the springhouse to get some cream."

"I enjoyed meeting Reverend Caldwell and some of Laurel's friends yesterday. Rachel Wilson seems to be a fine woman. She asked about you."

"She is a good friend to Laurel. Got a brood of kids already. Married to Josh Wilson, Laurel's cousin."

"She said she had little ones at her every step."

Shortly Laurel returned and called to the bedroom. "You ready for some breakfast now, Papa?"

"No, I ain't. Come in here. What did you decide about the proposal from Mr. MacLayne? Will you make this match in good faith, daughter?"

Laurel knew she had told Mac she would try to be the friend he wanted, but it was so difficult to give the answer to her father. He didn't want her to be Mac's friend. He expected her to speak marriage vows of love, respect, and obedience to the man who sat next to his bed. She lowered her eyes so he would not see her hesitance and fear. "Yes, Papa. If Brother Caldwell approves our vows, I will marry tomorrow."

"What do you mean approve your vows? What's wrong with the vows we always use in our church?"

"Mr. Campbell, please listen. We mean no disrespect to the pastor or to the tradition of the church; however, neither Laurel nor I can promise to love each other. Laurel doesn't feel she can swear to obey a man she has known only four days. I respect her choice. We take the vows seriously, so we don't want to start our marriage with a lie. We will write our own vows."

"Did Robert—Brother Caldwell—agree to that?"

"He will tomorrow after he reads them. Of course, he wouldn't agree to anything until he talked with you. Actually, he looked at me as if I were a kidnapper."

"We'll deal with that tomorrow. I need to eat now. Don't want those good biscuits to get cold and hard." Laurel was relieved her father seemed satisfied. She now had one day to pull together a wedding. Where to start? A prayer of thanksgiving and a request for guidance would be a good place.

"Come to breakfast, Papa. Mac, can you help him to the table? Please sit here." Laurel seated herself between the two men in her life. How strange that seemed. Mac reached for her hand as he had done at every meal they had shared together, but his touch remained strange. Laurel stiffened, but she held out her hand. "I'd like to say grace, please. Father, thank You for all Your tender care and for showing me Your will. Lord, I am grateful papa is able to sit with us at this table. I thank you for my new friend. Please guide us as we make our way to Shiloh. Bless the food before us as we use it to strengthen us for your service. In Jesus's name. Amen."

"Will you pass me that hot gravy, young man?" Together the trio enjoyed a meal and pleasant conversation until Laurel's papa fell into a particularly difficult bout with coughing. Mac helped him back to his bed where he passed the rest of the morning. Laurel didn't relax for about an hour as she waited for the cough to ebb. Finally, Mark Campbell slept again.

"When Papa's gone, Mac, I'll be an orphan. I shouldn't be afraid, but I will be alone with all my family gone."

"Laurel, you won't be alone. After tomorrow, I'll be your family. As long as God wills, I won't leave you alone. After all, what are friends for? They stand beside you when times are sad and laugh with you when things are good."

"I'll try to remember.

Laurel set out to prepare for the wedding. She was resigned she would speak vows with Patrick MacLayne. Even though the ceremony would be very small, certain minimal formalities would have to be in place. Brother Caldwell would insist on at least one witness who was not a member of the Campbell family. She needed to find time to ask Elizabeth to stand with her. She had to plan a wedding supper for Mac. Perhaps if there were enough sugar in the larder, she could bake a small cake. She would wear her mother's wedding dress and smiled thinking her mother would like that. The beautiful lace on the long sleeves had come first from her grandmother's wedding dress. The lace had aged to a soft ecru, where it had once been bridal white, but it was beautiful yet.

The straight skirt fell from the empire bodice that would have looked nice on her if it had been the right size and five inches longer. The fact that she had no white shoes only magnified the problems of the length. Resigned to her poor wedding attire, she finished her plans in the scope of a half an hour.

As she prepared the mid-day meal, Laurel realized she hadn't seen Mac since breakfast, but he was a grown man capable of caring for himself. She carried a bowl of warm soup to feed her father. He was awake when she entered the room.

"Laurel, I wish you could have a real wedding. I'm sorry things ain't what they should be. Sit here by my bed and tell me your plans."

"I've planned a simple ceremony. Once Brother Caldwell approves our vows, we will stand here by your bed and speak them to each other. Elizabeth and the reverend will sign the bonds as witnesses. They will be posted at our church and filed at the county seat."

"Sounds legal and that's fine, but I plan to get dressed in my Sunday suit and give you away. We'll stand there at the hearth. Daughter, go down by the creek and gather lots of those daffodils for the mantle and the table. I ain't seen any this year, but there's always hundreds of them down there by the creek. I wish you could have daisies because they are your favorites, but it is a mite too early for those. Have you thought about a wedding supper?"

"I don't want to make a big fuss, Papa."

"This is a special time, Laurel. Go to down to the smokehouse and bring us some of those nice pork chops. We have potatoes in the cellar to bake. Open some of those preserved peaches and the creamed corn Rachel sent at Christmas. Use the sugar to bake yourself a layer cake. I wish you had some cocoa, but vanilla will do." Mark Campbell showed more excitement and energy than he had in several days. Laurel was happy to see him excited about something.

"Yes, Papa." Within a short time, Mark Campbell slept again. At mid-afternoon Laurel got up and went to kiss his forehead. Without her awareness, Mac had entered the bedroom. He walked to her side and laid his hand on her shoulder. Laurel gasped and flinched. Immediately, she moved away from his touch.

"I'm so sorry I startled you. Please forgive my intrusion. I was touched, as I watched the two of you."

"I didn't expect you. I'm all right. You've been gone most of the day, so I hope it was some pleasant task you found to fill your time."

"Had a few things to take care. How's your father?"

"He was awake this afternoon so we got to talk a long while. Papa wants me to make some plans for tomorrow. He asked me to fix a nice wedding supper."

"Nice surprise to come back to."

"I have to ride to the Wilson place to ask Elizabeth to come stand with me tomorrow. Brother Caldwell won't sign the bonds if we don't have a witness who is not related to us. Really, she is married to my cousin, but I don't think that will be a problem. Is there anything I can do for you before I go? I expect to get back before dusk."

"I'll be fine here. I will stay close by in case your father needs something."

Laurel rode the short distance to talk to Elizabeth, rehearsing what she would say to her. Of course, the two were not strangers to woman-to-woman chats, but Laurel had never thought she would ask her friend to stand at her wedding, especially as she married a stranger who had entered her life only four days earlier. What would she say? *Guess what, Elizabeth, my papa gave me to this strange man so will you come stand with me when I agree to this madness?* Luckily, when Laurel did tell Elizabeth about Mac, her sarcasm had taken a back seat to the task at hand.

"Elizabeth, you know only too well that papa is dying and probably very soon. He and my uncle Matthew planned an arranged marriage for me. Mr. MacLayne is a good man of faith. My uncle told my papa that he is well able to support a wife. I am to speak vows with him tomorrow if the reverend will approve the vows we have written. Will you please come over in the afternoon and stand with me?"

"Laurel, can you speak vows with this man you don't know?"

"I will try. I can't disappoint my papa."

"Do you love this man, Laurel?"

"I don't suppose it makes any difference. I've never been in love, and the odds are that here in Washington County that will never happen. Truthfully, I'm not sure what that means. I guess Papa thinks that any husband is better than no husband."

Elizabeth agreed to stand with her friend once she understood Laurel's situation. After all, they had been close friends and confidants since Laurel's mother died. While the young woman had never been one to spend time in small talk, she had confided most of the painful events of her life to Elizabeth, all of them but one.

"Laurel, if you believe God is calling you to marry this man, I know in time you will be happy with Mr. MacLayne. God bless you and thank you. I am honored that you want me to stand with you tomorrow."

About an hour before suppertime, Laurel started home. On a couple of occasions, the thought of running away crossed her mind, but within a moment, she returned to her sanity. She could never leave her father when he was ill. When she arrived home, she was surprised, for Mac had prepared their supper. He had made a more than tolerable beef stew with some beef chunks she had preserved last fall. He had fixed a corn pone for Mark Campbell, who liked to eat his cornbread in a glass of buttermilk for his supper. He had even found a jar of cherries sealed with paraffin in the root cellar. They would make a nice addition to the supper.

"What a surprise. I don't know when I've had a meal I didn't cook. Papa will be happy because he loves cherries. You even remembered he likes his cornbread in buttermilk."

Mac went to the chair where Laurel usually sat. "Shall we have our supper?" Laurel nodded and sat as he pulled out her chair. He left the room and returned in a very few minutes with Mark Campbell who leaned heavily on his arm. He showed him to his chair and then sat next of Laurel on the other side of the table. "Mr. Campbell, will you ask the blessing?"

Laurel could see her father was pleased to sit with them at the table and that Mac had asked him to say grace over their supper. Surely, this man had been meant to become a part of the family. Mac reached out and took Laurel's hand. She tensed, but she did not pull away. Mac looked at her and smiled, but when Laurel saw him look at her, she turned away. She never seemed to know how to behave around strange men...and tomorrow this strange man would be her spouse.

The three ate and enjoyed the conversation. As usual, Laurel listened more than talked, but her father enjoyed a normal evening in his home, sitting at his own table. In a while, he'd reached the limit of his strength, so Mac took him back to bed and helped him dress for the night. Laurel began to clear the table and set the food away for a later meal. After several minutes, Mac returned. "Can I help, Laurel?"

"No, I'm nearly finished. Make yourself at ease by the fireplace. It seems a bit cool in here. Will you stoke the fire? I'll will join you in a while."

"Did you manage to get all your tasks done today?"

"Mostly. I have a few things to do in the morning. I hope Papa is strong enough to be up a while. He asked me to say the vows at the hearth. It's a sort of tradition. He told me once that he and mama were married by the hearth at Grandpa Wilson's homestead in February during a blizzard. A circuit rider spent the night at our homestead, preparing to hold services the next day. My grandpa Wilson often sheltered the circuit riders because he had an extra space in his loft. Lucky for my parents, he just happened to be at the homestead."

"It will be nice to carry on the tradition for your father."

"Tell me something about your family, Mac."

"Well, I'm the last living child. My older brother died when he was just seventeen in the Mexican War. He had left the Naval Academy to join the troops fighting in the Mexican War. His name was Sean Hays MacLayne...Hays is my mother's family name. My mother and father never came to Arkansas. They live in Ann Arundel County, Maryland, where I was born. My mama's family have lived there on the same land since Revolutionary times.

Part of my homestead in Greene County came from a land that belonged to my grandfather MacLayne...something about an Indian, but I don't know the particulars. We've paid taxes on those 150 acres for a long time. I bought another parcel and homesteaded the rest. I have title to about 280 acres, partly forest with some nice meadow land...nice little creek runs through the valley. Not too far from the ridge, but it won't be like your mountains here. Lots of nice rolling hills...so green and beautiful. The land is good for all kinds of crops, too. We'll have a good life there, Laurel."

Laurel listened, but she didn't reply to his last statement.

"Soon as we get home, I'll build us a cabin. We'll walk the homestead before we decide where to build. I have a place in mind about a mile from Shiloh church. We have the subscription school in the church, so it wouldn't be a long ride to school every day. You may want to build at another spot... but we can decide when we have time to look around our homestead."

"I can tell you really love your home."

"Well, it would be nice to have a house." They laughed together, and Mac leaned back into the arm chair. The silence that followed was neither strained nor tense as it had been during other times they had been alone. If this were a prelude to the life they would share back at Shiloh, Mac knew he had found a person to help him build a home. He was somewhat relieved because he wasn't sure if a home was possible without love, but Laurel would be an intelligent helpmate and a good companion. They could build a life on those things.

"Have you written your vows yet?"

"Not written...I have pretty much planned what I'll say. I didn't have any paper in my saddlebags so I didn't write it down yet. Have you?"

"No. My trip this afternoon took up a good part of my time. Last night before I fell asleep, I thought it all out. I think Reverend Caldwell will approve. I'll write my words in my Bible. Then I can carry it and not forget what I meant to say."

"You are a practical lady, Laurel. I think I'll do that too. That is a fine way to keep the important words we will speak to each other. If you have a pen and ink, I would like to write my mine now before I go to bed."

"I have them here. You can sit at the table there, and you may need to move the oil lamp from the bureau. Can I bring you another cup of coffee?"

"Yes, thank you." When Laurel returned with the cup, she put it down. Mac reached for her hand as she turned. She stepped back and quickly turned her back to Mac. She walked to the fireplace.

He followed. "Laurel, turn around and look at me." She turned but did not meet his eyes. "Laurel, if you pull away from me tomorrow when I reach for your hand, the minister will think you object to the marriage. Can you tell me what's wrong?"

"I'm sorry. I'm not used to being touched by other people. Please forgive me. It is just a nervous reaction."

"What can I do to stop that reaction tomorrow? In private times, we can work on it, but in public I don't want people to think you are afraid of me."

"I am frightened of you. I am not sure I can give you what you want from a wife."

"Laurel, I told you yesterday while we walked in the orchard that we will learn together. Let's just focus on tomorrow."

"I'm grateful you're a patient man."

"Let me suggest a way we can get through the wedding. I won't take your hand—I will offer you my hand and you can take it. That way you won't feel the need to pull away from my touch."

"Thank you." Mac emptied the coffee cup and sat it on the table. He took the pen and ink and wrote in his Bible the words he would speak the next day. Laurel was curious, but she made no effort to read what he wrote. After several minutes, he closed the book and returned the pen and ink.

"I'll say good night, Laurel. I hope you sleep well. I will see you tomorrow at 1:00."

"What about your breakfast?"

"I'm a grown man, Laurel. I can make do. Goodnight again."

Laurel felt the strain had returned, and she was sad that the easy, comfortable time they shared earlier in the evening was gone. She had no idea of how to bring it back.

"Good night, Mac."

Laurel sat at the table and opened the ink well. The words flowed from the nib of her pen onto the front page of her Bible, almost as if they had not come from her at all. Words certainly didn't come easily to her most of the time. Laurel blotted the page and closed her Bible. She walked to her father's bedside to see if he slept. He rested peacefully, so Laurel climbed the ladder to the loft. She looked at her mother's dress she ironed that morning. Everything needed to prepare the wedding dinner had been set aside. Everything, even the writing of her wedding vows, had fallen into place, as if all had been ordained. Laurel knelt by her bed and prayed.

"Father, I believe I am doing what you have willed. Too much has happened too fast and everything has fallen into place too easily for this to be coincidence. I know you want good for me always, but I am afraid. Tonight, I need the faith to believe what I already know. Please Lord, help me be gracious and kind to honor to my father, You, and the man you sent to be my husband. Even if this is not my dream, help me be a good wife to Mac. In Jesus name, hear my request. Amen."

Reverend Caldwell arrived just about noon, as he'd promised. Elizabeth met him at the door, and he asked to see Mark Campbell before he spoke to either Laurel or Mac. Mark Campbell had already dressed in his best Sunday clothes, a brown broad coat and blue cravat, and had trimmed his beard and dressed his long gray locks in a queue with a rawhide cord. The preacher pulled up the chair next to the bed where Mark reclined.

"Mark, what in Sam Hill is going on here today? Did you give that man your blessing to marry Laurel? Two weeks ago, Laurel had no prospects of marriage, and now she tells me you consented to her marriage with this stranger."

"Now, Robert, calm down. You know how the young men in this community treat Laurel. She has endured their gossip, name-calling, and rudeness for a long time. Besides, there is no hope she'll find a suitable husband if she stays here."

"I know Laurel has led a pretty sheltered life here with you."

"Well, my brother lives in the northeast part of the state. He's the pastor of a local congregation in Greene County. He arranged for a friend, a member of his congregation, to come here and meet Laurel. He wants a wife of good character and sound reputation. Laurel is a good match. If I wasn't dying, I'd have set a few months for them to court, but I don't have a few months. This is right. I need you to speak the words over my daughter. Then she'll be taken care of after I'm gone."

"You're sure this is what you want?"

"I am sure this is what the Lord wants them to do."

"Then I will read the vows. I guess they told you they won't speak the traditional vows."

"Yes, they told me."

"Well, I need to see if I can approve the vows they wrote. Where are they?"

"Laurel went to the loft about an hour ago. I haven't seen Mac today, but he has made a place in the barn." The minister asked for both sets of vows, and he sat at the table in the main room and read them. He took some time to read and re-read the vows the two had written. After careful study and comparison with several passages of scripture, he consented.

The little cabin was clean and simply decorated. On the mantle, Laurel placed two small bundles of daffodils. She dressed the table in the center of the room with a lace coverlet that had been one of her mother's wedding presents. Centered on the table were a small, vanilla wedding cake and two beeswax candles in pewter candlesticks. Leah Campbell's treasures served as decoration for her daughter's simple wedding. Elizabeth returned to the loft to help Laurel dress and to ease her pre-marriage nerves. When she reached the top rung on the ladder, she found Laurel at the foot of her bed dressed the gown made from the fabric of both her mother's and grandmother's wedding dresses. Because the dress had been fashioned for her mother, Laurel wasn't exactly the image of a beautiful bride. The dress was beautiful with its lace covered bodice and tiny pearl buttons. The fitted skirt was the latest fashion in 1820 when her mother had worn it. Unfortunately, the skirt was five inches too short, and the dress did not fit well in the bodice, since her mother had been more womanly than Laurel was. Worse of all, the worn work boots stood in stark contrast beneath the short hemline. Elizabeth could not let her friend walk toward her soon-to-be husband in those awful boots. "Laurel, don't you have some house slippers to wear? Those boots simply won't do."

"I hadn't thought about those. My mother did have a pair of light gray satin slippers with long gray ribbon that wrap around the ankles. They have no solid soles, though."

"No mind. You won't wear them outside." After she donned the house slippers, Laurel looked at her feet and was pleasantly surprised. The gray ties around her ankles presented a picture that the too short hemline had been planned just to show them off.

Laurel added a blue stone necklace and earbobs, Elizabeth's embroidered handkerchief and her Grandmother Wilson's wedding veil to her wedding ensemble. She and Elizabeth both looked for something new, but even together they were not able to find anything because Laurel hadn't bought anything new for herself in a long time.

Oh, well, it's only a silly superstition, Laurel thought to herself. "I'm ready as I'll ever be, Elizabeth. Please go down and tell Reverend Caldwell and Papa they can start anytime they are ready." Elizabeth climbed to the main floor, but she barely reached the last step when Mac handed her a small package.

"Can you give this to Laurel, please?" Elizabeth returned to the loft with the small wrapped package.

"What do you have there?"

"I don't really know. Mr. MacLayne asked me to give this to you." Laurel hesitated. Mac had thought to get her a wedding present, and it had not even crossed her mind that she should do something to honor him.

"Laurel, open the package."

"Oh, Elizabeth! What am I doing? This is ridiculous. Am I fooling myself to think this is the right thing to do?"

"It's only wedding nerves, Laurel. All brides feel nervous before the ceremony. You told me yourself that this wedding is an act of faith... and Laurel, you have great faith." Laurel closed her eyes and hugged her friend for a minute.... Then she opened the package Mac sent. Inside, she found a small bouquet of four apple blossoms, two nearly opened and two buds, nestled among several deep green leaves on two stems. The pretty pink and white blossoms would serve as her wedding bouquet, something else she had given no thought. The second item was a length of green silk ribbon. Mac had provided her something new, so she used it to make a sash for her dress. She turned to look in her peering glass over the bureau. She saw her reflection and sighed. *I'll have to do.* She bent to pick up the apple blossom bouquet and her mother's Bible. She and Elizabeth went down to the men who waited below.

Laurel approached her father as he sat in his chair. Mark Campbell took his daughter's hand and said, "You look like your mother, Laurel. I know she is with us today and pleased to see you in her dress."

"Thank you, Papa," Laurel bent down to kiss her father's cheek. "I'm ready."

With extreme effort, Mark Campbell stood and offered Laurel his arm. Together they walked the three steps to the fireplace. Elizabeth walked behind them, and Mac stood on the opposite side of the hearth with Reverend Caldwell.

"Friends, we're here this afternoon to join Laurel Grace Campbell and Patrick Liam MacLayne in marriage. Is there any objection to this union?" No one spoke though everyone in the room had concerns that could have raised several objections. "Who gives this woman to be married to this man?"

Mark Campbell spoke in a voice that reminded Laurel of the papa she had known before the wasting sickness had taken his vitality. "Believing in the providence of a loving Father God, I give my blessing to this marriage." Mark lifted Laurel's veil and kissed her cheek. "You are beautiful, Laurel Grace." He returned to his chair where he would watch his daughter speak her vows.

Mac stepped to his place at Laurel's side. He made no move to touch her or take her hand. She knew he would do everything in his power to help her get through this ceremony in a dignified manner. Reverend Caldwell continued, "Marriage is a holy estate and not be entered into without serious thought and prayerful consideration. Do you Laurel Campbell make this covenant with a willing and sincere spirit?"

"Yes, Brother Caldwell." Her voice was quiet with a touch of tremor, but the look in her eyes told him she was sincere in her decision.

"Do you Patrick MacLayne make this covenant with a willing and sincere spirit?"

"Yes, Reverend."

"Patrick, you may speak your vows to Laurel."

Patrick turned toward Laurel. She lifted her eyes to look at him. He smiled because her demeanor spoke to her resolve and faith. "Laurel, the pledge I make to you before your father, Reverend Caldwell, Elizabeth, and the Lord is sincere. I will honor your place as my wife. I will respect the extraordinary person that you are. I will support you and encourage your life's work. I will protect you and provide a safe home for you. I am honored you have consented to become my life partner. My covenant will remain as long as God wills."

"Laurel, speak your vows to Patrick."

"Patrick, I am humbled to become your wife. I pledge my respect to you at all times. I will honor your efforts to build a home together. I will work alongside you to create a home that will honor God. I will listen to your dreams and plans and share your efforts to bring them to completion. I will care for your homestead and stand beside you in all circumstances. This is my promise to you as long as God wills it."

"Laurel, will you have Patrick Liam MacLayne to be your lawful husband until death parts you?"

"As it is God's will, I promise."

"Patrick, will you have Laurel Grace Campbell to be your lawful wife until death parts you?"

"As it is God's will, I promise."

"Do you have a ring to give as a sign of this covenant you've made?" Laurel hadn't given any thought to a ring. Mac probably hadn't been prepared for this wedding tradition as the entire thing had happened so quickly. Mac took a black cord from beneath his green cravat. This caused Laurel to look at him, really look at him for the first time that day. He stood next to her, superbly dressed in his gray broad coat, an immaculate white lawn dress shirt and black trousers. His boots were buffed to a shine. He wore a green silk cravat made of the same fabric as the lovely wedding gift he had sent her. Laurel was ashamed that Mac had put more thought into this wedding than she had. She looked directly into his so blue eyes, and she saw no displeasure, condemnation or disappointment. He smiled at her. She couldn't believe how handsome he was. His chestnut colored hair was tied into a queue with a black leather cord. His strong square chin was softened with his close cropped, neatly groomed beard. His appearance was noble. It was solid. Laurel felt as if she were dreaming. In reality, she felt her inadequacy to her very core.

"Laurel, please wear my mother's wedding band. It has been in my family longer than I know. I offer it with respect and humility." Mac held out his hand to her just as he had told her. He waited for her to place her hand in his. She looked up and smiled briefly. Soundlessly, she murmured "Thank you." Laurel placed her left hand in Mac's. "I humbly accept your mother's ring. I will wear it proudly as long as you want me to. With God's help, I will strive to make you a good life mate."

"As Laurel and Patrick have made their vows and pledges to each other, I pronounce them to be husband and wife, in the name of the Father, Son, and Holy Spirit." Mac slipped the wide gold band on Laurel's finger, then raised her hand to his lips, and kissed the ring to seal their covenant.

They were married. Both Laurel and Mac turned to speak to Mark Campbell. Congratulations were offered by Reverend Caldwell and Elizabeth, and Reverend Caldwell wrote out the marriage bond and presented a copy to Mac. "I will file the others in the church record and at the county seat the next time I am in Fayetteville. God bless you both." For the next two hours, the couple with their wedding party enjoyed their wedding supper and the pretty wedding cake. Toasts were offered with cups of coffee. Just before four o'clock, Mark Campbell excused himself. He had spent all the strength he had left, and his cough had become continuous.

"Papa, I'll get your tonic right now. Mac, will you please help papa to bed?" Reverend Caldwell and Elizabeth spoke their farewells. Elizabeth hugged Laurel's neck and kissed her cheek. She whispered, "Don't worry about tonight. Mac is such a gentleman. He will be thoughtful of you." Laurel looked at her friend in confusion, but she had more immediate concerns. Her papa was in pain, and he needed the tonic so he could sleep and that horrible coughing would subside.

She helped him drink the tonic she'd prepared even stronger than usual because she saw the depth of his pain and fatigue. Her papa's worsening condition broke her heart. He had overdone himself to honor her at her wedding.

"Laurel, daughter, you are beautiful today. I know you will learn to be happy with Mac. He's a solid, faithful man. I know he will treat you well. You gave me a wonderful gift daughter. I won't leave you alone."

"Papa, please just rest. Please don't talk about that. I love you, Papa." He feebly sat up and kissed her cheek.

Laurel was nearly overwhelmed with the emotion from the day, and the unusual affection from her father fostered her tears. "You've always been a good daughter." Laurel helped Mark Campbell with the cup of tonic, and then she sat with him for some time. Finally, he slept and Laurel knew he was at ease.

About sunset, Mac came in and asked Laurel to walk with him in the orchard. She remembered his thoughtful gift of the apple blossom bouquet. "I really loved the apple blossom bouquet you sent to me. The blooms are lovely. Of course, you realize you killed four apples before their time."

Mac laughed. "And who said you have no sense of humor?"

"Did someone tell you that?"

"Yes...you did—that first day we met." Laurel relaxed when she understood that he appreciated her attempt to lighten the mood of the evening. He smiled at her.

"Mac, I am so humbled you gave me your mother's wedding band. This ring is so beautiful. You know, when I was a girl I dreamed that someday I would wear a ring like this...gold and wide and beautiful."

"That's good news, because I was about to apologize that I didn't get you your own ring. I didn't think I'd need one so soon. I hadn't planned to marry you without a courtship. When Matt and I talked about this, he suggested I come to meet you because we have so much in common. Neither of us knew how sick your father is."

"You are so good to ease my papa's mind, Mac. I am sorry you got pushed into this marriage. I know it would be impossible for a man like you to deny a man his last wish."

"Laurel, I am not sorry about our marriage. Honestly, I don't know what we we'll do next, but I'm at peace and blessed right now. All of this will work out for the best. We've been ordained to be together. And for right now, being good friends is enough."

"If you want to walk outside, I will have to change shoes..."

"I'll wait." When she returned, Mac held out his hand, just as he had during their wedding, and he waited for her to offer hers. She laid her land in his and, for that moment, all felt right and Laurel felt safe. They walked hand in hand for some time. The Ozark sky was dark now and filled with innumerable stars. A gentle southern wind spread the scent of the apple blossom buds across the valley. The night sounds of insects and birds provided their wedding serenade. They found no need to speak. Unaware, they arrived back at the Campbell cabin. Laurel whispered a silent prayer of thanksgiving. Today had been a nearly perfect day.

She went in and to look in on her papa. He rested and seemed to be without pain, another blessing. As she returned to the kitchen, she saw Mac at the table. "You want some leftover wedding supper?"

"No, but another piece of that cake and a glass of milk would be good. I'll go out to the springhouse for cold milk." While he was gone, Laurel went to the table near the hearth where she picked up the Campbell family Bible. When Mac returned, she would ask him to record their marriage. She brought the ink well and pen and laid these things next to the Bible on the kitchen table, and then set about cutting the cake. Mac entered and Laurel noticed how his presence filled the room.

"Will you please do me a favor? I would like you to record our marriage in my family Bible?"

"Don't you want to do that? It's your family."

"It has always been our family tradition for the man to fill out the record. I doubt a woman's ever written in that book." Laurel turned to the correct page and gave Mac the pen.

"You honor me, wife." Laurel smiled up at Mac...This was the first time she had been addressed as wife. In his bold, precise script, Mac wrote,

> *Patrick Liam MacLayne, 34, of Shiloh Station, Arkansas, married Laurel Grace Campbell, 27, of Hawthorn Chapel, Arkansas, on Tuesday, March 17, 1857. Witnesses included Mark Campbell, Elizabeth Wilson, and Reverent Robert Caldwell. The wedding was celebrated at the home of the bride's father.*

They laid the book aside and moved to the chairs near the hearth. Tonight, there was no fire, for the day had been so nice, and there had been no need to cook since the food had been prepared for their wedding dinner. They enjoyed the quiet, pleasant evening. "Laurel, did any of your wedding dreams come true today?"

Laurel sat for a minute...How could she tell him what the day had meant to her? "Yes...I had something old, borrowed, blue, and when you sent this lovely green ribbon, I even had something new. I truly loved the apple blossom bouquet. You were so thoughtful to think of them."

"They were your flowers, Laurel!" And Laurel thought to herself that only a kind person like Mac would think to make sure she had a bouquet at all.

"Well, you even sent me a wedding gift...that lovely green ribbon."

"To match those fiery green flashes in your eyes that show up when your emotions surface. I was lucky to find it at that mercantile in Fayetteville."

"So that is where you got off to yesterday when you were gone all afternoon."

"Oh, you missed me, did you?" Laurel lowered her eyes and a touch of pink touched her cheeks. "You know your eyes are really lovely when the green overwhelms the gray." Laurel didn't respond and she breathed deeply. She turned in her chair to look at Mac.

"You told me yesterday to speak the truth to you—only the truth. That has to be our cardinal rule. Mac, you are always kind, but don't flatter me. We will be good friends only if we speak the truth to each other."

"I don't like flattery either. It always has a hint of deceit in it. When I compliment you, Laurel, it will never be flattery. I like those flashing green eyes so much that I may have to keep you upset all the time!"

"All right..."

"You didn't say thank you, Laurel."

"What?"

"When you receive a compliment, you are supposed to say, 'Thank you.' I gave you a compliment...not flattery."

A hint of a smile touched Laurel's lips. "Thank you, Mr. MacLayne. Now can I answer your question?"

"What question?"

"Did any of my dreams come true? Remember?"

"Oh, yes. Well?"

"I just wanted to thank you again for your mother's ring. I would never want another to take its place unless you would like to have it back. I would understand if you do."

"My mother would want her ring on your hand, if she were here to bless our marriage. I have worn it around my neck since she gave it to me the day I left home. I know it is in the right place now. I'm pleased you want to wear it."

"The day has been special for me. I hope you feel the same."

"I am content and at peace. The day has been a good one. It is late, Laurel. As it is our first night together, I would like to establish a tradition for us, if you agree."

"What would you like?"

"Each night before we end the day, I want to share the scripture with you and close our day with prayer. That way, we will not end any day at odds with each other. Is this agreeable with you?"

"I can't think of a nicer way to end the day."

"And Laurel, when we pray together, I want to hold your hands."

"That is a lovely request." Mac picked up his Bible from the table by his chair. The leather-bound book was no show piece. Obviously, the book had been well-used. First, he showed Laurel where he had written his vows to her and where he had signed and dated the entry.

"What would you like to read tonight?"

"You are the head of the household, and I think the Good Book says that is your decision to make."

"I want to read about the first marriage." Mac read Genesis 2:18-25. When he finished, he looked up a Laurel, held out his hand, and waited for her to give him her hand. Laurel reached across the short distance and laid her left hand into his. Together they prayed. "Let's go to bed, Laurel. If you would like, I'll give you a few minutes to change from your wedding clothes. Then I will follow."

She was taken aback for a moment. Because he had told her he expected no physical union, she assumed that he would not want to share her bed. Laurel wasn't sure how to react, and the same doubt and fear that had inadvertently shown on her face several times over the past few days appeared again. She lowered her eyes for a minute, then the familiar jut of her chin and the green fire appeared. "Yes, Mac. Please come up in about ten minutes." Laurel went back to see if her father were still asleep. Satisfied he was all right, she climbed to the loft.

Mac returned the Bible to its place and turned down the wick of the oil lamp. He laid a fire for morning so Laurel would not have to do that before she prepared breakfast. He noticed the water pail was nearly empty so he walked the short distance to the well to replenish the water

PATRICIA CLARK BLAKE

in the house. When he returned, all the lights in the loft had been extinguished save a single candle. He blew out the last lamp on the kitchen table and climbed the steps to the loft.

Laurel had already lain on the left side of the bed and turned down the right side for him. He removed his boots, socks, broad coat, cravat, shirt and trousers. As he walked to the place Laurel had saved for him, she looked at her husband. He lay down and he pulled the coverlet to his bare waist. His chest was lightly furred and his broad shoulders and torso above his narrow waist were well-tanned. Obviously, Mac had spent a great deal of time outside without a shirt. When she saw he had noticed, she averted her eyes.

"Laurel, it is all right for you to look at me. I am not embarrassed. May I have your hand?"

In her nervousness, Laurel replied with wit... "I thought I gave that to you this afternoon."

"Oh, you're the funny lady tonight, are you? Laurel, please give me your hand."

"Thank you, friend, for this special day." He brought her hand to his lips. She felt the soft brush of his neatly trimmed mustache and then the warm touch of his lips. They were firm, yet soft and warm. The kiss lingered. "Goodnight Laurel." He turned to his right side and brought the coverlet to his shoulder as he blew out the candle.

6

Blessed are they that mourn: for they shall be comforted.

KJV c 1850, Matthew 5:4

Laurel MacLayne's first day began just before dawn. Her papa began to cough, and the episode did not quit but became stronger and harsher with each bout. Laurel jumped up and hurried down the loft steps. As she had awakened from a deep sleep, she gave no thought to the fact that she was a married woman. In the main room, the fire at the hearth was ablaze and the kitchen was warm. Fresh milk and eggs sat on the table ready for her to cook breakfast. Then she realized that Mac had not been beside her when she awoke. He had already been about the morning chores.

Laurel rushed to her father's bedside. Mark Campbell had dark circles under his eyes. The pillow cover showed large splotches of blood. He made no attempt to sit up. She hardly recognized this pale image of her father, who had once been the strongest man she knew. Laurel brushed her papa's forehead, and a brief touch told her his fever was dangerously high. She had hoped a good rest with less reason to worry would give him a restful night. Tears streamed down her cheeks, and she prayed, "Lord, please heal my father. Don't take him from me." Within a minute, though, she spoke again. "Lord, please don't let my papa suffer so. Your will, not mine." She rushed to the kitchen to make the tonic, but she found the pouch Elizabeth had left was all but empty. She grabbed her shawl and ran to the barn to saddle Sassy. Before Laurel had finished, Mac came into the barn.

"What? Are you running away already? Are you in so much of a hurry that you forget to dress?" A hint of laughter was behind Mac's teasing.

"I have to go. Papa needs Elizabeth now. Don't you understand?"

"Laurel, slow down. I was only teasing. I know you wouldn't run away. Tell me the way. I will get Elizabeth while you care for your papa."

"You have to ride as fast as you can. Papa's fever is too high. Ride down creek road for about a mile. At the fallen oak on the creek turn to the west for a few yards. Elizabeth's cabin is there behind a split rail fence. Please hurry, and tell Elizabeth the fever is too high."

"Calm yourself, Laurel. Go back to your father."

Laurel ran back into the cabin. She made a tonic of some honey, chamomile, cherry bark and apple vinegar. She knew this old remedy helped coughs, but she didn't think it would reduce the fever. She would be grateful if it brought any relief to her papa. Yesterday, her father had stayed up far too long through his sheer will to give her a wedding day. He had no strength left to fight the consumption. She spooned the tonic into her father's mouth between his bouts of coughing. She ran to the well for cool water to bathe him, praying the fever would fall. Mark Campbell slept fitfully. All she could do was pray.

As another half hour passed, Mac and Elizabeth rode into the front yard. Laurel cried out, "Please, come help me."

Elizabeth took over the nursing. She added extra herbs to the tonic she prepared and she added a dose of laudanum, so Mark Campbell would sleep.

"Laurel, you did a good job. The cool bath helped take down the fever. Let me take your place for a spell. You can go get dressed and have some breakfast. I'll call you when your papa is able to talk."

Laurel looked at the thin worn night dress she wore. The garment was certainly not warm enough for the cool March weather. She shivered... until that moment she hadn't realized how cold the cabin had become.

"Laurel, are you all right?"

"Yes, Mac. Thank you for bringing Elizabeth. Excuse me and I'll go dress.

"There will be time for that in a while. Come eat breakfast first. I have finished the eggs, and here are a couple of left over biscuits. Not as good as a meal you'd prepare but filling enough."

"I'm not hungry. I'll need to care for Papa so I need to dress."

"After you eat. Here, sit." Mac pulled out the chair. She looked up at her husband of less than one day and saw the determination in his face. She took the chair and ate several bites of the breakfast he put in front of her. When she had finished, he offered her his hand. Again, she looked up into Mac's too blue eyes. He smiled down at her. "Laurel, it's all in the Lord's hands now. We'll just trust and let go. Let me help you up." Hesitantly, she placed her hands into those of her husband. "Go on... get dressed. What kind of respectable housewife would be found in her bedclothes at noon?" Laurel knew he was teasing, but at that moment she felt nothing light or hopeful. Papa would see his end soon. Laurel wanted to stay strong in her faith as her father had asked, but the loss of her father was too much to bear.

Laurel climbed to the loft, where she saw the unmade bed with both sides rumpled. Mac's wedding clothes hung on the pegs. A carpet bag rested beneath the neatly hung clothes. Laurel made the bed and dressed in a black skirt and cream blouse she had taken from her mother's chest, not a very attractive "first day" ensemble, but at least it was functional. Laurel glanced into the peering glass and saw how disheveled her braids were. She didn't take the time to braid her hair, but she tucked a few tresses into her coronet. She returned to the kitchen. "Is my Papa awake yet?"

"Let's go ask Elizabeth." Together they entered the curtained nook that served as a bedroom.

"Laurel, your papa's fever is down now, and he's resting easy. He will probably sleep several hours. He is very weak, and I have no tonic or herbs that will make him well. I hate to speak such sad words on the day after your wedding, but your Papa will not be with us long. I will try to return tomorrow to relieve you with the nursing. I wish I could help more."

"Thank you, Elizabeth. I'll get your wagon ready." Mac left the cabin.

Laurel broke down in Elizabeth's arms. "Laurel, don't be afraid. Grieving for your Papa is not due yet. Rely on God and your new husband. Together we'll all take care of what's to be done."

"I know that's what Papa planned, but it is all too soon, and I'm so afraid. I guess it shows how weak my faith is."

"Not so. Your faith is strong enough. Just deal with one day at a time. That's all any of us can manage." Elizabeth held Laurel for a few seconds. "I'll be back in the morning."

Laurel sat at her father's bedside. Shortly, Mac returned and he brought a book and an old newspaper he had taken from the mantle. He also brought the arm chair over near the bed. "I found a copy of the Gazette. It's four weeks old, but I'd be happy to read to you for a while." It was a common to have an old copy of the Arkansas Gazette from Little Rock to surface in Hawthorn Chapel, always several days and well-read.

"Can you read?" She attempted some humor on that heavy morning.

He looked into her tear-streaked face. "Why, yes, ma'am. I learned how at my mother's knee when I was just a lad. Want to hear how good I say the words of this old newspaper?" A slight smile touched her lips. Mac skimmed the front page and began reading an article. "A bridge across a tributary of the Arkansas collapsed when a large woman in a carriage tried to cross at the same time as a heavy freight wagon and four jacks pulled onto the opposite side. There was no loss, except the bridge and a large six-layer butter cake."

In spite of her concern, Laurel grinned. "You made that up!"

"No, so help me. Look, see, it's here on the front page of the Gazette." He pointed to the column and put his finger completely through the paper. "Oops. Well, you can trust me, can't you?" Laurel smiled again, and relaxed a bit. The fear that had been so prominent in her eyes ebbed.

"My dear Mrs. MacLayne, please go rest a while. I'd be glad to sit with your father while you nap."

Before she could respond, Mark Campbell spoke from his bed. "Laurel, I'm thirsty. Can I have some water?" Laurel jumped up and hurried to check her father's fever.

"Papa, I am glad you're awake. Here's the water. Mac, please help him drink this while I go to the kitchen to make another cup of tonic. Your fever is up again."

"No, Sis. I need to talk... to the two of ya'll."

"Papa, please rest. You need your strength."

"My will."

She didn't know her father had made a will. He'd never mentioned one.

"I filed it a while back. You need to know what's in it. I'd give you the homestead, but ...but the law... Your brother took his part... sold off the part on the far side of the creek. You'd be alone here with no help... and not legal... sold the land ... dowry." Mark's ragged cough stopped the explanation. Laurel propped him up on his pillows and gave him another drink of water. "The mortgage payments ...next June ... seven years. Dowry...lien...bureau drawer." Mark strangled again.

"Papa, please just rest. Other things will wait 'til you're stronger."

"Mac, listen for her.... She won't listen. She never asked me for nothing.... Best daughter any man could want." Again, the conversation stopped.

"I understand, Mr. Campbell. I'll take care of everything. You can rest, sir. Laurel is in my hands and the Lord's now. You don't have to worry anymore."

"Laurel, Mac, come here." They walked the few steps to be with him. "Laurel, take Mac's hand." Laurel looked at her father.

"Papa?"

"Hush up, girl. My strength's gone." Mac offered his hand as he had done since they'd met. "No, Mac. That is not what I asked... Laurel, take Mac's hand." She reached out to take his hand. Again, Mark Campbell was racked with strong coughs. He lay back for a few minutes. Mac did not relinquish the hand Laurel had given him. Her father continued again. "Laurel, I made Mac promise four things... Thank you, son.... I saw you properly wed. Well, almost.... I heard no promise of love between ya'll, and I reckon I understand why. You need time... to know each other, but I prayed for love and passion of a man and wife for you both...I love your Mama, finest gift the Lord Father ever gave me.... I pushed you into a marriage of convenience...don't mean that love and passion won't grow." It was more than obvious that Mark Campbell had over spent his strength. He held his feeble hands toward the couple who sat at the side of his bed. When they took his hands, Mark Campbell bowed his head. In an almost inaudible voice, he blessed them both. "I thank You for the fine children with me here.... Awaken a great love and passion in them... Give them a full rich life. Father, please forgive me... all my sins. I praise You, in Jesus' name. Amen."

Mark Campbell didn't speak any more that night. Laurel prepared the herb tonic and helped him to drink the full cup. He would sleep better if he had more. Mac looked in on both Laurel and Mark and then went out to the barn. He returned to the kitchen to lay more wood on the fire and to stack extra logs nearby so the morning fire could be stoked without a trip outside. He filled the water bucket and carried it in to the dry sink. With no other chore to keep him occupied, he returned to the small room behind the kitchen. Mark Campbell slept, seemingly at rest.

"Mac, I'd like to stay down here with my papa tonight, if it is all right with you."

"I would expect no less, wife. However, before I go up to the loft, I would like us to share the scripture. We can't start a tradition if we stop after only one night."

"I guess I'd forgotten. This day has been a trial. I still can't believe you married me."

"That's a discussion for another night. I picked out Ecclesiastes 3:1-15 because I think those are good words for us right now."

The next two days passed in a blur. Laurel cared for her father, tried to learn more about her husband, finished household chores, read scripture with Mac, and napped when she could. On Friday morning, Laurel slept well past sun up, and she awoke with the sun shining in her eyes. The cabin was quiet. Laurel stood up, stiff from her night in the chair by her father's bed. The quiet unnerved her. Laurel looked at her father and understood why. Mark Campbell no longer rasped to breathe nor did he moan in pain. His struggle was over. She knelt by his bed and wept.

— ⌒

Shortly, Mac returned from the barn. He no more than opened the door when he realized that his father-in-law died in his sleep, and his bride of three days was grief-stricken. How he could support her? He would take her in his arms and hold her as he would any grieving friend, but she drew back every time he attempted to touch her without her per-mission. If he tried to comfort her, would she draw even farther from him? "Laurel, I'm sad we lost your father so soon. We'd have been good friends. Let me take you upstairs to rest for a while. You've not slept enough since I met you. After you've rested for a few hours, we'll do what has to be done."

Laurel leaned to kiss her papa's now cool forehead. Silent tears streamed from her red, swollen eyes. After several moments, she pulled the coverlet over her father's face. "Rest well, Papa, and please tell Mama I love her." She turned to her mate and offered her hand to him. He led her to the loft.

"Laurel, will you let me help you get your shoes off? It's hard to rest with shoes on your feet." She nodded. She sat on the side of the bed, and Mac pulled off the worn work boots and stockings. He rubbed her bare feet and calves for a few minutes, but Laurel responded very little to the attention. Mac pulled the quilt back and pulled her pillow forward on the left side of the bed they'd shared only one night. "Laurel, lie here and sleep for now." Laurel reacted to his direction without ques-tion. When she was settled, Mac covered her shoulder with the quilt. He turned to leave, and Laurel caught his hand.

"Please don't leave me alone. Won't you stay with me?" He lay down next to her, and as soon as he put his head on the pillow, Laurel spoke in her tear muffled voice, "Will you hold me?" She coiled up like a frightened child. Mac pulled her close and put her head on his shoulder. As he placed his other arm across her waist, Laurel began to sob again. He held her until she slept. Then Mac slept too.

Three hours later, they awoke to a knock on the front door. Mac went down to admit Elizabeth who had come to bring more herbs for the fever tonic. "Thanks, Elizabeth, but we don't need more tonic. Mr. Campbell passed during the night."

"My regrets, but thank the Lord, Brother Mark ain't suffering. He was such a good man, and he's meant so much to our community at Hawthorn Chapel. I just can't picture our neighborhood without Mark Campbell and Laurel."

"You've been a true friend to Laurel since her father's decline that I hate to ask for more favors. Elizabeth, I need your help to get through the services tomorrow."

"Anything I can do."

"Need you to stay with Laurel while I go to Hawthorn Chapel to talk with the pastor. She told me the day we went to church together that she wants to lay her papa to rest next to her mother in the churchyard." Mac donned his hat and coat, went to the barn to saddle Midnight, and rode to the church.

Elizabeth climbed to the loft and found Laurel on the side of the bed in the same clothes she had worn for the past two days. "Laurel, I'm so sorry about your papa. He's not in pain anymore." Laurel nodded and stood, walked to her peering glass above the bureau. She stared into the glass. "Laurel, can I make you a bath downstairs? Mac won't be back for a while." Laurel turned to walk to her rocking chair and sat. Once again body-racking sobs erupted. Elizabeth sat on the edge of the bed and remained there until Laurel's grief subsided.

"Elizabeth, I need that bath now. Will you help me?"

"Wait here. Let me heat some water."

Laurel was glad to have a few minutes to herself. "Father, please forgive my weak faith. My fear is unfounded, I know. You have provided all I need. Thank you for your loving care of my papa and relieving his pain. I need your help to get me through these heavy days. Amen." Laurel knew she had to make plans for her papa's service. She had to honor her father with a proper wake and then write to her brother Daniel. When she handled these major concerns, then she would think about the next things she must face.

Laurel went down to bathe. The warm water felt wonderful, and she realized how good it felt to be clean again. She remembered that she had given little thought to the way she looked since her wedding day. How long had that been? Seemed like a year, or perhaps she'd imagined it all. She certainly didn't feel married, but she did value the new friend who had found his way into her life. Mac's presence had been a godsend, and she knew he would take care of many of the funeral details. She also knew that when he returned, he would not be alone. Hawthorn Chapel was a close-knit community, and word of her father's death would spread quickly. People would come.

"Elizabeth, I need to wash my hair, too. It is worse than a mess, so can you help me undo these braids?" Elizabeth walked to the back of the wooden tub and unwound Laurel's coronet. Although they had been friends for many years, she had never seen Laurel without her braided coronet.

"Where is your hair brush, Laurel?"

"In the top drawer of the bureau in the loft." When Elizabeth returned, she brushed her friend's waist length tawny brown hair. She then helped her wash the mass of curled tresses. Even with the use of several towels, Laurel's hair would not be dry enough to braid in the limited time they had. "My hair is so thick it won't dry. I should have waited. I guess I will just have to leave it down for now."

"Do you have a band or ribbon to tie it back out of your face?"

"Only the green one Mac gave me. Won't look much like I'm in mourning."

"I don't think anyone will notice."

"I only have my Sunday dress to wear. It's only gray, but it'll have to do."

"Laurel, would you like for me to get your father ready?"

"No, thank you. I will do it. You can stand with me if you want. Papa took care of me all these years. It's the least I can do for him." Together, they entered the bedroom. Laurel hesitated briefly, but when she could, she removed the quilt she'd used to cover him. He was smiling. Tears once again spilled down her cheeks and she whispered, "Thank you, Lord, for taking my papa home."

After half an hour, Mark Campbell was ready. He wore his Sunday best, his hair was brushed and tied into a queue, and his beard had been brushed and trimmed. Laurel kissed his cheek one last time and left the room. She found a few things to occupy herself as she waited to greet her friends and family from the Hawthorn community.

Just before dusk, Mac returned, and he brought Reverend Caldwell, Jerald Wilson, who was Laurel's uncle, and the church elder, Martin Brand, her father's best friend. They removed their hats, and Laurel took them in to speak their farewells to her father.

Mac walked over and embraced Elizabeth. "Whatever you did to help Laurel was special. I was afraid she would not be able to stand up to the grief. I wasn't sure she could bury her father tomorrow."

"Don't underestimate her, Mac. She is made of sterner stuff than you know. She has weathered much sorrow in her years and has always managed to come through with dignity and faith. Laurel is much like a willow...able to bend with the storm and then stand tall to praise the Lord when the storm passes."

"Has she asked for anything since I've been gone?'

"No, but I think she will talk with you and the Reverend later tonight. You know that people will come in and out until late tonight. Just stand by her...she'll do what she has to."

"I almost didn't recognize her when I came in...she looks so different with her hair down. Her hair is beautiful. Why doesn't she ever wear it like that?"

"She'll tell you it's not the way plain women dress. That is a story for her to tell you sometime."

Shortly, Laurel returned from the bedroom with the preacher and her papa's best friends. Mac asked them to sit with them at the table. Both Wilson and Brand nodded a polite refusal. Martin Brand approached Laurel. "Laurel, your papa loaned me two dollars back last month. I'd like to return it to you, now." Mr. Brand handed the amount he had spoken of. "I just wish I could give it back to Mark. He was a mighty good friend to me." With lowered heads, the men left the cabin. Reverend Caldwell, Mac, Laurel, and Elizabeth sat down to a quick meal and talked through the plans for Mark Campbell's service. Between 7:00 and 9:30, a continual flow of people paid their respect to their friend and neighbor. Laurel greeted each family and returned the hugs and pats they offered. That night several more men returned loans her father had made to them. Laurel had no idea that her father had given so many people money. By the time the night was over, Laurel had received nearly $27 dollars from neighbors and church members. Laurel wondered if this was not all repayment of loans, but a loving congregation's way of helping her to get through this hard time.

When the cabin was quiet, Mac approached Laurel and gently pulled her close to him. He was not at all sure how she would react to this embrace, but he knew she needed to be held. She'd been strong and gracious all evening. She was quiet, but then that was her nature, he had come to know. However, her silence was also a blatant sign that she was near the end of her strength for the day. Laurel did not move away from Mac, but he did sense her stiffen for a moment. She relaxed quickly and laid her head on his shoulder. "You are very tired, friend. You did your father proud tonight in the way you welcomed his friends. He is surely smiling down from heaven at you, Laurel." Mac noticed his shirt had become damp. Laurel's reserve was gone. She wept again. Mac led her to the stairs of the loft and helped her climb up. Once she was settled, he went out to take care of the nightly chores, only to find they'd been done. He returned to the cabin and turned down the wicks to the lantern. He climbed the stairs to the loft.

He saw she'd changed into her nightdress. She began to separate her locks into lengths so she could reweave the braid her hair. "Leave it down, Laurel. I didn't realize how beautiful your hair is." Mac turned down the quilt and replaced the pillows in their places. "Laurel, come to bed. Tomorrow will be a hard day. We will both need to rest the best we can."

"You've been kind to me, Mac. Will you hold me again?"

"It will be my pleasure to hold you tonight. Let's read for a while." Mac picked up his Bible from the side table and read Psalm 100. Afterward the beautiful words of David's praise song, Mac took Laurel's hands and prayed. "Lord, we owe you so much praise for the gifts of fellowship and love from the Hawthorn Chapel family. We ask only for your strength to hold us up through these dark days ahead. Amen." He blew out the lantern and reached across the bed to cradle Laurel just as she had asked. He buried his face in her glorious curls and smelled the sweet scent of her loose, flowing hair. He felt Laurel begin to relax. Then he whispered, "Goodnight, wife."

At dawn, the friends who would serve as pallbearers arrived to take the body of Mark Campbell to Hawthorn Chapel. Laurel and Mac were prepared to attend the casket from the Campbell's homestead to a final resting place next to Laurel's mother. They spoke few words. By 10:00, nearly every member of the Hawthorn community had gathered to pay their final respect to one of their brothers and speak words of condolence to Laurel. Few of them knew the circumstances of her hurried marriage, and many of the women expressed their concern that such a sad thing as the loss of her father would ruin the happiness of the new bride. Laurel simply nodded at their kind, but mistaken words.

Brother Caldwell spoke boldly about the character of Mark Campbell, grieving the loss of a man who had been an important part of their settlement from the earliest days of the church at Hawthorn. He commended his spirit to Heaven and closed the service with one of Mark's favorite hymns. As the congregation sang *Rock of Ages*, the pallbearers lifted the simple casket and carried Mark Campbell to his place next to his wife, Leah. All repeated the words to the Lord's Prayer, as they did every Sunday while Laurel scattered a handful of soil across her father's coffin.

"I love you, Papa. Rest here next to Mama until I can be with you both." With those final words, Laurel turned and walked away from the grave, Mac at her side.

The ladies of Hawthorn Chapel laid out a fine dinner in the meadow just beyond the log church. Laurel walked through the motions of the event, nodding to comments, saying thank you, responding to congratulations on her marriage, and eating bites of the probably delicious food. Honestly, none of the experience had registered since she had walked away from the grave. Mac never left her side.

About 3:00, Laurel whispered, "Please take me away from here, Mac."

— ～

Mac pulled her shawl across her shoulders and then spoke to her church family. "Friends, we are grateful, more than we can say, but we have to return to the homestead. We appreciate ya'll and all you've done. We'll return to say a proper farewell on Sunday." Laurel waved and murmured a word of thanks. Mac helped her into the wagon and drove toward the Campbell homestead. Neither of them spoke as he drove away. When they'd driven quite a distance from the churchyard, Laurel broke into deep, jerking sobs and collapsed into his arms. He knew no words to comfort her, so he continued to hold her and make their way to her home.

When they reached the yard in front of the cabin, Mac reined in the horse and jumped from the wagon. He picked Laurel up from the wagon seat and carried her into the cabin. He placed her on her bed where she grieved. As she cried, Mac held her. Finally, when the sun was near the western horizon, she slept.

When he was certain Laurel slept soundly, he went to do chores as quickly as he could. He wished he'd remembered to bring Elizabeth back with him, but this was probably for the best. He would have to take on the support role as soon as they left for Shiloh, just the three of them... Laurel, him, and the Lord. But Laurel did not awake that night. Mac sat by the bed for a long while, reading. Laurel had developed a small library, and there were several good books to choose from. Just before he slept though, Mac did what was habit. He turned to pick up his Bible and offered a prayer. He found it very hard to keep his mind focused on anything except Laurel's grief. Helpless to comfort her, he asked God to comfort her and guide them both.

He knew it was not only the loss of her father that weighed so heavily on his new wife, but also the fear of a life with him. Though he did not know her well yet, he knew himself well enough to know he had already developed an attachment to the shy, quiet woman. Whether he felt duty or pity, he wasn't sure, but he knew she would be a part of his life from this time on. With a deep breath, he laid his concerns in the hands of the Lord and scolded himself for worrying. He knew the next few days would be a challenge for them both, but more than that he knew together they would meet every trial. He lay next to Laurel and he slept.

— ‿ ⁀

When the sun rose on Sunday, Mac awoke with Laurel gone from the left side of her bed in the loft. "Good morning wife. I love griddle cakes for breakfast. Do you know how to make them? Do you have any sweetening, maybe some molasses or syrup?"

"Of course, I'll make you some for breakfast if you will gather the eggs and milk so we can get ready for church." The casual, comfortable atmosphere of that day seemed a good omen for Laurel. While she didn't feel happy, she did feel at peace, even though she would have to say goodbye to her church family in a few hours. Mac had been very generous to give her the time she'd needed to be ready to leave, and she couldn't ask him for more time. Besides, Mac had spoken with the

Tomlins at her papa's service and told them they could move into the cabin on Wednesday afternoon.

"You seem thoughtful this morning, Laurel. What are you thinking about?"

"Just a bittersweet day. I love my church family, and they've always tried to look out for me, especially after my mama died. Saying goodbye to them will be hard." Laurel became very quiet and Mac left her to her musings.

As Laurel had said, the service was bittersweet. All her friends took special care to greet her and offer her congratulations on her marriage. The ladies of the congregation offered advice on life on a homestead, and tips to help her produce an abundant garden. Others promised to care for her parents' graves. Brother Caldwell met her on the porch and kissed her cheek as she entered the log church that her father had helped build only a few years earlier. The hymns were familiar ones she had always sung on Sundays. Reverend Caldwell's spoke of the journey all make in life, a topic so appropriate to Laurel's situation that Sunday morning. He quoted Genesis 49:10, where Jacob gathered his sons to teach them their roles in establishing God's kingdom in the Promised Land. *"The scepter shall not depart from Judah, or a lawgiver from between his feet, until Shiloh come; and unto him shall the gathering of the people be."* Three words caught in Laurel's attention...'til Shiloh come.... Of course, Shiloh had caught her attention since Mac had mention his home frequently in their short time together and later that very week she would set out on a long, dangerous journey to make that strange place her home. She saw that what she faced was not unlike the trek across wilderness the chosen people of God had made during the Exodus. Brother Caldwell compared the journey to every man's life, and emphasized the fact that the goal of each person should be paradise, a place of peace and contentment. Their aim was to reach Shiloh. Laurel realized with Brother Caldwell's amen that she felt reassured God had planned that life for her. She prayed the assurance would last. She knew under her calm reserve lay much fear and grief left unexpressed. At the close of the service the congregation sang a newer hymn with lyrics that Laurel was happy to hear. The beautiful words, *Blest be the ties that bind, our hearts in Christian love* lingered long after the people had gone out to the meadow to prepare for the dinner on the grounds.

Rachel rushed up before Laurel and Mac had reached the wagon to retrieve their lunch basket. She threw her arms around her dearest friend and hugged her so tightly that they were breathless when she finally released her. "I don't know how I will survive here when you are gone. I hope you will keep in touch. Of course, I know how the mail's slow most of the time but promise you'll try to write me. Please Laurel try to stay in touch." Laurel nodded her promise. Directly behind Rachel was Brother Caldwell's wife, Jane Ann, and several of the ladies from the church's sewing circle.

"Laurel, dear, we didn't get to have you a pounding with everything happening so fast. We just couldn't let you leave us without something to remember us all by. We decided to get together yesterday, and we worked late until we finished this coverlet for your bed. All the sisters crocheted the blocks, and we worked them together. It turned out real nice." She handed Laurel a sunny yellow bed coverlet so large that it would totally cover a bed and the pillows. Laurel was speechless at the gift of love her friends had made.

"Jane Ann and all of you wonderful sisters at Hawthorn, I'll cherish this gift always. I am honored to have this coverlet. Thank you all." A dozen hugs followed as Mac stood back and watched his wife, who smiled and was happy for the time. Shortly, Reverend Caldwell called, "Folks, it's time to eat. Let's bless this feast. And I'll ask for safe passage for Laurel and her new husband as they travel toward Shiloh." The meal was a typical dinner on the grounds, a potluck with far too much food to feed the number of people who were present. Three small cakes, canned fruit, and a flank of bacon and a couple of small smoked hams were not even touched and somehow found their way into the basket Laurel and Mac had brought with them. Hawthorn intended to help the young couple on their way. About 2:00 in the afternoon, Laurel spoke quietly to Mac.

"Mac, I have to go to the churchyard one last time to say goodbye to my family."

"I would like to go with you if you will allow me to." Laurel nodded and Mac rose and offered his hand to help her. As they walked among the grave markers, Laurel stopped at several to pick up fallen leaves and sticks or to brush debris from the stones of people she had known. Within a few minutes, she stopped at a stone marker on which the name Samuel Campbell and the year 1855 had been inscribed.

"This is my brother. He died too young. He planned to marry at Christmas that year. Sam was a headstrong Campbell, never listened to anyone." Laurel laid her hand on the stone briefly and walked on. The next marked gravestone bore the names of Leah Campbell and Mary. The date 1846 marked the date of death. Laurel knelt next to her mother's grave and spoke in a whisper. "Mama, this is Patrick MacLayne, the man Papa has picked to be my mate. He's a good man, and he has promised to take care of me. We're headed to Shiloh, and I may never be able to kneel here with you again, but I will always remember. You were the most loving mother." Laurel cleaned all the dead leaves, broken twigs, and other winter reminders from her mother's grave. Shortly, with her reserve gone, she stood at the foot of her father's new, unmarked grave and she wept. Mac laid his arm across her shoulders and let her cry out her grief. "Mac, Papa has no marker so others will remember him."

"Don't concern yourself. I left funds with Reverend Caldwell to have a marker carved. The back of the stone will say, Husband of Leah and Father to Daniel, Samuel, Laurel and Mary. The front will have his name and the date, like your ma's, and Romans 8:28. Your father said it's his favorite."

7

*By faith, Abraham, when he was called to go out into a place which
he should after receive for an inheritance, obeyed and he went out, no
knowing wither he went.*

KJV c1850, Hebrews 8:11.

Wednesday morning began as a beautiful early spring day in
the Boston Mountains. Light, wispy clouds drifted across
the high blue sky as a crisp breeze tugged at the budding
tree limbs. The sun shined and the scent in the air was clean and new
with the emerging life that comes with springtime. Laurel was up and
dressed early. She moved quietly around the loft, trying not to awaken
Mac too early. Laurel felt a twinge of anxiety, but even more a sense of
anticipation as she rolled a large pan of biscuits to bake, knowing any
they did not eat for breakfast would help make meals for the next day or
so as they traveled. While the bread baked in her mother's hearth oven,
Laurel sat in her father's armchair and began to work her hair into the
braids that she would weave into the dread coronet. She knew Mac didn't
like it, but it would be easier to care for on the trail.

As she pushed the last pin into the coil, Mac came down from the loft. He was dressed in buckskin, a look Laurel had not seen before. Frankly, she hadn't imagined Mac as a pioneer before, as he had always been so properly attired and groomed. He almost seemed to be a different man until he spoke.

"Good morning wife. Ready for an adventure?"

Laurel rose and placed an ample meal on the table. He pulled out her chair, and they sat down to breakfast. After blessing their meal, Mac tackled the hot biscuits and gravy, half a dozen slices of bacon, and several fried eggs Laurel put before him.

"Nothing like a big breakfast to begin a new day and a new life. Thank you, wife." He rose and went out the front door toward the barn to finish the morning chores that he would have to complete before they started their journey. Within the hour, he returned to load the few remaining items that Laurel chose to take to Shiloh. Mac carefully placed the carved bureau, her mother's spinning wheel, Laurel's grandmother Wilson's rocking chair, the bed frame from the loft, Mark Campbell's arm chair, Leah Campbell's side chair and the frame with the cuttings and saplings for Laurel's orchard. Laurel had wanted to take her parents' rocking chairs from the front porch, but the small wagon bed was full. She ran her hand across the back of her father's chair and went to the springhouse to bring the items she had packed to help feed them on the trail. Mac stored the carved box in the bottom drawer of the bureau along with the family Bibles and Laurel's small library. In the third drawer, Mac deposited the tiny box with Laurel's $700, the dowry her father had left her and the money from the sale of the homestead. The final few items to pack were fragile things wrapped in clothes and bedding: the mantle clock, a couple of crystal lanterns, and Laurel's peering glass. The last items packed away were the parts of the MacLaynes' meager wardrobe, including Laurel's wedding dress and Mac's small carpetbag with his suit and dress boots. He covered the beautifully carved bureau with the rag rug Leah Campbell had made to warm the floor in front of her hearth. The large, round rug would grace their home someday. Even the small amount of personal pos- sessions Laurel chose had almost overwhelmed the small wagon bed. Mac covered everything with a large oilcloth and secured the cover with ropes anchored around the wagon. Mac packed every last item Laurel had asked for. Carrying these things from her family's past safely all the way to Shiloh nearly three hundred miles east across Arkansas would be a difficult task, but perhaps they would help her settle in their new home. "Are you ready to leave, Laurel, or do you need a few minutes to say good bye?"

— ~

Laurel walked back into her father's cabin and looked around to assure herself she had taken everything she could not leave behind. After a several minutes, Laurel walked back to the porch, latched the door, and nodded to Mac. "I am ready."

As they drove from the yard, Laurel felt such a sense of loss, much as she had felt when they drove away from the churchyard on Sunday. Likely, she would never be here again--she would never again stand on this land, her home. The thought saddened her, but at the same time, she felt excited by the prospect of seeing new places and making a new life. She would have been lonely here without her father. Perhaps the Lord was showing her how to start over.

Laurel sat next to Mac quietly for some time, and they made good time for most of the morning. The well-travelled road to the east was a well-defined and fairly smooth. Even with the late departure of ten o'clock, they were well beyond Hawthorn Chapel before noon and on down the road toward Fayetteville.

"Are you hungry, Laurel? We could stop here, rest our mules and fix a bite of lunch, if you are."

"Yes, I will fix lunch if you are ready. We have left over chicken from yesterday and the biscuits I baked this morning. We may as well drink the milk while it is still good."

"Sounds like a fine meal. Let me unhitch the mules and take them and the horses down to the water in that small pond yonder. Need some help getting to the food?"

"No, you packed smart. I can get to the larder from the tailgate. I don't think I will even have to undo the cover." Within very few minutes, the stock rested and an ample meal waited on a quilt under an oak tree.

"You are very quiet today, Laurel. Are you well?"

"I am always quiet, Mac. I hope you aren't bored. I rarely think of things to chat about. I'm sorry.

"I'm not complaining, Laurel. I just wanted to know if you are all right."

"Yes, thank you."

Mac allowed half an hour for the animals to rest. "Well, I guess we should get back on the road. Will you store all this stuff? "

Laurel replaced the things that could be used later, but she placed the folded quilt on the plank seat of the wagon to make the ride more comfortable for them both.

"Here, let me help you up." Mac reached to help her to the seat, but she had already pulled herself up. "That was a good thought. The seat will be softer with the quilt there." Laurel nodded and took her seat next to Mac. "If I promise to avoid small talk this afternoon, will you talk to me? We might as well use the time because we have lots of it to fill on this trip home."

Laurel nodded her head and tried to relax. She turned slightly so she could see Mac when he spoke. She didn't know what serious things he wanted to talk about.

"Laurel, in our short time together, we have had little time to really get to know each other. Will you tell me how you feel about us?"

"Us? What do you mean?"

"Are you still afraid? I mean, of me?" She saw him frown. "I don't want to make you uneasy when we are together." She heard his voice change. "Hang it all, Laurel! Do you object to me sharing your bed?"

"What?"

"Our present situation won't allow much privacy. Sleeping together on a pallet on the ground at times or in rough public inns will be the best we can expect on our travels."

"Mac, I am not afraid to be close to you. Those first two days were awkward, but you've been very respectful. And it is your right as my husband to share my bed."

"My rights go far beyond laying my head on the pillow next to yours." Although he had spoken those words in a jest, Laurel squared her shoulders and her chin jutted out into its protective stance. A deep flush showed in her cheeks,

"I am aware of that. I am a spinster, not a moron."

"Laurel, you are not a spinster. You have been Mrs. Patrick MacLayne for the past eight days. I don't like that word much anyway. Why do you use it?"

"Sounds better than old maid, doesn't it?"

"Do you still see yourself as a spinster?"

"Not much changed except I changed hands. I went from belonging to my father to belonging to you." Mac clinched his jaw. "You were good to take me off my papa's hands and let him pass in peace, but as far as feeling different..." Laurel stopped. "I am sorry. That sounds so ugly. I meant no disrespect to you. I guess I don't know how to feel any other way. I have been a spinster for a very long time."

Mac didn't reply quickly. He drove around a curve in the road. "Let's change the subject for now. Tell me about your schooling. I noticed that there is no school at Hawthorn."

"We had a school some years back. You know how hard it is to keep a teacher." There was an edge in Laurel's voice.

"I didn't mean to criticize your community, Laurel."

"I didn't take it so."

"How did you get to be a teacher?"

Laurel realized the effort he made for them to have a real conversation...not an argument, but to really talk to her. She'd try, too.

"Just lucky, I guess." Mac laughed. "I finished common school in North Carolina, just before we moved to Arkansas. I was twelve when I passed my exams and received my diploma. Since then, I just kept reading whenever I could get a new book or an old copy of a newspaper. I helped the teacher at the Hawthorn school the couple of years I went to school after we moved here."

"You'll be a real treasure at Shiloh, Laurel. Few of our people can read or write. My friends will think I'm a real hero to our community because I brought you."

"Nice to be a treasure instead of..." Laurel didn't finish the sentence. "What about you. I know you've been to school. You speak well, and you can read the scripture, not just quote from memory like most of our people do. You are good at sums. How did you learn all those things?"

"Same as you, except in Maryland, where my family lived. Our town had a school taught by the priest, not a pretty woman like you." Before he had gotten the words out, Laurel's shoulders squared and her chin jutted out once more. She turned her eyes away.

"Stop the flattery, Mac. You were the one who made me promise the truth. I expect the same from you."

His careless words had ended the pleasant chat he'd been enjoying with his wife. He again had to pause to consider how to reply. Truth was the best route. "Laurel, I don't want to cause a rift. We've had a pleasant talk, but I feel I'm walking on eggshells with you every minute. I told you earlier that I am no flatterer, but I don't want to deal with that right now. Please excuse my choice of words. Let's just change the subject again."

"Fine." There was ice in her voice, ice colder than the brisk northern wind.

"I hope we find a good place to stop for the night. I think we saved some time by taking this road south of Fayetteville. We could have found shelter in Fayetteville, but I want to reach Shiloh in three weeks. Every mile we can save will help. We've a cabin to build and a garden to plant. Besides our orchard will do better if we can get the cuttings and saplings in the ground sooner."

"I'd like to see an orchard grow at your homestead."

The sun began to set behind the mountain ridge. About ten miles west of Fayetteville, Mac halted the wagon. On the other side of a small creek, he saw several small cabins clustered together. He jumped to the ground and walked the few feet to one of the cabins where he saw a light through a window. He knocked on the door, and a large, burly man came to the door.

"Howdy, brother. Can you tell me where I can find a good place for my wife and me to set up a camp for the night?"

"Surely can. About a quarter of mile down the road, you'll find a nice level meadow near a clean creek...not a stone throw from the cemetery. Nice enough place to pass the night. Wished I could offer you lodging but not an empty bed in this here whole settlement. When our circuit rider comes, we put someone out, just to make a place."

"That'll do just fine. We have what we need to shelter for the night. The fresh water will be nice, though."

"That place I told you about is our campground, here at Goshen community. We use the camp meeting ground as our church site. In a few years, we hope to have us a real church in that meadow. Brother Graham thought it'd be a good thing to start with a campground. Good Lord willing, we'll get us a church soon."

"Know how you feel. We felt mighty blessed when we got our church built back at Shiloh a couple of years back. We got our own preacher now too, so we can have service every week and don't have to wait for the circuit rider. Well, we'll head on before dark. Bless you, friend."

Mac climbed back into the wagon seat and drove a few minutes to a place near a tiny cemetery on a flat, grassy meadow. Within thirty minutes, the MacLaynes had made a good shelter under the wagon, using an extra oil cloth to create a shelter. Laurel retrieved an oil lamp and a small hamper with food from the rear of the wagon while Mac tended the livestock. He tethered them near the creek and filled a small keg and his canteen with the cold, clear water. Mac stretched his tired back and felt real fatigue. Even with his sore back, he was content to be headed home. He felt hope. Tonight, he believed Laurel was a person he could build a home with. God had been good to him, and he sensed a bond of friendship between them could grow into affection, if not love. And, he told himself as he walked back to the wagon, a true friendship was a far better foundation for a godly marriage than romance.

"Are you ready to eat supper, Mac?"

"More than ready. I didn't know how hungry I was until we stopped. Thank you for lighting a lantern. The moon and stars are hidden by the clouds tonight. I wish we could have a fire, but I don't think we should risk setting the wagon bed on fire, do you?"

"We have plenty of things already cooked. There are even a couple of small pieces of pie left over from last night. Eat your fill. Sorry there is no coffee tonight, but we still have a little milk."

"Lord, thank you for this place we stopped tonight, and the pleasant time we had as we learned more about each other today. Bless this food and grant us a good night's rest. Amen." They ate and talked about their day's travel. Mac seemed pleased with the first day's progress. When they had finished, Laurel stored the food that would keep another day and placed the small box at the edge of their makeshift tent so they could eat breakfast from it the next morning. Mac went to the wagon and reached under the seat to find his Bible. When he crawled under the wagon bed, he found that Laurel had laid blankets and pillows to make a bed for the night. In the pale light, he noticed the yellow coverlet made by the ladies of Hawthorn. "What'd you like to read tonight, Laurel?"

"I don't guess I have a preference. I just like to hear you read aloud. You've got a nice voice. You sing well too."

"Goodness, how do I deserve all these nice remarks from you?"

"Just speaking my mind."

"Well, you can thank your uncle Matthew for the singing part. That is one thing he requires...just like Wesley taught."

"What did Wesley say about singing?"

"You know those rules...we get a sermon on them quite often...Sing all...Sing lustily and with good courage...Sing modestly and don't set yourself apart from the body...Sing in tune and sing spiritually. Aim to please Him and not yourself."

"Are you sure those aren't just Uncle Matt's rules? He always loved to sing, and he did it very well as I remember."

"That is so, but Charles Wesley did write those rules for music during worship. I read it once." "Anyway, what should we read tonight?"

"You pick tonight." Laurel picked up Mac's Bible from his hand and let it fall open.

"Let's see what fate has in store for us tonight." The book fell open to the third chapter of Hosea.

"That is a good story, but I think we need to start at the beginning." Mac began to read. Laurel had heard the story before, but she had never really paid close attention to the text. She found herself engrossed in the tale.

After a while when he had finished Chapter 2, Mac laid the book aside. "Let's get some sleep, Laurel. Huntsville is still quite a long ride from here, but we can shelter inside if we are able to get there before nightfall. Goodnight, wife." He picked up her hand, held it for a minute and rubbed it against his bearded cheek. He kissed her palm tenderly and lay down. He patted the pillow next to him, drew back the yellow coverlet and then pulled it over them both. "Nice wedding present. We'll need it and the extra blankets to keep us warm. It's been really cool so far this spring. I hope you sleep well, Laurel."

Sleep came quickly. The MacLaynes were tired, but at least it was a good tired. About midnight, Mac was awakened by Laurel, shaking from the cold. The whole week had been unseasonably cool, but the temperature had fallen drastically during the night. Mac had not planned for the extremely cold night temperatures. The two blankets they had packed to use on the trip were not nearly enough to assure warmth on such a cold night.

"Laurel, why didn't you wake me?"

"I didn't want to bother you. Besides, we don't have any other blankets we can get unless we unload the wagon. I'll be all right."

"You'll get a catarrh, and if you get sick the trip will be slower and harder for us both. Will you let me hold you tonight? If we bundle together, we will both be warmer."

Laurel's teeth chattered from the cold, and she truly hated to be cold. She hesitated though.

"Laurel, I promised no familiarity the day you agreed to wed. It's not time for us yet. We have to get to know each other, and learn from each other...everything in its own time. Remember what we read the other night in Ecclesiastics. Tonight is time for us to keep each other warm. Will you let me hold you?"

Laurel nodded and moved nearer to where Mac lay. He pulled her closer and she rested her head on his shoulder. Mac pulled the blankets up so only their faces weren't covered. Soon both were warmer, and Laurel fell asleep when her shivering stopped.

For Mac, sleep did not come as quickly. He smelled the scent of Laurel's hair as she cuddled next to his side. He sensed the slightness of her body as she lay wrapped in his arms. He became aware for the first time of the very essence of her womanhood. Mac mentally scolded himself. *Patrick, Laurel is your friend. Remember. Just pull her close, keep her warm, and go to sleep. Remember you told her there is a time for everything. Well, this is not the time. He* wanted her, but he felt bad for his lust. It had to be lust, because he would not let himself fall in love. Laurel was a stranger to him, and he would never open himself to that hurt again. While Laurel rested in the warmth of his arms, Mac spent a fitful night, but at least they were warm. Mac made himself a mental note to unpack more blankets the next night they had to camp out.

At sunrise, both Laurel and Mac awoke. "I appreciate your holding me last night. I slept so much better after I got warm."

"My pleasure, Laurel. I hope you feel easier about me holding you. It can be a pleasant thing for both of us." Mac saw a touch of pink touch her cheeks as she sat up and began to tuck loose tresses back into her braids. She found her shoes and her coat.

The day's journey would be about twenty miles from the meadow near Goshen to Huntsville. It would be a fair trek for one day, so Mac had planned to leave early and drive as much as possible to reach the community before night fall. One thing in their favor was the good Carrolton Road across the top corner of the state. The way was a fifteen feet wide dirt road, well-travelled and well maintained. With luck, Mac and Laurel would sleep inside that night.

"Time to get a move on, husband. We have a long way to go. I'll get a bit of a meal together while you hitch up the mules and tie the horses to the back of the wagon." Laurel made a small fire and brewed coffee so Mac could start the day with his favorite hot beverage, and while she didn't know why he loved the bitter brew so much, he'd appreciate her effort. She also cut biscuits in two and warmed them in a skillet. She scrambled some eggs so she could offer her husband a warm breakfast.

Within half an hour, they were back on the Carrollton Road headed toward Huntsville. Mac had been told the town had a thriving Methodist fellowship there. The pastor would surely help them to find shelter for the night. He could get a good night's rest, which he badly needed after his fitful sleep from the previous night. "Laurel, will you read more of Hosea's story as we ride today? It'd be a good way to help pass the time."

Laurel read, off and on all day. When they reached the Huntsville settlement about 5:30, Mac was more than ready to stop. They had traveled more than ten hours. He saw a farmer mount his horse just as they reached the town and stopped to ask where he could find the Methodist church in Huntsville. "I will be obliged to show you the way, but afraid no one'll be there on a Thursday evening. Now on a Sunday night, you'd find half the town there. Well, never mind, as Brother Sumner's house is just beyond that rise over there. See the cabin just beside the church?"

"Yes, thank you, friend. You've been a great help."

They rode the short distance to the front of the cabin. They found the Sumners in their yard. Mac jumped from the wagon and made introductions. "Brother Sumner, can you tell us a place where we can board for the night? My new wife and I are fair tuckered after a day of travel."

"Brother, my wife Susan and I would enjoy your company, if you'll honor us. Our youngest girl left home two months ago. She married a fine man, but he moved them over to Jasper. We do miss the hubbub of our kids. We have room if you can climb a ladder."

"Indeed we can. I am Patrick MacLayne, Mac to my friends, and this is Laurel. We'd love the fellowship and the comfort of a room. We spent the last night camped out near Goshen just outside Fayetteville. It'll be nice to have a warm place to rest tonight."

Mrs. Sumner winked at her husband. "I'd bet you had your love to keep each other warm, ya'll being newlyweds."

Laurel knew her face turn bright red when Mac replied. "Indeed we did, Sister Sumner. It's a blessing to have a sweetheart to drive away the chill." Laurel couldn't believe Mac's reply, but Susan Sumner just put her arm around Laurel's shoulder and laughed. Reverend Sumner and his wife were excellent hosts. Susan prepared a fine meal, and the four new friends sat down to eat. Martin Sumner offered grace, and easy conversation flowed throughout the meal. Laurel found herself relaxed, and she had a wonderful time in adult company. For the first time in many years, Laurel forgot to be self-conscious and aloof. No one here knew she was the spinster of Hawthorn Chapel. She was a new bride headed for a new life.

Mac and Martin Sumner talked of their many common interests long into the evening. They shared a common belief about the contro-versy in the church, of which the slavery issue had been a primary rift for several years. Arkansas had made a formal statement of separation at the annual conference in 1844, yet the division of the Methodist church into the northern faction and the southern faction had done little to ease the heated discussion. "This doesn't mean a whole lot at Shiloh, Brother. So few of our people own slaves, but politics, especially in the church, will always stir people to a frenzy." Mac sighed. "It's a shame, too. There are so many other concerns for the community of faith." Sumner nodded in agreement.

While the men continued their discussion, Susan and Laurel en-joyed their own. As it turned out, Susan was an avid reader, too. "We seldom have new books here. Too many of our people don't read much or at all. Besides, books are expensive, and we ain't seen a copy of the newspaper from Little Rock for months." Susan continued, "We hope to start a school soon. It'd be a blessing for Huntsville. They got some schools over at Fayetteville, even got a college started over there, but it's too far to travel. We need to find us a teacher."

"I'll teach at Shiloh subscription school when we get there."

"They let a woman teach? Your husband will let you do that? That'll be a challenge for a new bride. How will you be able to take care of your homestead, take care of a husband, work a garden, and teach full time? And the babies will come in no time. Don't see how's you can manage all that."

"God will show us the way." Laurel didn't want to get involved in a conversation about babies.

"It's our routine, a new one, of course, to read the scripture together before we retire for the night. Would you join us, Martin? If I remember, we are in the twelfth chapter of *Hosea*."

"That seems to be a strange choice for newlyweds."

"Just the luck of the draw, but the book will make for some good discussion when we get done." The four friends read the next chapter, prayed together, and said good night.

— ~

Susan lit a lantern on a table and turned down the coverlet on the bed in the loft. "Sleep well. If you need another cover before morning, there is one in the chest. Goodnight."

Laurel turned her back and began to undress. Mac did not turn from her. In the well-lit loft, he watched Laurel as began to prepare for bed. He looked at her slim form as she removed her blouse and skirt. He watched as her well-worn nightdress slipped down her back, across her tiny waist and down across her hips to her mid-calf. He had not realized until then what a beautiful body Laurel had. In the nearly two weeks of marriage, this was the first night they'd prepared for bed at the same time in a well-lit room. When Laurel turned back, Mac had not looked away. She blushed and hurriedly slipped into bed.

"Do you plan to stand there all night? We have a long day tomorrow." Mac took a deep breath and slowly began to remove his shoes and outer clothes. He wasn't self-conscious about undressing in front of Laurel, as he had done it twice before, and she had not objected. He took a second deep breath, shook his hair loose, and sat on the edge of the bed.

"No, I'm not going to stand here all night. I'm tired. I hope we both sleep well tonight." He doubted he would, for as tired as he felt, he knew he wanted Laurel. Again, he scolded himself for his lust. His wife had a beautiful body. It was his right to take her, but he also knew he'd made a promise to her. Besides, he wouldn't return to his old ways. He would never use a woman to ease his needs, and he would never allow love to rule his ways again. He turned his back to Laurel and lay very still. "Goodnight, Laurel. I enjoyed your company today, and you were a fine companion as we visited with the Sumners tonight. I'm proud of you."

"Thank you. Sleep well."

Mac pulled the blanket over his shoulder and spoke a brief prayer under his breath. "Lord, give me the strength to keep my resolve. And please let me sleep." After several minutes, he did.

When he awoke the next morning, he was alone. Laurel had dressed and gone down to help Susan prepare breakfast. Disappointed to find her gone and with no reason for him to remain in bed, he got up, dressed, and headed down to the kitchen. Martin Sumner had just returned from his morning chores, which had included hitching the MacLayne's team to the wagon. "I see you're awake, friend. Pleasant night?"

Mac enjoyed the easy banter with his new friend. "Which road is a better choice from here? I heard there's a road to the north and an old military road goes to the south."

"Since it's rained so much of the spring, I think you'd find the road toward Jasper an easier trip. Carrollton Road is usually pretty good, but it gets real muddy when it rains too much."

"I understand. It's just like our dear governor says. 'We don't need railroads in Arkansas. We got good dirt roads.' I guess he doesn't get out of Little Rock enough to know that those good dirt roads turn into muddy impassible paths when enough rain is added to the dirt."

Martin enjoyed the joke. The time spent with the MacLaynes had been pleasant. Martin clapped Mac on the shoulder and together they went into a hearty breakfast.

Time to depart came too soon, but Mac's determination to reach Shiloh within another three weeks put them on a tight schedule. He helped Laurel into her seat and turned to wave goodbye to the Sumners one last time. As they reached the fork in the road, Mac chose the south trail, hoping the Military Road would be as good and as fast as the Carrollton Road had been on the two previous days. The distance between the two settlements, Huntsville and Jasper, was just less than fifty miles. Mac didn't know if he would find a Methodist congregation in Jasper. He decided he should share the news. "We may have to rough it for a couple of nights, Laurel. This is unknown territory for me. You'll have to help me keep the faith."

The morning was colder, and the temperature warmed little by noon. The ride was more uncomfortable than had been either of the previous days since they had left Hawthorn. However, the road proved to be in good condition, so the mules made good time. Because Mac hoped to cover half the distance to Jasper that he day, they stopped only briefly to rest the jacks. Mac and Laurel spoke little that morning and what they had said amounted to small talk and brief answers to questions.

"Laurel, why not finish the last few pages of Hosea?"

She read to the end and then she commented, "That is certainly an interesting story. Martin remarked that it's a strange choice for newlyweds. What do you think he meant by that?"

"Many believers find it hard to think that God would tell a man to marry a prostitute. It's not the usual picture we have of His will. But you know, part of this story is not unlike our story."

Laurel's chin jutted out, and Mac saw the green fire flash in her eyes. "First of all, I wasn't aware we have a story. And I can certainly assure you, Patrick MacLayne, that I am not an easy woman. That is an insulting comparison for you to make, especially since you know so little about me."

"Don't get mad, Laurel. I know you aren't Gomer, but if we reverse the roles, I do see us in parts of this story."

"Reverse the roles? I guess I don't understand your point."

"Gomer broke the laws of morality and decency. She turned her back on the goodness of her husband and God's law. That was me in earlier days, part of my past I will tell you about when we get better acquainted. Besides, you have many qualities of Hosea. You listened to God and followed his lead—even though you really didn't want to. In the end, Hosea received a blessing for his faithfulness. The same thing will happen to you in time."

"You give me too much credit. I didn't have many options."

"Laurel, don't belittle what you did. You chose to honor your father. You chose to step out in faith with me. Those are not small sacrifices."

"I hope it was a good choice for both of us. I still can't believe you married me to honor an arrangement you had no say in."

"What arrangement? I'd told your uncle Matthew I'd make a trip across the state to ask permission to court you."

"That is not what my papa understood. He told me you asked for my hand, and he even called you my intended. Someone didn't get the message straight. Either Uncle Matthew or Papa owes you an explanation. I don't reckon you'll get one from my father. I'm sorry you were put in such an awkward position."

"You owe me no apology. I told you I believe God ordained our marriage. We spoke our vows after your preacher asked if we did so with a 'willing' spirit. There was no gun at my back to make me say 'yes.'"

"Anyway, I am grateful you helped me ease Papa's last days. It was a noble act. I wish I were a more suitable mate for you. I'll work very hard to keep my vow to you."

"Why aren't you a suitable mate for me?"

"Mac, please. We have had a pleasant morning. Let's not spoil it. Find another topic for us to talk about."

"You brought it up. Now answer my question. Remember you promised to speak the truth."

"I can't talk about that right now. I guess I am mostly afraid your friends back at Shiloh won't think we are suited to each other. That's all."

"What difference does it make what anyone else thinks? Besides, I don't see how we are not suited to each other. We share our common faith, and we both have quite a bit of schooling. We have common goals, like building a home. I'd call that well-suited."

"How many people in Shiloh know my uncle Matthew arranged our marriage?"

"No one, even your uncle. He didn't push his spinster niece at me. I assure you that we are best friends."

"What will you say when friends wonder how you came home with me in such a short time?"

"I'll just say you swept me off my feet."

"I don't think you are a good enough liar to bring that off." Mac became very angry.

"You are right, Laurel. I am **no** kind of liar. I gave that up four years ago at a camp meeting, led by your uncle and our district circuit rider. I gave up lying, drinking, gambling, and carousing with women so I could live a new life. I wanted to be the new creature your uncle told me about because before that I lived no kind of life at all. I was just breathed and wasted all the blessings God lavished on me since the day I was born."

Laurel sat, speechless. Mac's personal, honest words came from within himself. He had not intended to share this story of his past with her in anger. His conversion was a precious memory for him.

"I don't know what to say, Mac. I appreciate that you trust me enough to say tell me. I'm sorry I angered you again."

"I am sorry I lost my temper when I spoke candidly about my life, but that is what I intend between us always, Laurel. If we are to build a marriage on friendship and faith, we have to trust one another with the bad things as well as the blessings."

"I know you are right."

"Look, Laurel, I know you wanted to fall in love and have a real courtship. I suppose every girl does. I wish you could've had it. Truth is we may never know that kind of love, but we can have a pleasant household and share a full life together. If we don't have love, friendship isn't a bad replacement."

"You are right.

"What? No comment from you?"

"You spoke the truth. What more can I say?"

"You could answer my question."

"No, Mac. I have no comment."

"Not that question. You know what I meant."

— ∼

Laurel didn't want to answer the question. The answer was too personal and too difficult to voice. She was not ready to broach that topic yet. She decided to make light of the situation and hoped Mac would let it pass. "It's been very cool today. This should be the warmest part of the day, and it's as cold as it was when we left this morning, strange weather for the last half of March."

"So, you changed the subject. Don't think I won't raise the question again."

"Tenacity, another quality I'll add to your list of good traits." Mac smiled, and they continued down the Military Road at a good pace.

Just before dark, they arrived at a large limestone outcropping not too far from a stream. The weather had turned even colder as the sun began to set. "Laurel, we'll need a fire tonight, and I can't build one under the wagon. I think we will make camp here, under this rock shelf. The outcropping is big enough to provide some shelter and allow us to make a large campfire. At least that will let us have a warm meal and provide heat for the night. I doubt we're half way to Jasper yet."

"If you think this is best, what can I do to help?" Together they took blankets from the wagon along with an ample amount of food. Mac unhitched the team of mules and their two horses from the rear of the wagon and led them to the stream. He found a small patch of early grass so the animals could feed. When he returned to the wagon, he found that Laurel had already made a good-sized fire underneath the ledge. The camp smelled of hot coffee and ham frying in the iron skillet. Laurel had warmed canned vegetables from her root cellar and fried potatoes for their supper. He broke off a stick and put two pieces of bread he'd sliced from one of Laurel's loaves over the flames. Warm bread would be a nice addition to their supper, and they quickly ate every morsel. They bundled together near the fire as the wind became brisker and colder. Mac added several more pieces of wood to the fire and then put the blankets nearby. They needed to bed near the fire under their rock shelter if they were to stay warm through the night.

Laurel began to remove her shoes. Thoughtlessly, Mac walked up and put his hands on her shoulders. Laurel jerked back in fear. "What are you doing?"

"Laurel, I'm sorry. I just wanted to say goodnight. I didn't mean to startle you."

"No, I'm sorry. I don't mean to act like a prudish old maid." There was a long silence.

"Come and lie down, Laurel. I'm afraid we don't have enough blankets to afford us much personal space. We will stay warmer if you will sleep close to me, like you did last night."

"I meant to explain that to you this morning. I didn't mean to awaken you. I just got cold. I wasn't aware I'd gotten so close to you while I slept, but I just wanted to be warm."

"I took no offense, Laurel. I like the feel of a woman's body near me. I knew you had done it unaware because when I touch you, you act as if I were Satan, and you want to run for your life, but I'm too cold to stand here talking." He walked over to the bedroll and lay down. He held open the blanket for Laurel to join him. "Just good friends, trying to stay warm." She hesitated but then joined him. After all, she hated cold as much as he did.

After a moment, Laurel began to relax. She even enjoyed cuddling, her back to Mac's chest. She smiled at the idea of "spooning" with Mac.

"See, I told you it could feel nice. One of the blessings of married life is a spouse to warm your bed."

"I guess it'll do if you can't find a heated brick." Laurel meant to keep things light, but she heard Mac moan in contempt.

"Laurel, I told you I didn't let things go. I'm not nearly sleepy so I want to talk awhile."

"All right. Where will we live when we get back to Shiloh? Since you haven't got a cabin, we may have a problem."

"Don't try to change the subject again. Tell me why you feel so unfit to be my wife?"

"I'm fit enough."

"I know that, but you don't. Every time I try to compliment you or point out a good quality I've noticed, you make a joke or apologize that you don't measure up. Let's get this issue out in the open. This afternoon, I got angry with you when you avoided answering me...that crack about me being a bad liar. Frankly, that is a compliment by the way." Laurel wanted to move away from Mac's embrace, but there was no place to move except into the cold.

"Please, Mac. This is too personal. The last time, the only time I ever spoke about this...well, I broke into tears. I broke down in front of my sick papa."

"That's all right, Laurel."

"Thank you for understanding, Mac. Goodnight."

"No. I meant it's all right if you need to cry again. What made you cry?" She knew Mac's tenacity would not let her avoid the answer that night. She felt trapped. "Lord, help me say the right and honest thing. Help me get it over, finally."

With a deep breath, Laurel spoke. "I am not a suitable wife for you because I am plain. My social graces are nil. I don't know the first thing about pleasing a man. People will take one look at us and see our poor match. There, I said it. Are you satisfied?"

"All right. Anything else you want to tell me?"

Laurel stiffened and pulled away. He may as well have slapped her. She bared her soul to him, and he had made a joke of it.

"Come back over here. It's too cold, and your pride won't keep you warm. Besides I am warmer if you are here."

She turned and met her tormentor, face to face. "How dare you make fun of me! I answered the best I could, and you laugh at me! What happened to the respect and honor you vowed?"

"Your eyes are beautiful when you're angry. There is just enough light from the fire for me to see those green flashes. I'm glad you don't have your glasses on."

"I asked you not to tease me. I'm serious."

"I know you are. You meant every word—you are serious about everything. You believe those things to be true. I just don't happen to believe those reasons you gave me."

Laurel started to vent her frustration when Mac reached up and pulled her into his arms. "Let's get under these blankets. It's too cold to get up." Laurel unwillingly lay down again, but Mac pulled her closer. "Laurel, you are the one who thinks you're plain. I'll not lie to you. I've known many women who are more outwardly attractive than you let yourself be, but that is a choice you make every day. You've built a very high wall around yourself, you know. Thankfully, walls can crumble in time."

Laurel asked bluntly, "If you've known so many women more beautiful than me, why would you settle for me?"

"I didn't say I ever knew any woman more beautiful than you are. I said physically attractive. I think beauty comes more from within than without. Who knows? When we get to really know each other, you may be the most beautiful woman I'll ever know."

"Mac..."

"Hush up now, Hosea. Gomer is cold and tired. Let me hold you so we can get some sleep.

8

And he said unto me, My grace is sufficient for thee: for my strength is
made perfect in weakness.

KJV c1850, II Corinthians 12:9

lthough the horizon was no longer dark, the sun shared no warmth and the wind was bitter. The fire had burned very low, and Mac felt the chill even though he still shared two blankets with Laurel. Heavy, gray clouds gathered quickly in the northwest, and he didn't feel good about the prospects of the day's travel. "Laurel, get up. We need to get on the road as quick as we can. Here are your shoes." Laurel awoke, stiff from her night on the hard ground. "Please pack up all these things, but keep out the blankets. We may need them. If we have anything we can eat as we drive, let's have that for breakfast."

With that, he pulled on his buckskin jacket and boots and hurriedly hitched the jacks to the wagon. As he tied the horses to the wagon, Laurel found some dried fruit, a small cheese and half a loaf of bread, somewhat stale but edible. She picked up the canteen and brought the breakfast to the seat of the wagon. In less than fifteen minutes, the MacLaynes drove east again.

"You seem edgy this morning, Mac. Did you sleep well enough?"

"I slept fine, wife, but this weather is not what you'd expect this late in March. We need to make good use of our time. I hope we can get make Jasper before the storm sets in." Mac motioned over his shoulder at the ominous clouds. When Laurel turned back to look in the direction Mac had pointed, the bitter wind stung her cheeks and brought tears to her eyes. She shivered from the cold northern wind. Mac pulled a blanket from the wagon seat and draped it across her shoulders.

"Mac, I found some cheese and bread. You should eat a bite." Together they travelled toward Jasper with Laurel huddled inside a blanket. Mac urged the team on at a strong gait. By mid-morning, a light rain began to fall. The drizzle was more of an annoyance than challenge to their progress. If the rain been the only matter, Mac may not have been as concerned, but with the temperature falling at the same time, travel became miserable. To make matters worse, Mac was driving into unknown territory, as he had not taken this path on his trip to Hawthorn. As they approached the Buffalo River, the road narrowed considerably. In places, only a wagon-width trail lay between the water and the rock cliffs around the river. In this area, the Buffalo River was far too deep to ford. Mac second guessed his choice of using the south road, because he was more familiar with the Carrollton Road that he used on his trip to Hawthorn. Since hindsight never helped much, he tried to refocus his attention to the tasks at hand, either reaching the Jasper settlement before nightfall or dealing with an early spring storm. He prayed for the first but feared the second. Except for brief rest stops for the mules, they plodded on toward Jasper.

By mid-afternoon, the stern scowl on Mac's face showed he was more than concerned. Laurel's whole body shook. Both the blanket and her clothes were soaked through. His buckskins had help repel the water so he hadn't realized that her clothes weren't much protection. "Laurel, we have to find something to repel the water. I should have thought of you sooner." He stopped the wagon and went to the back to search for something to cover his wife. Finding nothing else, he took his knife, cut a piece of the oilcloth from the wagon cover, and brought it to Laurel. "Here, drape this over your head and across your shoulders. It should help some." However, before Mac could reseat himself, the rain turned to heavy sleet. The temperature was at the freezing point now or maybe even colder. Mac had not planned for them to travel in these conditions. More than aware of the danger to travelers in winter conditions, he began to search the rock ledges for a place to shelter them and their animals, as he continued to push the team as much as he dared on the muddy roads. Their pace was much slower now. They would not reach Jasper by nightfall.

Mac continually looked over at Laurel. Each time he looked at her, she sat tall and straight with her shoulders squared. She never complained. Her posture reminded him of the girls in Mrs. Weatherly's dance classes back in Maryland. He could almost hear her repeat, "Posture, Ladies. Remember our posture." Mac smiled at the ridiculous thought that had come to his mind on a day like this.

Sometime later Mac noticed that Laurel shook from the cold, and he pulled the blanket from her shoulders. The water-laden cover provided no warmth and did more harm than good. Shelter was imperative. Even an outcropping like the one they'd sheltered under previous night would be better than their present circumstances. Again, he slapped the reins across the rumps of the mules to push them harder, as he scoured the rocks for sanctuary. Finally, near the bend of the road, he saw a dark area in the bluff and knew his silent prayer had been answered. Within five minutes, Mac handed Laurel the reins, jumped from the wagon seat, and ran toward the point that had caught his attention. He had indeed found a cave. "Laurel, we can shelter in this cave. It's deep enough for us, the team, and the wagon. I'll have to clear some of the brush to get the wagon to the cave, so just try to keep yourself as warm as you can for a while longer."

"I'll help. We can get inside faster and get our animals to shelter sooner, too." She was certainly not a hot-house rose he would have to serve and pamper. How different she was from Marsha Golden, who had never worked a day in her privileged life. Laurel would be a true helpmate for him as he built his homestead. Another blessing he'd been handed.

— ⁓

Within half an hour, the animals, wagon and two soggy MacLaynes were inside the cave and out of the spring storm. It was just before dark, and the rain and sleet turned to snow. Mac went out to find whatever dried wood he could. They would need a large fire to withstand the freezing chill and to dry their wet clothes and blankets. Laurel couldn't stop shaking, and her clothes were so heavy from the rain that she walked as if she were pulled feed sacks attached to her petticoats. Nevertheless, she set out to find ways to keep the wet and cold away. She removed the oilcloths that had covered the wagon, and with the rails from her bed, a broom, and hoe, she made a "wall" toward the back of the cave. The enclosure was small, but with a fire the space could be heated adequately, and there was plenty of room for a pallet so they could sleep. Laurel retrieved an oil lamp from the wagon, and she carried it along with two remaining dry blankets. She also found dry clothes for Mac and herself. On a final trip to the wagon, Laurel gathered their food in two boxes and carried them behind the makeshift wall.

Mac returned with armloads of dead branches and small limbs that he'd cut. He had brought anything that would burn. The wet, heavy snow fell even harder than when they'd entered the cave. "I hope this stops soon." Of couse, there was no way to know how long they would have to shelter in the cave. They must have heat.

Laurel was chilled, shivering from the cold and wet. Yet work remained to be done. "Mac, I will get us some supper while you make a fire. I know you'll want hot coffee. I'll go out to the river and get some water. No need for me to change clothes until I can stay out of the weather."

"No, Laurel. I'll get the water. You need to get out of those wet clothes."

"I'm no baby, Mac. Right now, we need heat. Build us a fire, and I'll walk across the trail and get water." Laurel's trip across the newly cleared path to the road went quickly, but the unbroken path from the road to the creek was not so easy. She stepped into several holes and filled both her shoes with muddy water. Just before she reached a place where she could fill the small keg with clean water, she tripped over a fallen limb and fell head first into the deep creek. When she tried to stand, she sank to her waist and fell again. Her head slipped beneath the surface of the water. Due to her heavy skirt and petticoats, she struggled to get back to the bank. When she could get back, she bent over, picked up the keg, and filled the container from the icy water. She picked up the heavy keg, and labored back to the cave in the twilight. The snow fell in blankets, and the huge flakes all but obscured the forest and the entrance to the cave. The road was now covered with a shimmering white sheet.

"Laurel, you are a mess."

"Thank you...for the compliment. I am cold, so I really don't care."

"Come over here to the fire. Take those wet things off, and we'll lay them out to dry." Laurel shivered uncontrollably. "Mac, please take this keg. I need to sit down a minute."

— ~

Her words were barely understandable through her quivering lips. When she got into the light of the fire, Mac saw her hair, her clothes, her face and her hands were all dripping water. He realized how unkind his earlier taunt had been. Mac took the keg, sat it near the fire, and sat Laurel down. He pulled her sodden coat from her quivering body.

"You'll warm up faster if you get out of these wet clothes. Let me help you."

She leaned against the wall of the cave. Mac knelt to help her take off her shirt. When he touched her, she whimpered. He touched her forehead and found she had fever. He had barely moved his hand when she fell against him. He picked her up and moved as close to the fire as he dared. He held her in his lap. He dared not lay her on one of the only dry blankets until he could get her wet clothes off. Laurel would need those two blankets for warmth. He undressed her as quickly as he could manage in the awkward way they sat together. When he got to her shoes, he found them both filled with water. He stripped the wet stockings and threw them into the heap with her other clothes. After he removed the last of her soaked underthings, he wrapped her in one of the dry blankets and laid her near the fire on the other. She continued to shake uncontrollably, and she didn't respond when he called her name.

Mac felt helpless. How could he get her warm? As he sat next to her, he realized that he was chilled, too. He had yet to change from his wet buckskins. At least he not gotten his boots wet. He bashed himself because he hadn't made Laurel remain in the cave. He could have gotten the water, but again, he realized the futility of hindsight. He had never been able to make Laurel do anything until she decided to do it. Besides, the problem wasn't solved by his remorse. He removed his buckskins and donned the dry shirt and dungarees that Laurel had brought from the wagon. They would help warm him, but they would do little to warm Laurel. Mac was worried because the chill continued. He'd never nursed many sick people so he really didn't know what he could do to warm his wife. He remembered how good a rub down felt when he was cold, so he decided to help increase the circulation in Laurel's limbs the only way he knew. He uncovered her arms and vigorously rubbed both. Then he turned her to the side and rubbed her shoulders and back. He then repeated his massage to her legs, praying all the time that his remedy would do some good. Mac rose and put more wood in the fire. Their little shelter was warmer, but Laurel still shook. He took her worn night dress and pulled it over her shaking body, removed his outer clothes and lay down next to her, pulling her as close as he could with her face to the fire and him holding her. He pulled the blanket over their heads with only their faces open. He held her for what seemed hours, and after a while, her chills became less intense. However, the fever remained. He knew nothing else to do, so he prayed and continued to hold her throughout the night, rising only to add fuel to the fire. As quickly as possible, he would return to warm Laurel with his own body heat. Laurel slept fitfully, screaming out in nightmares from time to time. Still, Mac held her. About dawn, Laurel's fever cooled, and she slept peacefully. Mac again stoked the fire, and only then did he allow himself to drift off to sleep with a prayer of thanksgiving on his lips.

Throughout the night, the snow fell. The landscape transformed into a beautiful tapestry of white and dark as the barren trees stood in stark contrast to the snow. The road disappeared under a pristine blanket of white. Travel would impossible until Mother Nature remembered it was already springtime in the Ozarks. Only warmer temperatures and dry skies would allow them to leave their makeshift home, and even then the thaw would pose new problems. His three-week goal to reach Greene County was in jeopardy. He didn't care at that moment, though, for Laurel seemed better as the morning light appeared at the cave entrance. He felt a weight lifted from his shoulders. How could he live with the guilt if she had suffered any permanent harm? If he couldn't give her love, at least he could provide her with safe passage to the home he promised her.

The woman who slept peacefully now under the sole dry blanket, little resembled the prim spinster he'd taken vows. This woman was almost beautiful in the firelight. He remembered from the night before how small her ankles and wrists seemed as he rubbed the circulation back into them. Strange that he would recall this in the morning light, when last night he didn't notice at all. Of course, last night he'd feared the worst. Laurel had fought off the chill and in the soft morning light, she seemed so different. Without glasses and her hair falling in wild abandon across her cheeks and down her back, Laurel in no way resembled the spinster of Hawthorn. Why did she hide that glory in those matronly braids all the time? Why did she scream out last night when the fever was on her? Why did she pull away when he touched her? He wanted to know many things about his stranger wife. Perhaps the snowstorm had provided the opportunity for them to get better acquainted. They certainly would have time for a day or two until the roads cleared.

Laurel slept for several hours after her fever broke. Mac had been up some time before she awoke. Because he had made coffee and fixed a breakfast of ham and boiled eggs, the cave had a nice aroma. The fire and oilcloth wall had made the little space quite cozy. Laurel stretched lazily, at ease and contented. When she realized what had happened to her the previous night, she blushed at first, and then realized Mac had simply done all he could to take care of her. All around their little cave home, their wet apparel and blankets had been spread open to dry. Even her shoes had been propped open near the fire. Mac had truly been her caretaker.

"Thank you, kind sir, for coming to my rescue. It seems I'm not much of a pioneer—falling into the creek in the middle of a snowstorm."

"I'm just pleased you suffered no permanent harm from your winter swim. You gave me quite a scare."

"I'd really like some breakfast, but I'm afraid I'm not properly dressed to sit in the company of a gentleman." Laurel hoped the light banter would lessen her embarrassment.

"Give it no thought...Your little night dress was the only apparel I could find among your things that would give you a hint of propriety while I attempted to warm you with my own bare form. Seemed to have worked all right."

"Mac! You're delighted when I blush. I apologize I was not able to see to my own needs last night."

"No apology owed. I rather enjoyed your company once you stopped shaking. Our one little blanket would have been a poor comfort had we not had each other to warm the night."

"Mac!" But then Laurel saw his impish too-blue-eyes and the up-turn of his mouth as he tried to hide a grin. "You're teasing."

"No, I'm not. You are so much warmer on a cold night than an old patchwork quilt." He then smiled broadly and Laurel relaxed, as she curled into the blanket. She smiled too. The easy companionship after the difficult day before was nice, and she realized how much she liked the openness with Mac. He let her be herself. Was she beginning to trust him?

"So, what will we do today? Travel is certainly out of the question. Actually, I think it is snowing again." Mac walked over and offered Laurel his hand. He pulled her to her feet.

"We can do whatever you like."

Mac smiled again. He ran his other hand down her long tresses and down to the nape of her neck. "Don't say that. As you look right now, I can think of a thing or two that wouldn't be on your list of things to pass the time." Mac took a stepped toward his scarcely clad wife. He stopped and pulled his hand through his hair and turned his back to Laurel. Then abruptly, he stepped back, picked up his drying jacket and spoke, "Laurel, I have to find more wood. I haven't watered the animals yet. Don't play the temptress dressed only in your night clothes. Find some dry clothes and make yourself decent before I get back." His tone had changed totally. Instead of the easy banter, Mac had spoken in anger. He moved past the oilcloth wall and went out into the cold.

Laurel didn't understand his abrupt change of mood. They had teased and talked and enjoyed each other's company, and then Mac's harsh remark cast gloom over the pleasant morning they'd shared in their cozy refuge. Laurel felt alone and rejected in the dim, cold cave. What had she done?

9

And bring hither the fatted calf, and kill it and let us eat, and be merry.
For this my son was dead, and is alive again; he was lost, and is found.

KJV c1850, Luke 15:23-24.

When Mac stepped outside, he welcomed the cold and the heavily falling snow. What had happened? He had smiled when he saw Laurel make the effort to relax and join in the small talk. He had enjoyed the quiet intimacy they shared. He loved the feel of her hair and the smoothness of her neck. Then he had made that thoughtless comment to her, and before the words were out of his mouth, Mac knew he'd not been joking with his teasing comment. In her state of undress, Laurel stirred emotions he didn't want to feel. He recalled the second promise he made to Mark Campbell. He had promised to respect her as a lady should be respected. He had would not treat her as he'd treated other women he'd used for his own pleasure. Wasn't physical intimacy without love wrong and perhaps a sin? Had he made a mistake thinking that he could ever take Laurel to his bed for the sake of bearing children when he didn't love her? He had bedded many women like that in the past...too many of them. He wouldn't treat Laurel that way.

Much later, when Mac returned he found Laurel dressed in her gray Sunday dress and her hair back in its customary braided coronet. She had replaced her glasses. She had taken on the appearance of the prim old maid he'd met at Hawthorn Chapel. She sat on one of the boxes from the wagon and read. Her demeanor had changed as drastically as his. Earlier in the day, when they bantered and teased each other, Laurel had been relaxed and open. Her head was high, and Mac had even detected a smile or two, but now she had moved back behind her wall. The damage was done, and his abruptness had been cruel and senseless. Nothing Laurel had done could be called into blame. She could never be the faithless temptress that Martha Golden was. She played no part in his pledge to never offer his heart to another woman. She wasn't to blame for the fear that destroyed most of his earlier relationships nor that his need for a family pushed him into a marriage of convenience. Laurel wasn't even to blame that his lust got out of control. She wasn't to blame, but she was the one whom he had hurt. He hadn't done it intentionally, but he hurt her anyway. "Please forgive my nasty mood earlier, Laurel. You didn't cause my foul temper."

"No forgiveness required. People can't help how they feel." Laurel rose from the box and checked the drying clothes. She folded her chemise and blouse. She moved other items nearer the fire. She pulled her wool shawl closer around her and went to the wagon to find food for a noon meal. With eggs and cornmeal she made corncakes in the skillet. She sliced the small piece of ham that was left and open one of her few jars of apple butter.

"If you'll bless the food, we can eat," Mac offered his hand, but Laurel closed her eyes and bowed her head. Mac spoke the grace, and they ate in silence. The remainder of the afternoon was no better. Laurel read near the fire, and Mac paced in and out of the cave, bringing water and then wood. He sought every opportunity to remove himself from the tenseness he had caused. Just before sundown, Mac decided he had to stop the damage before it got any worse.

"Laurel, come outside with me and look at the winter glory God has made for us."

Slowly, she followed him to the cave entryway and looked out at the beauty of the snow-covered Ozark Mountains. The dim light of dusk made the scene a fantasy. There was just enough light to observe the flakes of snow dance as the cold air blew the crystals into large drifts. The creek had frozen at its edges, and the snow created living, changing patterns as the currents moved beneath the surface pulling the small drifts from place to place. The scene from the cave entrance was breathtaking. Together they stood witness to the beauty of Arkansas in the icy storm, but while they stood side by side, they shared nothing of the glory before them. Laurel stood for a long while and looked at the mountains, but then returned to the campfire. She spoke not one word. She sliced bread for toast and four pieces of bacon from the slab, and fried the meat. She also sliced three small potatoes to fry along side the bacon. She brought the left over apple butter from their lunch. Laurel brewed herself a cup of tea and made Mac coffee. Then, she set the small, but adequate meal on a second box and waited for Mac to come in for supper. She refused to intrude on his privacy.

After dark, Mac came into the cave and placed an armload of wood near the fire. "Thank you for supper. Can we say grace?" Mac held out his hand to his wife again.

"Of course, you can."

"I can't until you join me." Laurel offered her hand. "Lord, we praise you and thank you for the beauty of this day. We ask you to bless this food. I confess to you my clumsy, stupid behavior that hurt my wife. Forgive my faults. In Jesus's name. Amen."

"There is your supper, Mac. Please excuse me." Laurel walked to the far corner of their cave and rolled herself into one of the blankets. In the dark, her silent tears flowed down her cheeks.

Mac ate a few bites of the supper Laurel had prepared. He could hear her cry quietly. How had he gotten himself to this wretched state? He pushed the pewter plate aside and picked up his Bible. Maybe he could find some answers there. He laid the book in his lap and it fell open to the center He noticed all the dates he had written there. His father was born in 1799 in Henrico County, Virginia. His mother's maiden name of Hayes was there and her birth date of 1801. They were much nearer the same age than he and Laurel. Then his brother Sean and his sister, now both gone. Only he and his parents had a marriage date recorded in the family Bible. He'd wrote the last date there only a few days ago, March 17, 1857. Did it belong?

After looking at the records he had written in his Bible, Mac laid the book in his lap. His guilt and remorse were more than he wanted to deal with. Mac groaned and put his face in his hands. He prayed for guidance as he began to search his conscience for answers. The last thing he wanted was to cause Laurel more pain. He rose and his Bible slipped to the floor. When he picked it up, it opened to the page where he had written his marriage vows less than two weeks earlier.

1. *I will honor your place as my wife.*
2. *I will respect the extraordinary person that you are*
3. *I will support you in your life's work.*
4. *I will provide a safe home for you.*

He read the words over and over, and he realized what had brought him to this place. Never once in his planning, traveling, and bargaining with Matthew Campbell or Mark Campbell or Laurel had he thought about her as a person with dreams and needs of her own. He had thought about himself, what he wanted, what he planned, and what he needed.... He'd never bothered once to ask what she wanted or what she needed.

He knew what he had to do. He would stop avoiding the problem he had made and return to the vows he'd made. He rose and walked over to the box where Laurel had set the supper. He poured himself a cup of coffee and then ate voraciously. He put away the leftover food and began to prepare the pallet for them to sleep on. He spread two blankets on the ground near the fire. He put two large pieces of wood on the fire, and then picked up the only other blanket which had dried during the day. He walked to the back of the cave where Laurel sat with her back to him and the fire.

Mac reached down to help her up, but when he touched her elbow, she startled and pulled away from him. "Don't touch me. Please just go away."

"No, Laurel. Come to bed. It is too cold over here. We will talk but not over here in the cold."

"Just leave me be. I can't see that we have anything to talk about."

"Heaven forbid, Laurel. We have too much to talk about. Now come over here and bring that blanket. I don't like to be cold when I don't have to be cold." She wadded up the blanket and threw it.

"That should keep you warm. I don't remember vowing to obey."

"Laurel, it's not an order, just a badly phrased request. Please come and lie down so we can be warm tonight. I want to talk to you and if you don't want to talk that's your choice, but I am asking you to listen to me."

Laurel shivered from the cold. When Mac saw the onset of another chill, he went to her, picked her up, and carried her to the pallet near the fire. He laid her there next to the flame and pulled the blanket and quilt over her shoulders. "I won't have another bout like last night. If you don't want to share a bed with me, just tell me. I'll manage."

"I won't deny you the warmth of a blanket. She turned down the opposite side of the cover and then turned her back.

"I asked you to listen to me, Laurel. I can't force you to do that, but I will talk anyway."

"I'm tired. Just leave me alone."

Mac lay down next to his wife, but he didn't find the warm, comfortable body from the previous night. Laurel had totally rebuilt the wall that had been so slowly coming down before he had let his emotions control his behavior earlier. "First, I'm asking you to forgive me. I have already broken the vows I made to you. My downfall wasn't intentional, but I know I hurt you. I'm sorry." Laurel made no reply. "I want to tell you why it happened. I want you to understand it wasn't your fault. None of it was your fault.

"Eleven years ago, I was in love, completely, passionately in love with a girl I thought was the most beautiful creature ever born. We were engaged to be married the summer after I turned 21. We spent four happy months planning a wedding, talking about our house, naming our children, playing together, having fun, and dreaming of married life. Our attraction for each other was almost overpowering. Short of taking her to my bed, we spent no small amount of time enjoying each other. That was not from my lack of trying. Many times, I pleaded with her to give in to our desires. I didn't see any reason to wait since we would be together forever. We wanted each other, so why should we wait?"

"That's enough!" Laurel's voice displayed the depth of her pain. "Why should I have to hear this? You have no need to taunt me and make me see my faults any more than I already do. I know who I am. No one ever wanted me. I've never been the object of any man's desire. I am sorry I am not the beautiful, desirable girl of your dreams, but I'm not the one who intruded into your life. Just leave me be. Don't tell me about something that I will never know myself? I don't deserve your cruelty."

"Laurel, you are supposed to listen to MY story. This story has nothing to do with you. You know I wouldn't say things to hurt you..." Mac paused and winced. "No, I guess you don't know that, do you?" He shook his head. He got up from the warmth of the pallet and went to the other side of the fire. He sat on the stone floor and spent several minutes beseeching God for the words to make Laurel understand. He had to tell her if they had any hope to live by the vows they had made to each other. He went out to collect some of the wood he'd brought to the cave for the night's fire. After a short while, with a sense of resolve, he continued his story.

"That was not the way I meant to say things, Laurel. A better explanation is that what happened between us this morning had nothing to do with your behavior. My foul mood is the product of an unresolved past. I wanted you to understand what brought me to where I am today. Can I come back to you?"

"I didn't ask you to leave." He returned and covered himself.

"Three weeks before our wedding date, I found Marsha in the stable with my best friend. Louis was the nephew of the governor of Maryland and a part of a wealthy family with a great deal of social prominence in our state. The girl I loved betrayed me. She destroyed my trust and badly bruised my pride. I'd begged for her favors so many times and she refused. She'd known my friend less than one month. She sold herself for money and social status."

"Sorry you were hurt." She could have been expressing her concern for any stranger who had experience such a disappointment.

"I know it is no excuse for my behavior today. I'm not a lovesick boy anymore. I thought I had grown up more than that since the Lord pulled me out of own personal hell. Maybe I am a bit arrogant about my sainthood. I never wanted to hurt you, Laurel."

"You never wanted to care for me either, did you?" Mac was shocked by her candor. For several minutes, Mac struggled to find the right way to respond. He knew only the truth could heal the rift.

"No, Laurel. That wasn't part of my plan."

"I appreciate the truth. Good night." Laurel turned her back and pulled her knees to her chest and wrapped her arms tightly around them.

"Laurel, we haven't read our scripture lesson yet today. You agreed to read and pray with me every night before bed. You were too ill last night so I offered the prayer for your healing alone. I want you to keep your agreement."

When she made no reply, Mac read from Proverbs 31: 10-31. When he finished, he prayed, "Lord, thank you for my wife, a special woman described by the prophet. She is a gift beyond measure. Please help me be worthy of such a mate. Amen."

⌐ ⌐

Tears rolled silently down Laurel's face. She didn't believe Mac meant the words he had prayed. She made no response. The sad event only went to prove what she knew about herself. She remembered how good Mac had been to her last night when she was cold and sick. How wonderful it would be if she could just turn back the time to yesterday. She would love to sleep next to Mac and feel warm, safe, and valued. Was it only yesterday that she had felt that way? Now she was sure she'd never feel that way again. She had heard the disgust in his voice, just as she had heard from the boys in her nightmares. She didn't remember why, but the beginning of those nightmares marked the time from which she had taken inventory of herself and found herself lacking in so many ways. Mac had begun to heal that hurt, and she'd allow him to begin dismantling the wall. She had let herself begin to care for him. How stupid she felt because she'd even dreamed of a relationship with him. Then this morning had happened! She scolded herself. *You ridiculous female. How could an attractive man like Mac care for the spinster of Hawthorn? You are truly a fool!'*

She held no bitterness toward Mac. He couldn't help how he felt. He'd been honest. Laurel felt exhausted, both mentally and physically. She was cold. She eventually fell asleep, shivering and too stubborn to seek the warmth that lay only inches away.

Monday morning dawned with a clear sky, and the sun made a bright reappearance after three snowy days. The temperature even edged up a degree or two, but travel that day would not be practical. Until the snow began to melt from the road, travel by mule-drawn wagon would be too dangerous. Surely one more day would see the MacLaynes back on their way toward Shiloh. After all, it was late March and not early February in the South.

Laurel dreaded another long day with little to do. She needed to act and not just sit. After breakfast was behind her, she checked her shoes to make sure they were thoroughly dry. She'd enjoy a walk alone in the wintry forest. She pushed her fingers into the toes of the old brown work shoes and was satisfied they were dry enough. She pulled on her woolen socks and laced her boots tightly around her ankles. She wanted to wear her coat, but the heavy wool was too wet for comfort, so she decided her shawl would do.

"Going somewhere, Laurel?"

"Just out to walk in the forest a while. I won't be gone long, and I'll be back in plenty of time to prepare lunch."

"I'll walk with you. I've been cooped up for too long."

"No, thank you. I am able to walk by myself."

"The terrain is rough here, and the trails are totally covered by the snow drifts. You don't know your way around this place. I won't let you go out alone. I promised your father."

"Do what you have to do to meet your obligations."

"Sharp as an adder's tongue."

"I promised to speak the truth to you. I try to keep my word."

"No, you are trying to justify your anger with me—and you haven't even heard the entire story. Stay angry as long as you want, but you will not go into this strange forest alone."

"It's a free country. You can walk where you please. I certainly can't stop you." Laurel picked up one of the blankets to put across her shoulders. She turned and walked out into the wonder of the snow-covered Ozarks. She had loved the mountains since her family moved to Arkansas. The snow only enhanced the landscape. At times, she stopped and stared at the view open to her. Mac was true to his word, and he didn't intrude on her walk, but neither did he let her out of his line of sight. Laurel lost track of time, but after a walk of some distance, she realized her feet and hands were very cold. Due to her practical nature, she returned to the cave and began to prepare a hot lunch.

Laurel became very restless after lunch. She'd enjoyed the scenery of the morning walk, but she knew she had been exposed to the cold enough, and she didn't want to risk another bout with the chills. She hated the thought of another afternoon of silence. How she wished she were back home in Hawthorn. She missed her home and her father. Grief was a hard thing to face alone. And Laurel had never felt more alone in her life.

Laurel finally took a sheet of paper from one of the boxes in the wagon and sat down to write a letter. She spent some time telling Rachel about the trip, describing the countryside, the people they'd met, and the sanctuary of the cave. She avoided writing anything about Mac or their problems. When she'd filled up all the paper she had, she folded it and put it in a book, planning to post it when they reached another town. The rest of the day was spent in silence. Laurel rose after a long time and checked the rest of the clothes that had been drying. Everything was again dry and ready to use, even the last coverlet.

"Here are your last two blankets, Mac. You'll sleep better if I'm not around to disturb you. I hope you sleep well. God willing, we should be able to make an early start tomorrow."

"Sorry, I can't let that happen. If we have four blankets now, the floor won't be so hard, and we will rest more warmly because we have two blankets if we share the cover. Besides, a separate marriage bed is against my religion." The tone of his voice suggested he spoke in jest, but Laurel didn't respond.

"I went to her house to murder her."

"What?"

"Marsha. I planned to kill her for the disgrace I thought she'd brought on me. I know now, of course, that it was my own pride I wanted to sooth. I went to her bedroom where she sat with my friend, but when I saw her there in her flashy jewelry, too low-cut dress, her overly made up face, I saw no beauty. She looked common and cheap. I knew then I'd never really loved her. I had lusted after her, but I felt no love. I was disgusted with myself. I left Maryland and started a seven-year binge, being the lowest level of human I could be. I wandered all over Tennessee and Kentucky, drinking too much moonshine, gambling away whatever money I could earn or win, and when none of that made me feel good, I took up spending my nights with whatever woman would invite me to her bed. Just call me Gomer. When I was broke and more than disgusted with the man—no, I wasn't a man then—with the animal I had become, I decided to go back home. At least my father's liquor was better than the moonshine, and it was free. I hadn't been back in Maryland two days, when Louis, my ex-best friend, called me out to defend Marsha's honor. I told him she didn't have any honor to defend, but he pushed me into a corner, so I killed him. It was a fair fight on the field of honor--stupid name for a dueling field--anyway, that was my breaking point. I either had to find a better life or end mine." Mac didn't say anything else. He went to the upturned box near the fire and sat down.

For some time, Laurel didn't know what to say. No one had ever spoken so openly to her. "I can see you've had too much hurt in your life. I am sorry about what happened to your friend. I understand why you said this had nothing to do with me. I guess I've been too wrapped up with my grief to think you have some too. Just like you said, it's not about me, but then in my life so little has had anything to do with me."

"Isn't that the way you want it?"

"This is your story, not mine. I don't want to talk about me."

"Well, then I'll finish mine. There isn't much left to tell anyway. My father took pity on my wretched state. He gave me some family land we had in Arkansas. He also gave me money to buy as much land as I wanted. Pa sent me off with this blessing. He said, 'Patrick, go live your passion, find your faith, and build a home.' Now you have the whole story of why my ill-temper fell on you yesterday. As I said...it has nothing to do with you at all."

"If you are finished, we can go to sleep. Tomorrow will be a difficult day with the roads so muddy."

"Laurel, you have really closed yourself in your fortress, haven't you? Is there a way I can reach you? We could build a good life together if we try."

"Being alone is just easier than being hurt. Good night."

10

There is no fear in love, but perfect love casteth out fear because fear hath torment. He that feareth is not made perfect in love.

KJV c1850, 1John 4:18.

The new day began with a noticeable chill. Both the temperature and the tension between Mac and Laurel were icy. Regardless, they worked side by side to pack the wagon so they could vacate their cave sanctuary and make their way east. As the sun rose above the horizon, Mac slapped the reins across the backs of the mules and headed toward Jasper. He had no idea how far the settlement was, and he dreaded the day's travel because the road was snow covered. Progress was slow, and at times both he and Laurel walked to lighten the load and to push the wagon out of icy ruts. Late into the morning, they met two travelers on horseback, headed west along the military road.

"Howdy, Stranger."

"Good morning, gents. We're headed to Jasper settlement. Can you tell me how far that might be?"

"You're nearly there now. About two miles on east, there. We sheltered there whilst the snow fell. Where ya'll headed?"

"Further east. Home to Greene County."

"Woo...eee! You still got a journey ahead. Headed to Huntsville, and we thought that was a far piece from here."

"You'll make it easy in two days if the weather holds. Good passage to you, friends."

"Same to ya'll." Mac was glad they had come upon honest travelers. The information they had shared proved true, and the MacLaynes reached Jasper just as the sun reached its zenith. Several small log buildings and even a clapboard structure or two made up the settlement of Jasper. One of the more substantial buildings was a trading post with the name John Ross printed on a sign above the door.

"Laurel, let's go inside and rest awhile. It'll be nice to warm ourselves by their stove. I'll ask a few questions and then we can decide if we will travel any further today."

"All right."

"Look around and see if they have some supplies to add to our foodstuff. I'm kind of tired of eating eggs."

"I'll look." The mercantile was larger than it had appeared from the street. The merchant had a variety of food, household items, clothing, and hardware stocked.

"Are you Mr. Ross?"

"At your service, sir. You're a stranger in these parts. Are ya'll gonna settle here abouts?"

"Name's MacLayne, and no, we are headed east. This is my wife, Laurel"

"Ma'am. Do you need provisions for the rest of your trip?" She nodded, but Mac answered.

"Probably want more than need. Gets old eating the same food after a few days."

"Well, look around. I'm sure you'll find some vittles to add to your stores. May even find a few fancies for the little lady." Laurel added several things to the larder. She took a small pail of lard, potatoes, several yams, a side of bacon, a small smoked ham, and a jar of preserved cherries. She added a small sack of coffee, a bag of salt, and cornmeal, enough to last until they reached Shiloh.

"Laurel, come over to this counter. Mr. Ross laid out several bolts of fabric for you to look at." Laurel walked over to where Mac stood. "You need several new dresses to wear to school. Why don't you choose two or three pieces for new clothes?"

"I already have three good dresses."

"I've seen them all. None of them fit right. They are too short and too big for your slight frame. They look like cast-offs from a missionary's barrel."

"They were my mother's." Mac grimaced.

"No offense meant to your mother. They probably looked fine on her, but on you, they don't fit. Go on and pick cloth for new dresses."

To prevent a verbal tug of war in public, she turned back to look at the fabric. She found a bolt of brown linsey-woolsey for a good practical day dress. She also picked up a bolt of gray calico with tiny white flowers. She would use it to make a new Sunday dress.

Mac walked over, looked at her choices, took both bolts, and laid them back on the counter. In a voice just above a whisper, Mac explained. "I want you to wear clothes that aren't so dreary and matronly."

"I always wear practical, neutral things. I prefer them."

"I know you do, Laurel, but you aren't the spinster of Hawthorn anymore. You are the wife of Patrick MacLayne. I want you to look the part. I like the blue calico with the white sprigs there. Over there, that green gingham check is good. And look at that gray sateen under the yellow bolt. That gray will make a nice dress for our town socials." Mac walked behind the counter that held the cloth. "Come look at these patterns. I like the looks of these." He picked up three before Laurel had a chance to say one word. Mac also picked up two bolts of lawn for chemise, petticoats, nightclothes, blouses and shirts. He added trim, lace, and buttons. "Laurel, try on shoes, too."

Laurel was appalled that Mac had chosen so much and at the cost. She didn't want or need all the things he'd carried to the front of the store, but if she put up a fight, Mac would be embarrassed and become angry again. Well, she told herself, Mac could spend his money if wanted. Of course, he wanted her dressed to suit him when he took her into his settlement.

"Mr. Ross, do you have a dressmaker or tailor nearby?"

"Well, my misses does a right fine job with ladies' clothes. Ya'll gonna to be around a week or so?"

"No, only one day. I wanted to get the dresses cut and fitted. Laurel can sew while we travel. Help keep her busy so she's not bored and testy from idleness." Mac winked at Mr. Ross as if they shared a secret about female behavior.

"Sarah is just in the back of the store, there in our house. Send your lady back, and she'll help you."

"Laurel, take these patterns and the fabric on back to Mrs. Ross."

"I don't like to follow orders today any better than I did yesterday."

"Excuse me, Laurel. I didn't mean to bark orders. I wanted to ask my wife to be good to herself for once. Please let Mrs. Ross help you." Red faced, Laurel picked up the patterns and cloth and walked to the back of the trading post through the door to the living quarters. Mac followed.

"Hello, Mrs. Ross. Your husband said you'd help my wife fit and cut some clothes. I would be much obliged if you have the time."

"I'll sure try to help. What's your name, dearie?"

"Laurel Campbell...MacLayne. It's my married name."

"Well, I'm Sarah. Make yourself at home, mister, whilst I do the fittin'."

"Mac, you could go load the wagon while I'm busy."

"Laurel, I'd like to rest a spell and watch the process. You don't mind, do you Sarah?" She shook her head and smiled at Mac.

"Mac, I have to remove my clothes for her to fit a new pattern."

"Just do what you need to do. I've seen your undies."

Laurel blushed again. "Sarah, please excuse my crude husband. He thinks he's funny."

"He can't offend me. John makes crude jokes too. I always tell folks who hears his silly remarks he's just bragging on his prize. Not everyone has such a shapely wife. Of course, right now I'm not very shapely. This new one will be here in June."

"You must be happy about a new baby in your family."

"We'd like us a boy this time, but a healthy babe will be a blessing regardless." She turned back to Laurel. "Do I need to make easement so you can wear these dresses for more than a few weeks?"

"I'm not sure I understand. I haven't sewn for myself in a while."

"Are you expecting? I can make you a bit of room in the dresses so you can grow into them."

Laurel blushed again and didn't have a quick reply.

Mac came to her rescue. "Not yet, Mrs. Ross, but we plan to grow us a passel of little MacLaynes when we get our cabin built."

Laurel didn't like the remark. She turned away knowing his eyes were sparkling with suppressed laughter. He purposely made that remark to see her fidget and blush. How would he feel if she told this woman that only one virgin had ever delivered a baby? Of course, that would have spoken more to her shame than his. What kind of wife denied her husband his due? What woman would be so stupid to reject a man like Mac? How could any woman be so undesirable that her husband didn't even want her?

Laurel wanted to run, but even that would be awkward and rude to a kind lady who offered to help her.

"No, Sarah, just make the clothes fit well right now. I will worry about other things if the need arises." Mac nodded and smiled at his wife.

The women continued to work for about three hours. Together they measured, cut, and pinned three dresses, two night dresses, two blouses and a skirt. When they got to the last piece of fabric, the silver-gray sateen for her party dress, Laurel balked.

"Mac, I can't wear this dress." The pattern Mac had picked was an off the shoulder, low cut bell-shaped ball gown. Laurel never owned a dress that showed that her cleavage as this one would. The bodice of this dress was so tight that her shape was more obvious than she'd ever allowed before.

"Laurel, that dress is beautiful. The material enhances your gray eyes. A dark green broach pinned right here will finish the dress just as it should be." Mac had put his finger where the two sides of the shawl collar met at Laurel's breasts. She gasped.

"What do you think, Sarah? Can't you just see Laurel waltz in this lovely gown? Lady, you are a miracle worker." He picked Sarah up and spun her around and then planted a kiss on her cheek. Both of them laughed with joy. Laurel stood in the pinned dress and watched the merriment. "Pack it up, ma'am. We owe you a huge debt for your work. I'll have the most handsome wife in Shiloh."

Mac left the room to settle his account with John Ross. He made two trips to the wagon to load the things he'd bought. He returned to the Ross house to pick up the sewing projects. He placed three silver dollars in Susan's hand. "Thank you for your help. I am keeping promises to my father-in-law."

"Laurel, keep the blue calico out to work on as we travel. I'd love to see you wear it for our first day home. I think you'll look right stylish." He left again to speak to John Ross. Laurel wrapped the cloth into two bundles, one large and one small. She thanked Mrs. Ross.

"Laurel, you are a lucky woman. That man is certainly smitten with you."

"You're kind, Sarah. I hope I'll find friends like you in Shiloh." Laurel picked up her bundles and headed out. She didn't want to have a conversation with Susan Ross, who thought Mac loved her. Obviously, the lady was a confirmed romantic or a poor judge of people. How could she believe Mac cared for her?

The tavern next door was crude, but they could get a room for the night and a warm meal before they left headed to the Lebanon community the next day. If Mac had been alone, he'd have travelled further that day, but Laurel was tired, and she would rest better in a bed after taking some semblance of a bath. They could spare the time and would remain overnight.

Mac arranged with the smith to care for their animals and store their wagon. Loaded down with Laurel's small bundles, his traveling case, his Bible, and a book from the wagon under one arm, Mac pushed the door to the tavern door open with his boot. He protectively took Laurel's arm with his other. She didn't object once she saw the occupants in the common room and moved a step closer to him.

The inn keeper approached them. "You want a table?"

"Yes, and a quiet room in the back for tonight." The man pointed to a table near the only window in the cavernous log room. The dining room was dark, musty, and cold, barely heated by a large fireplace on a back wall. Even in the middle of the afternoon, several lanterns were necessary to provide light.

"Only got one room left."

"Sure, he'd want a room in the back...with a doxy like her."

"She ain't no fancy woman, Ernie. She's got a weddin' ring."

"Maybe it's true what they say about the smart ones." Ernie poked his companion in the ribs with his elbow and together they made a vulgar sound.

"Wait there at the table, Laurel." Mac walked with a determined stride toward their table. "I'll accept an apology from you men for the insult you directed at my wife."

"Aww, get yerself away from here. We didn't mean no harm."

"It ain't like we touched her...." Mac grabbed the arm of the vulgar man, twisted it behind this back, and pushed him to the floor. He put his knee to the startled man's neck.

"Don't move or mutter another ugly remark to that fine lady. I'll move my knee just a touch and break his neck."

"Don't hurt my brother, mister. We're sure out of line." The shabby man turned toward Laurel and removed his hat. "Sorry, ma'am. We don't mean no disrespect. Don't get many ladies in here. We just mistook you, that's all."

"Please lady, tell your man we didn't mean no harm." Mac looked toward Laurel, and she nodded. Mac rose and jerked the arm of the man he'd put down.

"Remember, all ladies deserve to be treated well. Don't forget it, especially when my wife is near." Mac returned to Laurel at the table closest to the door where he would sit with his back to the wall. Together they ate hot beef stew and fresh bread. Blackberry cobbler made a tasty end to the good meal.

"Let's go to our room, Mac. I'm tired." The owner led them to a room down a dim hallway. The room was sparsely furnished with a bed, a crudely made rocking chair, and a bureau with a kerosene lamp in front of a cracked mirror. The small bedside table held a large bowl and pitcher with cold water for washing.

"Can we get a couple of buckets with hot water in here?"

"It'll cost you two bits."

"I'll be glad to pay for a little luxury." Soon the water sat inside the door. Mac lay on the bed with his back to Laurel so she could bathe as well as she could without a tub. "I'd leave so you could have your privacy, Laurel, but I don't think you'd be safe here alone."

"I don't guess it matters much. After all, you've watched me undress all afternoon."

Mac chuckled. "I like the banter, Laurel. It's fun to spar with your quick wit. I may have met my match."

Laurel began to unbraid her hair. She wanted to wash it, but the bowl was small, and she didn't think she could do an adequate job. As she began to brush the braids, Mac walked up behind her. "I'll help you wash your hair if you will let me." She looked up into his face. She didn't understand. Two days ago he couldn't bear to look at her, and now he offered to wash her hair. She nodded her consent.

Mac poured the warm water over her long hair and rubbed the soap bar through it several times. The lather was not much. He massaged her head and again poured water through her hair. Laurel didn't know when she had enjoyed such luxury. Never had she been pampered as she had been all day. Her confusion level continued to increase. Mac took the one towel from the table and began to dry her hair. Laurel felt...well, she couldn't name what she felt, but she liked it very much.

"Mac, you didn't bring any clean clothes for me to wear."

"I did. I brought your night dress and this." He handed her the thin, lawn nightdress and the dark green satin ribbon she'd worn at their wedding.

"This isn't very modest. The fabric is old and threadbare."

"But you like how it feels, and it is clean." Laurel quickly pulled it down. "Laurel, I am not uncomfortable with you in any state of undress. I want to see you dressed in feminine, pretty clothes, both night and day. Of all your mother's clothes, this is the prettiest."

Mac walked to her, took the ribbon and sashed the gown. Her figure was evident. Perhaps he'd overestimated the level of his self-control. The woman in front of him was far from the woman he'd first seen dressed in her father's work clothes only two weeks ago. He patted her head and returned to the bed to put some space between them; however, Laurel followed with the book he'd brought from the wagon. He went to the washbowl to wash away some of the trail dirt. He removed his shirt and stood with his back to Laurel. He attempted to clean as much of his shoulders and back as he could reach. Laurel walked up to him, took the small cloth, and began to wash his back and shoulders. Mac smiled, for her touch was unexpected and more personal than she'd ever touched him before. He turned and took the cloth from her hand. His eyes were the color of the bluest lake as storm clouds gathered. He gazed her eyes, trying to discern what she was feeling and thinking. How easy it would be to take her to the bed across the room and make love to her. *Would he always have to fight his lust!* He looked at her again, and with all the resolve he had, he spoke in a sarcastic tone, "Thank you for your help, kind lady." Mac bowed at the waist and kissed her hand. "Now if you'll give me a bit of privacy, I'll finish my bath."

Laurel's slight smile vanished as quickly as the words came from him. She turned her back and went back to her book, avoiding his gaze. Mac wanted to walk in the melting snow for a while, but he knew he could not leave her unprotected...he prayed she would not need protection from him.

Mac moved the lamp near the bed and lay down on the right side, which had become his habit. Funny how in two short weeks with almost no effort, the choice of which side of the bed they'd sleep on had become a habit, but all their attempts to communicate civilly had led nowhere. Laurel and he had much to settle, and perhaps he had more issues than she did. Abruptly, he got up and braced the chair against the doorknob. If he had been alone in the bed, he would have tossed and turned most of the night. As it was, every nerve in his body was edgy, ready to rush into action if the need arose.

"Laurel, what would you like to read tonight? Is there a book you haven't read?"

"I don't care. Just pick one. The Hosea story was helpful, don't you think, Gomer?"

"Who is the judge now?"

"Just let the book fall open. We'll read whatever fate gives us tonight."

"Luke 5: 37-42 wins the draw." Mac began to read from the Gospel of Luke, but Laurel heard few of the words of the scripture that spoke of criticizing others when we carry faults of our own.

"Mac, I'd like to talk with you about our day. I'm so confused I just want to run away, back home where I can make some sense of my life."

"I'll listen, but Laurel, I'm telling you now that I won't let you return to Hawthorn. I don't speak vows lightly and neither do you. Go ahead and speak your mind."

"Two days ago we were at odds. You told me you never meant to care for me. You turned away from me in disgust. You told me I was indecently dressed."

"Is that what you thought?"

"I think I reported the facts fairly."

"You repeated basically what I had said, but you don't know why I said what I did."

"I want you to understand my perspective of what happened. I am confused because one minute you loathe the sight at me, call me an unclothed temptress, and then you have me measured for new clothes and tell Sarah Ross lies about our relationship. What do you expect of me?"

"Laurel, I didn't lie to Sarah. I was predicting the future. I told you why I left home. Well, I didn't tell you everything. After I killed Louis in that duel, I was angry I'd been pushed by a Jezebel into a duel where I killed my best friend. Marsha still wanted to control my life, just as she had done to her now dead husband. I went to her parents' home to pay my respects to Louis and to see if I could help. Right then, with her dead husband lying in state in the front room of their house, Marsha approached me. She said now she was a wealthy widow and she could marry a man she truly loved. I picked up my hat, called her a few ugly names, and left her house.

"That night I vowed I'd never give my heart to another woman. I vowed I'd never trust any female. From that time to this, I've never let myself care about any woman. That is not to say I haven't had the company of too many, but I never let anyone close since. Truthfully, I've found it hard to make true friends. Until I met your uncle Matt, I didn't have a friend I could trust. That pledge has kept me a safe. I make acquaintances, but few friends." Laurel listened, but she did not respond. "What are you thinking now?"

"I answered that question last night. A person can't help how they feel." Laurel walked over to the cracked mirror over the bureau. She separated three lengths of her hair, ready to braid it back into her usual coronet."

"Laurel, I would like for you to leave your hair down from now on. Your hair is glorious. You should never tame this beauty in those horrible braids, especially those you wind around your head."

Laurel turned away with her back squared and her head bowed. "Mac, it's such a tousled mess. It's impossible to take care of this way. This mirror reflects my visage. I am not blind. It's not a pretty sight."

In a tense voice, Mac spoke, "Don't turn your back to me when we talk." Mac took the cracked mirror from the bureau and threw it against the wall above the lavatory table. "Laurel, I've threatened men twice for insulting you. I promised your father I'd protect you and help you learn your own worth. You're your own worst enemy. I have to protect you from yourself. From now on, the only mirror you need is here, in my eyes. When you learn to see yourself as you really are, then you can have another mirror."

"That's ridiculous. I can't put my hair up without a mirror."

"I told you, I want you to wear it down. You need to stop doing everything you can to cover up the lovely person you are. Laurel, your beauty comes from inside, not like Marsha who didn't have your kindness, loyalty, intelligence, or faith."

"But you turned from me yourself. You couldn't bear to look at me. You said to cover myself."

In a voice more fierce and intentional than Laurel had ever heard Mac use before, he responded, "Laurel, the other day when you were lying on that blanket, so full of life and enjoying our companionship... blessings to high heaven! I wanted you. I wanted to exercise my right as your husband."

Laurel stared at Mac in disbelief. "You never said anything, just your anger and nasty orders. I thought you regretted your decision to go through with the arrangement you'd made with my father."

"Far from it.... We have got to learn to communicate better. I have promises to keep and so many flaws of my own to deal with."

"Mac, I don't understand at all. If you found me somewhat desirable, why treat me so coldly?"

"My dear wife, you certainly know very little about men! It's not easy for a man to deny himself at times. Just like tonight when you washed my back and shoulders. Well, let's say the sarcasm prevented a very different outcome. In that moment, I wanted you, but more important, I vowed I'd never give a woman access to my heart, and if I took you in lust, is that not the worst kind of disrespect? That is why I told you that I had no intention of loving you, not because you are not worthy of love. Do you understand, Laurel?

"Once again, I appreciate your honesty. Even if I don't like what you say, I believe you're speaking truth. Perhaps tomorrow we can start over again. Friends shouldn't stay upset with each other."

"Honestly, Laurel...I don't know if I will love you, but I do want us to be friends, but more than that, I want to be your husband. I will work hard to keep the vows I made." Mac walked over to Laurel and laid his arm around her shoulders. He sensed her stiffen to his touch. He thought he should move away, but he didn't want to. Instead, he pulled her closer, put his other arm around her waist, and pulled her next to him. He buried his face in her hair and took in the scent of her clean locks, and the scent of the woman he'd married such a short time ago. Laurel didn't relax, but she didn't pull away either. "We had a very serious talk tonight, wife. Let's call it a day and get some rest." Mac led her to her side of the bed, helped her cover herself and got to his knees beside her.

He prayed, "Lord, thank you for bringing us through another day and past another hurdle. Bless us as we continue to learn about the other. Please Lord, help us know your will for us and show us the way to the life we will build together. Thank you for giving me Laurel. In Jesus's name. Amen."

"Thank you for Mac. Amen."

"Laurel, tomorrow we'll start over one more time. Even with our faults and shortcomings, with God's help we can make this marriage work.

11

*The aged women likewise...that they may teach the young women to
be sober, to love their husbands, to love their children, to be discreet,
keep at home, good, obedient to their husbands, that they word of
good not be blasphemed.*

KJC c 1850, Titus 2:2-5

The next morning, the MacLaynes made their way out of Jasper
headed east. The day was a long, tiring one, but at least the
mood between them was pleasant. They talked more easily
since they'd cleared the air. The effort to control the team of jacks and
keep the small wagon on the treacherous road took as much concentra-
tion as Mac could muster, but he found occasions to talk with his busy
wife. Laurel seemed to enjoy the work on the new dress he'd insisted she
make. When she tired of sewing, she read and the time passed genially.
Mac estimated that by nightfall, they'd traveled at least half the distance
to Lebanon. With no settlement in the area, they again found themselves
camped in the open. Their tiny oilcloth tent under the wagon provided
the shelter they needed. One more day had passed, and they were some
twenty miles closer to Greene County.

Anxious to reach Lebanon by midafternoon, Laurel and Mac arose with the sun breaking the eastern horizon. The sky was cloudless, and a gentle almost warm breeze hinted of a beautiful day. Laurel took cold biscuits and ham slices to make a fast breakfast, and Mac gave up his morning coffee so they could put miles behind them. The road was poor in many places with deep ruts and sloppy, wet low-lying areas. The spring rains and unexpected snow storm from earlier in the week had damaged some of the governor's good dirt roads. Mac was forced to rest the mules frequently and to focus his attention on driving the team so they didn't get mired in the bad places. He missed the pleasant conversation he had shared with Laurel the day before. He was beginning to believe he didn't have to have romance to make a good life. When he and Laurel really communicated, their friendship grew.

Laurel was busy and seemingly quite content, stitching the under-sleeves of the new blue calico dress she started in Jasper. When she finished the dress, the garment would befit the wife of one of Shiloh's leading citizens and more than suitable for a teacher to wear at school. No one at Shiloh would believe this woman to be the spinster of Hawthorn Chapel.

Even with the frequent rest stops for the mules, they made fair time and reached Lebanon community just before evening worship began. Although it had only been two weeks since they'd been at church in Hawthorn, it seemed much longer. Matthew Campbell had told him there was a growing church in Lebanon, and his friend from home in North Carolina was a local pastor in that settlement. He had renewed their friendship at annual conference a year or so back. A.L. Kavenaugh was the local pastor in Lebanon, and they had just finished a new church, which they had called Searcy Mission. This church had already affiliated with the Methodist Episcopal South conference, but Mac knew worship would be grace-filled, and the people there would give them a warm welcome. Finding the new church was easy. The settlement was small, and the words from the familiar Wesleyan hymns served as guide to the church. After several minutes of singing, Brother Kavenaugh delivered a strong message on the topic of joy. He read from the book of Philippians, Chapter 4:6-7. *"Be careful for nothing; but in everything by prayer and supplication with thanksgiving let your requests be known unto God. And the peace of God, which passeth all understanding, shall keep your hearts and minds through Jesus Christ."* His down to earth, positive message encouraged Mac for good reason. He and Laurel had spent two happy days together with not one angry word between them.

After the service ended, Mac introduced himself to Brother Kavenaugh and told him of his friendship with Matthew Campbell. "I miss that old rascal. Matt sure changed once the Lord got a hold of him. Did he marry that pretty little gal he was sparking back in North Carolina?"

"Well, he's married, but I'm not sure where he found Ellie. She is an angel. They got five kids now."

"Bless me. I never believed Matt would settle down. Guess it just goes to show what the Lord can do with a life if we let Him."

"Brother, this is my wife, Laurel. She is Matt's niece, and we've been traveling from Washington County for the last week headed back to Shiloh Station in Greene County."

"Heard your congregation is split about joining the south conference, Mac."

"That's so. We're talking a lot about it now, but we don't have many slave holders up our way. I'm sure they'll be a rift before a decision is made. Just hope it's not too big a one."

The good preacher nodded his understanding as his own congregation had dealt with the same problems over the slavery issue. That contentious issue had caused a split in many congregations and even the death of a few.

"Laurel and I are pretty weary from camping out last night. Can you recommend an inn or tavern where we can find lodging? We have quite a way to go before we reach Mt. Olive, and I am not sure we will even find an inn there."

"No decent place for travelers here about. Let me think a minute... I know just the place for you. I'll take you to Brother Abe and Sister Maggie. They're gifted with the spirit of hospitality. They love company.

They live in a fair-sized cabin. If you're lucky, Sister Maggie will have some of her excellent spice cake."

— ~

Within half an hour, Mac and Laurel were seated at the table of the friendliest eighty-year-old sweethearts in the state. Abe and Maggie Griffin had been married for sixty-four years, but their behavior was more that of newlyweds. As they sat together, they quietly held hands, and occasionally, Abe would lift one of Maggie's dear, wrinkled hands to his lips for a sweet kiss. They often spoke endearment to each other. Without any doubt, the two loved each other. Maggie tottered around her little kitchen and prepared a quick meal for her company. She apologized for the meagerness of the supper, but Laurel and Mac felt they had been served a feast when Maggie placed fried potatoes, greens, leftover chicken, and spice cake on the table before them. After the meal, Laurel helped Maggie clean the dishes while Mac and Abe went to the barn to complete evening chores.

"Well, Missy, I know you and Mac are newlyweds."

"How do you know that?"

"Just the way you act toward each other. You still walk separate paths."

"I don't understand."

"You haven't gotten to know each other well enough yet to plot a single way. It'll come in time."

"Being a wife is new to me. What do you do to make Abe a good wife?"

"So many little things, and some not so little things, I guess."

"I don't even know where to start. My mama died when I just a girl. I grew up in a house with my papa and brothers."

"Ain't you never been around womenfolk?"

"A few friends my age and some of the older ladies in my church. You and Abe certainly seem to have kept your love alive. You must have been truly in love when you married."

"Not the case, dearie. Back in '93 when I came over from Dublin, just sixteen years old, I was a bond servant. I pledged seven years work to get my passage paid to America. Just so happens that Abe bought my bond that same afternoon I landed in Virginia. That day he took me to the preacher because him being a God-fearing man, he wouldn't live in sin with any woman."

"You mean you didn't know him at all?"

"That's the Lord's truth of it. Took us a couple of years for me to know I loved Abe. The romancing part was quicker, but when the love was there, married life was so much better."

"How long did it take Abe to fall in love with you, Maggie?"

"He told me he knew the moment he saw me. That was why he bought my bond. Of course, I'm not sure if that was his loving me or his wanting me. You know what I'm a telling you."

Laurel blushed a bit and realized the talk was getting very personal, so she tried to change the direction of their conversation. "Tell me what I need to do that will make Mac happy, like you make Abe happy."

"Well, Missy, in all these years, I've found that my old man is happiest when I am happy."

"And what makes you happy, Maggie?"

"Just being with my old man. I thank the Lord for him every day!"

"Abe certainly shows you a lot of affection."

"That's a fact. It's always been his nature.

"You've been a dear to talk to me about being married. I like to think my mama would have told me these things if she'd been around. Thank you for sharing your roof with us tonight." Laurel felt hope rise. Perhaps Mac would learn to care for her. At least, she knew now that she wasn't the only woman in the world who had married a stranger.

Mac and Abe returned well after dark. Together the two couples, the newlyweds and the love birds shared evening prayer.

"Mac, you and Laurel will have to sleep in the loft. I'm afraid we'd never make it up that ladder if we gave you our bed."

"Plenty of blankets in the chest, should you need them, but as newly-weds, I'm sure you can figure ways to stay warm. Bless ya'll. Good night."

Though it was barely dark, perhaps seven o'clock, the elderly couple made their way to their room, leaving Mac and Laurel to fend for themselves. Mac had brought in Laurel's bundle when they arrived, but they had nothing to read, not even their Bibles to share, so they retired to the bedroom in the loft. Laurel went to the darker corner of the tiny room to change into her nightdress. Mac removed his outer clothes and slipped under the quilt. A single candle lit the space. Laurel made her way to the left side of the bed.

"Did you enjoy the Searcy Mission service tonight, Laurel?"

"It was good, especially the sermon. Brother Kavenaugh's talk about joy was something I needed to hear. I felt like he was talking just to me."

"He's a good man. He admires your uncle Matthew. Couldn't believe he'd changed so much. Our hosts are certainly a pair of sweethearts. Did you know they been married sixty-four years and raised seven children, all girls except for one son."

"No, Maggie didn't mention her children. She told me she married Abe the first day they met. Actually, he had indentured her and refused to live in the same house unless they were married. Strangely coincidental, don't you think?"

"I don't believe in coincidence, Laurel. God has a way of putting people in our paths all the time to help us find our way. I think that is why we are here tonight."

"It's sweet to see two people care about each other after all these years. Abe certainly has a deep affection for Maggie."

"More than affection. Abe told me that he loved her more now than he did the day he first saw her get off that boat from Ireland."

"She must have been very beautiful."

"No doubt, just like you."

"Stop saying that."

"I didn't mean to upset you, Laurel. What I meant was that Maggie has all the qualities of a godly woman. Abe couldn't help but fall in love with her and through the years he has been blessed because he obeyed God's plan. I hope the same for us, Laurel."

"I want to be a good wife for you, Mac. You've been kind and generous to me. You were so good to keep the bargain made with my family, even though it went far beyond what you'd promised my uncle. I know you did that to help my father pass peacefully. I hope somehow to repay your generosity."

"Laurel, no repayment is expected. This marriage is not all one sided… me giving and you taking. I want us to build a home. I can't do it without a wife. I've had my pick of women, more than my share, but you are the one the Lord has seen fit to yoke me with."

"I hope you feel that way in sixty days, let alone sixty-four years, like with the Griffins."

"I told you--as long as God wills it. If we are meant to experience romance together, I'll welcome it, but if not, our friendship and faith will do just fine."

"I will trust you to help me be a credit to you."

"You already are." Mac reached out to embrace her. He could sense her fear, and she pulled back almost as soon as his arms touched her. Mac had never had any woman react to him as Laurel did. She appeared to want affection, and she told him more than once she hoped to be a good wife to him. Why did his touch provoke such fear and anxiety in her? Under his breath, he prayed, "Patience and gentleness, Lord. Please send me a goodly supply."

"Laurel thank you for another good day. I hope you sleep well tonight. We have about eighty long miles before we reach the next community where we can hope to find shelter. Enjoy the bed. I'm afraid it'll be the ground for the next three nights."

"Goodnight, Mac." Laurel did not sleep well, tossing and turning the entire night. Mac heard her whimper in her sleep. Doubtless, her nightmare had returned. Perhaps soon, she would tell him what caused her so many sleepless nights.

When they awoke the next morning, the sun had yet to break the horizon. Regardless of the early hour, Maggie had prepared a hearty breakfast so her guests would travel with full stomachs. Fresh bacon, oatmeal, and hot biscuits with milk and butter made an ample meal. Mac went with Abe to the barn to help with the morning chores and hitch his animals to the wagon.

"Abe, we thank you for your hospitality. I'm afraid we won't find such comfort for several days."

"We're blessed by your visit. We'll keep ya'll in our prayers, and as for safe passage and a long happy life. You be careful when you get closer to White River. That'll come up 'bout half way to Mt. Olive. I heard rumors of foul play in that neck of the woods. God keep you safe, young friend."

"Again, I'm beholding to you and Maggie."

Laurel brought their few things from the cabin, pausing at the door to hug Maggie. "You've been such a dear, Maggie. I'm glad you told me about your life with Abe. Pray for me to be as good a wife to Mac."

"You'll be a good wife, Laurel...if you remember there are three in your marriage. And love comes when you trust. Remember."

"You are so wise. I hope some of your wisdom will rub off on me." She hugged her again.

"I don't know about wisdom, but you can take this grub with you. It'll help make the day's trip a little easier."

Laurel climbed to the seat next to Mac as Abe helped her up. The wagon moved eastward with Mac and Laurel waving farewell to two special friends they'd never meet again. Laurel was tired. She had slept so little the previous night, and she felt drowsy despite the bumps and jostling caused by the road conditions. To keep herself awake she worked on her new dress. The lawn undersleeves were finished so she plied her needle to the full, flowing outer sleeves. Mac hadn't picked a simple pattern. She would have to sew many hours to have the blue calico dress ready when they reached Shiloh.

Mac didn't sing that morning. Since they had left the Griffins' home, he hadn't spoken at all, except to ask her to do something or clarify what he needed. He wasn't curt or angry, but neither did he smile at her nor tease as he had the two previous days. Laurel missed his banter and the music. Perhaps she could break the quiet with a light natured question. "I hope you slept well last night, Mac. Did you enjoy Maggie's breakfast?"

"I did. Both Abe and Maggie are fine folks." Mac didn't add anything to encourage a conversation.

The silence was awkward. "I've made good progress on my new dress." There was no response. "The weather seems more spring-like today, don't you think?"

"Getting close to Easter, about time we have a bit of spring." Again the talk stopped.

"Have I done something wrong?"

"No. What makes you ask?"

"You seem a little distant today."

"Didn't mean to give that impression." Laurel stiffened her back and turned back to her sewing. They rode more than two hours in silence. "I've got to stop here to rest the animals for a while. Do you want to get down and stretch your legs for a few minutes?"

"Yes." Mac offered his hand to help her down and then left her standing at the side of the wagon while he attended the horses and the mules.

Laurel was weary from sewing all morning, so she went to the back of the wagon to find something to read. The only book she could see without unpacking things was Mac's Bible, which he always kept in easy reach. She picked it up and started to the wagon seat.

As she approached the wagon, Mac was there to help her up. He saw she had gotten his Bible from the wagon. "May I have that, please?"

Laurel saw that he had nodded toward the book.

"Yes. I'm sorry. I didn't think you'd mind. I wanted to read a while. It was the only book I could see."

"I'll get you a book if you want one."

"Mac, I'm sorry. I didn't mean to bother your things. I just didn't think you'd mind."

"What book would you like?"

"Never mind. I know we need move on."

After another hour or so, they ate a cold lunch made up of Maggie's grub. They drank cold water from a stream while the horses and mules rested for several minutes. Shortly, they were back on the road again, headed northeast. They traveled until nearly dark. Mac left only enough time to collect fire wood for the night and to put together a makeshift tent as a shelter for the night. Well after dark, Laurel laid out a cold supper, but she did make hot coffee for Mac. He hadn't had any all day, and he would like a couple of cups with the cookies Maggie had sent.

"Thank you for the coffee tonight, Laurel. I did miss it this morning."

"It was easy enough to make." They talked as if they were strangers.

"Are you ready to read scriptures with me?"

"Whatever you want."

Mac reached for his Bible and open to a passage in Luke, chapter 12: 1-3. "*He began to say unto his disciples first of all Beware of the leaven of the Pharisees, which is hypocrisy. For there is nothing covered that shall not be revealed; neither hid, that shall not be known. Therefore, whatsoever you have spoken in darkness shall be heard in the light, and that which you have spoken in the ear in a closet shall be proclaimed upon the rooftops.*"

"Strange choice. Did you pick it for a reason?"

"Yes, Laurel. I did."

"Would you like to share that reason with me? Or perhaps you'd like me to guess, just like I have been trying to guess all day why you decided to ignore me?"

"Why do you think I chose it?"

"Well, if we are going to have a philosophical discussion about it, I know the scripture says there is no such thing as a secret. Things should be open because eventually everything gets found out."

"You are a bright lady, well-versed in scripture."

"Sarcasm doesn't become you either. Tell me what I have done to make you so angry with me."

"I'm not angry, just confused.

"That makes two of us, then. I really tried to open a conversation with you this morning. That is certainly not my nature."

"Laurel, I'll speak my mind. We have to be honest if trust is to grow between us."

"I believe that, but how can we be honest when we don't talk? When we got to Searcy Mission and met the Griffins, I thought you were pretty content with me. Then this morning the good feelings of the past few days were gone again. Can't you tell me what happened between last night and this morning?"

"We have known each other now for nearly three weeks. We've been married more than two. Have I ever done anything to harm you or shown you in any way that I intended to hurt you?" Laurel didn't know how to respond. She didn't want an argument. She knew she would lose, and she was already exhausted from her lack of sleep the previous night.

"Well, not unless you count arriving at my house nearly twenty-nine hours before you were expected and finding me dressed like hired help." Mac didn't laugh at Laurel's attempt at humor. "No, Mac. You've always treated me with respect and courtesy."

"Do you find me unappealing?"

"What?"

"You heard. Please answer the question."

"Mac, I am too tired to get into an argument tonight. Can't this wait? I didn't sleep well last night."

"I am well aware of that. Am I unattractive or unappealing to you?"

"No. I think you are quite handsome. Now can we go to sleep, please?"

"When I get an answer that will let me sleep, too. Tell me why anytime I touch you, you pull away from me. You react as if you had been touched by a leper. Speak the truth. I need to know."

"I don't...still do that."

"You did last night. I'm required to ask permission to hold your hand or to help you into a wagon seat. I've only held you when you asked me to, and last night when I tried to hold you, you pulled away as it I'd were about to attack you, instead of offering an embrace."

"I didn't...I mean...I didn't know I did that."

"Laurel, friends aren't afraid of each other."

"I'm not afraid of you."

"Then you find my touch so repulsive that you pull away."

"That is ridiculous, Mac. That's not fair."

"I am being honest. Are you?"

"I've never lied to you since the moment we met."

"There are lies told and truths left untold. Didn't we just read that in Luke? They both break the trust, Laurel."

"I'm sorry, Mac. I don't mean to displease you. I told you from the start I am ill-prepared to be a wife for you."

"Will you answer my question?"

"I don't know what you want me to say. I don't have an answer."

"Laurel, Laurel, Laurel..." Frustration was so clear in his voice. "Can't you tell me what causes the barrier between us? I want you to trust me enough to let me through to the other side of the wall you've built around yourself."

"I don't know what you mean."

"Is that all you are willing to say to me?"

"I don't know what you want me to say."

"Laurel, I don't want you to say anything in particular. I want to keep my vows to you, and the promises I made to your father. I can't do either of those things alone."

Laurel was quiet for several minutes. Mac didn't speak to her. She stood up, walked away, and turned so she couldn't see his face. "I am overwhelmed."

Mac walked up behind her and took her by the shoulders and turned her to face him. "Laurel, look at me when you talk to me. I may not be your sweetheart or your lover, and probably not even your friend yet, but I am your husband. There is nothing you can't tell me."

"I don't know if I can look at you and say what I need to say."

"Look at me. I won't hurt you. I will listen." She raised her eyes to meet his.

"I'm overwhelmed with everything right now. My family is gone. My home is no longer my home. I am grieving and frightened. You are too good for me. I never intended to marry at all. Then you show up--attractive, intelligent, self-sufficient, and faithful. You've done nothing but show me compassion, respect, and courtesy. You honored my father's mistaken proposition. And all you got was me." Laurel breathed a sigh of relief. Surely, she had said enough to make Mac understand. She expected him to come to her and comfort her.

"Laurel, I was told you are a believer in the Gospel." Mac couldn't have surprised her more if he had laughed at her.

"Are you attacking my faith?"

"No, just questioning it." She stalked to the fire, sat on a log, and stared into the flames. She bared her soul and he'd attacked her. "Laurel, do you want to know why I took my Bible from you today?"

"I'm sure you just didn't want me to bother your things."

"I have no things, Laurel. Everything I have is yours now, but like you, I have some things I am not ready to share yet. Some of those things are listed in that book. Remember, I told you. Not everything is about you."

"I don't want to talk any more. I am tired. I want to go to bed."

"If we did, I still wouldn't be able to sleep. Right now, we're a hundred miles away apart, yet we share the same campfire."

"I don't know what else I can say. I tried to explain."

"Why are we're so far apart? Why are you not good enough? Laurel, no one but you can ever make you feel good enough. I wish I could say the right words and make you feel worthy, but that is not within me or any other human. That is what comes when people really understand the gospel."

"Do you think I need a sermon tonight?"

"I wish you understood. Your uncle Matthew taught me that lesson. I am so grateful that I learned. I was the least to be worthy until I claimed my worth in Christ. Not mine, but His." Mac sat for a few minutes. "Strange thing is—your name is Grace, not mine."

Laurel went on the defensive. Her words were full of venom as she directed them at Mac. "Yes, I know your name is Patrick...the noble one. Well, look what your nobility got you. Here I am--the spinster of Hawthorn. Aren't you blessed?"

In a voice solemn, he said, "I could be, if you'd let me. We both could be. Anyway, don't strike out at me when it's yourself you hate."

"How dare you speak to me like that?"

"Like what? In truth? That is our number one covenant, remember?" Laurel knew she had no defense against the truth Mac spoke to her. She looked at him, her eyes filled with hurt and confusion.

"Laurel, may I hold your hand?" She looked at him with questions unspoken. "Laurel, I want to touch you." She held her hand out to him. He took the offered hand and reached out with his other hand to caress her unbound hair. He did not pull her close, but he bowed his head, "Father, we have spoken very openly to each other tonight. Please Lord, let the words be understood in grace as I meant them. Please don't let us feel criticized or angry with each other. We have a long way to go to reach Shiloh and to find peace and understanding. Please keep us on the right road. In the name of Jesus. Amen."

Strangely, Laurel felt a sense of serenity. She didn't remove her hand from Mac's. When he bent forward and kissed her cheek, she did not pull away. She felt no threat. Within a few minutes, Mac had laid out the pallet for them. "Good night, wife. I wish you a more peaceful night than last night."

When the sun rose, the MacLayne's were packed and ready to start the second leg of the three-day trip to Mt. Olive. The weather was glorious, especially considering the short time ago they had been trudged through the ice and the snow of the early spring storm. Limbs were no longer bare, but everywhere Laurel looked she saw budding trees and bushes, the promise of the spring. Another week and the dogwoods would be blooming, heralding the coming of Easter. Laurel loved Easter, her very favorite holiday of the year. This year she would be at Shiloh, Lord willing. Of course, Laurel was still very apprehensive of what she would find there, but she knew Mac would stand with her, and a good friend would be most welcome in a strange place.

"Mac, would you mind if I ride Sassy a while? She needs some attention, and I would enjoy a ride."

"I think your saddle is buried underneath all those boxes. Besides, the roads may not be safe."

"I ride with a blanket sometimes. I promise not to get so far away that safety is a concern."

"Don't you want to be near me today?"

"That's not the reason. I just want to have some time to think about the past day or two."

"You are a grown woman. You don't need my permission to ride your own horse. Just be alert and watch for strangers." Laurel mounted Sassy Lady and trotted aways in front of the wagon. She was happy to be by herself for a time. Mac had confronted her with two things that demanded her consideration. She was truly puzzled he'd questioned her faith. Then he had really stung her conscience when he told her she was the only one who could make herself feel good enough. Laurel knew she'd think more clearly when she wasn't rubbing elbows with the source of her discomfort.

For two hours or more, Laurel rode, ignoring the world around her. Sassy pranced, galloped, trotted, and meandered at her own pace. Laurel was only a rider and in no way in control of the gait of her little mare. She was lost in thought. Why had Mac doubted her faith? She could quote scripture as well or even better than he could. She was faithful in her study and prayer time. She had always kept the commandments and honored all the saints she knew. What had he said about never claiming grace for herself? He had told her he was the least to be worthy, but he'd been given grace. What did it all mean? Mac possessed every quality that made him a servant of his faith. She tried to recall the scriptures and the sermons Brother Caldwell had given over the years, hoping to shed some light on her quandary, but still the meaning did not come.

Mac said she lashed out because she didn't like herself. She didn't realize she had become so transparent that a stranger saw her secret. She thought her haughty, independent façade was a good enough mask for the entire world. Her own father hadn't known of her opinion of herself until the night she broke down at his deathbed. Yet this man who had invaded her life saw what she didn't want anyone to see. She found little in herself to like and even less to value. Regardless, what did that have to do with that blatant statement he had made last night? *'I was led to believe you were a believer in the gospel.'*

Behind her, Laurel heard Mac singing *Amazing Grace*. The first verse was familiar to her, and she listened as he continued. Then she heard Mac sing a verse that she didn't know. To her memory, the congregation at Hawthorn Chapel had never sung the verse: *My conscious owned and felt the guilt and plunged me in despair. I saw my sin His blood had shed and helped to nail Him there!* Laurel heard in his words deep love and conviction. He was singing his redemption story. He continued, *"Twas grace that taught my heart to fear and grace my soul relieved. How precious did that grace appear the hour I first believed."* She had to ask him about that new verse.

"Laurel, come back to me." Mac's call pulled her back to awareness. She looked up and several riders were approaching from the east. Mac called again, "Laurel, ride back to me, please." Without hesitation, she turned Sassy and galloped to safety, back to Mac. Even in her concern, she realized that Mac did mean safety to her. The knowing felt good and she smiled. The riders proved to be a wagon train of freighters headed toward Little Rock, seeking provision for the settlements around Izard County. The men were a friendly lot and very anxious to share tales about the area.

One short, burly man called out, "How's about stopping for a rest and some grub?"

"We are ready for a break, stranger. Can you tell us how far it is to Mt. Olive?"

"Far piece from here. We left there two days ago. Headed on to the Rock to get provisions. What about you and your missus? Where ya'll headed?

"First stop is Mt. Olive. We hope to find some lodging and a hot meal. We've been on the road for nearly two weeks. Headed on east."

"Well, picking are slim in that little settlement. You can get a hot meal at the inn, but they only got a sleeping loft. You wouldn't want to expose your pretty lady to that." They spent the next twenty minutes sharing a lunch and some talk. Mac took to heart the concerns of the freighters. "Friends, be cautious when you get half a day or so closer.

There's a bad lot that hang around the creek. They don't take kindly to strangers. Been known to rob folks and steal horses."

"Appreciate the warning. We'll sure keep an eye out for them. Safe passage to ya'll." Mac tied Sassy back to the wagon, and Laurel climbed to the wagon seat. Mac sat beside her, picked up the reins and smacked them on the backs of the mules. "Did you enjoy your ride?"

"I enjoyed the ride, but I couldn't tell you anything about the trip. I'm afraid my mind was on our talk from yesterday."

"Did you reach any conclusions?

"Just a lot of questions. Maybe you will talk to me about it tonight when we stop. By the way, I enjoyed your singing. You have a fine voice."

"Thank you kindly." The afternoon passed into late evening. Mac stopped for the night in a tiny grove of maple trees. The terrain here was less like the forests Laurel knew in the mountains of the Northwest. The land here had more open spaces and reminded her of prairies she'd read about with tall grasses and rolling pasture land. She'd call the lay of the land rolling hills, not mountains at all. The horses and mules had plush grazing just beyond the camp. Mac made a secure area for them by putting a small fire between the trees and the wagon. He partially hid the fire by stacking a few boxes to block the view from the road.

"I'm sorry I can't make a larger fire tonight. I know cooking will be hard with such a small flame. Maybe you could just make coffee, and we can eat some bread and…"

"I think I can do a little better than that." Laurel went through the food box. She cooked bacon and potatoes in the lard and served it along with part of a loaf of bread and a jar of cherries she had bought back in Jasper. She made a hot, filling meal and hot coffee for Mac.

"You are a fine cook, wife. Even here in the wilds, you come up with a fine supper. I wander what you will fix in our own kitchen when you have a full larder."

"You are welcome, Mac." They sat for a while and listened to the night music of nature around them. Every part of their trip had brought them to beautiful places around the state. Her trek across Arkansas had been a special experience because she had not been more than thirty miles from Hawthorn since she was a girl of twelve coming from North Carolina. The foothills were not the mountains of Washington County, but Laurel realized the new terrain had a special kind of beauty all its own. "It's beautiful..."

"Shhh." A branch cracked loudly nearby. Both Mac and Laurel jumped to their feet, ready to protect their camp, only to find that the noise came from one of their mules moving nearer the tree where he was tied. They laughed. Laurel returned to clean up their supper and put the leftover food away. Mac tended the animal and laid out their pallet under the wagon. When they had settled themselves, Mac picked up his Bible and turned to the notes section in the middle of the book. He handed it to Laurel. In the very dim light of the campfire, she saw a list of several items written my Mac's hand. At the top of the list, he'd written <u>My Debt List</u>. Laurel looked at him with a strange expression on her face. Why had he written his financial obligations in his Bible? Why had he shown it to her? She looked back at him with questions in her eyes.

"Go ahead, and read the first one." Laurel looked back at the list. The first item listed was 'I murdered my best friend.'

"I don't understand, Mac. You told me you shot him in a fair duel. That is not murder."

"That is not the point, Laurel. Don't you see? I have drawn a line through each item on that list, all but the last one."

"Yes, I see the lines." Laurel looked down the long list of things Mac had written. Many of them were ugly, demeaning things, some of them minor by comparison, but all of them marked out.

"It's amazing grace. I have only one debt now...one I can never repay. This is the lesson I learned from your uncle."

"Grace?"

"I was a low life when I first came to Arkansas, Laurel. That's why my father sent me here. He watched me destroy myself because of what had happened with Marcia and Louis. I made a lot of stupid choices in my life. Do you think I didn't hate myself as much as I hated the events that led me to the place I had found myself?"

"Bad things happen to all of us. We aren't responsible for things other people do to us."

"No, but Matthew helped me see that we are responsible for what we do with the mess left behind."

"How do you fix it when it is over and done?"

"That is what you learn when you understand the gospel. I believed in God since I was a young boy, but I didn't find grace until I met your uncle, and he led me to the place where Jesus gave me grace."

"That is why you didn't mark out 'Christ's death on Calvary' from the bottom of your debt list."

"Yes, dear." Laurel became very quiet. After a while, she looked at Mac as he leaned against a tree.

"Those are words I heard you singing this afternoon that I hadn't heard before. 'I saw my sin his blood had shed and helped to nail him there.' I'd never heard that part of *Amazing Grace* before. I'm glad you shared your story with me. I see why you didn't want me to see your Bible without an explanation. Your faith story is a powerful one."

"Everyone's story is."

"No wonder you have such confidence. You know so much."

"I'm so far from perfect, Laurel. I have my scars to cope with. I just have to try every day to trust more and walk in faith."

"You said that when you asked me to marry you. You asked if I could walk with you in faith."

"I remember. Frankly, I was shocked you agreed. I shouldn't have been though. The Lord had told me that 'Grace is sufficient for you.' You know, if your name had been Sally, I wouldn't have made this journey across the state. You can thank or curse your uncle for that too. He calls you Laurel Grace."

"Goodness, if a person wanted to get theological about all this, my name that was given to me almost twenty-eight years ago, my maternal grandmother's name, lead you to me. Makes shivers on my arms."

"Pretty clear that God's plan to do good for us has been a while in the making." Laurel felt Mac wasn't such a stranger. She knew this man whose wedding ring she wore. She whispered a word of praise and thanksgiving that God was so much wiser than she. At that moment, she was pleased she had walked out in faith with Mac, who had given her friendship. "We'd better try to get some sleep. I figure we have about fifty or so miles to go. That is more than a day's travel, and we may not stay in Mt. Olive if the lodgings aren't safe. By the way, when is your birthday?"

"In June. Goodnight, Mac. I am glad you wanted to me see your Debt List and you told me about grace. I still have a lot to learn, but I think I have a good teacher. Sleep well."

12

Brethren, I count not myself to have apprehended but this one thing I do,
forgetting those things which are behind and reaching forth unto those
things which are before, I press toward the mark...

KJV c1850 II Timothy 1:7.

At midmorning the third day, the MacLaynes found themselves in Mt. Olive. Either they had made much better time than Mac had calculated or the distance was not as far as the freighters had told them. Both Laurel and Mac were disappointed they found with no suitable lodging was available, but they did find a small mercantile where they could refill their nearly empty larder. Prices were high in the little store. When Mac asked about the cost of flour and potatoes, the post owner explained that all the provisions were carried overland by freighters from ports like Little Rock, Jacksonport, and Batesville. Shipping costs almost doubled the price of any items they delivered. Laurel bought sparingly. When Mac questioned her, she simply said they needed little since they would be in Shiloh within a few days. He smiled knowing that Laurel's frugal nature would not let her spend the extra money. It also dawned on him that they had never spoken of finances at all. He wondered if she was concerned he may not have enough money to take care of a large bill.

Lawrence Crafton, owner of the trading post, told Mac the roads from this point to Powhatan were patchwork. The trail was not nearly as defined as the Military Road they'd been traveling. He warned that travelers often lost their way because many "roads to nowhere" carved out by local farmers led to a distant field or a favorite hunting area, and once they took the locals to place they were heading, they simply stopped. Many travel hours were spent backtracking the "roads to nowhere" in this part of the state. The store keeper complained that the Arkansas legislators were too busy carving out new counties from old ones, moving county seats to new towns, and arguing about secession to do the work of building roads.

"Dang politicians, they got no idea what we need out here in the frontier!" Mr. Crafton voiced his frustration. He told Mac about a recent article in the Little Rock newspaper about the coming governor's race. The present governor Elias Conway had questioned the need for a railroad in Arkansas. He had praised the "good dirt roads" that lead from one point in Arkansas to the next. "If he wins the election again in '58," Crafton roared, "that's what he'll give the citizens of Arkansas, more good dirt roads." The men standing around the counter nodded and laughed at his bark.

Mac looked at the man with some concern. Not familiar with this southern route he chose, he'd hoped the roads were more passable. The idea of losing time getting lost didn't suit him. Laurel saw the concern on his face. "Don't worry, wife. If we lose our way on the road, I have a compass, and the sun still rises in the east in the morning. East is our way home."

Mac asked Mr. Crafton about a local church community in town. He told Mac he didn't have time for religion, and he wasn't sure that he held with the behavior of a group of shouting Methodists who showed up for a camp meeting every month or so. He said he was fine not having a church in town, but he liked the increase in his business when the circuit rider came to town. "If those people weren't so noisy at the camp meeting, I might go myself to hear the singing." Mac smiled at Mr. Crafton. He obviously didn't know what the shouting was about or he would have joined them.

"You might give it a try the next time the circuit rider comes your way. You might like what you find at that camp meeting." Lawrence Crafton just waved off the comment and wished them safe travel. He did part with one final warning about travel in the area.

By noon that day, they were back in the wagon headed on toward Canton, the next settlement Mac knew about. They would be sleeping on the ground again for a day or two, but Mac didn't think any of the lodging he'd seen in town would be a better choice. Canton was supposed to be about thirty miles. If the roads were fair, they could be there before nightfall the next night. He knew from talking to Mr. Crafton, the distance on to Jackson in Lawrence County would only be a short day's ride the following day. The end of the long journey seemed to be almost in sight. Once Mac got across Black River at Powhatan, he would feel at home again since he knew that area well. Could it be possible in less than four days, he could be back in familiar territory? His spirit rose.

The afternoon spent together was a pleasant one for both the MacLayne's. Laurel worked to complete her blue calico dress. She and Mac spent a long while talking about their visit to Mt. Olive, and one of the news items in the Arkansas Democrat they'd found at the trading post. The slavery issue that had brought about a division of their church into two groups, the Methodist Episcopal South and the Methodist church wasn't news. The split had happened a few years earlier, but some churches had still not adopted the new name and church's stand on slavery. The article reported some of ministers who were opposed to slavery had even been forced out of the state due to their stand. The controversy hadn't impacted Shiloh yet, but Mac felt the time was short. They too would have to deal with the problem. He expressed his concern with Laurel telling her the two groups were based on the same scripture and the same teachings of John Wesley. How could any issue pervert the doctrine they had always lived with? The reality was that it was happening across the state and the entire country. Both Mac and Laurel regretted the hard feelings that were arising among members of their church. While the subject of the discussion was not a pleasant one, the opportunity to talk and share those feelings was a precious gift.

At sundown, Mac found a flat, somewhat sheltered area, much like the grove they'd stayed in the previous night. He set up camp in the same way and prayed that the camp would be secure and that no trouble would find them during the night. While Mac saw to the animals, Laurel prepared a good supper and made hot coffee for her husband. When they sat down to eat Mac decided it was time that he and Laurel had a serious conversation about setting up a household and taking care of business at their homestead. They had not had a practical conversation about those kinds of family matters. Mac realized they had not really talked about any topic that related to living as a family. "Laurel, we need to talk."

"I thought we had been talking all day."

"We have and I have enjoyed it, but we haven't done much talking about us."

"Us? That would be a very short conversation, wouldn't it? There hasn't been an us for very long so we can't have that much to talk about yet?" Laurel spoke in a lilting voice and the lighted-hearted tone was obvious to Mac.

"No, I mean a serious talk about us being a family."

"We've talked about that enough. The discussion usually ends up with hurt feelings. Let's don't talk about anything serious tonight."

"Laurel, you need to know about..."

"I trust you to take care of things. You've done well so far. Please just read to me from the Scriptures and let's get ready for bed. It's been a long day and I am tired. I know you must be too."

"Laurel, aren't you curious about..."

"No, not about anything right now. Let me get your Bible for you." She rose from the log where she was sitting and went to the wagon seat to get the book.

"All right. I will save the conversation for tomorrow." Mac chose a Psalm to read and then he took Laurel's hand and they prayed together. They spooned together under the wagon bed and within a few minutes, they slept warmly underneath two quilts and the yellow coverlet. Mac dreamed of his homestead and the tender family life he wanted. He saw himself with Laurel on their porch. A small boy who looked so much like him sat at his feet, and Laurel held another baby to her shoulder. The dream seemed so vivid to Mac, he didn't want to awake from the contented images he was experiencing.

~ ~

About midnight, the beautiful vision abruptly disappeared when Mac awoke to the sound of boots crossing rocky ground. He lay very still for a few minutes, then leapt to intervene. The taller of two men struck him with the butt of a rifle. Mac fell to the ground a few feet from the wagon.

Laurel ran toward the place where Mac lay, just as the man who had hit him was about to strike him a second time. "Stop. Leave him be." Laurel attacked the man to prevent him from striking Mac once more. She clawed at his face and kicked his shin. He turned his attention toward her and slapped her in the face, knocking her to the ground. As she tried to move toward Mac a second time, the shorter and older of the two men grabbed her shoulders and jerked her to her feet. He entangled his hand in her hair and pulled her back toward him. "Please, let me see to my husband."

"Ain't nothing to see about, woman. My friend done took permanent care of him." Laurel looked toward Mac. She jerked her arm from the man who held her and tried to run.

"Turn me loose. I want to see about my husband." The intruder grabbed her arm again and slapped across the face. When she tried to swing at his head, he lost his balance, and they both fell. Laurel screamed.

He put his hand across her mouth. "Shut up, you stupid woman." Laurel screamed again. "Lookasee here, Jackson. Got us a little entertainment for the night."

"She's scrawny. She ain't gonna to be no fun, Lester. Let's just get the money and horses and leave. That's what we come for."

"No, sireee.... I'm going to have me a little female company here."
Laurel screamed again, even louder. Lester jerked the front of her
blouse and ripped off the buttons. The garment fell open to reveal her
worn chemise. In the bright moonlight, the old garment did little to
cover Laurel. She cried out again.

"Please stop." Her pleading did little to stop the attacker. The intruder came toward her again, too close to her, and he pulled her into
an embrace. She flailed, writhed, and kicked. Laurel screamed over and
over.

"Shut her up, Lester. Someone could come by here. We ain't so far
off the road."

Laurel fought even harder. She swung her fists toward him, scratched
him, and bit his forearm. She'd never forget the acrid smell of the un-
washed man who held her down. With what seemed her last ounce of
energy, she jerked away and landed a fist in his face.

"Jackson, come over here and help me tame this wildcat. I'll give you
a turn if you want."

"You're a dang fool, Lester. We come here to get us some money, not
to take a plain, scrawny female." The two partners were clearly at odds.
Jackson turned his attention back to the bed of the wagon. Lester pulled
Laurel into his arms once again.

"When I want me a woman, she don't have to be pretty or willing...just
a warm body." He began ripping at Laurel's skirt and petticoats again.
Laurel screamed once more, so loudly that the horses were spooked at
the sound. "Shut up, woman." Laurel clawed at his face. In his pain, he
yelled, doubled his fist, and struck Laurel one last time. The blow ended
her struggle, and she fell at his feet.

— ⁓

Between the taller man's search for valuables, and the other's attempt
to claim Laurel as his prize, neither had paid any attention to Mac, who
appeared dead from the blow with the rifle butt. He had come around
just before Laurel's last scream for help startled the horses. He silently

crept toward the tree where he left the broad axe leaning after he had cut up dead limbs for their campfire. The axe was the only weapon within reach. He inched his way behind the tall man going through their things in the wagon bed. Mac used the sturdy oak handle of the axe to broadside him. Jackson fell to the ground. Mac then turned toward the man who was attacking his wife, and he used the sharp blade to cut through the thigh muscle of the older man. The blade stopped at the bone. Lester screamed and fell away from Laurel. He dragged himself toward his horse.

Mac yelled out, "Get out of here before I use this axe on your skull." He rode off back toward the settlement. Mac threw the other man across his horse and sent him in the same direction. Knowing there was no law officer anywhere near, Mac wanted to get the men as far away from them as possible. When Mac was sure there were no other intruders to deal with, he bent over Laurel who was still unconscious. The attacker had all but destroyed her clothes, but luckily, he was so inept, he'd not been able to complete his attack. Mac took water from the keg and part of her damaged petticoat, and washed her face, trying to arouse her.

"Laurel, come back to me...can you hear me?" Laurel lay still for several moments. When she awoke, she screamed and fought against Mac.

"Don't touch me. Leave me alone. Stop. Please don't hurt me again. Stop!" She continued to cry out and push Mac away. She curled herself into a tight ball and pulled at her tattered clothes, trying to cover her near nakedness. She rocked herself back and forth, crying out each time Mac tried to comfort her. He wanted to hold her and to assure her she was safe, but he found himself back at square one with her. Any touch sent her into a panic. All he knew to do was to build a fire and try to keep her warm. Perhaps she would sleep and let the trauma pass. Knowing he could not remove the panic, he prayed for patience and wisdom to help bring the Laurel back to him. The healing balm she needed, God alone could provide.

Four hours to sunrise, but this night was one he wanted to pass quickly. In the light, Laurel may be able to regain a sense of safety. He sat as close to her as he dared, knowing the slightest touch would send her back into the nightmare she'd experienced that night. The night lagged on even as he continued to pray for the dawn.

When the first tinges of red streaked the eastern horizon, Mac spoke softly, trying to rouse Laurel. "Laurel, can you wake up? Can I help you dress so we can travel?" No answer. She just curled up more tightly. "Laurel, let me help you dress for the day.

"Don't touch me. Don't hurt me anymore."

"Laurel, it's Mac. No one is here to hurt you. Those men are gone, with injury enough to keep them away. Please just wake up and look at me." Laurel opened her eyes. Outrage and terror were reflected in her gray-green eyes. "Thank God. Laurel, do you know me?" Mac reached over to smooth her hair out of her eyes. Laurel screamed a heart-wrenching cry, which evolved into body racking sobs. "Please, Laurel, let me help you get dressed. You will feel better when you get out of these torn things. We will burn them along with the terrible memories if you want. Please, Laurel. Can you see me? You are safe with me."

Laurel sat and rocked, back and forth. Mac knew he would have to let time calm this situation. As much as he wanted to leave this place and put miles between them and the lawless area, Laurel's welfare was more important. He went to the campfire and added more logs. He also took the coffee pot and pan out of the wagon so he could fix some kind of meal. Anything to get them into some semblance of a routine would be a step in the right direction. Maybe he could get Laurel to climb into the wagon shortly so they could leave. The previous night had proved the area was too dangerous for lone travelers. They couldn't stay another night. He offered Laurel a piece of bread with a bit of cooked ham they had bought at the trading post the day before. He also offered her a cup of water. She wouldn't take them from his hand so he sat them on a stone nearby. "Laurel, eat some, please. When you've eaten, I'll help you get ready to travel. We need to leave this place." She sat on the log and stared into the distance. He wasn't even sure she heard him. For some time, she sat, not eating nor talking nor crying. Mac had little hope he could get Laurel to change clothes because he certainly couldn't help her change clothes without touching her. Again, he made his plea. "Lord, help me. What can I do to bring her back to me?"

Shortly, Mac remembered the yellow coverlet, Laurel's favorite wedding gift. He wrapped it around her scantily clad torso and pointed the way to the wagon. He offered his hand to help her into the seat, but she moved away. However, she sat on the wagon seat and covered herself with the coverlet. Mac hitched the mules as quickly as he had ever hitched a team in his life. He packed the wagon and tied Midnight and Sassy to the back. The sun was high in the sky by this time, but he didn't believe it to be noon yet. He drove the mules harder than he had at any time on the trip across the state. He wanted to reach Canton before they had to stop for the night. Laurel needed shelter, a place to feel safe.

All during the day's drive, Mac tried to talk to Laurel, hoping she would answer. He sang to her, talked about the weather, pointed out buds on the dogwood trees, told her about her Uncle Matthew, and anything else that came to mind. He struggled to come up with any topic that might strike a chord and help bring her back to him. About two, Mac stopped for a brief time to eat. Within ten minutes, Mac motioned for Laurel to return to the wagon, and he set off on the last part of the trip to Canton. "Laurel, talk to me. Tell me what happened so I can understand. I'll listen if you tell me."

"Don't hurt me anymore. Leave me be." Laurel began to cry softly and then she turned toward Mac. With her face wet with tears, she begged him. "Please don't hurt me again."

"I'm here Laurel. I won't let anyone hurt you."

"Those terrible men! That man wanted to hurt me again, just like he hurt me the last time." Mac was confused. They had not met those intruders before they came to their camp. "Please don't let them touch me again. That mean boy Kenny broke my glasses. All those kids called me names and laughed at me. Can't you stop them?" Laurel again broke into sobs. He knew Laurel's broken words came from more than last night's attack on their campsite. Her talk of broken glasses and kids calling her names had to be images from sometime in her past. Perhaps in her babbling, Laurel had let him see into the fortress she lived in. The fear from last night had brought to the surface bad memories from some incident in her past. Yet, understanding was one thing, and healing another matter. Mac was determined to build a relationship with Laurel where she felt safe enough to share the painful secret from her youth. As amazing as it seemed, two bumbling robbers may be the keys to grace for Laurel. She had to get the horror out into the light so she could lay the fear to rest. Mac's mind went back to the scripture in Roman 8 that he and Laurel had talked about in the orchard the day they had met. Under his breath, he whispered, "Thank you, Lord."

— ~

Laurel looked with blank eyes directly at Mac. No sense of recognition came to her eyes. She saw only the face of intruders who had hurt her, humiliated her, and destroyed her youth. The faces she saw were not those of the robbers from previous night. They were faces of people who had assaulted her more than thirteen years ago. She cried. Silent, continuous tears ran down her face. The nightmare appeared all too real that moment. The scene was not a hazy, nebulous state that had plagued her since she was fourteen. The once vague feeling that had always been just beneath the surface of her awareness been played out during the attack and now it was real. Laurel remembered every terrifying minute of the ordeal her classmates had inflicted on her at the harvest celebration on that long ago November night in Washington County. She cried again.

"Laurel, it's Mac. Wake up and look at me. Can you see me? You are safe with me. Remember, I promised your papa...You are safe." The gentleness in the voice she heard and the concern for her were comforting. Laurel struggled to pull herself to awareness of the present. She touched her face, and she felt the dried blood in the corner of her mouth. Her body ached, and she knew she had bruises on her arms and shoulders. She rubbed her eyes with the back of her hand and looked down at her torn clothes. She became aware that only her yellow crocheted spread covered her. She understood where she was.

"Mac? Are you all right? I saw that tall man hit you with a rifle."

"I'm not hurt, Laurel. You're the one I'm concerned with. Will you let me help you get cleaned up and dressed now? I am hoping we'll be in Canton before midnight. We're going to travel as long as it takes to get to a settlement."

"Did they take anything from you?"

"No, they didn't have time. I got rid of them before they got what they wanted. I think they got more than they bargained for. Luckily, I'd left the axe out. Thank the Lord, too, that they were a couple of bumblers. He was watching after us. Will you let me help you change clothes now?"

Laurel nodded and Mac pulled on the reins to stop the mules. They deserved a rest after the quick pace Mac had been keeping. He tied them to a small sapling near the road. "What do you want me to bring you to wear? I am afraid there is little to salvage from that outfit."

"I'd like those work clothes that were my father's, please."

"Laurel, you will look like a man dressed in those things. Do you want to wear that to the settlement?"

"Yes, and I'm putting my hair back into braids. I don't want to be a woman right now. I'll be safer if strangers don't know I'm a woman." He retrieved the items she'd asked for. He led her to a small grove of trees to provide her with a bit of privacy. Shortly, she returned dressed in her work clothes, and her hair was back in the severe coronet atop her head. She had also put her glasses back on, the first time in many days. Laurel walked toward Mac, the spinster of Hawthorn again. She asked for his hat and used it to cover her hair and to shadow much of her face. Her attempt to hide was successful.

"Laurel, we need to move on. It will be late when we get to Canton, but I hope we can find some kind of shelter there."

"May I get a book to read?" Laurel wanted any distraction so she wouldn't relive the attack again. She didn't want to have to think about anything or anyone. It was so much easier to live in her fortress. When she was alone there, she was safe. Only people had ever hurt her. Books and work were always a refuge, and since she couldn't work while they traveled, Laurel wanted to get away into one of her books.

So, they began their afternoon trek. Mac tried to engage Laurel in conversation several times during the ride. She ignored his questions and did not respond to any comment he made. She was totally engrossed in the adventures of *Ivanhoe* that she had taken from her small stash of books.

The mules slowed after pulling the wagon up two particularly steep rises in the road, and Mac had to stop and let them rest often that afternoon. The animals could not continue much longer. Besides, at nightfall the road was too dark to travel safely. Clouds had obscured the moon and few stars were visible. In that area, there were no rocky bluffs like those of the Boston Mountains. No stone outcropping or a cave provided shelter. They were forced to remain out in the open for one more night. Mac whispered, "Lord, please keep us safe tonight."

Mac began to scan the road ahead looking for a spot that would provide some semblance of security. The dense black of the night sky made it difficult to see any distance. They traveled on very slowly for another quarter mile before a dense grove of hickory trees jutted into the bend of the road. The trees were so close together, they seemed to make a wall, and the bend in the road would let him sit sentry that night and see both directions. "Let's make a camp for the night, Laurel. I'm sorry you have to sleep out in the open again tonight."

Mac quickly set up a shelter under the wagon and used the oilcloth to create a tent on two sides of the wagon bed, leaving the sight of the road open on both sides. He did not to build a fire that would draw attention to the campsite. Instead, he took all their blankets to make a pallet and provide cover for Laurel. Laurel did manage to find some cold left overs to make a slight meal, but without a fire, of course, Mac would have to forego his coffee for the night.

"Laurel, can you try to sleep?"

"Can you read to me a while, Mac?"

"No, Laurel, I don't want a light. I just as soon not bring any attention to our camp. Lie here and let me cover you, and I'll sit here with you, and we'll just talk for a while."

"I understand. "

"Laurel, you've had a trying day. I don't want you to be upset, but do you feel like a serious conversation tonight."

"I don't know. I will try to listen."

"You remember Romans 8:28? I've been thinking about that verse a long time today. Do you remember when you first quoted it to me?"

"I quoted scripture to you?"

"More than once, really. The first time was in the orchard the first day we met. Then again on our wedding night."

"Yes, I remember."

Mac closed his eyes and quoted the verse from memory. "And we know all things work together for the good to them that love God, to them whom are called according to his purpose."

"Do you find solace in those words, Mac?"

"That whole section is pretty intense. I'm not sure I understand all the meaning. It talks about the Spirit making intercession for our groaning, and things we hope for are those things we do not yet see. The text says to wait patiently for those things we want and trust God to provide them according to his plan. Yes, I find a lot of comfort in the verse 28. When I'm troubled, that scripture comes to my mind. That is probably why it has come to me so many times today. It's been a hard day."

"I know. I often think of that verse. I don't understand how, but I know lots of times when I don't even know what to pray for, or when I pray for the wrong things, things work out all right. Like when I prayed for Papa to get well, I should have prayed for him not to suffer."

"I have to pray for patience all the time so I can just let time work things out. Did I tell you why I came to Hawthorn Chapel in the first place?"

"Papa said you'd promised to bring the school teacher back to Shiloh. He told me you'd talked about sending for a mail-order bride, but when you learned about me, you'd decided I'd do."

"That story surely took a beating in the retelling. That must have hurt you to think anyone would say that you'd do. I ask you to forgive me, Laurel, for I guess that is what I thought as I rode to Washington County. I gave so little thought to your feelings at all. I realized that the night before the wedding when I was walking about your orchard. Your uncle Matthew was teasing me about the mail-order bride thing, but I did want a wife. I was beginning to despair of ever having a home and a family. Your Uncle Matthew is my best friend, and he was concerned I had given up, so he arranged for me to come meet you."

"Some friend. Doesn't he like you very much? Well, you can get back at him for his practical joke when you get back to Shiloh."

"Laurel, this is not a joke. I hate your sarcasm. I know exactly what you are doing. You were putting yourself down again."

"I was trying to make light. I'm sorry."

"The more I see things work out, the more I understand the meaning of Romans 8. I hoped for a wife and with much waiting, prayer, and obeying, God gave me a wife. Some good may even come from that bungled attack on us last night."

"I don't want to talk about that. I thought God must have had a hand in our marriage. Everything fell into place so fast, but now that we are married, I am not at all sure this is what I was supposed to do."

"Don't you see? That is where faith comes into the picture...it is the part about things not seen. The other day when I asked if you believed in the gospel, that is what I didn't see. Faith is believing when you don't know. I have seen you live out that trait...after all you spoke marriage vows with me, a stranger. You walked out in faith. But then you turn back doubting that God intends good for you."

"I don't doubt God's ability to do anything He chooses to do!"

"No, you only doubt that He will do it for you, my dear. That is an extreme case of arrogance you carry around."

"Arrogance?"

"That's right."

"I am not arrogant or proud or haughty or any other term that puts me to thinking I am better than anyone else. Why are you being so nasty to me? Isn't it bad enough that I was attacked by those three terrible boys last night?"

"That didn't happen last night, Laurel"

"Anyway, I don't want to talk about it."

"That is exactly what you need to do. Secret things only fester and poison us. Get it into the light and the nightmares will go away."

"Say the prayer, Mac. I am tired. I am not talking anymore. We have a long way to go tomorrow."

"Please, Laurel, Let me..."

"Say the prayer or I am going to sleep without it." Mac knew the conversation was at an end so he prayed.

"Lord, we praise you as a God who wants to do good for us. I thank you we are safe and suffered no bodily wounds last night. I pray for those two ruffians who attacked us, and I hope their injuries are not life-threatening. Lord, thank you for getting us about 180 miles closer to home. Father, please give me the patience to wait for your promise. I ask you to remove the fear that Laurel lives with every day. Trust we need in our marriage can't grow where fear is strong. Keep us safe this night and allow us a good rest. In Christ's name. Amen.

Laurel muttered amen, but now instead of sleep, she wanted to ask Mac about his words. At times, he was the most infuriating man ever. A few minutes ago, all she wanted was to close her eyes and fall asleep, but now sleep had abandoned her. The thoughts running through her mind would probably keep her awake all night. How could he accuse her of being faithless, arrogant, and fearful? And hadn't he even implied that it was *her* fault that she didn't measure up? How dare he judge her! Patrick MacLayne didn't know her well enough to pass judgment on her.

"Goodnight, Laurel. I hope you sleep well tonight." Mac turned to his side and fell asleep within minutes. Laurel assumed he enjoyed the sleep of the innocent or perhaps the smug. As much as she tried, Laurel didn't sleep and found herself brooding well into the night. When she finally fell into a fitful sleep after midnight, she spent two hours tossing and turning. About two a.m., Laurel woke Mac with screaming and tears.

"Don't hurt me...don't touch me like that... Stop touching my hair."

"Laurel, wake up. You are having a nightmare."

"What? Oh." She sat up and stared at Mac. Her face was blank. Within a couple of minutes, she realized where she was. She slumped over and cried out. "Lord, please help me."

"He will if you will let Him. Laurel, please tell me what happened to you so long ago. Bring it into the light, and the hurt will go away."

As a result of the failed robbery and assault, Laurel had remembered the brutal attack that happened at the fall festival when she was fourteen. All the ugliness and humiliation came flooding back to her awareness. Now Mac wanted her to tell him the lurid details. If she did tell him, he could add other qualities to the person he knew. She could add tainted, ugly, and other choice labels she had carried around with her for more than a decade. The telling was beyond her strength to tell. "Mac, I'm all right. Just go back to sleep. I won't wake you up again. I am sorry that I bothered you. I will try to be very quiet so you can sleep."

"Have it your way. I can't make you cast out your personal demons. If you prefer to live with them, that is your choice. I am sorry for your pain, Laurel. Try to get some rest if you are able." Laurel lay back beside Mac. Instead of holding her, Mac turned his back and moved to the far side of the pallet. His actions again troubled Laurel, but she did not speak. After a few minutes, she slept. It seemed as if no time had passed before they were back on the road, and the sun was rising before them on a passable road that led to Canton.

13

*I am Hebrew and I fear the Lord, the God of Heaven, which hath
made the sea and dry land...Now the Lord had prepared a great
fish to swallow up Jonah, and Jonah was in the belly of the fish
three days and three nights.*

KJV c 1850, Jonah 1: 7, 17.

As they traveled that morning, the couple was quiet. Mac was at
a loss as to what he could say to Laurel. Throughout their travels, he had tried to open communication because he wanted to
build a relationship with the woman he had taken as his wife. Today he
was frustrated, feeling his efforts had been for nothing because Laurel
showed no trust in him regardless of his candidness and honesty toward
her. Obviously, she had chosen to shut him out rather than let him help
her. He didn't know what other recourse he had. He decided to wait.
Perhaps that was the whispering he was receiving from God. He thought
back to that day in the orchard when he had asked himself if he were
being selfish entering into this marriage of convenience. The choice
he made so he could have a wife and children at his home in Shiloh had
certainly not taken Laurel's interests into consideration. As a matter

of fact, Mac's assumption that he was doing good for all involved was a lie. He took care of Mark Campbell's problem. He provided a teacher for the Shiloh school for the next year. He had taken a mate, and after a time, perhaps a mother for his offspring. Never once had he considered Laurel's wants and dreams. He knew he had acted selfishly...not consciously...but thoughtlessly, bringing Laurel into the marriage without once thinking she may need something from him. The awareness brought fear because he didn't know if he could ever meet her needs. If she needed him to love her, he was trapped. He'd never to give his heart to a woman again.

H avoided intimacy with Laurel. In the two weeks they'd been married, he had never once kissed her, not the way a man kisses his new bride. He'd touched her in bed only to comfort her or to keep her warm, and he'd done that only when she allowed it. He didn't know if he could ever take her to his bed because he knew he didn't love her. In his past life that had never made a difference. After the ordeal with Marsha, but he'd found pleasure in the beds of many women, but he'd learned that pleasure was short-lived and left him empty afterwards. When Matthew Campbell helped pull him out of the mire, Mac lost the pull to the uncommitted, carnal lifestyle he had lived. Not that he had lost his interest in having a woman, but now he wanted a relationship with his mate. He hadn't asked himself how he could do that that without committing his heart to his mate. He had been physically attracted to Laurel more than once, but he wanted more than sex. Mac felt the dilemma he'd made. He realized he had cheated Laurel, and he was ashamed.

But then again, she had pushed him away since the first day they'd met. Mac knew Laurel had married him to please her father. With her father's failing health, she had one goal--to let him die peacefully, knowing she would be taken care of. She had not really taken Mac's needs into consideration any more than he had thought of her dreams, or perhaps, lack of dreams. What a mess they'd made, even though both declared they were acting in accordance with God's will. Had they misunderstood? 'Lord, help me' had been Laurel's plea only last night. Mac now felt the same plea on his heart.

After too long a silence, Mac broke the quiet. "I have to rest this team for a spell. Do you want to get down and stretch your legs for a few minutes?"

"Yes, please. Can we walk a while?"

"No. I want to take care of mules and get back on the road. The mules are tired, and the horses need water as much as Tripper and Dax need rest. Perhaps you could find us a bite to eat so we don't have to stop again too soon. It's still a long way to Shiloh, and I need to get back home as soon as I can. I have been away for too long already."

— ⁓

Laurel was stunned at Mac's aloofness and...well...rejection. She sensed none of the friendship she thought they were building. She turned to go to the back of the wagon and their meager larder. She knew well the role of the obedient housekeeper. She had done that for her father and her brothers more than a decade. She pulled together a fast meal, filling enough if not exactly a feast. She made a small fire and made coffee for Mac. Within the hour, they were back on the road. Mac still showed no interest in talking with Laurel. For some time, she pretended disinterest and started the first work on the puffed sleeves of what would become her Easter dress. The green gingham was so pretty, and the dress would be the loveliest dress she'd worn since she was a little girl. Laurel remembered how Leah Campbell had always dressed her as a perfect angel every Easter. The thoughts added to her mourning, and tears worked their way to her lashes. Why couldn't life just work out? She was so tired of the confusion, the hurt, and the unease. She'd given it all to the Lord, but He had not yet brought her to the promise of Shiloh. How ironic that the place Mac was taking her had the name which meant peace, contentment, and unity. Would she find those things at Mac's home? If so, there was still a very long way to go to get to Shiloh...and she didn't mean only the hundred miles or so left to get to Greene County.

The path down the road had become very patchy. Since they had taken the northern fork at the last split in the road, there were times when Mac slow the team and look on down the road ahead. The path would nearly disappear in weeds and scrub brush, and then a short distance on, the road bed would become more defined. The stretch they had followed the last quarter mile or so was some of the best they'd encountered since they had left the general store in the last settlement. They travel on for some time.

Suddenly, Mac stood up in the wagon bed. "Tarnation! Where did the road go?" The tone of his voice and the exaggerated gestures told Laurel that Mac was angry. She had never seen him in this state before. He jumped to the ground and kicked the wagon wheel and shouted. "My dear Lord, where have You led me?" Mac's flushed face and ugly scowl told Laurel that he had lost control of his temper. He threw gloves on the ground and stomped away.

Laurel sat on the wagon seat, looking down the barely discernible path where Mac had walked. The time seemed hours, but she knew only a few minutes had passed. Her surprise and concern at her husband's behavior added to the anxiety that she felt, not knowing what he intended to do. Surely, he would realize within very few minutes that they were losing valuable time they would need to retrace their path back down the "road to nowhere." After several minutes, she climbed down from the seat and walked in the opposite direction, just to stretch her legs. When she reached the curve that had obscured their view of road's end, she turned back to the wagon. In the distance, Laurel saw Mac walking back to the place where he had left the wagon and her.

"I apologize for the tantrum, Laurel. I can't believe I'd be so stupid as to get us so lost."

"Not knowing the area isn't being stupid, Mac. We all make mistakes."

"Well, be it so or not, I am sorry for the time I've wasted. I hope we're not going to have to sleep outside again tonight."

"I believe that temper fit was more than just you getting lost. I've never seen you so angry? Is it something I've done."

"I'm not angry... well, a bit, I guess. I don't want to start a word battle with you, Laurel, but we did promise no lies. So, yes, I am a little angry."

"If you will tell me what I have done this time, maybe we can get back to a civil mood."

"I told you I don't want to fight. Just let it be. We have to get this wagon turned around and make good time if we want shelter tonight." Mac offered his hand to help her back to the wagon seat. She took it and sat beside him. He turned the wagon and flapped the reins across the backsides of the mules, making fair time back to the split in the road where they had taken the wrong fork. When he got there, he didn't think either of the two forks seemed to be leading them east, toward the next community of Canton. "I'm pretty sure we came up that road from Mt. Olive, so I guess we will head down this fork. I sure hope that Canton is just a few miles down this fork." They drove on for over an hour, in silence.

"Mr. MacLayne, I have had enough. If I did something wrong, I can't fix it if I don't know what I did. Talking is better than...." Mac cut her comment short.

"I said I am not going to argue with you anymore. We will be back in Shiloh within the week. Then I'll let you go..." Before Mac finished the speaking, their attention was pulled to the trail in front of them. A single rider on a large horse rode toward them. The conversation died because safety was a more pressing concern.

"Howdy to you both, strangers." The rider ahead of them hailed them as he approached.

"Hello to you."

"Where be ya'll headed here on these backwoods trails?"

"Hoping to find Canton shortly. You know this neck of the woods?"

"Fair to middling, I guess. I hunt here when the game gets scarce closer to home. Mister, you done missed the road to Canton quite a way back. You live there?"

"No, just hoping to find some shelter for the night. We're passing through on our way to Greene County."

"You and your friend do look a bit done in. How you doing, young fella?"

Laurel just nodded. Her disguise had worked, and this stranger addressed her as a boy.

"Just my miserable luck? I want to get back home so much, I wasn't paying attention and wasted even more time. All this backtracking is testing my patience."

"No need to backtrack, if ya'll are willing to take another road. We just need to make tracks quick and find us some shelter...rain's coming and from the look of that western sky, we're in for a gullywasher."

"I guess I have been too busy trying to get east that I didn't take to time to look west. I should have been more aware. I know we get most of our bad spring weather from the west. You spoke true when you said we're tired. Got any idea where we can get out of this weather?"

"I know 'bout an abandoned cabin a couple miles or so down this here road. The cabin's sound, and there is a lean-to and barn. That'll give your animals some place to hold up, too."

"Thank the Lord! I didn't want another night in the open."

"If you don't care, I'll keep you company through the storm, and we can ride on together to Jessup. I'll take ya'll that far."

"I'd appreciate some company and help in laying out a trail to Black River if you can show me, since I've gotten us off our intended route home."

"My name's Lonnie Thomison. Lived in these woods most all my days."

"I'm Mac...that is Patrick MacLayne. I got a homestead over near Greensboro. This fellow you spoke to a few minutes ago is my wife, Laurel. We've been on the road more than two weeks. She lived in Washington County in the northwest part of the state."

Lonnie took his hat and placed it over his heart. He had such a strange look on his face that Laurel grinned. "I'm sorry, missus. I shore didn't mean no disrespect toward you."

"I'm not offended, Mr. Thomison. I was hoping my disguise would work."

"Let's get headed on. The sky is not looking good." The three traveled as quickly as their wagon would let them go. The rain began just as they eyed the abandoned cabin at the curve in the road. The homestead was in disrepair, as Lonnie had said, but both buildings had good roofs and shutters covering the oiled paper windows. They raced on into the clearing.

"Laurel, grab food and bedding. I'll get this wagon under cover." Laurel took two boxes of food and three of their blankets, trying to protect them from the rain as she ran toward the porch. She laid down her load and went back to help with the animals.

"You didn't have to come back out here. We can handle the outside chores. Go back and get a fire started if you can find dry wood. A hot meal and coffee would be more than welcome. We will share our supper with Mr. Thomison."

Laurel went back as she was told. Mac's tone had given her little insight to his present mood. She remembered her vow to be a helpmate to Mac, so she would do what he asked. She felt that Mac had dismissed her again. When she returned to the porch, she found some dry wood stacked on the porch. Some visitor from the past had left them a blessing. She began her work and built a large fire in the stone fireplace in the small main room of the cabin. After several minutes, Mac and Lonnie Thomison came in from the rain. All three travelers were wet through and through.

The cabin was warming, and the hearth was aglow with a roaring fire. The fireplace and hearth were wonderfully shaped for cooking. There was a spit for hanging pots and a small stone ledge that would serve for baking. Laurel decided she wanted bread so she took the corn meal and some eggs, lard and water to make pone. She knew the pone would be better if she'd had milk to use, but the water would suffice. She also put a pot of beans to soak on the edge of the hearth. They would not be ready to eat tonight, but she could cook them over night, and they would have food to take with them. For supper, she placed three yams among the embers and cut thick slices of ham to fry in the lard. Finally, she took some of her dried apples brought from home and soaked them. She would use the last of her oatmeal, butter, and molasses to create an apple crumble. They needed a hot meal. While the food was cooking, she kneaded biscuit dough so they could have hot bread for breakfast. She counted a half-dozen eggs left in the basket and just enough ham to make a good hot breakfast in the morning before they returned to the road.

The wind began to roar among the tree limbs. Lightening lit the sky and thunder rolled. Mac and the visitor went back to secure the barn so the animals would be safe. Both horses had been spooked already by the storm, but the mules were quietly eating the hay in the stall. Midnight was always anxious in storms. Mac calmed his stallion by giving him a handful of straw. He then went to the wagon and picked up Laurel's satchel and his Bible. He and Lonnie ran across the lot to the porch, just as a nearby tree fell across the road.

"Laurel, here's your bag. While the rest of our supper cooks, why not go up to the loft and get yourself dry. We need to dry these wet clothes and your hair is soaked, too. It won't dry in those braids. Please take care of yourself. I don't want you sick again." Everything that Mac had said to Laurel seemed a continuation of the aloofness and bad temper he had shown her before Mr. Thomison's arrival.

"I don't want to delay you again."

"I didn't mean to be so harsh with you, Laurel. I really don't want you to get sick again. You were so ill during the snow storm."

"I heard you. I won't cause any more problems. I'll change and then hurry to finish dinner." She found a candle and lit it in the fireplace. She carried her bag and climbed to the loft. She quickly removed all her wet clothes; of course, that was every stitch she was wearing. She put on her night dressing and took the pins from her hair. With her wet skirt, she tried to dry her hair somewhat and then used her brush to tame her curls as best she could. She tied the mass back from her face with her green sash. She looked down at herself and realized she could not go back to the main floor dressed as she was. She looked around and seeing the yellow coverlet, she tied it across her shoulder. Since she had no other choice, she picked up her wet clothes and returned to finish the supper for her husband and the stranger they had met that afternoon. In her absence, both men had stripped to the waist and now wore only their wet trousers. They had spread their clothes to dry. Laurel added hers.

When she stood up from spreading her skirt on the floor near the fire, Mac was staring at her. He continued to look at her, his surprise more than evident. Laurel was serene, feminine, and alluring. The yellow toga and the green band in her hair had transformed the somber peahen into a vision. Her eyes flashed, but not with anger or hurt this time. Her hair was glorious, loose and free, curling around her face, her shoulders and down her back. The yellow coverlet had draped itself down her womanly form in a very flattering way. Mac did not look away from Laurel, and she became uncomfortable with the attention. "I've lost my glasses somewhere. Have you seen them, Mac?"

"Uh...what...no, I haven't. Did you drop them in the storm?"

"I'm not sure where I had them last."

"We'll look for them in the morning light." Laurel turned to the hearth to take the supper to the table.

Lonnie whistled. "Golly, Man. No wonder you dress that woman like a man! She's an angel."

Mac made no reply.

"Where did she get that black eye? You didn't hit her, did you?"

"No, Lonnie. That's not my nature. We fell among a couple of would be robbers a couple days ago. Laurel got hit, but she is all right now. We were lucky."

"Dinner is ready, sirs. There are only two chairs at this little table, but I will sit on the hearth stone. Please come and eat." The men came to the table. "Laurel, may I have your hand, please?" Laurel was almost surprised, but then she remembered that Mac's strict observance of ritual. He also would expect her to help him keep up appearances in front of Lonnie.

"Yes, Mr. Thomison. Please join us in grace." She offered him her other hand. Mac smiled at her, and she saw his approval and smiled back.

"Lord, thank you for the shelter from this storm. We also thank you for sending our new friend Lonnie to find us when we were lost. We are so grateful for this excellent hot meal set before us by my good wife. Bless us, and the food we share. Continue to allow us to serve You. Amen."

The meal continued as the storm raged outside. They didn't mind the turmoil as they were dry, fed, and warm. The three enjoyed good conversation, though most of it came from the men. Lonnie knew the area well, and he was good company. It was good to have an additional person to share the road. There was security in numbers.

"Can I bring the dessert now, gentlemen?"

"I'd love some, ma'am. You're a fine cook. If this lucky husband of yours don't treat you good, just come looking for me. I'll find you a home in a heartbeat."

Laurel blushed. "You are kind, Mr. Thomison."

"I'd like it if you'd call me Lonnie. And I ain't a joshing. You're comely, smart, and set a fine table. What else could a man want?"

"Thank you, Lonnie, on behalf of my wife. You are right. She is that and so much more." Laurel was pleased with the kind words from both men, but especially those from Mac. He had stopped complimenting her when she had chided him about flattery. Of course, she had not done anything to earn a compliment in the past few days. The horrors of the attack had put a wedge between them. She knew most of the problems had been her doing. She carried the apple crumble to the table and returned to the hearth for the coffee pot.

"Mac, we only have enough coffee for breakfast. I hope we come across a trading post soon."

"Nice of you to think about such pleasure for me, when you don't care a whit about coffee." A loud roll of thunder interrupted the talk. Rain fell all the harder and continued to beat on the tin roof.

"Excuse me. I want to work on my Easter dress for a while. Go ahead and enjoy your coffee and the crumble." Laurel went to her satchel and took the bodice out. She sat at the hearth and sewed. Mac and Lonnie talked out a route on to Jessup and then on to Black River. Lonnie told Mac the ferry at Powhatan would carry them across the river, and on the other side, they'd be less than forty miles from Shiloh. He did warn that the roads were not good on that side of the river, and the trip through the Cache River bottoms could be treacherous in wet times. He told them that a wagon could not cross the swampy land if the rains continued.

"Well, Lonnie, the Lord will show us the way. Right now, all is well, and we got no concerns except enjoying good company and getting a good rest tonight."

Laurel had finished the bodice of her dress. The dress was turning out so well, she could hardly wait for Easter Sunday to wear it. She needed to remember to thank Mac for choosing the pretty green gingham. He would be proud of her when she wore the beautiful dress. Shortly, Mac joined Laurel at the hearth

"Mr. Thomison...I mean, Lonnie, it is our routine to close every day by reading the Word and having our evening prayers. Won't you join us?"

"Afraid, I ain't much of a praying man, ma'am."

"That is all right, Lonnie. The Lord invites all of us into His presence. We would enjoy your company, if you are inclined to join us."

"I'll listen with you, Mac, if you don't expect anything from me. I ain't much of a reading man neither."

"I'm afraid I will have to listen with you. I can't read much without my glasses."

"You seemed to do your sewing pretty well without them, but it would be my pleasure to read the scripture tonight. Let's see what would be a good passage to share."

"Do you know that tale about a man getting swallowed up by a big fish?"

"Yes, of course, that is the book of Jonah. Do you want to hear that story?"

"I'd surely like to know more about how that could happen." Mac smiled and turned to the book of Jonah and began to read. He didn't stop until he had read all four chapters.

"That is quite a yarn. Mac, do you think it happened just that way?"

"I'm sure the important things occurred just as it was written. We believe this book plainly tells us God's story. Jonah tried to run from the Lord, but he couldn't. When he obeyed, God took care of his needs, even a big fish to keep him from drowning."

"You really believe all this religious stuff, don't you?"

"We do, Lonnie. We have both experienced the loving grace of our savior, Jesus. It's the difference between a life and just living."

"Is your lady a preacher, Mac?"

"Well, she has preached me a lesson from time to time, but she is a teacher, by trade."

"I like that story. I wouldn't mind learning more."

"My friend, Matthew Campbell, told me that you have a fine congregation right near you. Do you know about the Shady Grove church? They've had a church family there for more than thirty years. One of the early circuit riders, Eli Lindsay, started the group, and he preached there for quite a while. Matt told me it is one of the oldest churches of any kind in Arkansas. They preach the same gospel there that Laurel and I share.

"Lord, as we prepare to sleep tonight, we offer you our praise and thanksgiving for a fine day. We are blessed to have the chance to share your word with a new friend. Please forgive my fit of temper this morning. Please keep me mindful always of my shortcomings and my blessings and vows. Amen."

"Amen."

"Laurel, you and I will sleep in the loft. Lonnie, I'm afraid you will have to keep warm by the fire. Here's a blanket. I'm sorry we don't have another."

"Plenty of comfort. Nice roof and a blazing fire. I could've been out under a tree. Sleep good tonight, you and your pretty missus."

Laurel climbed to the loft with the other blanket. Mac followed, his mind filled with things he wanted to talk with her about. He also knew he couldn't speak such personal things with Lonnie Thomison within earshot. Mac's emotions seemed to escalate with the storm. The rain had been heavy all evening and now into the night, the deluge continued.

Laurel was so different, and not just the way she looked. She seemed so happy sharing their beliefs with the nonbeliever they had befriended. The sweet nature she displayed so intensely seemed to be her very spirit. Regardless of the storm outside, their night together had been everything Mac had wanted to find in his home. Laurel had been at the center of it all. How different things can be in the scope of only a few hours.

When he thought he had nearly given Laurel an opportunity to leave him today, he paused and realized that Lonnie had been a God given blessing from the minute they had met.

If he had finished his comments he'd started when Lonnie had appeared, he would have told Laurel that while she could not return to Washington County, she did have options. He'd planned to tell her that it saddened him that she was so unhappy, but no life awaited her at Hawthorn so returning her to the home she knew was not possible. Mac would've told her that her Uncle Matthew would welcome her into his home and that she could earn her livelihood by teaching at the subscription school as long as she wanted. He'd nearly said she could choose whether or not she'd stay in their marriage. Of course, he knew she did not want them to stay in the sham of their contract. He would have let her out of her commitment. He'd intended to give her the choice he hadn't given her two weeks ago. Thank the Lord, Lonnie had appeared and stopped him.

"Laurel, we've had some strained times since those men attacked us. But I want to thank you for tonight. Lonnie told me how lucky I am to have an angel for a wife. He's right, but I need to tell him that my angel isn't luck but a God-given gift. I have so much I want to say to you when we have some privacy. I would be remiss, though, if I didn't tell you. Laurel, you are beautiful tonight. Don't you dare make light of it."

"Thank you, Mac. I feel beautiful tonight. Oh, not the way I look, but being able to share the scripture with Lonnie. That is such a special thing."

"I hate to disrobe you, wife, but we will need that coverlet to sleep under. If you don't mind, share your toga."

"Goodnight, Mac."

"Come over here, wife. Have you forgotten I don't believe in separate beds? Besides without a fireplace up here and one less blanket, I'll need you to keep me warm." Mac pulled Laurel close to him and laid her head on his shoulder and pulled the yellow toga over them both. He would never think of the yellow coverlet the same again.

14

Go, Ye into all the world, and preach the gospel to every creature.

KJV c1850, Mark 16:15.

Both Laurel and Mac slept soundly all through the night. When they did awake, the rain was still falling. They dressed and began their morning routine. Lonnie Thomison and Mac went out to tend the animals in the barn. The barn lot was waterlogged, and the road had turned to a stream in the overnight rainfall. Travel today would not be sensible or safe. Mac told Lonnie he would not chance going on.

"Lonnie, Laurel has been patient so far, but I can't drag her through this rain and mud. We'll stay here, at least for today."

"I'm thinking the same thing. You're a wise man. If you don't object, I will stay with you. I know my missus won't think nothing of me being gone another day."

"We'd enjoy your company, my friend. Sure am glad that the folks who left this place didn't take the hay. Our animals can eat—even if we're running low on food. Now the animals are tended, I'm taking a few things back to the cabin to make Laurel's stay a bit easier." Mac dug through the wagon bed and found a package of fabric Laurel hadn't worked on, a couple of books, and another small box containing the last of the food they had brought from Hawthorn. He also took clean clothes for all three of them. Lonnie and Mac returned to the cabin that smelled of baking biscuits and coffee brewing. The threesome enjoyed another pleasant time that morning. Shortly after noon, the rain stopped, and the sun began to shine brightly and a steady wind came up from the south. The roads would dry quickly if no more rain fell. The next day, their trip east could continue.

Mac and Lonnie decided to walk about the homestead to see if something could be found for an evening meal. While they were gone, Laurel began measuring the fine shirt linen for Mac's Easter shirt. She measured the drying shirt Mac had left by the fire earlier that morning. With the scissors from her satchel, she cut the pieces and pinned the seams so she could sew whenever she could steal a few minutes. Keeping the project a surprise would be a challenge, but she would try. She worked diligently until she heard the men returning. She quickly folded her work and returned to the kitchen.

Lonnie had shot a large rabbit a few hundred yards from the cabin. Laurel loved fried rabbit, but she could not fry without lard, so she cut up the rabbit and made brown gravy to stew the meat in. The gravy would be good with the last of the biscuits from that morning. They would not go hungry, and Lord willing, tomorrow they would find a place to buy more food as they traveled eastward. To assure they would have some food for the trail, Laurel added more beans to the pot on the spit and made fresh bread. The meals would not as flavorful, having no pork to season the beans, but at least she still had salt. It would do.

The afternoon passed and the sun was near setting. Both men left the cabin to do nightly chores and bring in more wood for the evening fire. Laurel took the few minutes to attach the cuff to the full sleeve on Mac's shirt. She used tiny, consistent stitches, wanting to make the shirt beautiful. She was so pleased that Reverend Caldwell's wife had taught her how to make the neat pin pleats at the cuff that allowed the sleeves to flow. She loved that style for a man's dress shirt. Her papa's Sunday best was made with those wide, flowing sleeves. Before she heard them returning, she had been able to finish the left sleeve. She was so pleased with the progress she had made.

Supper was sparse, but the rabbit in gravy was filling. The company was good, and there were high hopes they'd be heading out at first light.

"Thank you, Missus Laurel. You made a fine meal for us, even with little to use."

"You're the one to thank, Mr. Thomison. If you hadn't provided the meat, we'd had bread for supper."

"Call me Lonnie. Mr. Thomison is my pa. He lives just over the creek from my place."

"Do you have a family waiting for you in Jessup?"

"Surely do. Got my woman Mandy and four young'uns from ten to three. Fine family, even if I'm saying it. My ma and pa live near, as well as my in-laws. We like to stay close. We all came to Arkansas back in '36 from Tennessee. Family is the reason we're here. What about you, Mac?"

"Just me back in Greene County. My father gave me the land to help get my life back on track. I left Maryland to come to Arkansas in '53."

"That's a lonely life—no family around. How'd you find such a fine wife?"

"Oh, she is a gift from the Good Lord, her uncle, and her papa. It's a long story, Lonnie."

"You're a lucky man, Mac."

"No luck to it, Lonnie. Remember the Jonah story we read last night? Well, my life was kind of like that for a lot of years. I tried to live my own way, ignoring the Lord, using people—mostly being a wastrel. But when the Lord turned my life around, and I started to obey his calling, he began to give me what I need to build a good life. That is how Laurel came to be my wife."

"You really believe that, don't you?"

"I am living proof that the Word is true."

"I have to find out more about this religion stuff when I get the chance."

"It's the best life you can give your kids and rest of your family. The scripture says the man is to be the leader of his family, especially when it comes to faith."

"Problem is none of us can read the book."

"I'll bet you have a preacher around who can share the words with you if you want to learn."

Laurel sat quietly while her husband shared the good news with their new friend. She realized there was much about Mac that she didn't know yet, but watching him the past two days with Lonnie, she wanted to learn. He spoke with confidence and compassion. His personal passion for the Lord poured out with every word. Laurel found more reasons to keep her vows. Honoring and respecting this man should be an easy task.

Lonnie asked Mac to read another tale from the Book, so Mac picked out the story of David and Goliath to read that night. Lonnie asked a few questions about the sling, how big a giant is, and about David's courage. Mac answered them all with the same confidence.

"Mac, you sure know lots about the Book. You must be a saintly man."

"I wish that was the case, Lonnie. Truth is I murdered a man once. I've had more than my share of women I wasn't married to, and I have lied, cheated, and profaned myself in more ways than I like to remember."

"Then I don't get it. How can you be a man of God if you've done so much wrong?"

"Let me show you my debt list, Lonnie." Mac turned to the note section of his Bible. "See, I wrote down all the sins I could remember that I have done in my life."

"Yeah, but I see you marked them all out, but the last two."

"That's right. That's because I've been forgiven for all the bad choices I've made. That is what the Lord did for me."

"You still working on getting past the last two, Mac?"

"Well, I'll never repay this one." Mac pointed at the next to bottom item on his list. "It says Christ died for me at Calvary. I'll have to see about this last one as time passes."

"You sure open about your past, Mac. Ain't it shameful to do wrong?"

"No shame in forgiven sins. I got no reason not to tell. It's not my life anymore. I live forgiven, and so it's my story to share, but not my shame to hide."

"I'm glad you ain't no saint, Mac. If you was, you'd never want a friend like me." Mac just laughed and gave Lonnie a strong hand shake.

"I am more than glad to have you as my friend."

Laurel saw Mac was ready to end the discussion with Lonnie so she interrupted. "Can I get you boys the last of the apple crumble from last night? We got no coffee, but a little bedtime snack could help you sleep well."

"That's a nice plan, Laurel." They ate and within a few minutes the trio retired for the night.

When they were alone on their pallet in the loft, Laurel asked, "Mac, you added another debt to your list since the other night? When you showed me the list, Christ's death was the only thing you hadn't marked out."

"I realized I had another debt that I hadn't accounted for yet. I wrote it down two days ago, just a short while before we met Lonnie on the road."

"What debt do you owe that's come up since you showed me your list?"

"I wrote married Laurel." Laurel didn't respond. Did Mac believe their marriage to be a sin? Surely something was amiss. Just yesterday, he had said she was an angel, a good wife. He had held her tenderly during the night. She didn't understand, but she refused to give in to insecurities. She hadn't done anything to cause his remorse. She turned to her side and curled up to sleep. "Laurel, don't be upset. This is part of the long, long talk I want to have with you when we can talk in private."

"I'm not upset. This is your problem to deal with—not mine." Mac smiled. Laurel had not taken the blame for something she had not done. She took at least one step to stand up for herself

"Laurel, I am cold. Please come nearer and let me hold you."

"If that is what you want." Laurel moved near to Mac, but she did not take her cozy place on his shoulder. "Goodnight."

When the three were ready to set out the next morning, the rain was gone, the sun was shining, and a mild southern breeze blew across the foothills. Mac sang a bit and smiled constantly that day. Lonnie, on the other hand wore a scowl, obviously more worried than Mac. He knew the roads from the cabin to Sage and then on into Sidney were some of the worst they would have to travel. Horses were able to go along fairly well, but a moving the loaded wagon along these 'good dirt roads' would be proved to be a task, which would challenge the strength and civility of them all.

"Mac, how much of this stuff in the wagon you got to keep?"

"Everything in that wagon is Laurel's from her old home. She would not favor losing one piece of it. Why?"

"Roads here about ain't good during dry times, but we've had two days of hard rain. We may be able to get the wagon to Black River--not an easy task, mind you, but we can make it with lots of work and a heap of patience. No way that wagon's going across Cache River bottoms, at least until summer."

"Well, let's cross that river when we get there. Let's just get to Shady Grove church at Jessup, first. We have some ties there. Then we will see what the next step will have to be, but Lonnie, don't say anything about this to Laurel. She's lost a great deal in the last month."

The trail they travelled could hardly be called a path. The main road from Canton would have been much easier than the way they traveled. They should have gone into Davidsonville and returned to the military road. Lonnie had recommended the longer path for safety's sake. Mac shook off the option when he realized it would add two more days to their return. He didn't even consider the detour since they'd lost the time shut up in the abandoned cabin. The time had been pleasant until last night when Laurel had seen his updated Debt List. Her return to the protection of her wall made the draw of Shiloh even stronger. He would make the last leg of this trip disappear altogether if only he could.

"Laurel, if you are ready to go, will you please drive the wagon? I will walk and clear the path. The road's wet, and I'm sure we will find it blocked in places. Branches will have to be moved to let the wagon pass."

"I can drive a team." Laurel made a last walk through the cabin to make sure they had repacked all their things. Satisfied they had gotten all their things and left the cabin as they had found it, she went back to the porch to find Mac. He waited for her to climb into the wagon and handed her the reins. As the sun rose above the horizon, the mules pulled the wagon through the mud toward the path.

They travelled less than a mile when the first barrier had to be removed. A large tree limb had fallen across the path, and the forest was so near the road, the wagon was unable to pass. Mac retrieved the axe from the wagon bed and spent half an hour cutting the wood into sections that he and Lonnie could drag from the roadway. Lonnie explained that five or six miles on down the road, a settlement called Sidney lay at one side of the road. He told them there was no tavern or mercantile there so the chances of finding shelter were slim. He also confessed he didn't know if there was a church congregation in Sidney as he had never cared enough to ask.

"Cave City is on about another ten miles, but it's out of the way. They got a place to shelter for the night, though." Again Mac refused the additional distance.

"We can sleep out again tonight if we have to. We'll go the most direct route we can make our way over." Travel was very slow. The mules labored to pull the wagon through the muddy tracks, and the only blessing for them was the frequent stops that came because Mac and Lonnie were constantly moving the downed limbs and small trees from the path. The rain had turned the dirt path into a swamp in many places. They were making very little progress. Shortly before 11:00, they came to a creek.

"I didn't think, Mac. Usually, this little fork off Piney Creek is just a trickle. I ain't never seen the crick this far out of its bank before. Let me cross on horseback before you try to cross with the wagon." Lonnie walked his big horse into the rushing creek. The water was rolling so the current was strong. As Lonnie approached the midpoint of the creek, the water touched the belly of his horse. "Mac, the bottom feels soft and slimy, but the area I crossed ain't too deep for the wagon. I don't think you will get your stores too wet if you're real careful. Might be best if you'd lead the mules across by riding next to them on your horse."

"Do you think you can ford this creek if I lead the mules, Laurel?"

"I told you I can drive a team." Mac nodded and went back to put the bridle and reins on Midnight. Slowly, they started across the swift torrent, and the water swirled around the wagon wheels, but Laurel kept the team steady and the wagon didn't flounder. Shortly after the sun reached its high point in the sky, the MacLaynes and Lonnie Thomison were once again on a narrow trail headed to Sidney. Before an hour had passed, they saw the settlement down the road. Since setting out, they had traveled about six miles, at a rate of about one mile per hour. As they drove through the town, Mac called a stop so they could eat a cold lunch. While they rested, a farmer walked from a small barn.

"Hello, sir. Could we ask directions?"

"I was thinking ya'll needed some. Knew you were strangers when I saw ya'll pull into the settlement from that path there. Few folks try to use that path in the rainy times. Lucky you didn't lose a wheel. Where ya'll headed?"

"We'd like to be in Jessup by Sunday. Can you tell us the quickest route there?"

"You can't go by the quickest route. The roads won't take you there in a wagon, but there is a longer way that you will make better time. The road is better."

"Well, we will trust your call. By the way, my name's MacLayne and this is my wife, Laurel and our friends Lonnie Thomison from over Jessup way."

"Pleasure, ma'am, gents. Folks here 'bouts call me Ole Tom. Well, see that limb hanging over the trail down the hill? Take the road there to the east. I believe you can get to Maxville before night fall. Sorry to say, ain't lodging there, but you 'll be in good stead to make Calamine the next day. If you can get to Calamine, no problem in reaching Jessup by Sunday. Lots of folks in Calamine, and someone will tell you better about the roads on to Smithville. Good luck to ya'll and travel safe."

"Thanks for your good advice, Tom." Again, the three set out on the road east, planning to reach Maxville before nightfall. The roads were somewhat more defined, but no less muddy and just as littered with fallen limbs and branches left over from the storm. Mac and Lonnie continued the trek on foot, running interference so the team could bring the wagon safely over the roads. At nightfall, the weary travelers reached a settlement with a few cabins and no seemingly public buildings. If the information from Ole Tom was correct, they had managed to travel less than ten miles the whole day. Mac was frustrated and exhausted, having gone the entire distance not only walking but doing a great deal of chopping, hauling, and pushing. At least he had been able to spare Laurel from most of the heavy work since Lonnie had been with them to help. He'd need to remember to thank God for the blessing of a good friend that night. Laurel had also pulled her weight all day, never once asking him to take over the reins. She proved she could indeed handle a team. He tried to be grateful they were somewhat closer home, but he was not happy that they'd made so little progress in the almost twelve hours they'd travelled that day.

Anyway, it was near dark, and they had to find a place to set up a camp. While looking for a good spot, they travelled on about a quarter of a mile on down the road toward Calamine. Near a small creek, they found a flat, somewhat dry place with water for the stock and a small meadow to provide forage for the horses and mules. In fact, the livestock would eat better that night than the people they served. Being after dark, scouring up dry firewood would not happen. No wood meant no fire or warm food or heat for the night. Lonnie and Mac took care of the animals and returned to find Laurel had set up a campsite. She'd hung the oil cloth to create a tent under the wagon and used another panel to make a floor so they could sleep off the muddy ground. Laurel had also located the lantern and box with some food to make a meal. She brought out yams she had cooked in the cabin fireplace, sliced ham, jar of fruit preserves from her root cellar back home, and half a corn pone left from the previous night. Everything was cold, but edible. All three ate as if they had not seen food in weeks. Heavy labor did tend to make people hungry.

The area under the wagon was cramped with three people to share the shelter, but they made do. Mac pulled all the blankets from the wagon, and then handed Lonnie two of them. He and Laurel would share the other two. The cover would be enough to ward off the cold.

"Mac, did you see that back right wheel's wobbling pretty bad? Do you have another?"

"No, Lonnie, we didn't bring one. Bad planning on my part."

"Just wanted you to know. Maybe it'll hold. Guess I'll say goodnight to ya'll."

"We never do that, Lonnie. God has seen us through the difficult day. We owe Him some of our time. Mac, instead of trying to read in the dark, tell Lonnie the story of the children of God travelling to the Promised Land."

"Would you like to learn about some other travelers, Lonnie?"

"Sounds like a good tale, Mac." Mac spent several minutes recounting some of the highlights of the book of Exodus for their unchurched friend. As usual, he seemed fascinated with the telling. "God surely took care of them...what'd you call those folks?"

"Israelites...Yes, He did see to their needs, but no more than He does for us, Lon." Mac bowed his head after asking for Laurel's hand. "Lord, we are weary. It has been a long, difficult day. We thank You for getting us this far with no illness or accident. As Easter is near, we ask You to lay on our hearts our shortcomings and faults so we can ask forgiveness and then freely celebrate His great gift to us all. We ask for good rest and a successful day of travel tomorrow. Amen."

"Good night, Lonnie. I hope you sleep well. Laurel, come over here and try to rest. We have another long day ahead of us tomorrow." Mac lifted the blanket for her and pulled her close. "Sleep well, wife."

➹

Almost immediately, Laurel heard Mac's slow, steady breathing, and she knew he slept. Laurel too was very tired, but many things ran through her mind. During the long, hard day, no time came when she and Mac could talk. So many private matters between them had come up within the past few days, but those things would have to wait. Lonnie needed them right now, and heaven knew they needed him. Laurel sighed…the personal things would wait…Shortly she slept.

Laurel's sleep was fitful and filled with ugly images of the attack she'd survived. She cried in her sleep and fought with her attackers. Mac pulled her closer and whispered to her. "You are safe, Laurel. Sh-h-h-h. You are safe with me, wife." With his comforting voice in her ear, and his strong arms around her, Laurel rested.

Friday dawned with a beautiful, cloudless sunrise. The sun streamed in golden streaks across the greening Ozark foothills. Lonnie brought Laurel a branch of dogwood blossoms he found in the woods. Her mood lightened. The blooming dogwoods were the true harbinger of Easter. Mac had told her more than once he wanted to be home with his friends and church family on Easter. The weather had not allowed them to reach their goal, but Laurel still wanted to make the best of it. The new shirt she was making was about half finished so she needed a couple more hours to finish this gift before Easter morning. She had managed to finish her beautiful green gingham while they were shut in at the cabin. She could hardly wait for Mac to see her dressed in that lovely gown. She had saved the pretty new shoes she had bought back in Jasper, wanting to be an asset to her husband when he introduced her to his community. Shiloh was becoming more of a reality than when they had left Washington County. Perhaps she would find a new home at Shiloh.

"You are busy thinking this morning, wife."

"Oh yes. It's a beautiful day. Mac, I am grateful for your generous gift of the fabric you bought back in Jasper. I finished my green dress while we were waiting out in the storm. The dress is so pretty. I've never owned a more beautiful one. I can hardly wait for you to see it."

"I can't either. That green is the perfect match for the green in your eyes. Will you show me the dress tonight when we stop?"

"No. It's a surprise for Easter."

"Easter dress, huh? Do you have a bonnet too?"

"You know I don't. I'll just entwine the ribbon in my braids. That ribbon is so pretty."

"No, friend...No braids. Use the ribbon to tie those glorious locks out of your eyes and let the rest of it fall. That's what I want you to do for me. That is the Easter present I would like."

"Mac, no married woman lets her hair fall loose like that."

"That's okay, too. I'll just tell the people at Shady Grove church you are my mistress. Then your hair can stay down."

"That is not the least bit funny. First of all, who would believe a man like you would take me..." Mac put his fingers to her lips.

"You can't insult my wife, remember?"

They traveled on another half hour or so before Mac broke the silence again. "You didn't sleep well last night, Laurel."

"I'm sorry. I didn't realize I was restless enough to wake you."

"I'm not concerned about me, Laurel. I want to know about the nightmare. When will you trust me enough to tell me about that terrible fear you live with?"

Just as Laurel was about to respond, Lonnie rode back toward the wagon. "Hey, Mac. Tree's down over the road just a piece up the road. Need you to come and help me move it."

"Coming, Lon. And don't think this conversation is over. I want to talk with you about it as soon as we have a few minutes to ourselves."

—◦ ◦—

The delay was a short one. Before half an hour had passed, they continued on down the road toward Calamine, a thriving settlement due to the mining interests that had been developed in the hills. As they made the last turn into the town, both the MacLaynes were amazed by the size of the town they found nestled in the foothills. No fewer than fifteen houses and cabins were scattered along the dirt streets they found. They also saw a gristmill, a hotel, and a blacksmith shop on the main street. Just beyond, they saw a fair road crossing the creek.

"Thank goodness, we can get our wagon wheel fixed now. I was hoping we'd find a blacksmith here. Best take the wagon over and then see if we can find a decent meal. We haven't had a hot meal since we left the cabin. I am more than ready to rest for a night."

"But Mac, we're almost to Jessup. Being about noon, we can get to my cabin if we make good time. No need for us to stop over for the night."

"Lonnie, we've been travelling hard, and we have had little food and rest. We can get on to Jessup tomorrow."

"Well, I guess you know what's best for ya'll. Let's see to that wheel and get us some dinner."

Mac pulled the reins to halt the mules in front of the blacksmith shop.

"Hello, inside. Can you fix a mangled wheel for us?"

A tall, thin man with a trimmed beard came outside. He didn't look like a blacksmith, though. He was clean and dressed in fancy clothes.

"Surely can help with that. Been traveling a piece, I see."

"We have brought this wagon all the way from Washington County. We have traveled a good way in the past three weeks. This is the wheel that is causing the problems. Considering the roads we have traveled, I am surprised we have only one wheel that needs attention."

"Fine pair of mules you got there. They must be well-trained to have brought ya'll so far and still be in such fine condition."

"Thank you. They have served us well."

"I'd like to buy them, if you've a mind to sell. I got two hundred dollars in gold that I'd swap for the pair."

"Nice offer, but they still have a way to go to get us back to our homestead in Greene County. How long will it take to repair that wheel?"

"Only an hour or so. You sure I can't interest you in two hundred, fifty dollars for those jacks?"

"Just the repair. Is there a place nearby where we can get a hot meal? We would like to clean up a bit too."

"The hotel is just down that street to the right. Got nice rooms and a place for baths. The dining hall serves pretty good vittles. You staying overnight?" Something about the man's demeanor and edgy voice made the hair on the back of Mac's neck stand up. He didn't know what to make of this clean, well-dressed blacksmith.

"You don't seem dressed right for working on wagon wheels, Mr."

"Name is Marcum. I don't do the heavy work. I got a slave in there who's a first- class smith. He can fix about anything. Let me help the lady down, and ya'll can go get lunch while Mose fixes that weak wheel."

Marcum reached up to help Laurel down from the wagon seat. The leer on his face made her hesitate to take his hand. "Thank you, Mr. Marcum."

"Mac, we aren't staying here tonight are we? I would favor being home in my own bed tonight, if it is all the same."

"Lon, since we've only got five miles or so to go, I think we can make that distance after lunch. Mr. Marcum, I'll come back within the hour to reclaim my wagon and pay your charge. My haul won't be in your way here for an hour, will it?"

"No, sir. Take your time. We'll get your wagon ready." Mac could discern a sudden coldness in the voice of Marcum. He felt uncomfortable leaving their things with him. Lonnie had picked up on the awkwardness, too.

"Mac, I ain't feeling good right now. If it's okay with you, I want to take a nap here on the wagon seat. If you don't mind, bring me a bite of something when you come back."

"You sure, Lon?"

"I'd love me a good nap. Go on with the missus." When Mac and Laurel entered the dining room of the hotel, they were again surprised at the number of people eating their midday meal in the restaurant. Some of them were dressed in the clothes of shopkeepers, and many more were dressed in the dungarees of miners. Neither of them had any idea that a town the size of Calamine existed in the state. Mac's curiosity pushed him into a conversation with the man who took their order.

"I am sure surprised that a town of this size is here in the hills. Has Calamine been a thriving community like this for a long while?"

"Grows ever day, Mr. Ever since that geologist fellow from Philadelphia came through here a couple of years ago and found the zinc, the town has just doubled and doubled again."

"You talking about the Governor's geological survey of the state? I heard about that. I didn't know that much ore was found around here."

"Some investor types from St. Louis and Memphis have opened up four mines within fifteen miles. Calamine is one of the richest veins. Just out of town by Mill Creek, they got a new smelter going up. That chimney going up will be 150 feet high and totally made of brick. They say that when the whole thing is done, we'll be running two fires every day and two water wheels. We're planning for more than 1,000 pounds of zinc ore every day...maybe as much as 1,500 pounds."

"I guess the people hereabout will be getting rich with that much ore being processed. I know we have been importing that metal because we didn't have much being mined here."

"We do all right. The owners hire as many miners as they can get and pay them fair, I guess. I don't reckon that will make anyone rich, but it puts food on the table." Mac nodded and understood what the waiter was telling him. The locals didn't own any of the mines, but they were the labor working the rich lodes. The profits were going to absentee owners for the most part. He and Laurel ordered a hot meal and asked for food to take back to Lonnie. They didn't linger long over their lunch as Mac simply didn't trust the man who said he'd repair the wagon. Since he had refused to sell him the mules, the atmosphere at the livery seems strange, if not totally hostile.

As they left the dining room, they met with a constable on the board sidewalk. "Howdy, stranger. You looking for work in the mines?"

"No, we are just passing through on our way east. Can you tell me the least hazardous roads to get us on over to Smithville?"

"Easy traveling from the other side of Bear Creek. The old military road from St. Louis to Batesville has been tamped real tight in the past couple of years with all the ore wagons headed to port in Batesville and Powhatan."

"That is good news. The past three days, we have traveled in muddy tracks with brush and limbs covering the paths. We've cut up more than a few trees. I'll look forward to good roads for a while."

"Ya'll needing supplies before you head out?"

"Perhaps a few. We still have a way to go to get ourselves back to Greensboro. Do you have a good general store?"

"Well, pickings may be a bit slight right now because the storm has held up our supply wagons, but you can get some basics over at mercantile."

"Thank you for the help." Laurel and Mac made their way over to the store just up the road. The constable had been right. The shelves were nearly bare. They did buy a few items to add to their nearly empty food box, and the prices were indeed very high. They did not spend much time looking for more, as Mac wanted to return to their wagon and start for Jessup. When they returned, Lonnie was still reclining on the wagon seat, and the wheel had been replaced with a new one.

"Mose said that the old wheel would not be safe for a long haul. He knew you would want a safe wagon, so he put on that new wheel. Hope that is what you wanted."

"Surely do want a safe wagon. What is the charge?"

"Just swap the mules for the wheel and three hundred dollars gold and we'll be square. What do you say?"

"I'll just pay for the wheel. We have need for our mules. How much?"

"Well, that is good hard wood. Top quality. That'd be twenty dollars, gold." Marcum looked at Mac with a leer. He was trying to force Mac sell the mules knowing most settlers wouldn't be able to pay the ridiculous price for the new wheel. Mac reached into his pocket and pulled out the gold pieces that Marcum had asked for. When he did, a scowl appeared across the man's face.

"Thank you for repairing my wagon. Laurel, are you ready to go?" She nodded and Lonnie pulled her up to the seat. "I am going to ride for a while, if it's all the same to you, Lon." They turned and headed down the road toward the creek. "Lonnie, did they do a good job with the wheel?"

"I think the slave knew his craft. I sure didn't feel good about that other man, though. He kept running his hand along the backs of the mules and down their haunches. I'm thinking he planned to get those mules for his own."

"I think he did too. I am shocked he made such a big deal of it…a good pair of mules at home might sell for fifty dollars, but not for two or three hundred. He thought I'd have to sell them to pay for the wagon wheel."

"Well, I'm thinking I'm glad we'll be back at the Thomison homestead in a while. I am not sorry to leave Calamine behind us." Mac slapped the reins on the backs of the mules, and they made pretty good time for a mile or so when they came upon one of the zinc mine entrances. A dusty, bedraggled miner sat at the opening.

"Howdy, young fellers. Where ya'll headed in such an all fired hurry? You'll tire those good animals plumb out at that pace."

"Just trying to get home. You know how far it is to Jessup?"

"Only five or so miles on down that road you're on."

"Thanks, then. We'll be on our way."

"That's a fine pair of mules, and you got two fine horses to boot. Lucky man."

"What is it with everyone and mules in these parts?"

"Man alive. We need good animals real bad. A fine pair of animals like that'll bring $500 any day. I'll give you that much right now."

"No wonder Marcum wanted to take them for a wheel and three hundred dollars!" Mac and Lonnie both laughed, somewhat in relief that they had taken care to safeguard their team during their short stay in Calamine. Mac felt sure that if they had stayed in the hotel overnight, they would have found their animals missing the next morning.

"Thanks for the fine offer, but we need those animals to get us home. We appreciate the information. Thanks a lot." Again, they moved on toward the Jessup settlement, knowing they would be able to have shelter in Lonnie's cabin that night. The thought of another night on the ground was intolerable. Although the warm southern breeze felt good that early April evening, they were weary of travel. Shiloh could not come too soon.

15

For all the law is fulfilled in one word, even in this; Thou shalt love thy neighbor as thyself.

KJV c1850, Galatians 5:14

With better road conditions, the five miles passed quickly. Before the sun set in the west, the three travelers were on Lonnie's homestead. He pointed out some of the improvements he had been making, places where he was fencing a pasture, digging up stumps for a larger field, and even a couple of attempts to dig a well. "Dang ground up here is nothing but rock. I guess we'll just have to keep getting water from the crick. Mandy's been asking for a well, but I can't seem to dig through these rocks." As the wagon passed a stand of cedars, Lonnie grew concerned. He saw several horses and a couple of wagons tethered around his cabin. He handed the reins over to Laurel and jumped from the wagon seat. "Lord, please let my wife and kids be safe." He ran toward the cabin, calling out as he ran, "Mandy, what's wrong?"

"Lonnie. It is so good to have you home."

"What's all the commotion? You near scared me near to death."

"I got bad news. This morning, your pa's cabin burned to the ground. They saved the barn, but the house is gone. I said they'd stay here with us until ya'll can raise a new cabin for the family." Mandy Thomison threw her arms around Lonnie's neck and buried her head on his shoulder.

"It's all right, wife, as long as no one's hurt. We'll make room. That goes without saying. Ma and Pa and the two girls, they safe?"

"They didn't get burned, but Anna is real upset. You know she's fixing to get married on Sunday. She had been a planning her Easter wedding all spring. Now she wants to put off the wedding because her wedding clothes and things she was making for her house burned up in the fire."

"We'll see to that later. I've got friends with me." By that time, Laurel and Mac had arrived at the small cabin in the clearing. Mac got down and helped Laurel to the ground as Lonnie approached. "Mandy, this here's my good friend Mac and his missus Laurel MacLayne. We been traveling a way together and had to hold up in that deserted cabin over near Sidney when that storm came up."

"Glad to know ya'll. Please come on in." Mandy lead the way into her small, but clean home. She introduced the couple to her in-laws and other members of the Thomison family who sat around the table.

"Lon, you've got a full house. Laurel and I will go on and see if we can find the preacher at Shady Grove church. Being of our faith, he will help us find shelter for the night."

"Won't see it happen. You will be my guest and on Sunday, I will go with you and Laurel to the Easter service at Shady Grove, and I'll be a takin' my family."

"All right, but we will camp out there in our wagon."

"No way, my friend. I'll give my bed to my pa and ma, but you and Laurel are welcome to use the loft in the barn. Barn roof is sound, and bedded down on the hay, ya'll be nice and warm."

"Much obliged, Lonnie. You're a good friend." The Thomison women set about to finish dinner for the large family. The men sat down to eat and the women waited, sitting on the front porch. It proved to be a welcome retreat from the warm crowded main room of the homestead.

While the men ate supper, the ladies of the family were busy discussing how Anna could salvage her wedding day. Anna had set her heart of an Easter wedding, but her wedding dress and the shoes she had bought from more than two years of savings now lay in ashes just over the hill.

"Mandy, I am so mad. I don't want to wait a whole year to marry Lucas, but I've always dreamed I'd have me an Easter wedding."

"Anna, darling, please don't cry anymore. We will find you a dress for your wedding, and we'll have that ceremony just like we planned. I can get you a fine wedding supper pulled together. I know I got enough sweetening to make you a cake. Now don't you fret."

"I ain't got nothing to wear. This is the only dress I have left. Besides, look at these ugly old work shoes. All my pretty things are gone." Anna broke into tears again.

Mandy went over and pulled her sister-in-law into her arms. "Oh, I wish I had a new dress for you to wear. But even if I did, it'd be too short on you. You've always been a head taller than me. Your dress'll be fine. I'll wash and iron it real good, and you'll look nice. Lucas ain't going to care what you wear."

Anna shook her wheat-colored locks, with tears continuing down her cheeks. "Just ain't fair. I wanted to look beautiful on my wedding day."

Laurel remembered how she had felt the day she had spoken her vows with Mac. Her mother's dress had been far too short for her, and she looked at the worn work boots Anna wore and then down at her own feet. She got up from the porch step and walked toward the stable where they had stored the wagon. She pulled back the oil cloth and found the satchel. The pretty green gingham dress she had planned to wear to Easter services lay just beneath the lawn Easter shirt she'd made for Mac. She dug into another box and found the white leather shoes she had bought in Jasper. She had never had the opportunity to wear them on the trail. She laid Mac's shirt back in her satchel and then carried her precious gifts back to the porch where Anna and Mandy sat with Mrs. Thomison. They had just risen from the porch bench to return to the cabin to eat supper.

"Anna, this isn't a white lace wedding dress, but if you'll have it, I'd like to give you this new dress to wear for your wedding. I made it on our trip, and it's not been worn yet. I think it's pretty. Here, go try it on so we can make any changes you need. Here are some new shoes to finish your outfit."

"Laurel, it's too beautiful. I can't take your new dress."

"Anna, it would be a pleasure to share with you. My husband is a generous man. He bought me several new things when we started our trip east. Please accept this gift from us, if you want it."

Lonnie's mother began to weep. Anna stood looking at Laurel in disbelief for what seemed to be hours. "Oh, thank you, Miss Laurel. I will be the prettiest bride ever in this settlement. You're so kind to offer me this dress."

Laurel hadn't noticed that Mac was standing just inside the open door. He had witnessed the generous gift Laurel had given Anna Thomison, a girl she barely knew, the gift of her new green dress. She told him she had finished the dress she wanted to wear on Easter Sunday. Now she had given the gift of her 'most beautiful dress ever' to another bride. Mac smiled.

After eating the hearty supper of black beans, ham hocks and corn pone, and stewed potatoes with butter, the ladies returned to their wedding preparations. Anna tried on the new dress and it fit as if the dress had been made for her. Only a slight hem was needed as she was not quite as tall as Laurel. The hem was done in short order with three women there to work on it. Anna put the new shoes on and with a tiny wad of cotton in the toes, they fit well. She would be the beautiful bride she wanted to be when she married Lucas Crafton on Sunday.

A couple of hours later, Mac intruded on the wedding preparations. Laurel had gotten into the midst of the work and was having a wonderful time with the Thomison women. "Laurel, are you ready to make it a night? Tomorrow we can finish what needs to be done before the Sabbath. I am tired and I am sure you must be, too."

"Yes, Mac. I am sorry. We were so busy, we forgot the time. Goodnight, Mandy, ladies. I look forward to tomorrow." Mac took Laurel's arm, and they walked the short distance to the barn. Mac had already been out and laid out a blanket on the hay mound he'd raked together in the loft. He had also found a lamp and his Bible. He helped Laurel inside the dimly lit barn.

Saturday was a busy day. Lonnie, his father, and Mac rode over to the burned out cabin to see if anything could be salvaged for the new homestead. All the cast iron pots and skillets remained in the hearth, so Mother Thomison would still be able to prepare meals for her family. Lonnie's pa was pleased the fire had not gotten to the root cellar. True, not much had been left from their winter stores, but what was there would help them through the spring while their new garden grew food for the next year. There was also one window sash with the glass unbroken. Mr. Thomison took it down from the charred wall and stored it in the barn. Now all that had to be done was to remove the damaged cabin and rebuild. They would start on Monday.

Back at the Thomison cabin, the ladies worked quickly and continually to prepare the wedding dinner for Anna and Lucas. True to her word, Mandy prepared a pretty cake with white icing. Laurel remembered the last jar of unopened cherries from the food box in the wagon. That would make a nice finish to the white cake. They worked until well past dark, cooking, cleaning and making small decorations so Anna would remember her special wedding day. Again, just as the night before Mac intervened before Laurel was ready to quit for the night. "Laurel, tomorrow is the Sabbath. We have a few things to do to be ready for Easter. Are you ready to retire?"

"Yes. I guess it is late." As they walked to the barn, they didn't talk. Laurel was happy, and she was smiling. Her two days with the company of women who accepted her as a friend had been special. She enjoyed being a woman in the company of other women. Their shared task of preparing for Anna's wedding had quickly built a bond.

As the entered the dark barn, Mac spoke for the first time. "Laurel, be careful on the ladder."

"I'll be up in a minute, Mac. I need to do something at the wagon." Laurel went to her satchel and removed her blue calico dress to wear the next day. She also picked up the shirt she had made for Mac. During the day, she had sewed the buttons in their place to finish the project. She climbed to the loft and walked to where Mac stood. "Happy Easter, Mac. I hope you like this gift I made for you." She handed the folded shirt to him, and he unfolded the crisp lawn shirt. He had not been aware that Laurel had been making anything for him. He was so impressed with the detail Laurel had used to create this special Easter surprise for him.

"May I try it on?"

"Yes, of course. I would like to see if it fits or I can make an alteration if I need to."

Mac stripped off his work shirt. His bare chest and broad shoulders always impressed Laurel. Mac never seemed embarrassed to remove his clothes in front of Laurel. He pulled the new shirt across his broad back and across his chest. The shirt fit well. He was an attractive man, with or without his shirt.

"Laurel, will you do me the honor of buttoning my new shirt for me this first time?"

Laurel was pleased that the shirt fit so well. She ran her hands across the back of the shirt, smoothing the beautiful lawn fabric with her palms. From the shoulders, she ran her hands down to Mac's waist, feeling the fabric. She moved to the front and placed her hands on Mac's collar bones and smoothed the fabric across his chest down toward his waist. Laurel looked up into his face, realized what she had just done, and quickly moved her hands away. She lowered her eyes as color rose to her cheeks. In the dim lantern light, she was glad Mac could not see her blush.

—◦ ◦—

Mac was moved by the intimacy of her touch. She had no idea how her touch and gentle caresses moved him. Mac took both her hands and laid them back on his chest. He covered her smaller hands with his. Then he put each hand in turn to his lips. "Laurel, I have never received a nicer gift. I will wear it tomorrow with such pride, knowing you made it for me. Thank you, more than I can say."

"I'm glad you are pleased with it. Please excuse my boldness. I didn't realize..."

"Your smoothing my shirt was the nicest part of the gift. I enjoyed your touch. Now wife, what will you wear tomorrow? You gave your Easter dress away."

"It's nothing. I have two new dresses, and Anna was so upset with her wedding dress being lost in the fire. My blue calico is a very nice dress. It's new, too. I'll be dressed well enough. I don't think you'll be embarrassed to take me to church in that pretty dress."

"Laurel, I wouldn't be embarrassed if you walked into that church in your dungarees and work shirt. Look at me.... You should see what I see, a jewel of great worth. Your generosity and concern for other people is beautiful."

"Thank you."

"You are learning, my good wife. No argument for the compliment, just a sweet reply. Come here, and let's read the Easter story. Mac read in his strong voice from John 20: 1-18.

"Such a beautiful story. You know, Mac, in some ways I feel that I am living a new life. I never knew just being with friends and working on a celebration could be such fun. I loved making your new shirt. I guess that's kind of a resurrection."

"I know what you are saying, Laurel. Easter is my favorite time of year and such an important time for believers. It is a chance to remember what's happened to us since we began our new life. I know I made a trip to Northwest Arkansas. You have changed my life." Mac offered the evening prayer. "Laurel, thank you for your kindness to me and our friends."

"You're welcome, Mac. Goodnight and sleep well."

About 5:30, Mac woke Laurel. Dressed in yesterday's clothes, they climbed down the ladder and into the dark. As they stepped through the barn door, only a glimmer of light shown over the Ozark foothills, a thin glint of gold as the sun pushed its way above the dark. Minute by minute, though, new rays of light shot out turning the night to shades of spring. Delicate greens and tinges of white and pink sprinkled the scene before them on Eastern morning. As Mac and Laurel watched, night vanished entirely and a glorious morning replaced the black of only minutes ago. In the edge of the woods, a new fawn scrambled to shaky legs and nudged its mother to rise, and together they darted into a deeper part of the forest. A dove cooed in the distance and a robin dropped to a nest in a nearby tree to feed her nestlings. Witnessing God's glory, they stood in gratitude. As the sun rose boldly over the hills, both Laurel and Mac MacLayne dared to hope for a new life, together.

16

*Open rebuke is better than secret love. Faithful wounds of a friend, but the
kisses of an enemy are deceitful.*

KJV c1850, Proverbs 27:5-6.

On the Wednesday after Easter, Laurel, Mac and Lonnie found
themselves on the muddy banks of Black River. Mac's spirits
soared for many reasons. Easter had been a blessed day spent
among many brothers and sisters in Christ, worshipping in the Shady
Grove Church, and celebrating the resurrection in joy and gratitude.
The Jessup congregation lived out the commandment of hospitality.
Their long history beginning with the early work of Eli Lindsay and
other circuit riders in the early 1820's was a source of pride, and they
strove to carry on the tradition of sharing the gospel with all who wanted to learn. They lovingly opened their doors to the several travelling
strangers who worshipped with them that Easter morning, including
Lonnie Thomison and his entire family. Laurel and Mac were elated to
see Lonnie make his confession of faith that morning, and he had shyly
thanked Mac and Laurel for showing him what he had missed in his life.
He promised that he would be baptized soon as the river warmed up and

that he and his entire family would worship with the Shady Grove congregation. He'd told the preacher that if Methodism was good enough for his friend, Mac, it'd be more than good enough for an old sinner like him. Laurel had been the picture of a perfect wife that Sunday morning, too. Dressed in her blue calico dress with the tiny pleats down the bodice and the pearl buttons at the collar and at the sleeves, Laurel looked and acted the part of Mrs. Patrick MacLayne, and Mac was awed by the serene, comely woman who sat across from him in the pews of the log church. Her loving, generous character was mirrored in the outward appearance, from the totally appropriate wardrobe to the happy, kind expression on her face. Mac knew that the spinster of Hawthorn was no longer the true nature of his wife. He prayed he would not find her again. That Easter morning, the dream he carried in his heart of a real home in Shiloh was closer than ever. Four more days were all that stood between that dream and the reality he wanted. He could hardly wait to present his help mate to his family at Shiloh.

After the worship service, Lonnie and Mandy invited the entire Shady Grove congregation to their homestead to attend the wedding of Anna Thomison and Lucas Crafton. They had intended to have the local justice of the peace perform the marriage ceremony, but the minister volunteered to read the traditional wedding service for the young couple instead. Anna was indeed a beautiful bride—happy, glowing, and grateful. A large group of the community accepted the invitation to the Thomisons' cabin and stayed for the wedding supper that Laurel had helped Mandy and her mother-in-law prepare. The evening was filled with music, laughter, and conversation. Laurel especially enjoyed the dancing that closed the festivities. Mac was a fine dancer, and he held Laurel tenderly, relinquishing her for only two dances, one to Lonnie and then the preacher of the Shady Grove church. Laurel felt cherished, but truthfully, she wondered at the attention Mac had showered on her that evening. What had she done to deserve so much attention?

Although they'd planned to leave for Powhatan the next morning, the Thomisons wouldn't hear of their departure so soon. The community and the members of the Shady Grove church decided the next day would be one of thanksgiving and reclamation. An impromptu cabin raising would fill the entire day on Monday when the community of Jessup would meet at the site of the burned cabin to ready the site to rebuild the senior Thomisons' house. Of course, a building day meant a party too. Mac and Laurel had to be a part of that celebration. Threatening storm clouds on Tuesday meant another delay. Thankfully, the day passed without a single drop of rain. The fellowship and joy of that long weekend would be a long cherished memory, and strangely, it had all started with the tragedy of a family losing their home.

Lonnie spoke and broke into the memories Mac was reliving from the previous days. "Well, Mac, there's the river and just on the other side, you said you'll feel at home."

"Thank the Lord! I'd wondered if I'd ever get here." Mac knew only three hurdles remained for them. First, they had to get the ferry to carry them across the muddy river. With any luck at all, a day and a half ride across Cache River bottoms would happen without incident. Both of those should be quite simple, but Mac's greatest difficulty would come in getting Laurel to leave most of her precious things behind to be delivered later by freighters. Lonnie had convinced Mac the wagon could not cross the bottoms. Too much rain and practically no roads would make the effort dangerous and foolish, but Laurel cherished the few things she had packed to bring to her new home. She would protest and their happy time would come to an end when he tried to convince her. He'd had several wonderful days with Laurel, and he certainly did not want them to end. They'd enjoyed the lighthearted banter, the dancing, the fellowship with the Thomison and their family in Jessup, and they'd shared an easy friendship since arriving at the Thomisons' homestead. None of the issues they'd argued about since their marriage had surfaced. He had begun holding her hand at times, even when they weren't praying. At the wedding party, he had casually laid his arm across her shoulders a time or two. When he pulled her close to him while they waltzed, Laurel had not flinched from his touch. He knew she enjoyed the attention. Hoping the good feeling would last a few more hours, he waited to tell her.

In Powhatan, Mac found the hotel almost immediately. He got down from the wagon and walked in to rent a room and to ask about the ferry crossings. The clerk inside handed him a key and told him the ferry owner was on the last run for the day and would return from the east side of the river about 5:00. He also suggested Mac go down and book his passage for the next day. "Never know how many folks will want to cross in the morning, and the ferry can only take four or five horses at a time."

Mac returned to Laurel and Lonnie waiting with their wagon. Both Laurel and Mac were sad, knowing that Lonnie, their constant companion since they had gotten lost between Sidney and Sage more than a week ago, would be leaving them to return to his life in Jessup. His word had been true. He had led them to the banks of Black River. Now they would go on east and perhaps never encounter their good friend again.

"Mac, I'll hate not having you and Laurel to tell me all those stories from the Good Book. We ain't known each other very long, but ya'll been 'bout the best friends I ever had."

"You've been a life saver to us, Lon. I wish you were coming to Shiloh with us."

"Not a chance...only one puny ridge over your way. I need me some hills to wander. I'm a thanking ya'll for showing me the way to the Lord. I'll be owing you and Miss Laurel all my days."

"You've been a blessing to us both, Lonnie."

"Miss Laurel, I'll never forget what you done for my little sister, neither--giving her your Easter dress to get married in. You're an angel, no doubt."

"It's only a dress, Lonnie. Every girl deserves to feel beautiful on her wedding day. It was a small thing for me to do after the gift you gave us. We have made a lifelong friend and a new brother in the faith."

Mac embraced Lonnie and tossed the reins to his horse up to him. "I hate to see you go, but it's a long way back to Jessup. I don't want you getting lost in the dark."

Laurel brushed away a tear. "God bless you, friend."

As Lonnie rode back toward Smithville, the MacLaynes felt the loss of their companion, and in his absence, they felt a sudden shyness. They hadn't been alone together for more than a week, except those nights they slept in the barn, and even then, two of Lonnie's children were sleeping below in one of the stalls, having given their bed to their aunt Anna. Now there would be time to get back to the business of getting to know each other. Perhaps they could even do it without the hurt feelings and arguments that had come up so often. They carried their satchels to their room and lay down for a short nap.

About five, they walked the raised plank sidewalk of Powhatan down to the ferry dock. They could see flat log raft had nearly reached the west side of the river. As they got closer, Mac saw the ferry was large enough to hold several passengers and their horses in one crossing. He felt reassured they could easily get across the river on the morning crossing, making it possible to travel at least half the day. When Laurel and Mac reached the bank, level with the dock, Mac stopped in his tracks. Unloading at that moment was his best friend, Matthew Campbell. Mac ran to the dock and threw his arms around Matthew. "I can't believe you're here. What a sight!"

Equally delighted Matt returned the embrace. "I thought I'd sent you off the edge of the earth, Mac. Where in tarnation have you been the last two months?"

"As glad as I am to see you, don't be exaggerating the parting. I've only been gone forty-three days."

"Forty-two too many." Matt and Mac walked arm in arm up toward Laurel. "Mac, what have you been doing all the time you've been gone? I'd convinced myself you'd died along the way. I set out Easter afternoon on my mission to bring your ornery hide back to bury at Shiloh."

"I'm not quite ready for the cemetery yet. I just did what you told me to do. I saw the western part of this beautiful state, and I went a courting."

"Took long enough. So, are you going to continue to court my spinster niece in Washington County?"

"Think my wife will let me?"

— ⁓

Laurel saw Mac embrace the man leaving the ferry. She stood in disbelief. The man was the image of her father. She stared for a time, but as they got closer to her, she realized she'd mistaken her Uncle Matthew as her father. There was a striking resemblance between them. Her uncle was somewhat taller, but otherwise he could have been a twin. Like her father, he was a striking man. He stood about 6'5'' tall and his shoulder length salt and pepper hair fell across his shoulders. He wore a trim, neat beard, just like her papa, and it softened his almost too square jawline. She made herself stop staring.

Just before they reached Laurel, Matthew Campbell stopped and stared at his friend. "Your wife? That was kind of sudden, don't you think? Did you find a bride along the way?"

"No, Uncle. He found and married the spinster of Hawthorn."

With her words, Matthew Campbell looked squarely at the young woman who spoke to him.

"Laurel Grace! My dear Lord. Thank you, Father! This reunion with my long lost niece is a blessing this day." He pulled Laurel into his arms. "I am so happy to see you. I can't believe your papa let you come all this way. He'll miss you. I'll have to convince him to move east and join us at Shiloh."

"Uncle Matt, Papa has gone to be with Mama. Didn't he tell you he had the consumption? I know you two wrote often."

"Mark's gone?" Mac nodded to affirm his friend's question. Matthew pulled Laurel close again and together they wept. Seeing the grief in the face of her uncle, Laurel also grieved. After a while, Matthew took Laurel's arm, and they walked back to the hotel. Together they went to the dining room for a hot meal and a long overdue conversation.

"Has it been a hard trip, Mac?"

"At times, very. We got caught in a snow storm and lived in a cave for about three days. We got attacked by a couple of bungling outlaws outside of Mt. Olive. We took a "road to nowhere" between Sidney and Sage, and we nearly drowned in a heavy rainfall and had to hold up in a deserted cabin. There's more but those are the major events, don't you think, Laurel? Let's just say I am more than ready to be back at Shiloh. I know Laurel is very tired, but she's been a good helpmate. She's earned a good rest."

"Laurel, has the trip been too hard on you?"

"I'm fine, Uncle Matthew. I was a bit taken aback when I saw you on that dock. For a split minute, I felt I was seeing Papa. You two look so much alike."

"My brother was a good man, always thinking about other people. Even me. He didn't tell me he was sick. I could've come with Mac if I'd known."

"He hated wasting away like he did for the last six months. The last three months, he was almost bed ridden. He's in Heaven now with my mama, Samuel and my baby sister, Mary. He's not hurting anymore." Laurel felt her cheeks were wet again. Matthew Campbell gently brushed her tears away with his fingertip.

"Don't grieve, little one. God has put you in caring hands. Shiloh Station will welcome you with open arms. All is well with our family. They're with Jesus now."

They talked for some time, sharing stories about the good and bad parts of the journey through the Ozarks. Matthew told Mac news from Shiloh and about the planting conditions he'd asked about. Well after dark, they left the dining room.

"Laurel, would you enjoy a bath tonight and a chance to wash your hair?"

"That would be heaven sent. Can I do that here?"

"I'll arrange for the hotel clerk to bring you hot water."

"Goodnight, Laurel Grace. Enjoy your bath. I'll send this one back to you when you've had some private time."

"Goodnight, Uncle Matthew. I feel better now that you've shared some tears with me."

Mac and Matthew Campbell went out to the porch and found empty chairs not directly in the path of the foot traffic. "What on earth have you done, Mac?"

"What you wanted me to do. I married Laurel."

"Just like that? When we talked about this, I thought you just needed to get away for a while…to get some perspective on your life at Shiloh. If things had worked out well, I thought you'd start a courtship if you two had anything in common. Never in my wildest dream did I think you'd marry her—a stranger."

"Circumstances didn't allow any courting time."

"Do you love her?"

"We're getting to be great friends. We work well together. Things just fell into place. We think it's God's will."

"Do you love her, Mac?" He didn't answer his best friend. "Well, your silence is the answer to my question."

"Look, Matthew…don't be judging me. I told you I never wanted that heart and cupid stuff again."

"Did you ask Laurel Grace if she did?" How had Matthew looked into him and seen the shame he felt.

"Matt, we're good together. Share a common faith. We like talking to each other. We are equally yoked."

"That yoke may get mighty heavy someday soon, when you understand that a marriage is dry, lonely, and just plain hard work without the joy and passion meant for a man and a woman."

"It's not like that, Matt. We are getting to be really good friends."

"Have you bedded my niece, Mac?"

"Except for the night before her father died, we've shared a common bed every night."

"I'll take that to mean you sleep together, but you've been no husband to her yet."

"Matt, you're getting personal."

"I should take you out behind the livery and show you how personal it is. I can't believe you stood before a minister of the Gospel and spoke marriage vows. I've never known you to be dishonest."

"We didn't."

"You brought Laurel Grace all the way across the state without benefit of clergy?"

"No, Matthew. You know me better than that. We spoke vows. We didn't pledge to love each other. Laurel didn't promise to obey either, but we did take solemn vows that Reverend Caldwell honored, and he declared us man and wife."

"Can I honor those vows as leader of the Shiloh congregation?"

"We have a legal marriage, Matthew."

"Did you give one thought to how Laurel Grace must feel, knowing you married her to take her off her dying father's hands? Bless her, Lord. What a load she must be carrying around!"

"I didn't think about it like that, but I didn't intend to hurt her."

Knowing he had to share part of the responsibility for the sham of a marriage, Matthew Campbell sat with his head in his hands for several minutes. After a while, Matthew raised his head and spoke, "Mac... regardless of the problems, I am happy to see you again. We will deal with this together. Pray with me?" He laid his hand on Mac's shoulder and spoke quietly, "Lord, I know your grace is without limit. I'm grateful you brought my niece and my best friend safe across the rugged paths of this state. Give us the wisdom to make all this work out in your will. Watch over us all and take care of my family for me for a couple more days 'til I get back to Shiloh. Amen."

"Good night Matthew. I'm glad you're here. I've missed you and your good advice."

"Well, next time, let's just get that mail order bride." Matt had hoped to end the evening on a light note since he and Mac had just had the most difficult moment they'd ever shared. However, Mac did not see the comment as light.

"There will be no next time. We've made our covenant, and it will remain as long as God wills it. I need you to help me deal with a more pressing problem, namely, separating Laurel from her family things that we brought from Hawthorn. We can't take that wagon through the Cache River bottoms right now. She'll be angry when I tell her."

"Well, you can't take that wagon right now for sure. I just came over those paths and traveling was hard on horseback. The wagon can't cross right now...too much flooding."

— ⁓

Mac returned to the room where Laurel was relaxing in her bath. Neither of them expected a real bath tub, but that was one luxury the booming port town could offer. He called to her quietly, not wanting to startle her. She didn't respond. When he took a couple of steps inside, he found his wife had fallen asleep in the warm bathwater. Her wet locks lay down the side of the tub nearly touching the floor. He became sharply aware of the lovely woman he saw across the room. Again, like the night he had watched her dress for bed in the loft, he knew he wanted her. He looked away and spent a few minutes reigning in his emotions. He would not allow himself to sink to that level ever again in his life. He refused to let physical desire win out over his dreams of family life and home. He went back to the hall and ran directly into Matthew Campbell.

"Did she throw you out for the blackguard you are?"

"She's asleep in the bath. I didn't want to embarrass her."

"I can't say as I understand the first thing about you, brother, but this is your problem. I'm headed to bed. I'll see you in the morning."

Mac turned and knocked loudly on the door and called out, "Laurel, can I come in?"

She startled when she heard Mac. "In a moment, I'll get dressed."

"No hurry...." Mac leaned against the door, recalling the image of his sleeping wife. He couldn't understand how she'd hidden behind her façade for all the years.

Shortly, Laurel opened the door, dressed in her old ill-fitting night dress and her hair wrapped in a towel. "Come in, Mac. I'm sorry I took so long. The bath was such a luxury, I guess I just relaxed too long."

"I'm glad you enjoyed your bath. You've earned a little pampering since our trip has been long and difficult. You haven't complained of the hardships...not even once."

"Would you like a bath, Mac? There is no clean water, but the water in the tub is still a little warm."

"If you don't mind, I'd love to get some of this grime off." Laurel went to the side of the bed away from the tub and sat down.

"I'll just sit here until you're finished." Mac stepped out of his dirty clothes. He slipped into the water and sighed. Even the tepid water was relaxing. "Thanks for sharing, Laurel. This is a little piece of paradise."

"The bath was nice. Thank you for arranging it."

"It's good to give you some of the things you like. You'd told me a while back you wanted a bathing space in our cabin, remember? I surely need to find us one of these tubs. We'll feel like wealthy people if we have a copper tub in our house."

"I'd settle for some privacy and access to water. I don't expect a mansion, even if you promised my papa."

"I didn't, but I'd give it to you if you want it." Laurel smiled. "Laurel, will you do me a favor?"

"I will if I can."

Mac took a deep breath and decided to take the risk. "If I cover myself, will you come over here and wash my back?" She'd seen him bare to the waist several times, including the special day he had removed his old dress shirt to change into his Easter shirt. Mac realized she hesitated. "You don't have to if you are uncomfortable."

"No, Mac. I'll wash your back." Laurel walked to the copper tub and knelt behind him. She dipped her hands into the water and moved her wet hands over his bare skin. "I'm not sure you'll like the scent of this soap. I used my own, because the clerk didn't bring any with the water.

"It's fine. I like the way you smell when you're close to me." Laurel rubbed his back and shoulders with the soap and dipped her hands back into the water to rinse it away. When she finished, she rose. "Don't stop. I'm enjoying your touch on my skin. Nice present from my best friend."

Laurel continued to massage Mac's back and shoulders. "I thought my uncle is your best friend."

"Don't see Matthew doing me such a special favor. I think I will just leave that up to you, if you don't mind."

"I don't suppose I'd mind."

"Would you like me to return the favor?"

Laurel blushed bit, "No thanks. I've already finished my bath." Together they laughed.

"You'd best turn away, wife. I can't stay in this water forever. I'm getting waterlogged."

Laurel threw him a towel and teased, "You'd best make yourself presentable."

Mac knew it was time for him to remove himself from temptation. He took the towel and wrapped it around his torso, and he stepped from the water. He took clean clothes from his satchel and dressed for bed. He made a mistake in opening such an intimate talk with Laurel and found himself fighting his feelings again. He squared his shoulders and turned. "Better get to bed. We got a lot of work to do tomorrow." In a tone was much harsher than he had intended, his words sounded as if he were barking orders.

— —

Laurel didn't know what she had done wrong. She thought back over the last few minutes. Unless Mac had taken offense at her telling him to make himself presentable, she couldn't understand his sudden change of mood.

"Mac, what did I do to anger you?"

"I'm not angry. Let's not get at odds with each other. I've got something I need to discuss with you."

"You're angry. Everything points to it--your posture-- the change in your voice. We were laughing, enjoying each other, and then you're giving me orders."

"I apologize. Didn't mean to bark."

"Tell me what I did. I want to know."

"Nothing. I just have something important to talk to you about."

"You're not telling the truth. You've forgotten our first rule...speak the truth, always."

"Just like you do, every time you close me out after one of your nightmares?"

Laurel turned, walked to the bed, and lay down. She started to turn down the lantern wick.

"Don't turn the light off. Laurel, I need to talk to you before you sleep. I know you aren't going to like what I have to say. Hear me out."

"I don't want to hear anything you have to say tonight."

"Laurel, this can't wait."

"I said no. I don't deserve your nasty mood. Go to sleep and try to get into a better humor before tomorrow. I don't have to put up with your foul temper."

Mac walked to the right side of the bed and sat down with his back to Laurel.

"Laurel..."

" Mac, I am tired. I don't want to argue with you."

"Laurel, I wanted you."

"What? Wanted what?"

"You don't know anything about the nature of a man, do you?"

"Leave me be. I told you that before you pushed your way into my life."

"I wanted to take my rights as your husband. I saw you in your bath, and when you bathed me.... I had to push you away or break my promise to you."

Laurel had no words. "Forgive me, Laurel. It's my problem. You don't deserve my temper, but I do have to talk to you tonight." Mac hesitated and then he spoke, "Laurel we can't take the wagon across Cache River bottoms. Matthew has just crossed the route from Lorado. There's just too much water. It's rained nearly every day in the past week."

Laurel stiffened and sat up. She glared at Mac, her eyes much more green than gray. "So now you are punishing me because I have displeased you. You and your lies about finding me desirable!"

"Laurel, you know I never say things just to hurt you, nor have I told you a lie. I may have kept things from you, but I haven't spoken a lie to you."

"There is little enough of my family and past life in that wagon. You can't want me to discard the little I have. I won't do it. My uncle Matthew will help me."

"Matt told me about the road conditions. We can cross on horseback, but the wagon can't get across the swamps right now."

"I'll stay here and wait for dry weather."

"No. This is no place for a woman alone. Besides, you are my wife. You will go home with me."

"No, I won't leave my things behind."

"Listen to me. We will go through the wagon and take the most valuable things we can pack on the mules. Then I'll have the other things stored until freighters can bring them in the summer. By the time I get our cabin built, you'll have all your family belongings."

Laurel began to cry softly. Mac tried to brush away the tears on her cheeks, but she pulled away. "Laurel Grace, please understand?"

"I don't see that I have much choice."

"I promise you'll have your family things for our new house."

"Don't make promises you can't keep. I'm tired. I want to go to sleep." Laurel sounded so defeated.

"Yell at me if you want. I know you don't believe me. I'd prefer an angry tirade to your silent rejection."

Laurel turned away. She knew he'd not found her desirable. He'd used the words as a ploy to get her consent to leave her things behind. She hated the deceit. If he couldn't be honest with her, they had no hope for a future together.

"All right, Laurel. I'll get the Bible out of your satchel. Let's read our scripture and then we can go to sleep."

"Leave me be. I am not in a frame of mind to read tonight."

"I'm sorry, but that covenant we will not break." Mac strode across the room dressed only in his underwear. He was always so confident, regardless of his state of dress. Laurel watched him as he picked up her satchel and looked for one of their scripture books. Finding Laurel's first, he carried it back to the bed. Laurel had left a marker at one passage, so Mac decided to read that one.

"First John 4: 10 -19. Now that is very interesting, don't you think? 'There is no fear in love, but perfect love casteth out fear because fear hath torment. He that feareth is not made perfect in love.' Why did you mark that passage, Laurel? Does it mean something special to you?"

"I asked you to leave me alone. Just add to the list of failings you've already made for me. I am faithless, arrogant, and now fearful. I suppose I'm afraid no one can love me. I am sorry you've been shortchanged in a marriage partner." The jut of her chin and squared shoulders made it clear nothing would come of a talk tonight.

"Laurel, give me your hand."

"No…"

"Laurel, you promised. Give me your hand." Reluctantly she did. "Father, please forgive my failure to make my wife see her worth. She is a gift beyond anything I deserve, and yet I fail to let her see I value her. Please teach me to mirror that worth, just as Christ Jesus does for us all. I ask you to protect us in this last leg of our journey and bring us to Shiloh. In Jesus name, Amen. And Lord, I certainly enjoyed my bath. Thank you for my wife's touch. Amen."

"Arghhhhhh." Laurel beat at her pillow. Why did she and Mac have a few good days when their friendship seemed to grow and then one brief episode would pull her back to loneliness and self-doubt? What was missing in her? She hated living in the constant turmoil. She sighed deeply and tried to sleep, but about the time she'd dozed off, an image of her throwing her family Bible in the Black River or a feeling that she was pulling the leaves and roots off the orchard cuttings she'd carried across the state would pull her back to consciousness. Well after midnight, Laurel was finally slept, but even that was short lived.

Three hours before dawn, Mac sat upright as Laurel screamed so loudly that she could be heard down the entire hallway. He watched her pull at the blankets as if to protect herself, and she slashed out in all directions around her. Mac knew he'd heard those same desperate cries for help on at least four other occasions. He tried to comfort Laurel. Holding her had worked in the past, but this time, she wouldn't be held. She called out to her father and wept uncontrollably, great wailing sobs. She shoved him away. Mac was helpless, unable to wake her or comfort her.

Within minutes, Matthew Campbell crossed the hall. "Mac, what's happened to Laurel?"

"Another nightmare. She's had them before, but I can't get her to wake up this time. When I try to hold her, she fights back at me."

Matthew Campbell approached his hurting niece. "Laurel Grace, it's Uncle Matt... It's safe, little one." He brushed her hair back out of her face. "Wake up, Laurel Grace...Shhhhhh." He sat down next to her and pulled her into his arms, as if she were a small child. He rocked her and continued to whisper to her. He began to sing to her, *Jesus Lover of my Soul,* in a tune sounding more like a lullaby than a hymn. Shortly, her tears subsided and Laurel laid her head on his shoulder

"Stop that caterwauling in there. Don't ya'll know people are trying to sleep?" Loud yelling accompanied the pounding on the door." The intrusion awoke Laurel, and she screamed again. Mac jumped up, ran to the door, and jerked it open to see an angry man.

"Stop! My wife just had a nightmare. We'll get her quiet in a minute. Stop pounding on the door. Go back to your room."

"You'd better shut that harpy up...now."

"Just leave. Your angry words don't help."

The frustration showed in Mac's voice, and the stranger left without further complaint. He shut the door with a firm hand. Matt continued to hold Laurel, singing the quiet words of the old hymn. Within minutes, Laurel slept again.

"What's the nightmare about, Mac?"

"I only know part of it. Laurel was attached once, a long time ago. She'd blocked it all out until one night on the trail. A couple of bungling thieves decided to rob us, and one of them took a shine to Laurel. He attacked her, but I stopped him with a broad axe. Laurel's been mixing up those two events in nightmares since then. I can't get her to tell me about it."

"She won't get rid of the demons until she'll talk about what scares her."

"I've told her that, but she doesn't trust me enough to share that with me."

Matt continued to rock Laurel and sing to her. When her gentle breathing told him, she was asleep and the nightmare was gone for the time, he laid her head on the pillow and covered her shoulder with the blanket. "Why do you think it came up tonight, Mac? She should have been relaxed and sleepy after her warm bath."

"We argued again. Seems like every time we have two or three good days, something always puts a wedge back between us. You know, she tried to run me off the first day we met, and four days later, we were married. I should have known better. I've used people over and over since Marsha. Laurel didn't deserve to be one more person on that list."

"It will be all right, Mac. You didn't set this up yourself. I think I had a hand in it...the Lord did too. I see his work here. Laurel needs you, just like you need her. Keep your faith. Remember, grace is enough."

"Yes, I told myself that...and there she is, my portion of grace. I have to find a way to let her know."

"Sleep some, Mac. We need to head home in a couple of hours. Today will be hard enough without you being dog tired."

17

Therefore if any man be in Christ, he is a new creature: old things are
passed away; behold all things are become new.

KJV c1850, II Corinthians 5:17

*L*aurel woke before sunrise. She had dark circles under her eyes, and her hair was unusually wild. Laurel quickly braided her long hair and twisted the braid into the ugly coronet Mac so disliked. She donned a skirt and long sleeved blouse, needing functional clothes for the journey across the river and into Greene County. She'd worry about making a good impression later. She walked carefully so as not to awaken Mac and slipped out and down the stairs. On the front porch, she met a man walking toward the ferry. "Sir, can you point out the blacksmith's shop?"

"Silas Dawson owns the livery down the street and to the right." He tipped his hat and continued.

Laurel followed the directions and found herself looking at the parts of her life she had to keep. When she remembered the scene she'd made the previous night, she was mortified. How could she have reacted so to Mac? Dragging a fully loaded wagon into the swamp would be foolish. She'd lose everything if she stubbornly demanded that he bring her things. Yet, with her good sense telling her what she had to do, she knew there was a very real possibility she'd never again see the things she'd leave behind. She'd pick up one item and then put it back in its place only to do the same thing to a dozen more. A mule couldn't carry her furniture. Some of these things could not be left in the hands of strangers. Who would take care of her great grandmother's painted china tea cup? It was precious only to her. She must take every item in the Campbell family box. If she had to carry it every step of the way, she would not leave it behind. Laurel even stowed several more things inside for safekeeping.

She pulled back the canvas covering from her orchard cuttings. To her dismay, they looked wilted, so she took a bucket to a rain barrel outside and gave them a hefty watering. She refused to leave the fragile plants and carefully wrapped cuttings. Within a week, they would only be a memory because no one here would see their value. To guarantee her future orchard must be be watered regularly, so she'd take her orchard cuttings with her—somehow. She set the canvas-covered box aside with the family's box. When she took back the next oil cloth, she saw her grandmother's spinning wheel, her mother's rocking chair, her papa's arm chair, and her mother's handmade walnut bureau. Laurel broke into tears as she ran her hand down the side of the bureau. When she reached out and touched the cool stoneware of her mother's churn, she felt as if she was losing the last of her family. *Lord, please don't make me give up the last part of my home.* Laurel's grief for her father and for Hawthorn overwhelmed her.

As the sun rose over the muddy river's eastern shoreline, Laurel ran from the stable. She didn't know where she was going, and at that moment, she didn't care. She just had to go—run from the pain of her loss, the fear of her future, and the hopelessness she felt. *Father, where are you? You promised never to leave me, and I am so alone. Please, Lord, show me that you see me and will not leave me alone."*

She walked on a long time. Finally, she became aware that she was near the bank of the river. She looked at the sky and noted the sun well above the horizon. She heard someone calling her name.

"Laurel Grace. Where are you?" She was holding up their departure. She hadn't planned to miss the morning ferry. She'd only wanted to run away from the hurt. Now she would have to apologize to Mac for keeping him away from his home. She knew how much he wanted to get home. She wanted that too, but unfortunately, she had no clue where her home was.

"I'm here, Uncle Matt. I am sorry you had to come looking for me. I didn't realize how long I'd been gone."

"Where you running to, child?" How strange that he always treated her as if she were a child. Was it her uncle who had held her last night? She had such a vague memory of it all...just a nightmare and the singing.

"I wasn't running anywhere, Uncle. Just trying to clear my head. I tried to choose between my things in the wagon. I just couldn't do it. Those aren't just things--they are the only remaining pieces of home. That's all I have left to connect me to the people I love and are gone now."

"Bless your heart, child. The last few months have been a trial for you. I hate that you had to deal with it alone. Wished I had known Mark was so sick. I would've come if I knew."

"It doesn't matter. Mac helped when he could. He's has been very kind to me."

"But truthfully, he's part of the problem, isn't he?"

Laurel didn't answer, thinking a reply would be disrespectful to her husband.

"Laurel Grace, I'm partly responsible for Mac's trip to Washington County. Please forgive me for not thinking this thing through."

"You didn't know. Mac told me what you two had planned. I am afraid Papa was the one who misunderstood. Mac had not been in our cabin two hours when Papa made him promise to marry me. Being the good man he is, Mac couldn't say no to a dying man's last request. It's not his fault that he is stuck with me."

"Laurel Grace, if you think Mac was stuck with anything he didn't want, you don't know him."

"You're right about that. I don't know him."

"We have to go back now, child. As hard as it is, we'll have to choose what we can haul by mule and find a place to store your things until we can get a freighter to move it to Greene County when the road's better. Don't lose your faith. The Lord will take care of everything if you will turn it over to Him."

"Papa said that to me...'Laurel, keep hold of your faith.' I am glad you came to find me. I think you are an answer to a prayer."

"Maybe so, but I know everything will work out." Matthew Campbell pulled his niece into his arms. She felt a sense of safety and wellbeing in his warm embrace. "I want you to know that I love you, and God loves you, and he doesn't know it yet, but Patrick MacLayne loves you, too."

"Uncle, our first covenant is to speak the truth always. I believe you love me. After all, you are my uncle. You are so much like my Papa that I feel safe with you. I know God loves me, but Mac is my friend. Truthfully, I doubt I even deserve that much. Let's go back."

As they topped the bluff, Mac was coming to meet them. "Laurel, are you okay? I was worried when I saw the wagon. When I saw the cover off and some of the things taken out, I thought you'd been robbed or kidnapped."

"I am all right now. I'm sorry I delayed the crossing. I'll hurry."

"No need to rush. We will try to cross this afternoon. Let's see what we can load onto the mules."

"Mac, will you..." Before Laurel could ask, he responded.

"Yes, wife. I will find some way to bring your orchard with us." After an hour or so, Laurel had pulled the things she had to bring from the wagon. Together they packed her family box, Laurel's new calico dress and her small satchel with her night dress, brush and both their Bibles. She wanted to take her books, but the weight would be too much. On the second mule, Mac and Matthew mounted a small box filled with soil and an oil cloth lining to hold the precious cuttings for the orchard.

He stuffed the precious seedlings, the cuttings of the fruit trees and the grape vines among the wet burlap he had used on the trip across the state. He stowed his broad ax and a small satchel with his clothes. Mac also stored two large pieces of oilcloth and three blankets along with Laurel's yellow coverlet. Everything else was repacked and covered to wait for better days. In a heap on the stable floor remained their saddles, horse blankets, reins and bridles. Those things would be used when they set out on the last leg of the long trip.

"Let's go to the mercantile and get a few things to eat for the next couple of days. I want to ask some questions too." A short way from the hotel, they found Smart and Brothers Mercantile on Main Street. Fronting the businesses along the main street of Powhatan was a sturdy boardwalk, a welcome site for the patrons of the town who found themselves walking in mud and water in areas not on Main Street. This plank walkway led all the way to the docks of Ficklin's ferry, which was less than 100 feet from the center of the village. Having a little time to look around this settlement, the travelers noticed a thriving population. On the outlying area of the town, several cabins, both of hewn logs and rounded logs, were visible. Some of the larger cabins had porches across the front of two pens. Laurel was pleased to see a school near a small clapboard church. The sign at the front of the yard read, *Powhatan Male and Female Academy*, est. *1854*.

Once inside the mercantile, Mac and Matt went to the counter to speak with the owner. Laurel browsed around the generously supplied store. The store not only had food, farm implements, yard goods and household needs, some shelves were stocked with items that had been shipped from Europe and England. One shelf held colognes, laces, and hats that most of the customers could certainly not afford. Laurel was surprised at the exorbitant display of finery and even more at the prices. The green felt chapeau with a net and sweeping feathers had a tag marked $21.00! A person could buy 15 acres of good farm land for the price of that hat. Laurel was also pleasantly surprised that salt, milled flour, and potatoes were very reasonably priced. She wanted to ask about the difference.

"Laurel, we need some food for a few easy meals. See if you can find a few things that will be easy to carry and won't spoil too fast. We'll be home in two days or less, depending on the weather and the trail."

"Mac, why don't you go back and get the coffee pot. You don't have to give up all life's blessings."

"You are a thoughtful wife. And I thought you were upset with me."

"Shhhh. We won't talk about private matters in front of others." Laurel picked up a pound of coffee at .75 a pound, ten pounds of potatoes, a sack of flour and cornmeal, a small smoked ham and three pounds of bacon. That would suffice until they could get back to Greene County. When she laid the items on the counter, she asked the clerk. "How is it that you have so many things from Europe and England? The cologne and lace are surely not in big demand as costly as they are."

"We get some business from passengers on the steamboats. They often want goods that have been shipped in. We got enough steamboat traffic that we seldom get stuck with the things we stock for the travelers. It is true that our local ladies would never think of buying those things, but Powhatan is an up and coming place. Why, I'd guess that we got close to 400 or so folks living here about since the zinc mines were opened last year. We got us a doctor over in Black Rock and a couple of lawyers living right here in the town."

Laurel's bill was nearly five dollars. She'd have to tell Mac that she'd have made the bill five times higher if she had bought the hat! She smiled at the thought. Just as she was about to pick up the items she'd bought, Mac walked up to the counter and laid a pair of men's trousers next to her basket.

"You need something practical to wear in the swamp. That skirt will never do. Please change and we'll head to the ferry."

— ~

While Laurel and Mac shopped, Matthew had gone in search of the local pastor of the Powhatan Methodist congregation. He had met the preacher at a conference two years back. On the bank of the river was a framework of what would someday become a new Methodist church. Jacob Runsick was busy measuring another board for a rafter that was going up. He was young and afire in his work to grow his congregation. Matthew liked the new pastor who reminded him of himself during his own early ministry.

"Hello to you, brother. You're building a fine church here by the river. How goes your flock?"

"Matthew Campbell. Good to see you. We are trying to get us a building. Whenever we get some extra offering, we buy some more lumber. Not too expensive here since we got us a couple of lumber mills just up the river. I hope to have a roof up before summer's over. What's brought you all the way to Lawrence County, Brother?"

"Helping a member of my flock move his new bride across the state. We have a problem though. They have a wagon of family keepsakes to take back to Greene County. With all the rain in the past couple of weeks, Cache River bottom is a swamp."

"That's true. I know the river's up here. No way you'd get a wagon across the bottoms right now. Some of our farmers told me they're having to replant their cotton. The rain has washed out their fields again. Yeah, I know a freighter that brings our supplies from St. Louis, Jacksonport, and as far away as Wittsburg. He makes his routes regular. This spring he's had to make changes his routes using only the main roads. Eli is a member of my congregation and is honest as the day is long. I know he's going north to Pocahontas and south to Batesville. I am sure he told me that he'd be going to Greensboro in the second quarter, about midsummer."

"If you vouch for him, I'm sure he'll get my niece her things. I'd like to book carriage for the wagon. We are headed across the river this afternoon. Could I give you funds to store and book that delivery to Shiloh Station whenever he comes east?"

"It'd please me a lot to help you, brother." The two ministers found themselves in a good discussion about the conference they'd attended together, enjoying the opportunity to talk with a fellow clergyman. Both Matt and Jacob were growing their congregations, but they both felt uneasy about the increasing talk of secession around the conference. Like Matthew, Jacob had spoken adamantly against the split and against slavery, and as Matthew had done, he'd gained himself a few adversaries in the process.

With the wagon delivery booked, Matthew returned to find Mac and Laurel sitting on the porch of the tavern where they would eat lunch. "Mind if I join ya'll?"

"Of course not. You've been gone for a long time."

"Just doing a little business with a fellow clergyman. Your wagon of treasures will be safe. Brother Runsick will store your things and arrange for a freighter to bring it when the roads are passable. Just as I said, everything will work out if you keep the faith."

The sun was well past its zenith when Laurel, Mac, and Matt walked up to the loading dock waiting for the ferry to cross to the east side of Black River. The ferry owner had promised them room on the trip, and Mac counted out the crossing fee. The fee was dear, but everyone who knew the area was aware of the treachery of Black River. Unusual currents, sudden drop offs in the bottom, and hidden debris made crossing by ferry the only safe way to get from Powhatan to the east bank. Even if the rainy spring had not added several feet to the depth of the crossing, Mac would have chosen the ferry crossing, regardless of the cost. Matt had a meeting on the Sabbath, and Mac just wanted to be home. Both were more than happy to pay the three bits for each of their animals and a dollar a piece for the three of them.

The ferryman greeted his passengers as they waited to load their animals. "Where ya'll headed folks? From the looks of the little lady, I'd say you plan to spend a couple of days on the road. Mighty brave of you, ma'am. Not many females are willing to cross the sunken lands. Fewer still would wear trousers."

Laurel blushed, as she was not entirely comfortable with her attire... not that she disliked pants for she wore them frequently at home when she did outside chores, but the trousers Mac had bought for her were far too big and were held up by a wide brown belt that he'd loaned her. She had to roll the legs up several inches to keep them off the ground, but she straightened her shoulders and smiled at the ferryman. "Don't you like the new style created by my husband?"

"How do you do? Name's MacLayne. My wife and I are headed across Cache River Bottoms to get home to Greensboro. Got any advice on a safe route?"

"Well, the safest route would be to go up to Pocahontas and cross at DeMun's Mill. That crossing leads to DeMun's Road, which connects to the old Southwest Trail. Good road all the way to Greensboro. It'd cost you a couple, three days in travel time. If you go across the bottoms, when the plank road ends you'll find patchwork between here and Fontaine. The plank road only goes a few yards, then its dirt...I should say mud. Probably meet other folks coming west. They should be able to tell you about any trouble along the road. Biggest problem is the rain. River's up and so you know the road'll be poor, if you can even find it. Good thing, you didn't overload your mules. MacLayne, make sure those jacks are tied. If the water gets rough, I don't need cantankerous animals trying to scuttle my ferry."

Mac walked up behind Laurel and laid his arm across her shoulder. He felt her stiffen at his touch, and he remembered the tiff from last night. He decided to ignore the rebuff. "We are so much nearer home, Laurel."

"I am happy for you, Mac. I know you've been homesick in your absence from Shiloh."

"I'm more hoping for safe travel. The distance ain't so far, but the road and swamps here will be some of the worst we've traveled."

"That's certainly discouraging. I seem to remember some pretty difficult paths already."

"Keep your faith, niece. The good Lord didn't bring you all the way from the mountains to drown you in the swamps of Cache River." Matthew smiled at Laurel and patted her shoulder. "What happened to all that glorious hair of yours?"

"Still there...just tamed for the trip across the bottoms. Mac doesn't like my braids, I'm afraid." Laurel turned her attention to the crossing.

"Why is the river so brown here? We've crossed several that were very clean and beautiful."

"Rich dirt in these parts. Why you could grow a crop of shovels if you left one in the dirt overnight. Soil washes into the river cause of the hills and low lands. Lots of creeks carrying the soil run off, too, but our farmers are blessed to own the bottom land. They grow plenty unless the river floods on them."

"So different than the mountains where I lived."

"Well, Missy, you'd better take one last look at them hills on the west bank...that's the end of the Ozark foothills. Thanks to that quake back in 1811... I think that is when it was... from here to the Mississippi you'll find the delta. Old fellers call it the Sunken Lands. Of course, over your way, you got that scrawny little ridge where Crowley put his homestead. You'll find it poor comparison to the Boston Mountains where you lived."

The river crossing was uneventful and took only a short time. Mac and Matthew led their livestock across the dock and on to the east landing. Mac figured they'd have at least four hours of good light before they'd have to stop for the night. With luck, they'd make it to some community before dark. Laurel mounted Sassy while Mack took the lead reins of the mules and mounted Midnight.

"I'll lead one of those mules, Mac. They'll travel better that way." Matthew took one of the mule guides, and they headed down the road toward Fontaine. The pace was very slow, because the mud was thick and deep in places. Laurel understood why so much of the soil wound up in Black River. Before they'd gone a bit more than a mile, the men dismounted and lead the animals. Only the noise of the boots and hooves sloshing in the mire broke the silence of the afternoon. Before they had reached Bunson, the only settlement between the river and Fontaine, Mac insisted they stop for an hour. The animals needed rest. Travelling under these poor road conditions could permanently injure an animal.

Laurel got off Sassy Lady and sank ankle deep into the mud. She should have been more careful, but she hadn't dreamed the earth was practically liquid.

"Laurel, I'm sorry conditions are so bad. If I had known, we could have gone the long way around with much better roads. I was only thinking of myself...my wanting to get home. Forgive me again."

"Not a crisis. It's only a little mud. It will wash off with a little clean water."

"As if you had any clean water. When you get back to my homestead, Laurel, I'll have your Aunt Ellie make you a grand tub of hot water."

"That'd be wonderful. How is your family, Uncle Matt? It's been forever since we've been together."

"Well, you know that Susan got married about eight years ago. She made me a grandpa already three times. Beautiful kids, blonde and brown eyed, like Sue. Then we got two boys near grown. Mark is twenty-two now. I named him for your pa. He's got his own farm, a homestead neighboring mine. John is sixteen, and he's thinking about preaching the gospel, too. He's a might young, but I believe he's been called. We'll see what time brings. Then we had a little surprise about five years ago. Named her Mary after my ma. She's got me wrapped around her little finger...one of those special gifts from the Lord."

"Sounds like you've got a wonderful family. Do you live near Mac?"

"Our place is about a mile the other side of Shiloh Station from Mac's homestead. Of course, right now I'm not sure where Mac is going to build your cabin."

"I told Laurel we'd walk the place in a few days and pick a site for the house. She should have a say. We need to be headed on now. Daylight is a wasting." They remounted their horses and continued to ride east along the road, but at a very slow pace. They arrived at Buncom Ridge within an hour. In the settlement, they talked to a couple of travelers and one of the residents and decided to move on. While they had good light, they rode, taking special care since the travelers they'd spoken with had told them of sink holes and deceptively deep waterways, especially those around Running Water Creek. Near dusk, Matt told Mac they'd have to make camp. They would not be able to reach Fontaine before it was too dark to travel. They had learned for themselves that that the path was too dangerous to ride when they couldn't see clearly.

The rain had made it impossible to find a dry place to set up a camp. Mac rode up a small incline and found a grove of white oak trees growing at the top of the knoll. The ground there was not dry, but at least it was not oozing. He chose the site as close to the top of the rise as he could find room. Together Mac and Matt unpacked the mules so the animals could rest through the night. The following day would be another long difficult trek. Both men knew they hadn't reached the bottoms yet. Mac retrieved the three blankets and oilcloth to spread on the ground. Unless it rained again, they would have a dry place to sleep. Matt scoured the area, looking for dead branches that were dry enough to burn. If they could build a fire, they could heat up their food for a light meal and make coffee. Matthew knew Mac's habit...coffee in the morning and coffee at night...

By dark, they had made the semblance of a camp with a small fire. Laurel put three potatoes among the ashes to cook for supper. She sliced pieces of ham and divided the small pone she had bought at Smart's store that morning. She warmed the meat and bread over a spit on the campfire so they would not have a totally cold meal that night. At least they would not sleep hungry.

"Mac, where'd you intend to let the new bride sleep when you got back to Shiloh? You know you don't have a roof of your own?"

"I guess that is another one of those things I didn't given much thought to. Things happened pretty fast back in Washington County."

"Seems to me, you need to think about it soon. Laurel ain't going to want to sleep on the ground, you know."

"I'll find us some shelter. First, we 'll get a garden planted. Laurel also brought back those seedlings and cuttings to plant our own orchard. We have a lot to keep us busy when we get back."

"You know school is set to start at the end of the month. We have our school during the slacks times for farming. Most of the crops are in and not near ready to harvest so the kids have time to go to school in the late spring and early summer."

"We'll handle it, Matt. But now it's time to get some sleep. It's too dark out here to read. Matt, will you share some scripture from memory?

It's a tradition we started. We close every day by reading the Bible and praying together. We decided it would assure we'd never go to sleep at odds with each other. Hasn't worked that well yet, but it'll be better when we get home."

"Laurel Grace, you been quiet since we stopped. Is something amiss?"

"No, just tired. Go ahead with the scripture, Uncle Matthew."

"There is a passage in Proverbs that Ellie reminds me about once a week. She tells me it's a good marriage reminder. *Who can find a virtuous woman? For her price is far above rubies. The heart of her husband doth safely trust her so that he hath no need of spoils. She will do him good and not evil all the days of her life. She looketh well to the ways of her household and eateth not the bread of idleness. Let her children rise up and call her blessed and her husband also. He praiseth her.*"

"Any particular reason you think I need to hear that, Matthew?"

"Just thought a little encouraging would help you both. And Mac, you are family now, and you need to know we Campbell take care of our own. Learn to make her happy, my friend. She is a gem of rare value, probably more than you deserve. I love you, brother. I want ya'll to be happy."

"Thank you, Uncle. I appreciate your kind words, as undeserved as they are."

"Laurel, when someone gives you a compliment, you just say thank you. You know it's really an insult to call people who care for you a liar. Give it some thought." When Mac finished scolding Laurel, he picked up her hand.

"Lord, it's been a long, hard day, but we are feeling the call of home. Thank you for all the blessings of the day and help us get through the swamp tomorrow. There is much work to do at Shiloh, and with your help, a good life waits for Laurel Grace and Mac. We praise Your Son for his gift of salvation, and the opportunity to be new creatures in Him."

"Uncle Matthew, Mac told me a week or so back that you had helped him find a new life in Jesus. That's a strange idea to me. I fully understand the idea of salvation, but I've never heard about being a new creature. I'd like to know more about that someday."

"Easy lesson, Laurel. When we lay down our past before Jesus, we have the chance to start over again. I see Mac hasn't told you much about his past. You need to have that conversation with him sometime. From what I know about you, you need to leave a lot of bad memories and start a new life. You will find what you want in life when you do. Well, enough preaching for tonight. Hope ya'll sleep well. I know I will. I don't think I ever been this tired before."

Matthew moved to the far side of the oilcloth, roll himself into his blanket, and lay his head on his saddle. Matt fell asleep almost immediately. Too little sleep the previous night and the drudge through the wet lands made sleep easy.

Mac laid out one blanket on the other side on the oilcloth and took the other to use as a coverlet for him and Laurel. The saddles they used as pillows didn't allow much snuggling, but they would keep their heads up off the wet earth. "I hope you sleep well tonight, Laurel. Regardless of what your uncle thinks, I do see you as a gem of great value. I've seen your hard work and your willing spirit. I am blessed and I will call you blessed. I made that promise to your father, and I make it to you."

"Thank you, Mac. We haven't been talking much lately. I thought you were upset with me."

"We'll have some private time soon. Good night, Laurel."

When they awoke at dawn, no sun was visible. Ominous clouds hid the sun, and there was little hope the day would be dry. Laurel pulled out a meager breakfast from the leftovers she'd kept. The fire was out, so Mac wouldn't get hot coffee. All of them realized they had to ride on as quickly as possible. The rain would be with them, hindering their progress before noon. About two hours into the morning, they arrived in the community of Fontaine, but they found no trading post or mercantile. They rested the animals for half an hour and then moved on in the pouring rain. The next community was Lorado. The weather was uncomfortable but not severe enough for them to seek shelter. This was the last stop on the road home, and Lorado was only eleven or twelve miles. Mac didn't tell Laurel the down side though...the distance between where they were and where they had to cross was the worst part of the Cache River bottoms. It was swampy, dangerous, and with almost no discernable path.

Mac stopped in the shelter of a grove of cypress trees, seeking shelter. Matthew and Laurel lead their horses near enough to hear. "If we were being smart, we would go back and try to find some shelter."

"Are you sure we could find a place to get out of this weather? The settlement looked awful small. I don't know any congregation there we might get help from."

"We have two choices. We could make camp here in the wet and mud, or we can continue at the slow pace and pray we can get to Lorado before dark. I figure with these clouds and rain, we have about six hours before we will have to stop for the night.

Laurel was already soaked from head to toe. She had no hat as she never had worn one, and she just hadn't thought about needing one. "I think we are as well off traveling and hope we can find shelter before nightfall. I'll not be any wetter. At least it's not freezing out here."

"Laurel Grace, you sure are a plucky girl. On ....let's go home. I can almost feel Shiloh, can't you?" So they rode on through the uncomfortable spring rain. In many places, they dismounted and led their mounts through low areas filled with water. By mid-afternoon, the three came to Village Creek. The usually small, lazy creek had turned into a swift moving, murky river, which they would have to ford. Mac and Matthew rode across, testing the bottom and the depth of the water. While the trip across was touch and go, both men felt it was passable for Laurel and their pack mules. They returned to the west side of the creek.

"Laurel, just keep your eyes on the other bank. Hold unto Sassy's reins. A soft bed and a hot bath are only about seven miles from that opposite bank. We will be home tonight." Mac's words were reassuring, and Laurel nodded to him. She was cold and miserable, but she told herself to be happy, at least for Mac. He was nearly home...even if she wasn't.

Matthew successfully led both the pack animals across the rolling stream. He tied them to a nearby sapling and dismounted. The animals would have to rest before they could continue across the rest of the swamp. Mac tried to lead Sassy Lady across the same path that Matt had used. Sassy was skittish, though. She had never been ridden in such terrible conditions. In the mountains, there were no wet marshy grounds to learn on, and Laurel had always pampered her little mare, rarely taking her out of the barn in bad weather. Sassy did not take well to storms. As they neared the eastern bank, a loud clap of thunder rolled across the swamp. Sassy reared, pulling her lead from Mac's hand. The little mare stumbled on the rocky, uneven bottom of the creek. Mac jumped from Midnight's back and tried to catch the lead which was swinging wildly as Sassy continued to rear and stumble, desperately trying to get up the slippery bank. Matt headed into the water, attempting to help, even as Laurel grasped Sassy's mane and bent forward, trying to calm her frantic mare. Just as Mac caught the lead, Sassy reared once again and sidled away from Mac. Laurel screamed and tried to secure her seat by holding Sassy's neck. Sassy wouldn't be calmed, for at her hoof was a cottonmouth, mostly submerged in the water, but whose snowy white mouth gaped wide and easy for all to see. Laurel fell. Mac took two fast steps toward Laurel as he slid his large knife from its sheath. The snake struck out at his attacker. Laurel screamed again, but not in fear this time. Mac slashed at the water, and took the head off the venomous snake, but not before the snake had found its target. The cottonmouth had landed a strike at Laurel's ankle, just at the top of her shoe. He picked Laurel up from the edge of the creek and carried her to safety on higher ground.

The saturated clothes encumbered her. "Laurel, you'll be all right. Just hang on to me." Mac yelled for Matthew, who had managed to secure and calm the frightened mare. "Matthew, help me. I've got to get Laurel down so I can look at that bite." A cottonmouth bite could be deadly, not always from the venom, but from infections that followed bites. He rushed to Mac's side.

"Here, give her to me." He sank to the muddy bank of the creek, rain streaming from the brim of his hat. "Mac, cut those pants off at the knee and get that shoe off. Good, now cut a gash just below the bite and let it bleed to get some of the venom out."

"Laurel, I am sorry to hurt you again. Just hold on to your Uncle Matthew. Matt, hold her." Mac grimaced as he cut into Laurel's ankle, trying to follow the direction as quickly as he could. He was grateful his friend had come to find him, and he was not facing this problem alone. Laurel screamed in pain as Mac cut into her flesh. Even in the few minutes since the snakebite, her foot had begun to swell, and the discoloration was growing around the fang mark. "Matthew, help me. I don't know what I can do to help her. What else can I do? Lord, help us, please. I can't lose her."

"Mac, there is little else you can do. Let me see to the wound. Hold her while I try to find a dry cloth to use for a bandage." Matt went through the pack on the mule to find Laurel's satchel. He found the length of lawn Laurel was sewing into a new nightdress. He ripped it into strips and bound the wound, hoping he had let it bleed long enough to expel part of the venom. He tied the gash tightly, attempting to prevent further loss of blood. They needed to head toward Greensboro and a doctor. "We are about three miles from Lorado, and Greensboro is less than five more across country. Get her to Greensboro and a doctor. After you pass Lorado, the roads will get better, not so muddy and water covered. The land's higher. Laurel is in shock, and she can't ride. Put her in front of you, cover her with one of these oilcloths, and ride as quick as you can. I'll follow. I'm taking your pack animals to old man Ellis, his homestead is just a mile or so back. Now go, I'm praying already."

"Pray hard, Matthew. I can't let her go now." Laurel had fainted during the time Mac was trying to tend her ankle. Laurel moaned in delirium. Mac mounted Midnight and pulled Laurel close to his chest. Matt handed him a section of oilcloth, and he pulled it over her head to protect her from the drenching rain. He pulled on the reins and rode, probably too fast for the safety of his horse, and he held onto one thought. "I won't fail her again. Lord, help me find help for Laurel." The moments passed like hours. Mac felt he was getting nowhere. In the downpour and dim light, it was impossible to identify familiar landmarks. Mac prayed he was still on the road home. Before two hours had passed, Laurel had a high fever. Mac could feel the intense heat through his wet shirt.

"Laurel, we are nearly home. I know you will be glad to get off this horse for a while. You've been brave and spunky during our journey. You've been the strongest helpmate." Mac knew Laurel hadn't heard anything he said, but he felt compelled to talk to her. "Have you read Proverbs, Laurel?" There are so many practical pieces of advice in that book. Remember, your Uncle Matthew quoted that one passage to us last night? We'll study that book together when we get home." Laurel groaned in the pain as Midnight ran on. Mac feared the worst. He'd promised to give Laurel a safe home and twice on this trip he had seen her close to death. The severe chills and ague that came from her fall in the frozen creek had frightened him, but now a bite from the cottonmouth threatened her life. He had failed to protect his life mate. He would not lose her now. He had no recourse but to turn her life over to God, so he prayed, not words--for he didn't know any words--by releasing his fear and guilt. Mac rode on.

At last, Mac saw a lantern flickering in the distance. He decided to leave the road and ride directly across the open field. He would ask for help. Laurel's fever was worse. He had to get the fever down because fever unchecked was as deadly as a snake bite. In what seemed an eternity, he rode into the yard of a double pen cabin. "Hello in there. Please help me."

A man dressed in buckskin opened the cabin door. Behind him were a small woman and two toddlers. "Hey to you. What's the problem, stranger?"

"My wife's been snake bit, and her fever is too high. Can we shelter with you for a while until I can get her fever down?"

"Surely can. Come on in. At least we'll put a roof over your head."

The buckskin clad man approached Midnight and reached up to take Laurel from Mac's arms. "You go and shelter your animal in the lean-to there and I'll get her in."

Before Mac could return to the cabin, the woman started peeling off the wet layers of Laurel's clothing. "I could use your help here. Take that wet shirt off her, and I'll get her shoe. She lost one somewhere and her stocking, too. Get those wet trousers off." Mac did all she asked. Laurel had not roused at all. She moaned and winched when they moved her, and cried out, lost in her pain and fever.

"Papa, where are you? Papa…"

"Here, cover her with this coverlet. She won't need a quilt until we can get that fever down. Let's get some water and try to wash down the fever."

"Papa, come and help me… hurts too much." Laurel continued to call out in her delirium. She called out names that Mac had heard only once before. "Robbie and Jimmy, stop it." She thrashed and struck out, but with less energy than in other nightmares. The woman returned with a bowl of rainwater and several strips of cloth.

"Mister, your lady needs that fever down quick. Wash her with this cool water. I'll help you. We'll just keep at it 'til we feel less heat. I'll get more cold water when we need it."

Mac began to wash Laurel with the cool water. He continued for what seemed like hours with the tiny lady on the opposite side of the home-made bed. Every few minutes, she would take the bowl and toss out the warm water and return with cool rainwater which was pouring off the roof of the porch. Mac continued to ply her forehead, neck and shoulders with the cool water, all the time whispering prayers for Laurel's fever to fall. The fire in the hearth was burning low, but Mac knew it was not yet 8:00 p.m. His hostess had not taken time to tend the fire nor cook supper for her family. She continued her gentle, quiet ministering to the sick stranger who lay in her bed. After some time, Laurel roused briefly.

"Could I have some water? I'm very thirsty."

Mac lifted her head from the pillow and gave her sips of water from the dipper. "I'm so hot. Take that blanket away. Stop hurting me, Jimmy. Don't tear at my blouse like that. Papa, make him stop hurting me." Laurel had slipped back into a feverish sleep, but Mac could feel that the fever had ebbed. He moved the lantern to the foot of the bed and removed the bandage from the wound. The red swollen ankle was twice its normal size. Mac could plainly see ugly red streaks moving out from the site of the bite. As he examined the wound, he saw there was only one puncture, not the two he had expected. The snake must have sunk one its fangs into her shoe. That was a good sign. Perhaps the amount of venom was too small to cause any permanent damage. He muttered, "Thank you, Lord" under his breath. Laurel slept on, and the agitated nightmare passed. She no longer fought the elements, the ugly memories, and him. She rested.

Mac walked to the family room where the buckskin clad man sat drinking coffee.

"Want a cup?"

"I'd be grateful, and I am more than grateful you were here to help. My name is Patrick MacLayne. Laurel is my wife. She was bitten by a cottonmouth around noon or so. I don't think she would have made it much longer had you not sheltered us and your wife had not helped me lower the fever. I am in your debt."

"No debt here. We're glad to help a brother in the faith when he needs it."

"How did you know I am a brother in the faith?"

"Not hard to figure when I saw how you prayed for your wife. By the way, I'm Russell Lamb. This is my wife, Shirley. She's always been a good help when healing's called for."

"You're a godsend."

"How ya'll come to be out in such a storm?"

"We've been travelling more than three weeks. Headed for Shiloh. The storm's so bad, I'm afraid I lost the way. Your lantern was a beacon to us. Again, thank you. Laurel is resting better now. I know you put her in your bed. Would you allow me to put a pallet on the floor of the loft? We needn't take your bed for the night."

"Nonsense, brother. We will bunk with our babies in the loft for the night. We have beds up there. Call us if you need anything during the night. Everyone will sleep sound tonight with the rain dancing on the roof."

Mac returned to Laurel's bedside. He sat next to the bed and took her nonresponsive hand in his. He tried to recall some scripture he'd tried to memorize, but his fatigue was overwhelming. He laid his head near Laurel's hand, and he slept.

When dawn came, Mac was still at the side of the bed with Laurel's hand in his. Laurel had slept through the night and while she still felt warm, she wasn't nearly as hot as she had been. Mac pushed himself off the floor, somewhat stiff and sore. He walked to the foot of the bed and gently pulled back the coverlet to look at the wound again. The ankle was still swollen and ugly; black, blue, and red streaks radiated out from the infected wound on her ivory skin. Laurel needed a doctor, but Mac could not go so far and leave her alone. Nor did he think carrying her so far on horseback would be to her welfare. He thought for some time but no answer came to him. He once again turned their fate over to the Lord and within a few minutes Mac sensed the answer, "My Grace is sufficient for you. Return your gratitude with faith. Give her to me." He didn't understand totally, but he did obey. "Lord, I give my wife to your care. Your will be done, not mine." Mac didn't know if he had lost his bride to the snake bite, or whether God would be merciful and heal her. He would just wait and pray, but in his resolve to turn everything over to God's care, he hoped with his whole being that Laurel would be spared. He didn't want to live without her. She had become too much a part of his dream. He needed her. He was not the rescuing hero taking care of the helpless orphan. Mac needed Laurel. The friendship that had begun to evolve had become the very core of his hopes for home and family. As he thought back over the events of the past few weeks, he realized every time he talked about his homestead, he referred to it as their place, and Laurel had never set a foot on the land. Laurel was the image of the life mate he pictured in front of the hearth in the cabin which did not yet exist. When he thought of family suppers, it was Laurel who sat at the opposite end of the table. As he planned the house, he always did so thinking of what she would like. When he thought about the future, it was always 'their' future. He didn't know how or when, but Laurel had infiltrated his world. He wanted her friendship, and he didn't want to lose her. He didn't love Laurel, not the kind of love he had felt for Marsha, but he liked her. Even more he liked the man he was when he was with her.

Mac shook his head, rousing himself from his thoughts. He pulled his hand through his hair and sighed. Surely, his plans he'd made when he'd promised Laurel's father to honor and respect his daughter had been fulfilled. A marriage based on a rock solid faith and friendship could work, and they would build a good life together. Mac smiled to himself. Matt Campbell didn't know everything. He knew God would intervene and bring Laurel back to health.

"Mac, are you here?" He walked toward the head of the bed. He placed his hand on her forehead. The fever had returned. "Mac, I'm so thirsty. Can I have a drink of water?"

"Yes, of course." He lifted her head again and let her drink her fill. "I'm relieved that you know me this morning. Are you in pain?"

"Burns...my leg and I am so hot. Please take away this blanket."

"I'm afraid your fever is rising again. Can you remember how you made that fever remedy we gave your father? Maybe I can find some for you."

"Just so hot, Mac ... the burning." Laurel again lost her connection with the world around her.

"Mrs. Lamb. Can I have more cool water? Laurel's burning with fever again."

"Let me bathe her for you. Mac, you've not slept much since you got here last night."

"No. I'll care for her, but thank you. Do you have any fever remedy? Laurel used to make something for her father, some kind of tree bark and honey. I think it was cherry bark."

"No, we got no cherry trees here abouts. I do have some honey and some herbs the doctor left when my little ones had an ague last month. I'll get her a cup."

"Thank you." He returned to wash Laurel's feverish body with cool water. He washed her legs and feet, careful to avoid the area where the bite was even more swollen and discolored. The red steaks moving outward from the puncture wound had grown more pronounced and thicker. Infection had set in. He continued to apply the wet cloths until Mrs. Lamb returned. He took the tonic and spooned it into Laurel's mouth. Shirley Lamb took the cloth from Mac and continued to cool Laurel's burning body. Within half an hour of drinking the tonic, Laurel's fever ebbed once more, and she slept again. Knowing Laurel would rest awhile since the tonic had worked so well, he left her side to speak with Russell. The red streaks gradually rising up Laurel's leg brought more fear than the fever. Infection grows quickly if left untended. What did Mac know about that kind of wound? He needed to get word to Matthew to bring a wagon so they could take Laurel to the doctor in Greensboro. Matthew would know the name his wife used to stem infection. "Russell, are you familiar with Shiloh community?"

"Sure, Mac. We go through there when we go to Greensboro to the mercantile or the blacksmith. Not a bad ride from here when the roads are dry."

"I know you are busy here at your homestead, but I need to get word to Laurel's uncle. He's the pastor of our church. If he could come get us with a wagon, I could get my wife to a doctor."

"I'd give you mine, except it's got a broke wheel. I was headed to the wheelwright until the rain set in yesterday. If you want to go find the doctor, we'll take care of your missus."

"I can't leave Laurel now. If she thought I deserted her... Anyway, if you can go and bring back help, I'll gladly pay you for your day's labor."

"I'd like to help you, but my milk cow is birthing her calf right now. My family needs this calf. We'll sell it when it's weaned. The cash will let me get new shoes and winter coats for my kids. We'll be able to get staples to restock our larder. It's pretty thin after the winter."

"I'll tend to your cow. I fear for her life."

"Course, I'll go."

"Wish I knew how to get the swelling down and stop the infection. What do ya'll use for infection? With kids, I know you have to have something."

"We all use yarrow in these parts. Don't you know about yarrow? We mix it with butter and make a salve, and we also brew teas from the root to help with sickness."

"Yarrow. Yes, that is what Ellie Campbell uses with her kids. Is there yarrow around here?"

"Oh, yeah. The stuff grows wild here by nearly every ditch in the county. I'll have my wife collect some for a poultice and to make a tea for your missus before I leave. Go on back and see if she's awake." Mac nodded his thanks and turned to walk the distance to the porch.

When he returned to Laurel's bedside, Laurel seemed to be sleeping, really resting. While she was still warm, she didn't display the high fever that had scared him when they first arrived. Mac lifted his eyes and let the fear go again. If he had kept to his resolve, he wouldn't have lived the last several hours in fear. "Thank you, Lord. Thank you for Laurel's life and please fortify my faith. You told me you would take care of us."

Mac returned to the barn where he spent the next few hours waiting for the Lambs' milk cow to birth her enormous calf. Russell had little to be concerned with. Mac's assistance to the cow during the process was emptying one bucket of water into an empty water trough. When he was sure the calf was healthy and the mother was well and caring for her newborn, Mac returned to the cabin. Russell had not yet returned from Shiloh.

He found that Shirley Lamb had made yarrow salve and used it with a piece of Laurel's chemise to make a poultice. She had tied it to the wound and Laurel had no trace of fever, and her steady breathing told Mac that she was resting. He tried to lie down next to sleeping wife, but just as he turned his put his head on the pillow next to hers, Laurel awoke.

"Mac?"

"Hello, Sleepy head. Did you decide to wake up?"

"I slept well. I didn't want to wake up. The dream was nice. I was safe with you holding me."

"Must've been a nice dream," Mac mused, as he stifled a yawn.

"I need some water, and I am really warm. Please take this quilt off."'

"How immodest of you, wife, to flaunt yourself without your clothes, and you want me to remove the only cover you have?" Laurel was bare under the coverlet. Of course, Mac was teasing her.

"Mac, couldn't you have left me some modesty?"

"Your life was more important than your modesty, my dear. Besides, from what I saw there was nothing to hide. I don't see why you would be the least bit self-conscious. You are beautiful, Laurel. You'll know it someday."

"Mac, can we go to Shiloh. I am so tired of the road."

"We need another day to make sure you are strong enough to ride that far. I'm thinking we have less than five miles to reach your Uncle Matthew's place."

"Isn't he with us?"

"We got separated when I left him behind with the jacks and Sassy. I think he took them to a friend to get them out of the storm. I am sure he's home by now."

"I'm sorry. I really ruined your homecoming."

"Laurel, you didn't cause the delay. There was an accident, and we are handling it."

"Well, is there anything left of my clothes? I can't go to meet my relatives and your friends, riding on Midnight in the fashion of Lady Godiva."

"I think that would make a very memorable entrance for the new school marm. I know my friends wouldn't stop talking about it for years." They laughed. The easy banter was pleasant, and the problems they'd had earlier seemed far away at that moment.

"Mac, I'm tired. Can we go back to bed?"

"You are surely a brazen hussy...inviting a man you've know only three weeks to your bed."

"Oh, you. Read me some scripture, and let's call it a night. Tomorrow, I'm taking you home."

18

*And all things, whatsoever ye shall ask in prayer, believing, ye
shall receive.*

KJV c1850, Matthew 21:22.

As the sun rose on that April morning, Mac and Laurel said a
heartfelt thank you and goodbye to the Lamb family. Russell
had returned with the Campbell wagon in the middle of the
night. "Russell, you were a life saver for us. I wish I had some way to repay your kindness. I'd have lost Laurel if you hadn't offered us shelter.
Shirley, you have the healing gift. God bless ya'll."

"Ain't nothing to repay. I know sometime ya'll do the same for another traveler. I hope the last leg of this journey will be easier. Ms. Laurel, I
know you'll like our part of the state. It'll make you a good home."

Laurel nodded and then she hugged Shirley Lamb, almost as a re-
flex. "Shirley, you are an angel. Your medicine has made it possible for
us to finish our trip today. I'm glad we aren't so far apart. We'll be able
to visit from time to time."

Mac flapped the reins on Midnight's haunches as they drove out of
the yard. He looked over at Laurel in the concocted outfit of remaining

clothes he and Shirley Lamb made. She had stitched another leg to the torn side of Laurel's dungarees, not the same color as the older pants, but it did provide some protection and modesty for Laurel as they rode toward Shiloh. She put Mac's jacket on over her torn shirt. Accept for being too warm on the beautiful spring day, her new apparel was acceptable. She looked like a homeless waif, but the end of the trip was in sight.

Mac left his last three dollars on the pillow. Russell had told him of the struggle to get through until harvest time. Without doubt, their generosity in sharing their food would leave small stomachs growling at times. He wished he'd had more of his traveling money left to share, but he'd not planned for the expense of bringing Laurel back across the state. Mac smiled as he thought to himself that he was totally broke at that moment and didn't know when he had been more content. He was home.

The ride to Matthew Campbell's homestead, less than two short miles from his own land, passed quickly. The road was clear, and the sunshine had dried much of the mud. With every mile, Mac's mind went back continually to one thought. Home. The restlessness that had sent him to Washington County was missing. He began to sing, "God is on his throne and all is well in the universe." For the last mile of the trip, he even urged Midnight into quicker gait. He couldn't contain his enthusiasm. He pointed out all the local landmarks, told Laurel names of the neighbors, commented on the seasonal changes around him, praised the progress he saw in planting and the greening of the ridge. He rambled on as they rode the last few miles that morning, relaxed and yet excited. A broad smile shouted his joy to be home.

"Look, Laurel, there is Matt's house. We are finally home. Thank the Lord."

━ ⁓

Laurel smiled at his comment, but she found herself an alien at Shiloh. This wasn't her home. She saw no mountain peaks, nor valleys surrounded by lush green hill sides. Although Crowley's Ridge was visible, Lonnie

Thomison had been right. Compared to her home, Crowley's Ridge was one puny little rise in the delta landscape. She did see a few flowering trees, mostly redbuds and dogwoods blooming here and there, but she didn't see one apple blossom or peach tree. She wondered if her Uncle Matthew had remembered to care for her orchard cuttings after they'd become separated. Just as quickly, she realized how selfish she felt. She hadn't commented on Mac's joy of returning nor did she know if her uncle had found refuge from the storm or been able to reach his home safely. She sighed.

"Are you all right? Are you too tired?"

"Not overly so. I was just hoping Uncle Matthew had made it home safely."

"I am so glad I brought you home, wife. I hope in a day or so you will feel like going out to the homestead. I want to show you our valley and the creek and stands of so many different trees. I know you'll love our home. The sooner you choose a home site, the sooner I can build you a house. The sooner I can build you a house, the sooner you can make us a home."

"I am grateful you're home, Mac. I can see how happy you are. Except for being tired of sitting on this wagon seat, I really believe the worst of my encounter with the cottonmouth is past us. I guess I need to be thankful he had a bad aim."

"I'll get you to your uncle's and let you rest a spell. I'm betting your Aunt Ellie will be happy to offer us lodging for a couple of nights."

"Where exactly do you plan to live until you can build us a cabin? We can't stay with Uncle Matthew long term. He already has a houseful."

"The Lord will provide, wife. Don't worry about it." They rode into the yard, and Mac jumped down to the ground. "Hey, Matthew. Ya'll home? Thank ya, Lord, I am home!"

His joy was so obvious that Laurel again felt selfish that she did not share his joy. She thought of the story Mac had told Lonnie Thomison about the children of Israel who had spent forty years crossing the desert, but still they were not able to claim the Promised Land. They had survived the trek across the rugged mountains and foothills of Arkansas, and her husband had reached home, but she hadn't conquered her personal enemies, so she wasn't able to claim the promise. She'd like to think she'd find a home, if only she knew where that was supposed to be.

"Thank the Lord, you've made it back. Laurel Grace, are you all right?"

"I've been well taken care of. We found help with a family near Lorado. I'm so happy to see you safe at home, Uncle Matthew."

Matthew walked over and helped Laurel from the wagon seat. He carried her to his porch.

"Ellie, come see what just stumbled into our yard."

Matthew Campbell's wife was a pretty woman, even at the age of 45. Her blonde hair was pulled up into a loose coil and her clothes were well-fit homespun. She wore a smile of welcome that reached to the depths of her eyes. "Welcome home, Laurel Grace and Mac. I can't believe it's you, niece. I wouldn't a known you, after all these years...How long has it been? Twelve years or more."

"I am happy to see you, Aunt Ellie."

"Niece, welcome to your new home. I know you'll like being part of the Shiloh family. On Sunday, I'll be proud to introduce our school marm. Come on in and let me get you into a chair."

"Laurel Grace, you'll need to prop up that foot for a spell."

"Where are your children, Aunt Ellie?"

"Well, two of them have places of their own, but the younger ones are out and about. They'll be home for supper. Goodness, you need some different clothes. Should I have Mac bring in your satchel?"

"Unless Uncle Matthew has brought our pack animals, I'm afraid I don't have any other clothes."

"Well, Mac, Laurel Grace, to tell you the truth, I headed home as fast as I could. I wanted to be here when Mac got back. I was hoping for the best but planning for the worst. You're a miracle, Laurel Grace. I guess I'll have to ask forgiveness on giving up hope. I was afraid the Lord was taking you home, niece. At least, Ellie sent the wagon with that Lamb fellow to bring ya back."

"I still have a bit of life yet, but I appreciate you wanted to be here to take care of Mac had he returned alone."

"I didn't totally forsake you, Laurel. I was just in the barn, caring for your orchard. I knew you'd never forgive me if I let those twigs dry out."

Laurel and Mac laughed at the determined look on her uncle's face.

"Matthew, that was the only thing Laurel asked about since she awoke. She wanted to know if we'd taken care of those silly sticks. Well, she did ask if she had any clothes to wear once."

"Mac! My aunt Ellie is a lady."

"Yes, one who is well-acquainted with how men often speak without thinking what they're saying." Laughter followed and marked the beginning of a wonderful evening. Talking, teasing, eating, and enjoying the company of people who cared about her made Laurel forget how tired she was. Laurel had experienced such an evening like this only one other time in her adult life, that being the night they had boarded with the eighty-year-old sweethearts in the middle of the Ozarks, but this night was somehow more comfortable. Except for an occasional twinge and stinging sensation at her ankle, Laurel reveled in the companionship. She felt more a sense of family than she had known in a long time. Again, she felt that others were treating her as an adult, as one of them. Before the end of the evening, Matthew Campbell picked up his guitar and together they sang hymns. Laurel remembered how as a little girl she'd loved to hear her uncle sing at family gatherings. When they'd finished, Mac asked Matt for a Bible, and he read a Psalm of thanksgiving.

Then he prayed, "Father, I believe I have lived this Psalm. I was ready to give up the dream you gave me until I was willing to obey. Thanks to a friend and a good woman, Lord, my dream is alive again. Thank you for bringing us home, and I am grateful Laurel is healing. Keep us, Lord, as we continue to build our earthly home here at Shiloh. Amen."

"And Amen! Brother Mac, maybe you should consider the call."

"No. I'll leave that to you and your boy John. I've got my hands full now. I got a house to build."

"You men can talk later. Can't ya see Laurel Grace is nearly exhausted. You do recollect the girl had a serious injury just three days ago."

"Forgive me, Laurel. I did forget for a moment. It's just so fine being back home with my family."

"It's is good to see you happy, Mac. Aunt Ellie, could I have some warm water. I need to get some of this dirt off before bed."

"Of course, come back here to our room. We'll bunk in with our youg'uns tonight. I'm sure that climbing to the loft wouldn't be an easy task for you."

Laurel started to object, but her uncle Matthew walked between her and her aunt. He took his wife in his arms and pulled her close. He kissed her, not a peck on the cheek, but a deep loving kiss that spoke soundly of the love he carried for his wife of nearly thirty years. "Excuse the interruption niece. I make it a rule never to end a day without my goodnight kiss. I'll go up and get us a place ready for the night. Come on, John and Mary. It's been a long day. Let's get some rest."

Laurel hugged her uncle's neck and said good night.

"Sweet dreams, Laurel Grace. I am truly glad to have ya'll here. We are all thanking the Lord ya'll made it safe."

Ellie took Laurel by the arm and led her to small space curtained off from the cabin's main room. The room served as the bedroom she'd shared with Matt. Ellie brought her a large basin of very warm water and some lavender-scented soap. She hugged her niece good night and turned to leave. Just as she was about to go through the curtain, she stopped and spoke. "Laurel Grace, Mac is a good man. He is favored in these parts by lots of people. He's always doing good for someone or the other, but I think the best thing he's done is bring you to Shiloh. When Matt got home day before yesterday, he was sad. He told me how his brother died and how you'd suffered from the long trip and the in-jury. He was afraid you had been taken by the snakebite. Today when he carried you to the porch, the light came back to his eyes. He will not mourn so deep for your pa, now that he has you here to look after. Bless you, Laurel Grace and Mac. I'll pray you'll always be happy with your love for each other." She handed Laurel a lace-trimmed nightdress and went to the main room, pulling the curtain behind her.

Laurel paused before she began her bath. Uncle Matt had obvi-ously not told her aunt about the arranged marriage. She was a wom-an so loved that she had assumed that Mac felt the same for his wife.

Laurel thought ...*how lucky to have a husband who would love me like my aunt is loved.* Momentarily, she shook her head and pushed the low feeling away. She would not let the circumstances of her marriage spoil the lovely evening she had enjoyed. She returned to her bath.

Mac gave Laurel several minutes to finish. When he did enter the room, he found his wife on her knees, beside the bed. She was dressed in Ellie's lace-trimmed nightdress. Laurel's tawny hair cascaded to her waist in an array of curls. Her words were inaudible. Mac stood and watched, storing the precious sight with other special moments he'd observed in the short time they'd had been together. He remembered that first tongue lashing Laurel had delivered in the orchard in Washington County and the grief-stricken girl he'd held all the night that her father had died. Her generous gift to Lonnie's sister and the terrible ride through the storm after she was bitten by the cottonmouth also returned in startling clarity. So many memorable things had already happened between them. Had he not been on the receiving end of her sharp wit and tongue, he would have believed an angel knelt here before him.

"Amen."

"Laurel, you are lovely tonight. I've been standing here watching. I'm grateful you're better. I was afraid I'd never get you home." He walked to her, and for once, she didn't move back from his approach. "This has been one of the best days of my life, wife, sharing good times with my best friends...both of them. Thank you."

"I've enjoyed this special time too. It's the first time in my life I felt accepted among my family, as an adult. I love being a part of family life again. That wasn't supposed to happen to the spinster of Hawthorn."

"Laurel, we left that person behind. I told you before we came here that you could only see yourself through my eyes, until you learned to see your own value. Look at yourself now, the way that I see you. Do you see the lovely woman standing here before me? Can you see how like a jewel of great value you are?" Mac offered his hand to her, and she took it. She looked at him and saw her value reflected in his eyes. Mac kissed her hand tenderly and then her palm. He pulled her to him and wrapped her in a strong embrace. "Wife, I think it's time we started courtin' again."

Mac raised her lips to meet his. They shared the first real kiss of their marriage. Laurel didn't pull away. Mac picked her up and laid her gently on the left side of the bed. He sat next to her and bent to give her a second kiss, a long, lingering, gentle kiss. Laurel moved her hand to back of Mac's head, returning the kiss. Abruptly, Mac stood and walked to the curtains. "I've got to go out and check on Midnight before I can sleep. He had a long, hard haul today and he's not used to pulling a wagon. I should have already tended to him. Goodnight, Laurel. Thank you for an almost perfect day."

Laurel had so enjoyed the unexpected embrace of her husband, but then his abrupt departure left her confused and hurt. What had she done to make him run away? Then the anger surfaced. She had done nothing to deserve his rejection. Why did he thank her for a nearly perfect day? What had she done to keep his day from being perfect? She grabbed the coverlet, pulled it over her shoulder, nestled her head deeply into the feather pillow, and she prepared to sleep. She didn't care what had made Mac leave her again. It is his problem, not hers. At least, those were the last thoughts that crossed her mind. Just as she was about to drift into sleep, a sharp pain ran up the side of her leg. She rubbed her ankle just above the bandage, and the pain subsided again. Laurel nestled herself once more on the left side of the bed, and fell asleep.

— ~

Mac had rushed from the room, putting some distance between himself and Laurel. He had promises to keep, and he doubted his will power was strong enough to reject the temptation he felt. Laurel was his wife, worthy of all the respect he could ever give her. He would not treat her as he had treated other women from his past. He argued with himself that his marriage sanctified before a minister of his faith had given him any marital right he wanted, but in his heart, he knew that fulfilling his needs at the expense of his innocent wife was wrong. He would not return to using people. If only he had met her before he'd given his heart to Marsha Golden so many years ago. He tried to shake the thoughts away, but a wry smile crept onto his face. He knew that if he had met Laurel when he was the selfish, wild man of his youth, he'd never had given her a second look. Audibly, he moaned and then cried out, "Lord, I don't know what you want me to do. Did I sin in this marriage and then openly declare it had been your will?" No one was in the empty barn to hear his anguish. "So be it. I'll be patient and wait. Forgive my doubt."

An hour or so later, Mac returned to the bedroom where Laurel slept. A walk in the gentle, warm spring night had provided him a reprieve from his self-condemning thoughts. He quietly lifted the coverlet and lay beside Laurel on the right side of their borrowed bed, but he made a deliberate effort not to touch her. He had held her several nights while she was sick, or when they needed warmth, or when she grieved. Never had he held her just because she was his wife, and he wanted to be close to her. Yet tonight, when he had held her and kissed her for the first time, he had not wanted the embrace to end. He would need to be more distant to her if he were keep his vows. Mac slept fitfully, when he slept at all.

Midway through the night, Mac sat bolt upright in the bed. Laurel was screaming the same fearful cry he'd heard several nights on the trail. He reached over to comfort her and found her hot to the touch. She had been awakened by a nightmare and once again, her fever had returned. She pushed at him and continued to toss and fight against her imaginary attackers. Mac rose from the bed and went to her side to hold her and try to awaken her so the terror would go away. His touch only brought another scream, even stronger than the first. "Laurel, wake up. You're having a nightmare again. Sh-h-h. Laurel, you are safe here."

Within seconds, both Matthew and Ellie came from the loft. Ellie lit the lantern on the bureau. Mac was still not able to arouse his wife. He knew the fever delirium had returned. "Matthew, please help me calm her. I am afraid the fever has returned."

Matthew Campbell moved to take his niece from Mac. "Mac, she's burnin' up. This is a high fever. Did she complain of feeling bad before ya'll went to bed?"

"She seemed fine when I went out to tend to Midnight. When I got back, she was sleeping. I know she was tired, but I thought she beat that snakebite."

Matthew sat next to Laurel and pulled her against his shoulder as he had done that night at the hotel in Powhatan. Laurel continued to fight and push him away. He remembered the soothing came when he sang to her, so he began to sing very softly. "Rock of Ages, clef for me. Let me hide myself in thee." After a few minutes, Laurel began to relax and her crying stopped.

"Matt, why does she fight me so? When I try to calm her, just as you are doing, she screams and pulls away."

"I'm afraid I got no answer for you, brother. I'm just glad she is calm again."

"Matthew Campbell, don't you remember how Leah used to sing hymns as lullabies to Laurel Grace? She is comforted because the singing helps her feel close to her mother again... Men!"

"What's brought back the fever?" Mac unwrapped the bandage from around Laurel's wound. The wounds from both the snake bite and the cut where he had allowed the blood to flow were both swollen and red again. While the yarrow salve had begun the healing process, the potency of the salve had worn off, and the infection had grown again. Mac turned a looked at Ellie. "Ellie, do you know where yarrow grows nearby?"

"Course, everyone in these parts keeps yarrow at hand. I have dried leaves in the larder. I can make up a salve for the ankle. Mac, come brew a cup of yarrow tea to help take down that fever. Matt, just keep her quiet. I don't know why, but she seems to like your singing."

When Ellie and Mac returned to the little bedroom, Laurel was asleep in her uncle's arms again. She was not fighting, screaming, or tossing, but the sleep was not a natural rest that could help her heal. Mac had seen the delirium sleep twice before. The pall on her skin was frightening. He spooned several ounces of the healing tea into Laurel's mouth. Ellie discarded the old dressing and packed the wound with salve and wound a clean cloth around the swollen ankle. Mac had seen it work miracles before, and he prayed he would again see Laurel respond to the God-given plant.

"I'll take her again, Matt. Sorry we woke ya'll and I'm sure your kids too. Thank you for being such a good friend."

"No thanks needed. Family helps family. We'll relieve you in a couple of hours. Try to rest some. Just call if you need us."

Mac held Laurel throughout the night. When the Campbell's awoke and came down from the loft to see about Laurel, they found Mac and Laurel propped in the bed, just as they had left them the night before. Laurel's fever had not broken, nor was she conscious. Mac had spent the night rocking her, bathing her in cool water, and praying that his wife's life would be spared.

"Mac, it's been too long. We need a doctor. Dr. Gibson is over in Greensboro. It's about five miles by the road, but only about three and a half across country. Do you want to go bring him back?"

"I can't leave her, Matt. Will you ride Midnight and try to get help before..." Mac could not finish his sentence. He could not bring himself to voice his dreaded fear. Ellie approached him and pulled back the coverlet.

"Mac, I'll bathe Laurel Grace with cool water again and put on a clean dressing. You and Matthew go get that horse ready."

"Thanks Ellie, but that is my job. I promised her father I'd get her safely here and build her a secure home. I'll watch over her."

Matthew and Ellie went into the main room of their cabin and sat at the table. Matt took Ellie's hand. Together they prayed for Laurel's return to health. "Ellie, darling, go take Mac some coffee and maybe spoon some broth down Laurel's throat. I'm riding to Greensboro, and I'll be home as soon as I can." Matthew took the wife of his heart and kissed her goodbye. "I love you, Ellie Campbell." Then he was gone.

Time seemed to have stopped in the Campbell household. The two children came down from the loft, subdued and somber. Mac refused to leave Laurel's side, and Ellie continued her daily routine, quietly and ably. Mac could have sworn that days passed before Matt returned with

Dr. Gibson. Of course, the few hours seemed so much longer, but they were blessed to have a doctor so near. Outside Greensboro, the next doctor that Matthew knew of lived in Jacksonport or across the Cache River bottoms in Black Rock. A trip to either of those places would have taken days, not hours.

"Matthew, take this scarecrow of a man out of here. I need to examinee this young woman." He asked, but his efforts to get Mac out of the room failed as had Ellie's attempts to feed him earlier. Mac stayed.

"Doctor Gibson, please help her. I'll do whatever need be to get her well again. Just don't let her die, please." The doctor laid his palm on Laurel's brow. The fever was still dangerously high. He checked her pulse and breathing with his wand-shaped stethoscope. He was encouraged by a strong heartbeat and steady breathing. He cut the bandage away from the injured ankle. He need look no further. The infection around the two open wounds had spread. Dr. Gibson feared the infection would lead to blood poisoning within the day if he could not stem its spread. He worked quickly to clean the wound again, and he took a small scalpel and removed small areas of dead tissue, fearing it would become gangrene if left attached. Laurel moaned and tossed when he excised a bit of the tissue. He knew that flesh was still alive. He rewrapped the wound with an ample dose of salve. He covered Laurel once again. All this time, Mac had not left the place he had taken on the other side of the bed.

"What coulda happened, Doc? Yesterday she seemed much better."

"MacLayne, this young woman is very ill. Ya'll have done as much for her as anyone else could have done out there in the swamp where this happened. I think that the venom was below the fatal level, but infection from the swamp is a hard thing to prevent without the proper care. That infection has grown by some degree. If we can stem the growth of the infection, I believe she will recover in a few weeks. Our biggest threat now is blood poisoning."

"What can I do to help her?"

"You are doin' it already. Keep her warm, but keep the fever down. Keep that wound clean. Let Ellie put hot compresses on that wound every two hours. MacLayne, you eat something and get some rest. I'll have two patients instead of one."

"I'll be okay if she is."

"Thanks, Ed. I'll get your horse."

"Matthew, I'll come back tomorrow to check those veins near the cut. That is where the most infection seems to be. Tell Mac not to worry. His wife seems to be strong. You don't think she's in the family way, do you? Fever that high can harm a baby in the womb."

"I don't think there is a child. I'll ask Mac later. We'll see you tomorrow."

Mac did not seem much relieved by the doctor's visit. Words like infection and blood poisoning were fearful terms to hear from a doctor. He continued to sit by Laurel's side, refusing to release her hand. She had to know he was there with her. Ellie came in with the heated cloths ordered by the doctor. When she applied the heat, Laurel cried out in pain.

"Ellie, don't hurt her, please. I have caused her to suffer too much already. Ever since we met, I have brought trouble."

"Mac, the doctor is trying to prevent the infection from turning into blood poisoning. Laurel Grace won't remember any of this when she wakes up."

"Mac, let Ellie tend to Laurel Grace this afternoon. There's nothing you can do here. Let's just ride over to Lorado and bring back Laurel's things. That will make her feel better, just having her family things around her."

"No, Matthew. I can't go. I would appreciate your going, if you want to, but I won't go away from her 'til I know she'll be all right." That was the way it would be. Mac refused to leave her, and at the end of a long, strained day, Laurel awoke. The doctor's knowledge, the salve, the hot compresses, and continual cleaning had helped Laurel overcome the fever, but Mac knew Laurel had been spared through prayer and Christian love. Once the word had spread, members of Shiloh church had begun a prayer vigil, all asking blessings on Mac and Laurel. That had been the best treatment for Laurel's injury.

"Mac, I am very thirsty. Please give me some water."

"Yes, Laurel, yes. Praise the Lord. Ellie, she wants water." At that moment, Mac knew his wife would live.

— ⁓

Sometime well after dark, Matthew Campbell returned with the two pack mules in tow. As he rode into the yard, he saw his wife, Mac and Laurel sitting on the porch. The evening was warm, and the family had come out to get a breath of fresh air while they waited for Matt to return for supper. Matt smiled to see Laurel seated in his rocking chair. He called out across the lot, "Ellie, I'm back. Come out here and show me how glad you are to see me, woman."

With a mischievous smile, Ellie walked down from the porch and walked to the corral where her husband had tied the mules. He pulled her into his arms and kissed her. "Will you behave yourself, Matthew Campbell? Is that any way for a man of the cloth to act in public?"

"This ain't public. It's my front yard and if I want to kiss my wife, I'll do it. I'd do the same thing on a Sunday morning on the church porch, if I have a hankering to do so. I love you, woman. The world just needs to know it."

Laurel watched from her chair where she sat covered with a small blanket. She'd only been up about an hour, but she was weak from her bout with fever. She felt good, being up and outside, but she knew she couldn't stay up long. She was pleased to be up when her uncle returned. Again, he seemed so much like her papa, and the intimate scene between him and his wife brought back powerful memories of her own parents. They too had shared a passionate love for each other, and many times, Laurel had witnessed intimate embraces between them. Part of her fondest memories of her parents had provided the foundation for the dreams she'd held in her youth. Those dreams had been discarded in the light of reality, but the memories were precious all the same. Laurel knew she envied her aunt the love she shared with her Uncle Matthew.

"Laurel Grace, all your things are on those mules. Here is your satchel, but your husband can go out and unload the rest of that stuff. We'll find a place to store it until he finds you a place to board while he builds a house."

"How fine...a change of clean clothes and my hairbrush." Laurel started to pick up the satchel that Matt had set at her feet. Her lack of strength would not let her lift it. "Mac, I'm afraid I'm going need some help. Will you take my things in, and I will unpack a..."

"No, I think you need to return to bed. I let you get sick the second time, because I didn't make you rest enough." He picked her and then her satchel. He carried both to the back room.

"I wanted to eat supper with everyone tonight. I'd enjoy the adult company again."

"Not tonight. We'll have lots of those times. We have the rest of our lives to enjoy our family. I don't intend for you to get sick again. We have orchards to plant, a garden to till, and a cabin to raise. You have to get well."

"I'm more tired than I thought."

"Here, lie down and I'll read to you awhile if you like."

"Actually, I'd like to eat first. Since the fever's gone, I've gotten hungry."

"All right. I think it's a good idea." Before he left the room, he turned and sat on the bed. He reached to take Laurel in his arms. She allowed him to embrace her. "I am thankful you're better, Laurel. When you got sick, this second time, I felt I'd really let you down."

"You weren't to blame. Infections are common with serious wounds. Anyway, I am fine now. I expect to be up and back to normal in a day or so."

"I'd love to be able to take you to our homestead tomorrow. I want to show you the creek, and the meadow that edges next to the ridge. We can walk our land and you can show me where you want to plant your cuttings. I'll break the garden so you can plant in plenty of time to harvest our winter food. We should be able to get our cabin up within a couple of months. All our friends and family will help. I wish I could make it all happen overnight."

"Nice to see you excited about your plans, Mac, but I think I said I am hungry."

"Oh, yeah. I think I remember something like that. Come to think of it, I am hungry to." He rose, took Laurel's face between his hands and kissed her gently. Laurel didn't pull away from him, but neither did she respond.

"Mac, supper, please."

"I'll bring you supper, Laurel. You rest."

As Mac turned his back to leave, Laurel sighed. She dreaded spending time with Mac again. She was so confused by his behavior that she didn't know how to react anymore...the easiest way would be to avoid any more private time. Her request for food had been a ploy to get Mac to leave her for a while, but she found that she was somewhat hungry. Once she started the food, she found that she was very hungry, and she ate every morsel he brought her.

Yet, Mac found he had little appetite for the hearty meal Ellie had put on the table. He glanced over his shoulder several times since he came in to supper. He picked at the food on his plate and spent most of his time watching the Campbell family at supper. He listened to them sharing the day's activities, a few items of local gossip that always came to the preacher's attention, and even a silly joke shared by Mary. He observed how casually Matt stroked Ellie's arm as she sat next to him and bent over to whisper in her ear a time or two. Once when she had gotten up to retrieve more biscuits for the meal, Matt swatted her behind as she came near his chair. The children were comfortably at home with their parents in the cordial, peaceful atmosphere. The picture he was witnessing was everything he wanted in his home. Unfortunately, he didn't have a clue how to get from where he was to the place he longed to be. It seemed the more he did to win Laurel's acceptance, the more problems he created. In his mind, he was pleading, *Lord, help me...I feel the fool!*

When they finished, Mac asked Ellie to let him help her clean up from the meal. "No need for that here. That is one of the chores the kids take care of for me. They do a right nice job with the dishes. Just go sit a spell, or go out and help Matthew with the night chores. You've got livestock that needs tending and a waiting bride."

"Thanks for the nice meal, Ellie. After three weeks of trail food, you prepared us a feast."

"Stop flirtin' with my wife, brother Let's go get our chores done." The two friends left the cabin to tend to the stock in the barn. The feeding and milking were quicky finished between the two of them. "You're really quiet tonight, Mac, and you didn't eat a quarter of what you normally put away. You can quit worrying now. I am sure Laurel is on the mend."

"It's not that, Matt. I guess I just have a lot of questions, too much remorse, and even some shame I am trying to justify and...well... I am jealous of you. If you weren't the best friend I ever had, I think I could almost despise you. Brother, you got everything I want."

"I know I have been blessed, but I ain't got a thing that's you can't have. You just have to reach out and take it, Mac."

"That's an easy thing for you to say, but not so easy for me to do."

"Tell me about the remorse you're carrying around, Mac."

"I shouldn't have married Laurel like I did. I've put her in harm's way more than once, and I am sure she isn't happy. I thought, I was doing good. Her papa was distressed because she'd be alone and not able to care of herself. I told myself God meant for us to be, but now? Oh well, I went a'courtin' and got me a pretty good deal in the process!" Mac's laugh was dry and scornful.

"Do you love her at all, Mac?"

"I respect her. Sometimes we have entertaining conversations. We like a lot of the same things. She is an understanding companion, but being with her is like being on a see-saw. For a day or two we are up, and I think finally we are going to make it. The next day, I put my foot in my mouth or what's worse, I do something to hurt her or make her angry, and I don't even understand what I did. I don't know how to get passed her defenses."

"Do you think you can ever love her, Mac?"

"I told you I'd never give my heart away again. No woman will ever control me again the way Marsha did. Laurel and I can grow a strong friendship and with our mutual faith, surely we can build a good life. We agreed to that before we spoke the vows together."

"Well, how's that working for you, Brother?"

Mac was so frustrated with Matthew's words, he was tempted to punch him, but he knew Matt had the courage to be a real friend and speak the truth to him. "You know how it's working. It's not."

"So, try a different tack."

"And just what might that different tack be?"

"We'll get to that. You said you are feeling ashamed. You know better than that, Mac. You are strong in your faith...you have been since you let the Lord have your past. There is no room for shame with grace."

"That is exactly where the shame is...with Grace, Laurel Grace. She has been brave and has worked as hard as any man ever since I've known her. She thinks that I've intruded into her life. I know she agreed to my proposal to let her father die in peace. She told me she had all the dreams that girls have about marriage. Laurel didn't have much of that dream. I never thought about her side of all this. Now we have made vows that are eternal."

"Laurel Grace is a good woman, Mac. She's no China doll you put on a shelf and admire. She wouldn't have agreed to marry you if she hadn't found qualities that she liked. You said your marriage had been directed by the Almighty. Laurel said almost the exact same words to me while we were walking down by Black River the day I meet you in Powhatan. Mac, if you want a home and a family, you are going to have to build a different kind of relationship with Laurel Grace. Being friends don't make babies."

"I've tried to start courting Laurel. When we are getting along, I think we are becoming closer and then something happens, and we are strangers all over again. Like, I kissed her before she got so sick the day we got here, and...well...I think she like it. Anyway, I kissed her again tonight before I brought her supper. She may as well been a statue for the response I got. I don't even know why she is upset with me now."

"At times you find her attractive, don't you?"

"Of course, I do. Matthew, you got eyes. When Laurel wants to, she can look really nice, very feminine, and quite comely. Of course, she hasn't had much opportunity, crossing that God forsaken swamp and then getting snake bit. Only clothes she has with her are those torn dungarees, a ripped shirt, and one nice calico dress she made on our way across the state."

"Nice dodge, brother. Have you wanted her?"

"Blasted, Matt. I promised Laurel and her father that I would protect her sanctity until I earned the right to be her husband. And now, I'm not sure I'll ever want to take her to me. I gave up carnal relationships when I repented over my old life. I have had too many encounters like that, all lust and no love. I don't want to dishonor Laurel by treating her like a prostitute. Watching you with Ellie certainly makes a stark contrast. You're a lucky man." Mac turned his back to his friend and pastor. He started to walk to the door. "Matthew, do you think a physical union without love is a sin?"

"Tarnation!!! Mac, you always ask me the hardest questions to answer. I'll have to pray on that one. And no, Mac, I am not lucky. I am blessed, and I believe God intends to bless you too."

"Well, we've been gone a while. I'd best go back and check on Laurel. Thanks for listening."

Matt clapped Mac on his shoulder and prayed with him. "Lord, just show us the way and we'll follow. Bless my brother, Mac. Give him patience to see and build the blessing you have for him."

Mac walked back to the cabin, ready to face Laurel. He didn't know what to expect. Of course, that was not new. He told himself that they would just start over...honest, open talk aimed at getting to know each other, no problem solving, no planning for the future, no explaining the past.

"Laurel, are you awake still?"

Only one candle lit the backroom where Laurel lay. She was dressed in the lacy, feminine nightdress Ellie had loaned her the previous night. Laurel had taken advantage of having her hairbrush again and her curls bounced across her shoulders and down her back. She sat with her back against the headboard, and she held her Bible in her lap. She was as comely as any woman he'd ever seen. He realized he was not looking at her physical beauty though. He saw so many beautiful things he'd learned about her in the month since they'd met. Her saw her love of the Lord, her generosity, her charity, her kindness, her industry, her modesty, and her loneliness. He remembered the day they'd spoken their vows, and he heard in his mind the words Laurel had spoken to Lonnie Thomison the day they parted in Powhatan. Laurel had said that every girl deserved to feel beautiful on her wedding day. Mac knew Laurel had not felt beautiful. Shame reared its ugly head briefly. Mac consciously pushed it aside and returned to the vision before him. He sat next to Laurel on the bed and bent to kiss her goodnight.

"I'm not asleep."

"Good. We can spend some time together tonight then."

"Mac, I am too tired for small talk tonight."

"I promise. We have several serious things we need to work out. Of course, we also have no privacy to talk about all those serious things. Do you realize how long it's been since we've had any time alone?"

"Travel is difficult."

"Tomorrow, I have to find us a place to stay while I build our cabin. You've got to regain your strength because school starts in less than two weeks. Life goes on even when we aren't ready."

"I apologize for being a burden these past few days. I thought I was made of sterner stuff."

"I didn't mean you'd been a burden, Laurel. I am more than grateful you're better. If I could, I'd take you to our homestead tomorrow, but I know we'll need to wait for a few more days."

"Let's see how I feel in the morning. Right now, I am feeling a bit weak, but I know I'll be well in the next couple of days. I will try hard not to slow down your work."

"Laurel, let's talk about building our cabin. Finish telling me what you need in your home."

"I told you already, remember."

"I vaguely recall something about a porch with rocking chairs. Just tell me again."

"Real glass windows to let in the light would be nice. I know the cost will be too much, but maybe we can use the money from Papa. We will have the loan payments for the next seven years. We could use that to buy real windows."

"Wait a minute…that is your money."

"Some Bible scholar you are. Don't you know what a dowry is?"

"It's security money for you, Laurel. I'll build you a house. I promised your father I'd build you a safe, secure home."

"What about my vows to help you build your homestead?"

"You will…you will do all the things that you did for your papa." The look on Laurel's face told Mac what she felt the minutes the words had cross his lips. What he had meant to say had not come out as he intended.

In a tone, more subdued and colder than any Laurel had spoken to him, she said, "All right." "What…no Laurel. That is not what I meant." A tear ran down her cheek, and Mac rose to walk to around the bed. He sat and put his head in his hands. "I am always saying I am sorry to you. I never say things so you understand what I want to tell you. You are right. We are strangers. Even when I plan to spend a little quiet time talking to you, I hurt you."

"It's not your fault, Mac. We've had so little time to get to know each other. You have been kind and generous to me. From the beginning, you have been honest and open with me. You can't help how you feel. I wish you didn't feel so obligated to me because of the promise you made to my father."

"I don't have an obligation to anyone, not to your father nor to you. I have a responsibility that every husband has to his wife. I want to get to know you, and I want to provide you with a home. We will have to take the time we need to get to know each other. No more serious talk tonight.

Good evening, young lady. I'm glad to have you here in my neck of the woods. Name's MacLayne. I believe you're new here abouts. Won't you tell me about your favorite things."

Laurel laughed at Mac's silly attempts at playing the suitor. Obviously, he was trying to make her relax and play along, too. "I haven't really thought about it. I guess I like daisies, as flowers go. Do you know how to grow daisies? That green gingham dress I made was the best dress I ever owned. I like fried rabbit for a Sunday dinner when I can get one. I enjoy reading in my mother's rocking chair first thing in the morning. I sound pretty boring." Mac put his finger to her lips.

"Just stick to the facts, ma'am...just the facts." Mac was making every effort to keep the conversation light and out of conflict's way.

"What about you? What things are special to you?"

"Not much better than riding a good horse. I'm pretty fond of Midnight. I love walking around the homestead. As a matter of fact that is all I've done with my land in the four years I've been here. I especially love the meadow near the creek. It's surrounded by all kinds trees just at the edge of the ridge. I've kinda thought it was my own person Eden. I'll share it with you, though. I like reading Scripture. That's been especially nice since I've been able to discuss it with you. I don't think I ever talked about things like that with a female before, except perhaps my mother. A nice handful of pecans makes a great snack. My favorite piece of clothes is that fine shirt you gave me for Easter. Green has become special to me of late."

"Favorite hymn?"

"Amazing Grace. You?"

"Me, too." The couple spent half an hour or so just sharing simple things together and enjoying each other's company. Mac sensed that his plan was the right one. If he could make times for them where they felt no tension, no hurt feelings, no tears and no guilt, there was real hope they could learn to live together.

The next morning, Mac got up at dawn when he heard the Campbell family coming from the loft. Laurel still slept. Mac felt her forehead just to assure himself the fever had not returned. Laurel brushed his hand away, turned to her side and slept on. Mac went out to the barn to help Matt with the morning chores.

"Morning, Matt. Beautiful spring day, don't you think?"

"Well, you seem in a better frame of mind this morning. How's Laurel Grace today?"

"Still sleeping. We stayed up a while last night just talking. Nothing serious...just getting to know each other some. That is what we should have done in the first place. Mac, we appreciate your hospitality, but we need a place of our own. We need some privacy. Do you know of a place we can board or rent, while I build Laurel's house?"

"I'll ask around today while I'm out and about. Let's hurry with this business. Ellie is making sausage gravy and biscuits to go along with our eggs and oatmeal. Man, that's a breakfast for a king. If she will give me a couple of kisses to go along with the feast, I'll have enough blessings to get me through the whole day. What about you? Hungry?"

"Since I picked at supper last night, I'd say I could eat about a dozen biscuits. I only hope...well never mind. It'll be a happy day. When Laurel is up and about again, I'd like to borrow your wagon and take her to the homestead."

"Don't have to ask." The men went to the kitchen to find Laurel sitting at the table, and Ellie pouring coffee. "How are feeling, Laurel Grace? Think you are ready for a short wagon trip?"

"If that is what Mac wants to do, but I think I could ride Sassy Lady."

"Not yet...Let's take it easy another day or two. As a matter of fact, you're still looking a little pale. We'll play it safe. Anyway, Dr. Gibson is coming back to look at your ankle this afternoon." Laurel wanted to complain, but Ellie asked the family to sit down for breakfast. They shared the morning blessing and Matt, Ellie, John, and Mary joined Laurel and Mac in a filling, enjoyable breakfast time. The morning fellowship was every bit as enjoyable as that first supper they'd share two days ago.

"Mac, I am stronger today. I think I could go for a ride with you, if we don't do too much. We could at least mark off our orchard and garden plot."

"I know. You do seem stronger today, but I want you to take a couple more days to rest."

"We need to go pick out a site for the cabin."

"We have time, and I want you well. Just humor me today."

"Whatever you say. I'll find plenty to occupy me. Maybe Ellie will let me help in her garden."

Laurel was restless, and she certainly was not used to lying around. She sat at the table and wrote a letter to Rachel. She didn't tell her much about the difficulties they'd encountered during the journey east. She did tell her about the difference she'd seen in the changing terrain she'd seen from the Boston Mountains to the Ozark foothills to the swampy sunken lands. She also told her of the great joy she'd had in finding her Campbell family. When she finished the letter, she realized that Mac had been right. She was very tired, and it was only mid-morning. As much as she hated to admit it, Mac's request for her to stay there had been the best thing for her.

"Aunt Ellie, I think I need to lie down for a while."

"I'd think that'd be a good plan. Mac will be upset with me, if I let the fever come on again. He wants to get that cabin up." Laurel went back to the tiny room and lay down. Her head hardly reached the pillow before she slept. About noon, Ellie Campbell came to see if Laurel was awake, but she found her sound asleep. About an hour later, Dr. Gibson arrived, and Ellie gently shook her. Laurel roused up, looked about the room where she was and felt embarrassed when she realized that she had been asleep more than three hours. She'd never slept so much during the day...not once in her whole life.

"Good morning, Mrs. MacLayne. How do you feel today?"

"I thought I was well, but Mac wouldn't let me go with him today. Then I got very tired. He said I was pale."

"Quite natural, young lady. You have been pretty sick. I am pleased you stayed in. Let me look at that wound. Need to make sure no blood poisoning has set in'." When the doctor removed the bandage, he was pleased to see the improvement. "I believe you are well on your way back to health. I meant to ask you yesterday, though you weren't exactly up to conversation when I was here. Is there a possibility you are with child, Mrs. MacLayne?"

Laurel startled at the question. She had never spoken about such personal things with any man, not even her father. She felt herself blush and she lowered her eyes. Dr. Edwards observed her awkwardness and said, "It's quite all right to answer me. I'm a doctor and more than used to talking about such matters."

"No, Doctor Edwards. Mac and I have only been married since the seventeenth of March."

"Ma'am, babies frequently happen unexpectedly."

"Well, they don't happen to me." She had taken a stance for what she thought was an insult to her character. Of course, Dr. Edwards had not meant to embarrass Laurel."

Ellie spoke up to defuse the awkward feelings in the room. "Laurel Grace, please don't get upset. Doc meant no disrespect, and he wasn't making a judgment of your character. Fever can cause problems with babies."

"I didn't mean to offend. I only wanted to take precautions."

"When can I get up and be about my business, sir?"

"If you experience no more fever, you can go to church on the Sabbath and then ride to your homestead in a wagon. I'm right pleased you're healing so quick."

— —

While Laurel was getting a good report from the doctor, Mac had met up with Matt who was coming back from the general store. They rode back to the church and sat on the steps of the porch. "Mac, I've got good news for you. While I was in the mercantile, Widow Parker came into the store to place a notice. She is looking for someone to take care of her homestead, while she is visitin' her daughter in Bolivar. She'll be staying 'til her grandbaby is born. Are you interested?"

"Where is her homestead? "

"About two miles north of me. She's a member of the Cumberland Presbyterian community over near Herndon."

"Any roof will do. Let's go make arrangements."

"Glad you said any roof will do, because I told her you'd take care of it for her. She's pleased to have your help...she said if I trusted you, that she'd accept your offer even if you are one of those shoutin' Methodists." Both the men laughed.

"When can we move?"

"Whenever Laurel is able to travel. Mrs. Parker's leaving tomorrow."

"Praise be...all things work for the good....Will you help me move Laurel into the Widow Parker's homestead in the morning?"

"If the doctors says it's all right, and the sun is shining."

19

And the multitude of them that believed were of one heart and of one soul neither said any that aught of things which he possessed was his own, but they had all things in common...Neither was there any among them that lacked.

KJV c1850, Acts 4:32, 34.

Regrettably, the sun did not shine, nor did it shine on Thursday. Rain is common in the springtime in Northeast Arkansas, but the normalcy of the climate did not please Mac. He was restless, and in a surly mood much of the time they were pent up in the cabin together. After the long two days, everyone was pleased to see the sun rise bright and warm on Friday morning. Mac walked out onto the porch and took a deep breath in the warm spring air, and then he called out to Laurel. "Mrs. MacLayne, it's moving day. Get to it." One tiny wagon carried all they possessed and a small collection of supplies to start their larder, a gift of Matthew and Ellie.

The widow's homestead was located higher on the ridge than the Campbell's homestead, and more than three miles from the Mac's homestead. He didn't mind the temporary inconvenience, for this tiny cabin nestled near Crowley's Ridge would allow them privacy they hadn't had since the afternoon they had met up with Lonnie Thomison over in Searcy County.

The cabin was a small single pen structure with a porch spanning the front. At the back steps was a stone-faced well. A small outhouse stood in a grove of trees at the back of the yard. The tiny barn was barely large enough for the four animals they brought with them from Washington County, but the loft did provide space for winter feed. Mac thought to himself he'd not have to fill that loft space, for their cabin would be done long before winter came. Then if the widow needed forage for her animals, Mac could return and help her while he settled into his own home.

For all the shortage of space, the cabin was a homey, comfortable place set in the natural beauty of Greene County. Besides the gifts of Mother Nature, Mrs. Parker had added to the glory of her yard by planting different flowers around the path to her porch. Inside there was a main room and a half loft over the kitchen portion of the single pen. There was a large hearth on the left wall of the cabin with spits and hooks for cooking, but there was no hearth oven in the fireplace. Baking bread would prove a chore. The dry sink stood on the back wall, just beside the door. Drawing water could be done without having to leave the porch. Toward the back of the cabin was a small table with two chairs and a double bench. The room was immaculate, obviously scrubbed the day before. Near the fireplace was an arm chair covered with well-worn once golden-colored fabric. Next to the chair stood a single lamp table with a tin and glass lantern with a well-trimmed wick and a tiny vase with two blossoms. Next to the table a cane bottom rocking chair sat. All the furniture had been built from native pine and oak. The rustic cabin suited two people despite the size. A cabin this small would not have housed many children.

"Mac and Laurel Grace, I'm leaving you in this little house to get settled. I got a sermon to finish and chores left for when I get home. I will look forward to seeing ya'll at Shiloh church on the Sabbath."

With that parting, they were finally alone.

"Well, wife...it's not home, but at least it is ours temporarily. Is this place suitable for you?"

"The cabin is cozy. We can make do very well while you get your house built." Mac was annoyed. *Why did she always refer to their homestead as his place?* He hoped he would someday make her see that she was the reason for the homestead. He remembered clearly his conversation with Matthew in February when he said *I don't want a house. I want a home. A family makes a home.* Today, they were far from being a family. Then he remembered, Laurel had not even seen the land he would build on. Of course, she would not be able to imagine a home in a place she'd never been. He shook off the low thoughts and tried to bring himself back to the present.

"We sure have a lot of work to do. For tonight, we need a fire, some water from the well, and the stock cared for. Guess I'll go to work."

"If you'll bring me that box of food, I'll fix dinner for us

———

Laurel explored the tiny cabin. She climbed the ladder to the loft where she found the only real bed in the house. The bed was beautiful. Mr. Parker had obviously been a master carver. The massive four poster bed was carved from the foot to the ornate newels on each poster. The footboard and the headboard of the tall bed were detailed with scenes that could have been copied from the view outside the cabin. Beside the bed stood a two-step footstool that would allow a small woman to climb to the top of the quilt-covered mattress. Laurel had never seen a more beautiful bed, and she remembered the carved walnut bureau her father had made for her mother. How nice they would look together, but then the family treasure remained in Powhatan, waiting for better travel conditions. Laurel climbed the two steps and perched on the edge of the bed. She felt like a princess she'd heard stories about in her childhood. How Mr. Parker must have loved his wife to create such a gift for her. Laurel wondered how that must feel.

With a brief sigh, she set about changing the bedcovers. She removed the sheets and blankets belonging to the Widow and carefully folded them and stored them in the cedar chest at the foot of the bed. She used the bedding loaned to her by her aunt, and then she took her yellow coverlet that Mac had wrapped around her during the long trip across the bottoms. After a good washing and drying in the open air, it was like new and smelled of the spring breezes. She unpacked Mac's Bible and laid it on the small table next to the oil lamp at the right side of the bed. She laid her hair brush and her own Bible on the small three draw bureau, the only other piece of furniture in the loft.

Only one task remained upstairs. Laurel unpacked their meager wardrobe. She hung Mac's suit coat and his classically styled trousers on the pegs beside the window. She put his tall handsome boots on the shoe shelf below. A few pieces of underclothes and two shirts went into the top drawer of the bureau. She placed Mac's Easter shirt on the top. A comb, a straight razor, and a hair brush completed the unpacking for her husband. Laurel wondered if he had more things that had not made the trip across the state. She would need to ask. Laurel's unpacking was even simpler, as she had so little left. Laurel placed one chemise, her mother's nightdress, two pairs of pantaloons, and her torn work shirt in the second drawer. She wore her black skirt and ecru blouse, and the only other things she had were her dungarees and her blue calico dress. Mac had thrown away the torn pants he'd bought in Powhatan. She had no dress shoes to place on the shoe shelf next to the peg wall. Thanks to her uncle Matthew, who had remembered to pick up the shoe Mac had removed on the creek bank, she at least had a pair of shoes to wear. Looking around to assure herself she had done her task well, she smiled and went to prepare dinner in the tiny cabin.

Mac returned to the cabin shortly after Laurel finished setting the table with Widow Parker's pewter dishes. The dishes were very old, probably wedding gifts. As she prepared dinner for Mac, Laurel felt very close to the old woman she'd never met. The meal was a simple one, as she had no way to bake fresh bread, but it was enough.

They sat down together to share their first meal in the Widow's cabin. Mac took Laurel's hand and offered a blessing. At the amen, Laurel squeezed his hand. He looked up at her and she smiled. "Amen."

After supper, Laurel cleared the table and Mac went across the room and moved the chairs away from the hearth a bit, placing the rocking chair nearer the armchair so he and Laurel could share a pleasant evening together. "Come join me, Laurel. I'm excited we have an evening for ourselves...no audience. I love those kids of Matt and Ellie, but they were too full of energy and always under foot when I wanted some adult time. Speaking of private time, the past couple of evenings I enjoyed the time we spent getting to know each other."

"That time was good. We need to share a lot more of those little things before we tackle some of the bigger issues. Over the past weeks, we have found too many things to fight about, and I don't like conflict."

"I don't like fighting with you either, but in good time, we will get to know each other better and I'm sure lots of those things will just go away."

"What's wrong with this time?"

"I don't suppose anything is wrong with it, but I'd like to have a peaceful night or two here in the Widow's little cabin."

"If we will keep our tempers in check, I don't see why we should fight about anything. Mac, that first night we arrived at Uncle Matt's house, you kissed me—twice. You said it was time we started courting. Then you pulled away from me and left the room for almost two hours. I know you wanted me to fall asleep before you returned. What did I do to upset you?"

"You didn't do anything wrong. I had chores to do."

"I don't think you are being truthful with me. How can I try to fix things you don't like about me if I don't know what you don't like?"

"I don't want you to change anything about yourself. Well, I'd like to forbid you to ever wear those blasted braids again."

"That's a petty thing, Mac. I doubt that's the reason."

"Laurel, you are good and one of a kind. Only a fool would want you to change, and for all else I may be, I'm no fool."

"Why do you reject me if you don't want to change anything about myself?"

"Laurel, I told you before, back in the cave, I believe. Not everything is about you."

"What was it about?" Mac picked up Laurel's hand and brought it to his lips.

"Laurel, I haven't earned the right to be your husband yet. That night you were a beautiful sight, kneeling by the bed dressed in that pretty nightdress of Ellie's. Your ivory shoulders and neck were bare and your gorgeous curls fell to your waist. You looked like an angel. I knew I could not guarantee my promise to you if I stayed...so I left."

Laurel was surprised by Mac's answer. "I don't understand. You told me that you didn't love me, and you don't intend to fall in love."

"Laurel, you are too sweetly naïve. What I was feeling had nothing to do with love and everything to do with lust. I won't dishonor you. I promised you and your father. I made a wedding vow to honor you, remember?" Laurel did not respond. "Can we leave it at that for right now?"

"It's your house. Whatever you say."

"This wasn't how I planned this night. I don't want you upset. I just want our friendship to keep growing. I want to build you a cabin so we can get on with life here at Shiloh."

Laurel went to the boxes Mac had brought in from the wagon and picked up one of the partially sewn blouses she was making. She wanted something to occupy herself while they sat together in the living room. Mac had gone to the loft to get his Bible, looking for something to read so he didn't feel the need to start another conversation that would probably end in another dispute. So, the MacLaynes spent nearly two hours in silence. Laurel was sewing and Mac was reading. Anyone who saw them would think they were a contented, comfortable married couple spending a pleasant evening in front of their hearth, but both Laurel and Mac both felt the tension between them.

The fire in the fireplace had nearly burned itself out before Mac decided to break the silence. He had a question he hoped would bring a simple answer. "Laurel, do you have enough clothes to be a proper school teacher, or do we need to make a trip to Greensboro so you can get another dress or two?"

"I have my blue calico that I wore at Easter and this skirt and blouse. That was all I packed when we left Black Rock. I hope they meet with your approval."

"I wasn't criticizing your wardrobe. I only asked if you needed anything. Is there anything we can talk about that isn't going offend you?"

"Just another of my short comings. I'm tired of apologizing to you with every other breath. I told you I'm not a suitable mate for you."

"What can I do to make you see that you are a suitable wife. I've tried to tell you more than once. We have two or three good days, enjoying each other's company, talking, laughing, and sharing...then everything falls apart between us. The rifts are always about petty things." Mac turned to the center of his Bible where he had recorded their marriage date. He had written his marriage vows to Laurel on the next page. He read them aloud. "I will honor your place as my wife. I will respect the extraordinary person you are. I will support and encourage your life work. I will protect you and provide you with a safe home. These vows I make to you as a gift to the glory of our Lord. My covenant will remain as long as God wills." He closed the book and laid it aside. "Laurel Grace Campbell MacLayne, I am beyond frustrated. I don't know how to make you see that I meant these words. Do you believe I'm a liar?"

Momentarily green lightening met the blue storm in Mac's eyes. "No, Mac. You are honest and faithful to the vows you spoke.... I am at fault. Being married to a stranger is hard. I don't know how to talk to you or how to please you. I didn't realize I was questioning your integrity, but I know I have done that time and again since we started to your home, haven't I?"

"Yes." That was his response, abrupt and to the point. No conversation broke the empty silence. Shortly, Mac rose from his chair, picked up his Bible and went toward the ladder to the loft. "Laurel, when you are ready to join me, we will read our scripture for the night." He climbed the rungs and in a short time, a soft glow came from the lamp. Laurel stayed in the rocking chair for several minutes. She didn't want to anger Mac, and she didn't know why she always became so defensive with him. Did he really think she doubted his honesty? She rose and climbed the ladder to the loft. She stood waiting for Mac to acknowledge her presence. He sat on his side of the tall bed with his back to her. His head was bowed, and she knew he was praying. When he lifted his head, he spoke, "Laurel, we have to learn to talk with each other if this marriage is going to work. When I say things to you, you need to understand I'm never going say things to insult you. How could I honor you as my wife if I put you down when I speak to you? I will not dishonor you to your face nor behind your back."

"I'm sorry."

"Tell me why a question about your clothes puts you on edge so quickly. Please start the dialog you asked for. We have private time and space where we can really talk. No one is here to hear our words, and Laurel, no one is here to judge or criticize what you say."

"I did ask you for this didn't I? It was all for selfish reasons. I wanted to ask you why you had done this or criticized that. I know you don't have any answers for those kinds of questions. You aren't the problem. It's me that has to change."

"Well, dear lady, let's talk. You ask me a question, and I'll tell you the truth every time. Then I'll ask you a question and you tell the truth. We'll get all the secrets out in the open, one conversation at a time. You can go first."

"Can you tell me why you put me on your debt list? I was hurt when you told me you had written 'Married Laurel' on your lists of sins to be rectified and forgiven. Do you think marrying me is a sin, like...well... some of the other things on your list?"

"You don't give a fellow any breathing room before you jump right to your point."

"I told you several times, I don't like small talk. This is one of those issues between us that keeps me from knowing where I stand with you. I want to know why you wrote that in your Bible."

"No, Laurel. I don't believe our marriage is a sin. I think it's God's plan for us to be together. I've never had anything fall into place so quickly in my life. I am not sure he meant for us to wed so soon is all. You're the person I owe a debt to. I've already talked with Matthew about this, and he agrees. I made a poor choice when I failed to talk all these things over with you. I should have found a better way to ease your papa's passing without pushing you into a marriage before you were ready. Because I took it on myself to make the decisions without your input, I treated you as if you had no say about your own future."

"I could've said no."

"Could you? With your papa telling you to marry me, with me telling you how it would be, with the world we live in saying you can't live alone? No, Laurel, you had no choice, and for that, I am sorry. I wish it had been different for you."

Laurel was touched by Mac's honest reply to her question. She had never known any man so candid and willing to talk of personal matters. Not even her own father had taken her wants and dreams into consideration. "Thank you for that, Mac."

"Now it's my turn, and I have so many questions I want to ask you... where should I start?"

Laurel turned her back to Mac and silently made a plea to the Lord... *Please don't let him ask me about the nightmares. I don't want to talk about that. How can I explain that I don't know why those images frighten me so badly?*

"Laurel, tell me why you wear those glasses all the time? I've looked at them when I picked them up out of the dirt outside the deserted cabin the day after the rain storm. They are very weak. I've seen you read without them, and you often do needle work without the glasses. Tell me what charm those silver-rimmed ovals hold for you."

Laurel sighed. "To be honest, I do need them to read for any length of time. Eyestrain has been a problem since I was a child, but I guess the real reason is they are part of my mask—just like the braids you hate so much and mama's old clothes. My papa would've given me as many new dresses as I'd ask for, but I never asked."

"Thank you for telling me the truth."

⁓ ⁓

Mac rose from the foot of the bed where he'd been sitting and walked to the left side of the bed Laurel had claimed as hers. He inhaled deeply, reached over and took Laurel's hand and laid his other arm across her shoulder as he sat beside her.

"Laurel, relax. Do you realize most people spend months courting before they call each other by their Christian names? We have known each other barely six weeks, and we've been married more than five. We are still in our courting stage. I'll bet when we get acquainted, we'll like each other just fine." He smiled and tousled her hair.

"I think it is time we called it a night. I am tired, and there is a lot to do tomorrow to make this tiny cabin a home for the time. I'd like to have it done before Sunday. We promised Uncle Matthew we'd come to church."

"I'm looking forward to being back at Shiloh and to a good night's rest. I saw this beautiful bed when I came to get my Bible. So much nicer than a pile of hay!"

"I think so, too." Mac walked to the small table and turned up the lamp to add to the light so he could read their scripture. "Mac, turn down the lamp please, or turn your back."

"I want to watch you get ready for bed. Do you mind?"

"I hadn't planned to be the entertainment."

"Sharper than a serpent's tongue....Here, sit on the edge of the bed and let me help you take your shoes off. We need to get you another pair of shoes. I seem to recall a beautiful gesture at Easter when you gave your new shoes to a bride. No one did that for you, so will you let me buy you shoes?"

"I would be pleased to have new shoes, if we can afford them."

"New shoes it will be." Mac continued to unlace the old brown work shoes Laurel wore. He then removed her stockings. He rubbed her bare feet and looked at the scar on her ankle. The wound was healing well, finally. Mac bent down and kissed the bruised area on her ankle. "Thank you Lord. You saved my life mate." He massaged her calves and then her other foot. Laurel enjoyed the attention. Mac was honoring her role as his wife, and she liked the feeling of being a wife. "Laurel, will you unbutton my shirt for me?"

"If that is what you want." Mac leaned back against the carved headboard of the tall bed and watched as his wife undid the buttons of his shirt. Laurel was a bit hesitant at first. Of course, she had seen Mac in a state of undress before. She had caressed his shoulders and chest last Easter eve, but she had never removed his clothing like this. She straightened her shoulders and continued. She was enjoying the domestic scene too much to let her timidity spoil the evening.

When Laurel had undone the last button, she helped Mac remove it. Then Mac captured her hands and placed them on his chest. "I sure wish we had a copper bath tub. I'd love to have another of your special baths."

"I believe I can still take care of your massage." Laurel turned so she could rub Mac's back and shoulders. He began to experience the same urge he'd had that night in Powhatan, but he refused to let it spoil this good night. He breathed deeply for a minute and then relaxed. He let Laurel touch him as she would. He wouldn't leave her this night.

"Wife, I think it's courting time." Mac pulled her into his strong embrace, and he kissed her long and tenderly. He pulled his hands through her long tousled locks, and he kissed her again and again. And to his pleasure, Laurel returned his kisses. There was no shyness or tension to separate them. "Laurel, I like it when you are courting too." Mac picked up his Bible and read Laurel the wedding story from Genesis again. "When Shiloh come, Laurel...when Shiloh come."

That night, Mac held Laurel close—not from a need to stay warm nor to comfort her from a nightmare. He held her just because she was his wife--his friend, and he wanted to hold her. He knew she wanted to be held. He spoke an evening prayer, grateful for the excellent day and for their privacy. He ended by mentioning the extraordinary carved bed they lay in. He blew out the lamp and cuddled with his wife, and the two slept, peacefully and contentedly for the first time in many days.

— ᵔ ᵔ —

The first Saturday at the widow's cabin didn't turn out as Laurel had planned. She arose early and dressed in the only 'home clothes' she had, what she had worn yesterday. She had slept so well, she felt an abundance of energy. She had enjoyed the night in Mac's arms, and this morning, she wanted only to please him. She would not taunt him with the braids he hated. She pulled her locks into a loose knot at the nape of her neck and tied her green ribbon around it to keep it out of her face. She was ready to set up their temporary home in the widow's cabin. She began to unpack the few boxes they'd brought across the swamp. Precious little awaited her attention. She realized why Mac had asked if she needed anything from the town. If the widow had not left the cabin filled with her household goods, they'd need practically everything. As it was, they could live quite comfortably when they restocked their larder.

Laurel smiled. Every bride had to make her home. She would do the same. She remembered how flustered Rachel had gotten when she had begun to process of converting the cabin that Jason had built for her into a home. For a minute, Laurel felt a pang of loss. How she would have loved to have Rachel here to share this time. Laurel brushed the melancholy away. She would make the day another good one. No sad thoughts allowed and no spat with Mac. At the end of the day, there would be no regrets. Laurel planned to claim the promise her Uncle Matthew had told her about. She would be a new creature, and she would grow beyond the past, which she resolutely laid down that morning, again.

Mac came in from the barn where he finished his chores and retrieved the last of their belongings. "Good morning, Laurel. Did you rest well in that tall bed?"

"I did. I see you found some fresh eggs. The widow has certainly left us a well-stocked house, even breakfast, but if we are going to eat for the next few days, we will need to lay in some food. The larder we brought with us is meager."

"Well, we can eat this morning, at least. Then, we'll see what the Lord provides. Perhaps I can go find us a plump rabbit for supper. I remember you have a knack for cooking rabbit in gravy that makes a filling meal."

"Rabbit and gravy is a lot better with potatoes and bread, I believe."

"Let's explore and see what we can find in the root cellar." Mac started to the back door when he heard a quiet rap on the front door. "Must be Matthew." Mac opened the door to find Mrs. Whitlow and her three children on the porch. "Morning Margie...kids. Nice to see ya'll this morning."

"Praise be to the Lord, Mac. We're right pleased to see you got home safe. We sorely missed you at church. And lookie here, you brought home a sweet wife. Welcome to Shiloh, Mrs. Mac."

"Thank you, ma'am."

"No ma'am here, dearie. Name's Margie and these here's my young'uns...Tommy, Billy and Lafe." Before Margie Whitlow finished her introductions, a second wagon drove into the yard. A middle-aged man and woman pulled their wagon under the tree near the fence.

"Hello Ransom, Lilly. What brings ya'll out so early?"

"Came to welcome ya'll home, friend. We thought you'd fallen under the spell of the mountains and decided to stay in the Ozarks."

"Looks like he just fell in love." Lily Nolan laughed as Mac shook hands with her husband.

"Friends, this is Laurel. She graciously decided she would marry me." Before Mac could finish his statement, Matt, Ellie and their children drove up followed closely by Susan, Randall and their family. Susan stepped down from the wagon as deftly as a mother with a two-year-old in her arms could, hurried to the porch, placed her toddler in Mac's arms, and threw her arms around her cousin.

"Laurel Grace! How blessed to see you again. It's been years, but I'd of known you anywhere!" Those green eyes and those tawny curls. You've not changed one bit."

"Susan. How wonderful to see you, again. I can't believe you are here."

"Mornin' Mac. Welcome home." Matthew Campbell clapped Mac on the back. For the next hour, the members of the Shiloh community arrived by foot, horseback, mule drawn wagon and even a few in buggies. Gradually, wood plank tables went up in the yard and bright cloths began to cover the planks. Pots of every sort of victual filled the tables. A keg of cider and a large urn of lemonade sat at one end of the table with a tin dipper hung on each. Sweets of every variety were covered with clothes to keep the flies away and sat at the shaded end of the makeshift table. Mac and Laurel just stood and watched. How could all these people even know they'd taken up residence at the widow's already? They'd been there less than one day.

An elderly matriarch planted herself in one of the rockers on the porch. "Mrs. Mac, we're dearly blessed to have you here. We've been a needing a school marm for a good spell. Our kids have been hurting—too many bad teachers, temporary fill-ins, and mean school masters who didn't care if kids learned as long as they obeyed. My name's Maddie O'Neal. My kin settled this area nearly three decades ago, so I'm prideful of our home. We knowed if Mac brung you here, you'll be the answer to our prayers. If he loves you, we'll love you too!" Laurel lowered her eyes to Mrs. O'Neal's comment.

She had no way to respond, so she nodded and spoke quietly. "Thank you, ma'am."

Before noon, several families of Shiloh were represented at the widow's cabin. A huge dinner on the grounds was laid out on the plank tables and a small group of musicians had gathered near the porch. The little band, including a banjo player, a fiddler, a tall, thin man with a guitar, and a toothless fellow shaking out his brass plated harmonica, had gathered at the porch. They were ready to strike up the music when called on to do so. It seemed that a spontaneous party had developed, but Laurel was sure it had not happened without some outside instigator.

"Uncle Matthew, this is quite a gathering for one short day. How did all this happen?"

"Shiloh loves any excuse to have a party. I just mentioned to a couple of our ladies that you were setting up a household for the first time, and the party grew."

"Word spread mighty fast."

"Well, Shiloh is a close-knit community. You know that, Mac." Matt Campbell climbed the three steps to the front porch. He bent and planted a kiss on the check of Maddie O'Neal. "Friends, if you'll let me bless the food, we'll eat." The group applauded their approval briefly and then quieted for the blessing. "Father, thank you for the return of our brother Mac and the arrival of his wife, Laurel Grace. We welcome this chance to celebrate together. Bless our food and the ladies who cook it so well. Please smile on our fellowship. Amen."

Laurel's introduction to the community at Shiloh was joyous. All the ladies welcomed her as if she were a long-lost relative returned home. They told her stories about Mac and her Campbell family, most of them aimed a poking fun. Laurel was not surprised by all the kind acts people recounted, telling her of times when Mac intervened in their lives. She fully understood why her Aunt Ellie had told her Mac was the favored son at Shiloh. All who spoke of him told of his generosity, tireless efforts, and love for their community. Laurel felt a kinship with these people already. They were much like the church family she'd known at Hawthorn. Laurel found herself, laughing, visiting, and sharing stores of their trip. She was at ease and content, with only one shadow on the otherwise beautiful spring day. All the woman who spoke to her remarked how lucky she was to have a man like Mac love her. Each time Laurel would lower her eyes and nod or whisper a thank you. She wondered if they would have welcomed her so warmly if they'd known the truth behind her coming to Shiloh. Again, she consciously pushed the melancholy away and returned to the moment.

After lunch, Laurel's Aunt Ellie invited the women to sit in a circle under one of the larger oak trees. As they approached, each carried a small container, a wrapped package or a dish covered with a cloth. Ellie Campbell placed a chair near the tree and motioned for Laurel to take her place.

"Ladies, I'm thanking all of you for coming out today to welcome a new member to our church family. As we take turns around our circle, please tell Laurel who you are, a bit about your family, and one piece of advice to keep a happy husband. Laurel, this is a pounding party. We usually do this for new preachers, but we ain't had one for a long while so we decided to help our new teacher set up a household instead."

"Aunt Ellie, these ladies hardly know my name."

"Well, that's not a problem. After each piece of advice, you tell 'em about yourself and by the time we get around, everyone will know you and you'll have lots of fine things to help you set up your new home."

"I don't what to say."

"Then just sit here under this tree and listen." Margie Whitlow was the first to speak. "Mrs. Mac, please accept this loaf of bread that your house will never know hunger." Laurel accepted the golden loaf, which still held the odor of bread freshly baked in the early morning.

"Thank you. The bread smells wonderful."

"You know my name is Margie Whitlow, and you met my kids this morning. My husband Ben is that fellow leaning against the well there by Brother Matthew. One piece of advice I'd give to keep your husband happy is feed him well and on time." The ladies laughed as they were intended to do.

Maddie O'Neal, who had taken her seat on a split log bench next to Laurel, handed a cloth-wrapped container to her. "Missy, this is a gift of salt that your home will never be without the flavor of life." Laurel unwrapped a carved wooden saltcellar in the shape of an acorn. Laurel commented on the fine carving and put a touch of salt to her tongue.

"I love salt. It's one of my very favorite foods."

"My advice is simple. Just love him. Everything else will take care of itself."

Susan handed Laurel a fine paper-wrapped oblong object. When she did, she said, "Candles that your home will never know darkness." Laurel unwrapped the package and found two honeysuckle scented beeswax candles...just the perfect size to ornament their table.

"Did you make these, Susan?"

"Of course, Silly. We have our candling day every fall, in late October or the first of November. Lucy Martin has candle molds that she lets us all share, and we do our share of dipping too. Sometimes we use dried flowers to help scent them, but most are just plain for everyday use. You'll enjoy candling day. It's another excuse for a party. My advice to you is to speak your mind to your man. They never can figure out subtle hints—just tell him." All the women laughed, and this time the commotion was so loud that several men looked across from different parts of the yard, wondering what could be so funny.

Every lady in the circle presented Laurel with a gift of a cup of sugar, a small crock of butter, a pound of flour or cornmeal, a pail of milk or half dozen eggs. All had shared from their own pantries to help Laurel begin to fill her own. The last lady to bring her gift was an elderly woman with bowed shoulders and a huge smile on her face.

"Little Missy, my name is Elizabeth Dunn. I didn't know what I could spare so I made you this here bread cover. Tain't much, but welcome to Shiloh."

Laurel took the foot square of linen cloth from the elderly woman. She had embroidered a very ornate "M" with vines, leaves, and dainty blue flowers. Each stitch was precise and perfect. Laurel had never seen a more beautiful piece of needlework.

"My gracious, what a beautiful gift. Surely, you made this for someone you love very much. What time it must have taken!"

"Thank you. I did it last evening while the kids and me sat by the hearth. But you owe me no thanks. My grandkids, Catherine and Roy Dunn will be in your school. We need you here so much, and we are grateful you come here to teach our young'uns. We owe you a huge debt."

Laurel was dumbstruck that such a beautiful gift had been made especially for her. "I am very grateful Mrs. Dunn. I'll use it on our table every day. Such a beautiful gift!"

Matthew Campbell stepped up with Mac and handed Laurel one last gift, a bottle of mulberry wine. "One last gift to assure that prosperity and joy always fill your home. I know we Methodist frown on the consuming of too much alcohol, but we all know our efforts to preserve our good berries and grapes shows good stewardship of God's gifts. Remember, all things in moderation." Everyone laughed. "Hey, fellas strike up the reels."

The dancing began and the laughter, storytelling, and good times continued until near sun set. Kids ran through the yard, men pitched horseshoes and had dart-throwing contests. The women sat, gossiped, shared recipes, and comforted their infants as they sat beneath the shade trees. Laurel danced with Mac, her Uncle Matt, and nearly every other man and even a couple of the boys from her school. What a happy day that Saturday had become!

When the families began to return to their own homes, Laurel and Mac remained on the Widow's porch. The sun was just below the tree line, and the light streamed through the tree branches in an array of black, gold, red and blue. Laurel savored every memory from the day. "Did you enjoy the party, Laurel?"

"Yes. Your friends made such effort to welcome me. They must love you dearly."

"Just plain good folks. They opened their hearts to you, and they're grateful you are here for their children."

"I know. Mrs. Dunn made us a beautiful bread cloth with your initial embroidered on it. She said she was happy I'd be here to teach her grandchildren. Imagine she'd do this for me!"

"Where are we going put all this food?"

"We'll be able to fill our pantry now. That is what a pounding is all about."

"To think this morning, we didn't know how we'd eat tonight. The Lord did provide, didn't he?" Laurel smiled, and they walked into the widow's cabin just as the last hint of color slipped below the horizon.

20

By faith, he sojourned in the land of promise as in a strange country...

KJV c1850, Hebrews 11:9a.

Laurel awoke when the sun rose above the horizon, excited and nervous all at the same time. Today her Uncle Matthew would introduce her to the Shiloh congregation—Mrs. Patrick MacLayne, wife of the favored one and new schoolmistress. She'd been well received by the people who had able to visit the day before, but the entire community would be at church that morning. The typical Sunday was much like the Sabbath back in Hawthorn. Nearly every Sunday when the weather was good, people shared dinner on the grounds and held afternoon singing, which ended in an early evening service. Mac had promised that they would go on to the homestead after lunch if she wasn't too tired. Of course, Laurel had no intention of getting too tired. Mac had his heart set on showing her his land. He wanted her to choose the site for the cabin he would build.

Mac still lay asleep on the right side of the tall carved four-poster. Laurel moved over to him and ran her finger across his jawline. The touch would wake him, but she didn't want to arrive late for church on her first day there. When he opened his blue, blue eyes, Laurel leaned down to whisper into his ear. "Good morning, Mac."

"Come over here, wife."

"Mac!" This is the Sabbath. We have to get ready for church so we'll be on time. Besides it is the Sabbath."

"And God is in His heaven and all is right with the world." Mac pulled Laurel to him and kissed her, softly, tenderly.

"Enough of that. Uncle Matt is expecting us."

"All right, Laurel, up and at 'em. I can't wait to take you to our homestead this afternoon." Mac pulled the yellow bed coverlet off the bed and pushed Laurel off the left side of the bed. "Make us a nice lunch, please. I'll get dressed for church after I take care of the stock. I left you water for a bath before I came up to bed last night. Rise and shine. Make yourself beautiful for the Shiloh congregation."

Laurel scowled at his comment. "Mac...well never mind." Laurel kept back the scolding that was on the tip of her tongue. She refused to break the peace.

"You'll look fine in your blue calico this morning. I'll be proud to have you on my arm as we walk into the church."

Morning chores were finished quickly, and they were dressed and on their way to the Shiloh church before 8:30. When they reached the churchyard, several families were already gathered about the log building. Laurel was relieved to see her aunt and uncle with their children on the church porch. Laurel waved and smiled to them. She was determined the day would be a special one for her husband. The spinster of Hawthorn was gone, and today Mrs. Patrick MacLayne would make her entrance into her new church family. No one there was acquainted with the spinster. Only Mac knew of her true nature so she would pretend to be a different person, one Mac could be proud to have as his wife.

Mac helped Laurel down from the wagon and tethered Midnight in a shady arbor. He took her hand, and they walked together. Matthew Campbell came down to meet them. He kissed Laurel's cheek and said, "Welcome, niece. You look mighty fine today. The kids will be happy to see a nice teacher coming to teach them."

"Thank you, Uncle Matt. I am nervous. I want to make the right impression."

"Just be yourself." Matt walked with Laurel to the porch where his wife waited. Mac had not followed them. A pretty, blonde woman, wearing a straw bonnet decked with pastel ribbons had stopped him. The ribbons fluttered across her face and down her shoulders as she preened in front of him. She laid her gloved hand on his arm. Laurel was more than a little jealous.

"Uncle Matt, who is that girl?"

"Her name's Willa Ferguson. She's had designs on Mac for over two years."

"She's a slow worker. Only took me four days." Both Ellie and Matt smiled at her remark.

"Laurel, she doesn't mean anything to Mac. He is just being courteous." Willa Ferguson's beauty was not lost on Laurel, though. She wore no flirtatious, beribboned bonnet, lacy gloves nor fashionable shoes. As a matter of fact, looking at the well-dressed young woman caused Laurel to glance down at her worn work shoes. She hoped the hem of her new dress covered her unsightly shoes. Mac continued to talk with the girl.

"Excuse me, please." Laurel walked over to Mac and took his arm. "Husband, dear, won't you introduce me to your friend." There was not one hint of meanness in her voice, nor did her jealousy show in her request. She was poised and friendly. Mac grinned.

"Laurel, this is a good friend, Willa Ferguson. Willa, this is my wife, Laurel."

Willa's tone of voice was not as pleasant. "Your wife?" The well-dressed young woman looked at her rival who had taken Mac's arm. The expression on her face suggested she was not impressed. She looked with pleading eyes at Mac. "When...why...uh." She turned to look at Laurel again. "Nice to meet you, Mrs. MacLayne." The chill in her voice and the terse words told Laurel that this pretty child thought that the title of Mrs. should belong to her.

"Mac, Uncle Matthew is waiting for us. Shall we go to worship?"

Mac nodded. Laurel had been the picture of grace and composure. She hadn't let the situation push her behind her wall. He bent and whispered into Laurel's ear. "Well done. What a lady I just saw! Thank you, Lord. Please let me get that cabin built soon." Laurel blushed and smiled at her husband. The day was beginning so well.

Matthew Campbell's congregation was a growing one. Presently twenty-nine families attended Shiloh church regularly. Among those families was a good number of children. The music was strong and beautiful. "Oh, for a thousand tongues to sing, my great Redeemer's praise," rang through the log church. Laurel loved that the families sat together, because Mac sat next to her and held her hand. Matthew preached a message from Philippians 4: 6. *Be careful for nothing; but in everything by prayer and supplication with thanksgiving, let your request be made known to the Lord.* The congregation stood and sang the touching hymn *Alas and Did My Savior Bleed.* Matt closed with a benediction from John Wesley. "The Lord's will is good and whether God gives or takes away, a follower of Jesus equally blesses His name. In ease or pain, in sickness or health, in life or death, we give thanks from the bottom of our hearts to God who orders everything good. They have wholly committed body and soul into the hands of the faithful Creator. They cast all cares on God who cares for them. Because of this, they fear nothing and in all things rest on Christ, having made their requests known to God with Thanksgiving. Amen. Brothers and Sisters, as we begin to live this promise with Jesus, our brother, we begin to enjoy life. He can bless us, and we don't have to depend on our woefully lacking selves. Praise be to God."

Matt's words were powerful, and Laurel felt her spirit uplifted, as if her uncle had crafted his sermon just for her. This was the lesson she had tried to grasp from Mac. Laurel began to understand the concept of becoming a new creation, though there was still so much she didn't understand. Was it truly possible that all she had hidden, feared, and denied could be left behind her? How could a person learn to be grateful for ugliness that happened to them? So many questions remained, but today she was happy. As the congregation began to sing the familiar old song of invitation, *Just as I am*, Laurel took Mac's hand and they sang together.

"Brothers and Sisters, before we part for our dinner, I want to introduce all of you to the newest member of our Shiloh family. Our own Patrick MacLayne has finally made the commitment. Ya'll thought he was a confirmed bachelor, but Mac has brought his new wife Laurel to join us. I'm especially pleased as she is my own niece. Laurel will also serve as our new teacher here at the subscription school. Please make her welcome."

With the end of the service, slaps on the back, congratulations, gossiping among small groups, and a couple of ugly snarls filled the small sanctuary. Mac took Laurel's hand and led her outside to the picnic area and into the midst of his friends and church family. Laurel had thought she had met most of them yesterday at the pounding, but many new faces surrounded them. She took a deep breath and squared her shoulders, refusing to retreat into her shell, and she greeted everyone Mac introduced with a smile and a kind word. Laurel was playing her role quite well, she thought. Even the day before at the pounding, she'd taken some time in warming to the notion of being the center of attention. Today, she seemed to take it all in stride, and she was every bit the serene, professional that a teacher should be in public. She displayed a sense of confidence and kindness that she wish she felt. Mac simply stood by her side and watched.

"Laurel, ya'll come join us for lunch. Bring your basket and eat with Matt, the kids, and me."

"I'd like that Aunt Ellie. That'll be fun." And it was.

Family after family came to welcome Laurel and congratulate Mac. Many youngsters came forward to tell their new teacher who they were and what grade they were in. Laurel knew she would never remember all the names, but she was happy they wanted to meet her. Only a few people in the congregation declined the chance to meet Laurel. Three of them were females, from age nineteen to twenty-one, all Mac's former girlfriends. One pretty woman with dark brown hair glared at Laurel throughout lunch. Laurel smiled back at her when they made eye contact. Laurel felt uncomfortable, but she didn't let her anxiety hinder the good times. She felt a bit of sadness for the young women, though. Laurel wanted to leave the possibility of friendship open with these girls, but she made sure they knew Mac was no longer the best catch in the community.

After a fine meal marked with great fellowship, Mac pulled Laurel aside. "Hey, Lady, have you seen my wife? She's a shy little thing, hardly lets me touch her. She claims to be the spinster of Hawthorn. You notice her around anywhere?" Laurel laughed at his coy remark.

"She's gone. She told me to treat you well, because she wouldn't be around much anymore."

"Thank you, Lord."

"I am pleased you are happy with me today." Mac pulled her into arms and held her for several minutes.

"Don't you think it is time we build a house?"

"Are you sure you aren't too tired to go on the homestead this afternoon? It's already been a pretty full day."

"You promised. I want to see this place you love so much."

— ⁓ —

They rode about mile east of the Shiloh church. For most of the ride, they were quiet, just experiencing the beauty of the spring and the serene mood the morning had left with them. At a sharp bend in the road, Mac pulled Midnight to a halt and jumped from the wagon seat. He walked around to help Laurel down.

"Laurel, this is where our land starts. Together we made a long, treacherous trip across this state and for the first time you have your feet on our land. We own about 370 acres, the best homestead in this whole state." He took her shoulders and turned her so he could see into her face. "Honestly, more than once I doubted I'd ever get you here. Between that winter swim and the cottonmouth in Cache River I wondered if nature was against us. All those angry words we spit at each other. It is a miracle we didn't poison each other with our own venom.

I don't think I told you, but the day we met Lonnie Thomison, I was mid-sentence in telling you that I'd let you go to Texas if you wanted to go because I thought you were so unhappy with me. Thank God, Lonnie interrupted us when he did. The time we spent in the cabin with you wearing that yellow toga was what made me know letting you go would be the worst mistake I could make. Laurel, I don't know what lies ahead of us. I still haven't kept all my promises to your father, but we are so much closer to having a home than I've ever been." He looked at her with hope in his eyes. "Do you still want to keep the vows we made in March?"

"Mac, the time since we have moved to the Widow's has been a good time for me. I hope for you. I want to keep my vows and build a life on our friendship and faith as we promised, as long as you want me."

"You don't feel slighted by the marriage vows we made?"

"Mac, you have lived up to each promise you made to me...well, except I still don't have a house of my own."

"Laurel, what a life mate you are. Let's ride down to the stream, and then we'll walk through the meadow. If you see a place you want to build a cabin, just tell me. I'll build your house wherever you want it."

"Your land is very beautiful, Mac."

"Laurel, this is our homestead. Understand, it's a place for us, not for me. I was ready to sell it, give it back to the state, or let squatters have it before I met you. Don't you see? This is where I want us to build a life. I can hardly wait to start a life here with you. You've done this for me in the short month we've been together. Your friendship has been an answer to my prayers."

"Beautiful words, Mac." Laurel was quiet for a few minutes. "Tell me where you see a cabin when you dream of your homestead."

"There is a grove of oak and maple trees standing at the top of that hill. At the center of that glade stands the grandest oak tree I've ever seen. I believe it's stood there from the moment of creation. From the top of the knoll, you can see the entire meadow and the creek. Whenever I stand there, I'm I awe of God's creation and the beauty of this place. Laurel, I often come here just to sit when I need time for myself. What a perfect site for a house!" Mac turned the wagon in the direction of the glade, and Laurel saw why Mac loved the knoll.

"The beauty is more than anyone can describe. Destroying such glory would be sinful. Building here would destroy what makes this place so perfect."

"I suppose you are right, but what are you thinking?"

"I am thinking we have to leave it the way God made it. Let it stay our special place, if you'll let me share it with you, our own private Eden, just for the two of us to enjoy together."

"That sounds too good to even imagine. If we leave Eden, where will the MacLaynes live?"

"We passed an area in the meadow set back among several trees that would be a good place. It is not so close that we'd worry about flooding from the creek, but near enough we could make a spring house. The valley would provide shelter from storms. The creek would be handy for watering our orchard and our garden. If we had a long porch, we could sit out there and see a huge piece of this beautiful homestead as we end each day."

Mac drove back toward the road across the meadow to the grove of large trees. Pecan trees, red oaks, and a few maple trees formed a natural windbreak to the north. "So, Mrs. MacLayne, walk to your home site, and let me mark an outline for the foundation. Show me where to start."

Laurel felt as if she was watching herself in a dream. Nothing of that day had seemed real to her, and the gift was so precious it was almost painful. Laurel knew that any minute she would wake and all she'd experienced that day would prove to be only a joyous dream, but for that short time she would not give in to her doubts. She would savor every moment of being happy.

"Where do you want your hearth, Laurel, on the side wall or on the back wall?"

"Put it in the center the north wall, Mac. We can put our chairs near the fire so we will be comfortable on the coldest days of winter. Don't forget, I want a hearth oven too."

When he'd paced off an outline of the first pen, he went to the other side and walked through a second pen. "Come help me, wife. We gotta have a bedroom."

"This will be a large house. If you put a loft over the second pen, we'll have space for others to stay with us from time to time."

"No. I will build a half loft over the kitchen area, like at the widow's place. We'll make space for company there. The second pen will be our place. I won't share this space with anyone else."

Mac looked at the space they'd chosen to build Laurel's home. He smiled and yelled aloud, "Praise the Lord. What a perfect day!" He recalled each part of the day—from Laurel's sweet whisper before they got up, to her confident, serene way of handling his past lady friends, to her acceptance of his friends, and now the feeling that his dream was within reach. Laurel was the reason he was happy. His plan of the arranged marriage with a good friend was a solid one. "My friend, you have made this a very wonderful day. Thank you, Lord, for bringing this special friend to help me build a good life here on this fine land."

Mac tousled Laurel's curly tresses and tilted her head up so he could look into her eyes. What he saw was green fire and through his mind ran the scripture he had thought of so often since he'd met Laurel. *All things work together for the good of those who love the Lord.* It would have been impossible not to kiss the woman in front of him. He made no attempt to avoid the need. *How long does it take to build a cabin?* Too long, he thought as he held Laurel and kissed her again. She returned his kiss.

Mac took the pointed stake he'd tied with green ribbon. He handed it to Laurel, and she placed it where he'd lay the cornerstone of their cabin. With one blow, he marked the site of their home. Their journey across Arkansas had ended, but the MacLayne's dream of home at Shiloh was only beginning.

About the Author

 Patricia Clark Blake holds a BSE in English, an MSE in reading, and an EdS in counseling psychology from Arkansas State University. Now retired, she spent her career in Arkansas public schools teaching English, Spanish, oral communications, leadership, and as a secondary-school counselor. She taught psychology and supervised counseling interns at the college level.

Known as Pat to her friends, Blake has published in juried psychological journals. Her proposal for the Shiloh Saga won an award from the Blue Ridge Christian Novel Retreat in 2016. *In Search of Shiloh* will be followed by the next book in the series, *The Dream of Shiloh*.

Blake volunteers at her church, teaches Sunday school, and leads water-wellness classes. She is passionate about genealogy and loves Arkansas history. She is blessed with a wonderful daughter and son-in-law. She is Nanna to a beautiful granddaughter and a fine grandson. She resides near the Greensboro community, the source of inspiration for her Shiloh stories.